By Royal Decree

MARIE DONOVAN
MARGARET WAY
OLIVIA GATES

MILLS & BOON

First Published in Great Britain 2018
by Mills & Boon, an imprint of HarperCollins*Publishers*
1 London Bridge Street, London, SE1 9GF

ISBN: 978-0-263-26716-7

05-0518

FSC
www.fsc.org

MIX
Paper from
responsible sources
FSC™ C007454

This book is produced from independently certified FSC™ paper to ensure responsible forest management.

For more information visit: www.harpercollins.co.uk/green

Printed and bound in Spain
by CPI, Barcelona

Marie Donovan is a Chicago-area native who got her fill of tragedies and unhappy endings by majoring in opera/vocal performance and Spanish literature. As an antidote to all that gloom, she read romance novels voraciously throughout college and graduate school.

Please visit the author's website at www.mariedonovan.com.

Margaret Way, a definite Leo, was born and raised in the subtropical River City of Brisbane, capital of the Sunshine State of Queensland, Australia. She currently lives in a harbourside apartment at beautiful Raby Bay, a thirty-minute drive from the state capital, where she loves dining *al fresco* on her plant-filled balcony. No one and nothing is in a mad rush, and she finds the laid-back village atmosphere very conducive to her writing. With well over one hundred books to her credit, she still believes her best is yet to come.

Olivia Gates has always pursued creative passions such as singing and handicrafts. She still does, but only one of her passions grew gratifying enough, consuming enough, to become an ongoing career—writing.

When she's not writing, she is a doctor, a wife to her own alpha male and a mother to one brilliant girl and one demanding Angora cat. Visit Olivia at www.oliviagates. com.

[illegible]

[illegible]

[illegible] She currently lives in [illegible]

Olivia Gates has always pursued creative passions such as singing and handicrafts, [illegible] but only one of her passions [illegible] enough to become an enduring career—writing.

[illegible]

ROYALLY ROMANCED

MARIE DONOVAN

To Dad,
A prince in a book for a prince of a man in my book.
Happy reading!

1

"You're what?" Giorgio's gold pen dropped from his fingers and rolled forgotten off his polished wooden desk as he gripped his phone.

His sister, his *baby* sister, Stefania, giggled from four thousand miles away in New York City. "I'm engaged to be married." She repeated it in Italian to make sure he understood. *"Fidanzata."*

"But, but…" he stammered, normally not at a loss for words. "To whom? And when?"

"Well…" She drew out the news teasingly and then her excitement bubbled over in a rush. "His name is Dieter von Thalberg and we met a few months ago when he traveled here for business."

"Only a few months?" Giorgio interrupted. "And you want to marry him already?" Stefania was impulsive sometimes, but not foolish.

"Of course." She giggled again. "Oh, Giorgio, I can't wait for you to meet him." She lowered her voice. "He's German nobility from a little place in Bavaria. You have to trust me, I've never felt this way about any other man. When he kisses me and we…well, anyway…" He practically heard her blush as she continued the catalog of wonders that was Dieter.

Giorgio fought the urge to start an international incident over Dieter, his future brother-in-law, for showing her the wide world of womanly delights. Giorgio couldn't think of it in more specific terms without his fine lunch of sausages and polenta sitting uneasily in his stomach.

He sighed and wished he had finished the rest of the bottle of wine rather than restraining himself to the two glasses he normally imbibed.

Rotten Dieter.

He hoped the man's ancestral holdings were overrun with mold and rats. But then Stefania would be unhappy, and that was the last thing in the world Giorgio wanted.

Actually, he hoped Dieter had some money of his own for the ancestral holdings and wouldn't constantly hit Giorgio up for loans. Giorgio had enough trouble with his own palazzo, *molto grazie.*

"But, Giorgio, you must realize none of this will be official until you give us your blessing. Dieter insisted it be so."

Hmm. He quirked his mouth. It was true. As ruling head of the Most Serene Principality of Vinciguerra, Giorgio had the right to approve or deny betrothals of members of the royal family, i.e. his sister, Principessa Stefania Maria Cristina Angela Martelli di Leone. It said so on his business card. Well, not really.

The only other members of the royal family were his grandmother, who at eighty was not expected to seek permission to wed again, and himself: Giorgio Alphonso Giuseppe Franco Martelli di Leone, Prince of Vinciguerra. Long ago, Giorgio had decided that if he never wed and had the requisite heir-and-a-spare, he would pass the title to Stefania and her children. After all, he was an enlightened, twenty-first-century monarch. One with the power to send Dieter the Dunce packing. He snickered.

"Giorgio?" his sister asked nervously. "Are you still there?"

"Si, si." He lapsed into silence, pondering what to do and how many heavy items Stefania would hurl at his head if he refused her undoubtedly golden-haired, Teutonic Prince Charming.

"Come to New York," Stefania commanded.

"What? Now?"

"Yes, now. I called Grandma today and she told me to get you out of her hair. She says you're driving her nuts." Having spent most of her childhood in New York, Stefania had a definite command of American idioms.

"What?" Giorgio sat bolt upright in his ergonomic Corinthian leather chair. "I am doing no such thing!"

"She begs to differ. She says you poke your nose in on her day and night so she can't get any rest."

Now he was insulted. Their grandmother had had a nasty bout of flu that had settled into pneumonia. After a couple touch-and-go weeks of around-the-clock care, she had pulled through but still needed nursing visits, respiratory therapists, physical therapists and doctor visits. And it was his job to make sure they were doing their jobs. He was more at ease if he could be present for all their consultations.

He reconsidered. Maybe that was a bit too much. After all, his grandmother had run Vinciguerra while he was off at university and had absolutely no trouble making her wishes known. He could also have his assistant text him updates on her health.

"Yes or no, George!" his sister shouted. She only called him his American nickname when she was either very pleased with him or very annoyed. No bets on which it was this time.

"Fine, Steve!" he shouted in return, his matching temper surfacing. "I want to meet this German Romeo who thinks he's good enough for my only sister. If he's not up to snuff, forget it! You can finish your master's degree instead. I'm not paying university tuition to have you moon over some man you barely know."

"He is not *some* man! He is *my* man, and I know him very well."

Giorgio gritted his teeth at her implication and forced himself to take several deep breaths. If he pressed his sister too hard, she was likely to elope to Vegas with the guy. "If you think so highly of him, Stefania, I will be happy to meet him."

"Fine." She sounded mollified, for the moment at least. With Stefania, you never could tell. "And I *am* finishing my degree, you know. If I take an extra course each semester, I'll be able to graduate next spring."

"That's wonderful news." He checked his schedule on his phone. "I can fly into New York Wednesday if that would work for you. And Dieter," he added grudgingly.

"Great! We'll meet for dinner Thursday, just the three of us."

"Great," he parroted, with much less enthusiasm. "I look forward to it."

"No, you don't, but thanks for saying so."

"Insincerity has its place, Steve. I would appreciate a tiny bit more insincere flattery from you, for example. 'Oh, my princely brother, if it pleases you to meet the unworthy specimen who has asked for my dainty royal hand in marriage…'"

She snorted. "If you wanted me to be dainty and insincere, you should have left me in Vinciguerra after Mama and Papa passed away."

"You know I couldn't do that, *piccina mia.*" *My little one*—it was what their papa had called her, at least when she wasn't raising hell. Some things never changed.

"I know, Giorgio, and I love you for it."

He cleared his throat, which was developing a sudden lump. "I love you, too," he muttered. Words of love never came easily for him, even for his beloved sister.

"*Ciao,* Giorgio." She made a kissing noise into the phone and hung up.

He spun his chair to stare at the terraced vineyards beyond his office, the land still leafy and green in the April sun after a wet spring.

Springtime and young love. Giorgio's lips pulled into a wry smile. He remembered how romantic New York City could be in the spring. Unlike Stefania's Dieter, though, he had never been tempted to propose to anyone. He'd been busy with his education and bracing himself to return to Vinciguerra.

And now he would return to New York. It had been so long since he had been a foolish young student in the city. He straightened in his chair, the idea sounding better by the minute. He hadn't even had a free day in what seemed like forever, his every action in Vinciguerra witnessed and gossiped over by his loyal subjects. And to date any of them? Unthinkable.

He grimaced and tried to roll the kinks out of his neck. It wasn't as if he had any free time to date anyone, Vinciguerran or not. He pressed the intercom to call his assistant. "Alessandro? Please make arrangements for me to join Princess Stefania in New York tomorrow." He rubbed the back of his neck. Stefania would give him grief if she thought he looked scruffy for her big dinner.

"Oh, and also make an appointment with my barber." Women always loved a fresh haircut.

"RENATA?" RENATA PAVONI's assistant, Barbara Affini, who was also her aunt, stuck her perfectly coiffed, poufy head of black hair into Renata's workroom.

"Hmm?" she mumbled around a mouthful of straight pins as she pinned the white satin hem of a wedding dress. The dress dummy stood on a carpeted platform, high enough that Renata didn't have to crouch to work with the fabric.

Barbara tsked and came into the room. "Your mama would have a fit if she saw you like that. If you swallow a pin, I'm going to call your brother's firehouse to take you to the hospital and you'll never hear the end of it."

Renata spit out the pins and stuck them into a tomato-shaped pincushion. "Okay, okay. Hey, how does this look?"

"Short."

Renata sighed. Why did she bother asking? It was the same answer every time. "It's supposed to be short, Aunt Barbara. It's a vintage-style wedding dress." Nineteen-fifties and -sixties fashions were hot as hell, thanks to several hit TV shows and movies set in those time periods.

"Your cousins' wedding dresses, now those were classics," her aunt reminisced.

Renata pulled a face, glad her aunt was behind her. Her petite cousins had rolled down the aisle in dresses wider than they were tall, looking like those plastic doll head and torsos on top of crocheted toilet paper holders. Thank God wedding dresses from the eighties were still out of fashion. She'd go broke buying miles of satin and tulle and pounds of sequins.

Why had she hired her aunt? Oh, yeah, her uncle Sal had begged Renata to get his wife out of the house. She needed someone to mother once their youngest married, and the newly retired Sal wasn't about to volunteer for the vacancy.

Plus, Barbara was a fantastic seamstress and put the *p* in punctual.

Renata finished pinning the hem and stood, her knees popping. "The bride is coming in for her final fitting tomorrow. Will you have time to hem this?"

Her aunt sniffed. "Child's play. I even have time to add some sequins on the skirt if you'd like?" she asked hopefully.

Renata shook her head. "No sequins." Her client was an avowed hipster and would bite the sequins off with her teeth before wearing them down the aisle.

"Seed pearls?"

"Nope."

"How about some white-on-white satin-stitch embroidery?" But her aunt knew when she was beaten, her plump shoulders already slumping.

"Sorry." Renata *was* sorry. Her aunt would like nothing better than to hand-bead, hand-sequin and hand-embroider a gigantic ball gown with a twenty-foot train. But customers for gowns like that didn't come to Renata's design studio, Peacock Wedding Designs.

Instead, the dress in front of them was pretty typical of her sales—a fifties-style vintage reproduction with gathered halter straps and a full-circle skirt complete with a tulle crinoline. The bride was planning on a short, wavy fifties 'do and a small satin hat with a tiny net veil to drape over one carefully made-up eye.

Renata smoothed the skirt and carried it into the alteration workshop for her aunt. She caught a glimpse of herself in the three-way mirror and sighed. She loved vintage clothing but it sometimes didn't stand up to the modern workday. Her ivory linen blouse was wrinkled and her navy pencil skirt had twisted around her waist so the back slit was somewhere along the front of her thigh. She patted her auburn hair back into its nineteen-forties-style roll.

Her aunt noticed her self-grooming and finally smiled. "You look just like old photos of my dear mamma, God rest her soul."

"Thanks, Auntie." She blew her a kiss and fixed her skirt. She probably needed to touch up her lipstick, too. While lush red lips were historically correct, they did require more maintenance and she had to be careful that she didn't trip over her feet and plant a big red smacker on her pure white fabric. The things one did for fashion. Or at least her grandmother's fashion.

Renata hopped onto the elevated chair at her design table. Before she could uncap her cherry-red tube, the phone rang. "Peacock Wedding Designs, this is Renata."

"Hi, I've been looking at your website and I was wondering when I could come in to look at your dresses." The New York voice was young but confident, typical of her clientele. Brides who wanted a vintage look were not shrinking violets.

Renata flipped through the appointment calendar. "We can see you Friday."

"Are you free tomorrow afternoon?"

Renata wrinkled her nose. She'd been planning to take the afternoon off for the opening of a new art exhibit at a gallery in Manhattan. Her friend Flick knew a couple of the artists.

Her potential client hurried on. "I want my brother to come with me, and he's flying into town tonight."

Business was business, and maybe Brother was paying for the dress. "No, that's fine. What time is good?"

"Noon?"

"Great." Maybe she could see the opening after all—it started at two. "And your name?"

"Stefania di Leone." She had a perfect Italian accent when she pronounced her name.

"Ah, Stephanie of the Lion." Renata laughed. "My full name is Renata Isabella Pavoni—peacock. That's where I got the name for my salon."

"I think your designs are wonderful," Stefania enthused. "I looked in the bridal mags, but everything there is too over-the-top. I don't want a gigantic, poufy dress, or a corset-slip that looks like I forgot to put the rest of my dress on. And don't get me started on the mermaid style. I want to be able to *dance* at my wedding." She ended in a plaintive note.

Renata penciled her name into the calendar. "I'm sure you can find something you love. Have another look at my website and jot down some styles you'd like to try on." She gave Stefania directions to her salon in Brooklyn. Renata wished she could afford space in Manhattan, but even marginal neighborhoods there were exorbitant.

But Stefania didn't seem fazed. "My brother and I will see you tomorrow. Oh, I'm so excited! My first time wedding dress shopping!"

That could be good or bad, depending on if she made up her mind quickly or liked to browse. Either way, it was an opportunity. They said their goodbyes, and Renata hung up.

Barbara appeared in the doorway again. "Who was that, dear?"

"A bride is coming in tomorrow at noon to look at the dresses."

Her aunt made a disappointed face, her penciled eyebrows drooping. Since Renata had planned to take the afternoon off, her aunt made an appointment for Uncle Sal's annual colonoscopy. Lucky Sal.

"I'll be sure to keep you posted. And who knows? She may want a little more embellishment on her dress."

Barbara brightened. "That would be wonderful! I have lots of ideas."

"Great. Write them down. Or draw them."

She made a dismissive gesture. "Renata, you know I can't draw worth a lick."

"Ask your granddaughter Teresa to draw it for you. Isn't she a good artist?"

"Oh, well..." Her aunt fluttered her fingers at her bosom. "I'll have to see...my ideas probably aren't very good."

"You won't know until you try." Her aunt was a product of her times, discouraged from attending college and encouraged to marry straight out of high school. It was about time her aunt focused on herself instead of her family. Her family would be grateful, too.

"But I *can* hem that dress. I know I'm good at that."

"You are indeed." Renata gave her an encouraging smile and checked on the selection of samples she had in stock. Kick-ass. Her new bride would love them.

Unlike her aunt, she didn't have any doubts about her abilities. Renata loved vintage clothing, but she sure didn't have a vintage attitude.

2

"OUR LITTLE STEVIE's getting married?" Giorgio's old friend Francisco Duarte das Aguas Santas was obviously as dumbfounded as he had been. Once Giorgio's call from the VIP lounge in Leonardo da Vinci Airport in Rome had reached Frank at his ranch in the Portuguese countryside, it had taken several minutes to explain the situation.

"Yes, she's engaged." It was getting somewhat easier to say the words aloud. Giorgio's grandmother had been ecstatic at the prospect of a royal wedding in Vinciguerra, especially since his own parents' wedding had been the last one celebrated, and that had been over thirty years ago. They had been returning from an anniversary trip when they died tragically in a car accident. Giorgio hoped his sister's nuptials would distract his grandmother from asking him when he would make some lucky woman his *principessa*.

"And to some guy we've never met." Frank sounded nearly as disgruntled as Giorgio had been.

"I'm leaving in a few minutes for New York, so I'll meet him tomorrow."

"Does Jack know?" Jacques de Brissard was the third member of their trio.

The three men had met their freshman year at the university in Manhattan. Although Giorgio technically outranked Frank, a duke with a large estate in Portugal, as well as Jack, a count who owned a lavender farm in Provence, they had much in common. Their bachelor apartment had turned into a home when Stefania had come to live with them—home, something Giorgio thought he'd lost when his parents died.

"No, I left a message for him, but he's traveling to Southeast Asia to do medical relief for that cyclone that hit the coast."

Frank made a sound of dismay. "He just got back from the earthquake in Turkey and sounded exhausted. I told him he needed to take some time off to recuperate. What is he thinking?"

"He's a doctor, and his patients come first." Giorgio didn't like it any better than Frank, but Jacques had always been single-minded about his medical career.

"He's going to wear himself out," Frank predicted gloomily, breaking off to shout instructions in Portuguese. Giorgio must have caught him as he was supervising the farmhands. Frank was always experimenting with new crops in addition to the olives and grapes his family's land produced. "But what are we to do with Stefania? She's not old enough to marry."

Giorgio shook his head to decline a second glass of wine from the lounge attendant, a pretty redhead. "I don't like it, either, Frank, but she's twenty-four. At least she's finishing up her graduate degree first. Besides, if you think she was stubborn when she was eleven…"

Frank snorted. "Remember when she refused to go to that fancy prep school you had all picked out for her and insisted on going to the academy of the arts? You even threatened her as her principality's sovereign ruler and what did she do?"

"Called the State Department and requested legal asylum on grounds of persecution." Giorgio sighed. He had tried to forget that little incident. His grandmother had not been amused to receive indignant phone calls from various human rights and refugee organizations.

"*Amigo meu,* maybe it *is* time to turn our girl over to this German fellow. After all, they are the orderly sort." He laughed, and Giorgio had to join in at the idea of anyone keeping Stefania in order. "And when is the blessed event? If she wants to come to my island out in the Azores she and the German can have a private honeymoon—consider it my gift."

Giorgio smiled. "They haven't set a date, but I'll be sure to tell Stefania when I see her Wednesday."

"Give her my love, and make sure this fiancé of hers is a decent guy. If he isn't, then you and Jack and I will talk some sense into her."

"Or I'll just drag her back to Vinciguerra and put her in the dungeon." They had three actually, one cleaned up for the tourists and two that hadn't been used since the Napoleonic Wars.

"Human rights organizations be damned." Frank sounded more cheerful. "We're just living up to the time-honored European tradition of locking stubborn princesses in towers and such."

"Do the time-honored traditions mention princesses with black belts in tae kwon do cleaning their brother's clock?"

"You can only blame yourself for that. You insisted she go to those self-defense classes if she was going to travel to the arts school in that awful neighborhood." Frank laughed. "Come on, things will be fine. If her young man is okay, then pick a date. Jack and I will help you plan her wedding—don't worry."

"The three of us?" Giorgio yelped. "Since when are we wedding experts?" He had fought very hard to be the exact opposite.

"Once you get the dress and the date, everything else falls into place. My mother planned my sisters' weddings. We run large estates—hell, you even run a whole country. How hard could it be?"

"You weren't even living in Portugal at the time—you merely flew in for the weddings and missed months of preparation."

"I did see some of what my mother and her wedding planners did." Frank sounded a bit hurt. "They have notebooks at the bookstore that explain what to do."

"Fine, okay, Frank, we'll all help Stefania as much as we can." Giorgio had no intention of being the lead wedding planner. It sounded like a nightmare in the making.

"*Maravilhosa.* Great." Frank cheered up. "I'll fix up the island however she likes. And I'm good for several barrels of the family sherry."

Giorgio could use a barrel of sherry about now, but his flight was about to board. "Thanks again, Frank. I'll keep you posted."

"Send me the report on her fiancé from the private investigator when it comes in. *Adeus!*" His friend hung up.

Giorgio wasn't sure if Frank was kidding or not about having Dieter investigated. Probably *not* kidding. He tapped his fingers on the small glass table. Should he? Stefania had several million euros in trust funds, some of which were to be released on either her marriage or her twenty-fifth birthday, both coming up within the next year.

He sighed, remembering the trouble some other European royals had run into with their unwise marriages.

Maybe erring on the side of caution…he quickly called his assistant. "Alessandro? Please call that private investigator from that insurance fraud case last year and have him research my sister's fiancé."

Oh, well. If Stefania found out and lost her temper with him, it wouldn't be the first time—or the last.

"Welcome to Peacock Designs—you must be Stefania." Renata came from behind her workstation and warmly shook the bride's hand. She would be a dream to dress, slim but not too skinny, with rich brown eyes and olive skin. Her dark hair lay in curls on her shoulders. She looked like she should be modeling for an Italian tourism poster.

"Yes, I'm Stefania di Leone." Her bride gazed raptly around the salon. "The dresses are all so wonderful. I can't wait to get started." She made a beeline for a full-skirted, tea-length dress.

"Would you like to try this one?" May as well jump right in.

"Absolutely!" She pointed at the other dresses. "And that one, and that one, and that one."

Renata took her client's expensive leather coat and hung it next to her. "The changing room is right here." She ushered Stefania across the pearl-gray carpet into the large curtained alcove that served as her changing room and hung a couple of dresses on the hooks.

Stefania pulled off her pine-green sweater and then stopped. "George! I almost forgot."

"George?"

"My brother—he got a phone call right before we arrived here so he dropped me off. He should be here by now." She pulled an expensive phone out of her leather purse and rapidly sent a text. "There. I told him to get off the phone and get his butt in here."

Renata tried to hide a grin. Good luck with trying to get a guy off his phone and into a bridal salon.

"Do you mind sticking your head out to see if he's here?" Stefania unbuckled her belt. "George is definitely out of his element in a place like this."

"Aren't they all?" Renata backed out of the alcove and made sure the curtains were closed before she went looking for the missing George di Leone. Poor guy. She had conjured up a picture of the hapless Italian brother of the bride, nice enough but not a clue about fashion—just like her own brothers. Probably about average height, maybe running a bit thick around the middle from too much of Mamma's lasagna and cannoli—like her own brothers.

And then *he* walked in.

Renata forced herself to close her jaw at the specimen of exotic Italian manhood that had stepped into her humble little shop.

Not like her brothers, thank the good Lord. A couple inches over six feet, black wavy hair and emerald-green eyes set against the same olive skin as Stefania and no lasagna potbelly in sight. His hair was perfectly cut, short over the ears and slightly longer on top.

He was dressed like Cary Grant in a fantastic suit tailored in Italian charcoal wool by a master. Renata couldn't even begin to guess how much that would have set him back, combined with the finely woven snow-white shirt and expensive gold silk tie.

Renata smoothed her hands along her hips, fiercely glad she'd worn her high-waisted, ruby red 1950s "wiggle" skirt and snug-fitting black blouse. "Are you George?"

"George?" His honeyed voice positively dripped sex, even with that one syllable. "Ah, yes. Stefania has wasted no time. She calls me George." He spoke perfect English with a charming Italian accent.

"I'm guessing you're actually Giorgio." Giorgio di Leone—the lion. Rrrrawwww. She'd purr for him anytime.

"You may call me whatever you'd like, *signorina*. And what may I call you?"

"Renata Pavoni. This is my shop." She offered her hand and he took it, bowing slightly in a European manner.

He released her hand slowly and looked around the shop. "And these are the bridesmaid dresses?" He gestured at a short strapless number in blush pink satin and tulle.

"It could be—but that's a popular style for many brides, as well."

He stared harder. "That is a wedding dress? And so is this?" One had black leaves embroidered on the white satin skirt with a black-trimmed chiffon petticoat.

"Those are perfect for an informal wedding, not necessarily a church wedding. For example, one bride who sang in a rock band got married onstage in a gown much like this to her lead guitar player. They gave a concert after the ceremony."

"A rock band wedding?"

"Lots of fun," she reassured him. She had attended that wedding and had enjoyed the trip down memory lane when they played several hits from her Goth-girl phase. "But not for everyone." She wouldn't tell him about the tiny embroidered black skulls the rocker bride had requested for one of her petticoats. Aunt Barbara had flatly refused to do that embroidery—the handwork of the Devil, she called it, so Renata had sewn skulls until she saw reverse images of them when she closed her eyes at night. Not exactly sweet dreams.

"Not for Stefania. She is having a church wedding." That was Big Brother putting his foot down. Renata hoped that was Stefania's plan, as well. She had a feeling brother and sister were evenly matched in the stubbornness department.

"Many of the dresses are quite appropriate for a church wedding, if that is what Stefania has in mind. Excuse me, I need to check on your sister." She'd been so wrapped up in the brother that she'd almost forgotten about the bride. And if the bride wasn't happy, nobody was happy.

Renata poked her head through the cubicle curtain. Stefania sat on the gray velvet chaise texting someone. She'd been interrupted while undressing and wore a lacy bra and jeans. She looked up from her phone. "Sorry. Dieter is flying home from England and wanted to text me before they make him turn his phone off."

"No problem—let me know when you're ready." Renata wasn't exactly unhappy to return to Giorgio. He still stood politely, waiting for her. She'd forgotten that some men still had old-fashioned manners and would not sit down while a lady was standing. She gestured to the white leather—okay, it was vinyl—couch. "Please, Giorgio, have a seat. Your sister is texting her fiancé before his plane takes off."

"Only if you sit with me for a minute."

Renata hesitated. She never sat down during an appointment, was usually too busy to do so. And she never, ever sat with the bride's family, even if it only consisted of an extremely sexy older brother. She was there to work, not flirt.

"Please, *signorina.* I will not sit unless you do. My grandmother taught me better manners than that, and what kind of man would I be to embarrass my grandmother?"

Okay, now he was flirting, but subtly, not in a wolf-whistle, kiss-the-tips-of-his-fingers type flirting. Maybe she'd flirt back, if she wasn't too rusty to remember how. "If you insist, but only until Stefania needs me."

"Of course." He waited for her to settle onto the couch before sitting about eight inches away from her.

Renata rested her hands on her knees, acutely aware

of his presence. He was the epitome of men's elegance, his silk-clad ankle resting on the opposite knee, his black leather shoes immaculately polished. Even his cologne was classy and masculine, the scent of star anise and sandalwood rising off his warm caramel skin. Her nipples tightened under her blouse and she shifted on the couch to distract herself—in vain, of course. Well, she was a warm-blooded American woman with the male equivalent of an all-you-can-eat Italian buffet sitting next to her, complete with dessert. Mmm, Giorgio as dessert…she thought about that until she realized his delicious lips were speaking.

"Stefania is quite the whirlwind. She did not give you any information about herself or the wedding?" For some reason, he leaned forward, almost as if to gauge her reaction.

Back to business. "None at all. She told me over the phone that she'd just become engaged and was bringing her brother to shop for a wedding dress. I assumed the rest of your family was back in Italy and couldn't come over right away."

He sat back and sighed. "The rest of our family is our grandmother, who is indeed back in Italy, recovering from pneumonia."

If his grandmother was all he and Stefania had left…oh, dear.

He must have read her growing dismay. "Yes, unfortunately, our parents were killed in a car accident many, many years ago." He shrugged wide shoulders. "*Nonna* and I raised Stefania as best as we could, but searching for a wedding dress to wear on what I hope will be the happiest day of my sister's life?" He clenched his hands on his knees. "This is for our mother to do, not a stupid older brother."

Renata grabbed his hand, wrapping her fingers around his tense ones. "You are not stupid. Stefania waited to come in because she wanted you here with her. I know you both must miss your mother, but you are the person she loves and needs for this."

He looked down at their entwined fingers. She inwardly groaned. Her impulsive nature had gotten the best of her again and now she was holding hands with her client's sexy brother whom she'd met, oh, approximately twelve minutes ago. Talk about professional and businesslike.

She tried to tug her hand away, but he tightened his grip. "Signorina Renata, how did such a beautiful, young lady become so wise?"

An unladylike snort escaped her. "Years of foolishness."

The curtain rustled. "Renata, how do you zip this?" Stefania called.

Renata leaped to her feet as if one of her straight pins had fallen into the cushion and stabbed her in the butt. "Excuse me, please." He was there for dress-shopping, not getting mushy glances from the hired help. Giorgio released her hand and stood politely as she disappeared into the dressing room.

The bride held the bodice against her and Renata zipped up the back, slipping into sales mode. "All right, this is a tea-length, white lace dress over a white tulle petticoat. As you can see, the skirt is very full." So full that it was pushing Renata away from the bride as she fastened the hook-and-eye closure at the top of the zipper. "It has three-quarter-length sleeves that reach about to the middle of your forearm and a wide neckline that shows off your neck and shoulders nicely." She backed away so Stefania could get the full picture of how she would look.

"Is it the lighting or is there some pink at the bottom?"

"Yes, the neckline and petticoat are hemmed with a pale pink thread for decoration."

Stefania shook her head. "Not for me."

"No problem." Renata helped her out of the dress and carefully hung it up. "Here's one without the pink." Renata fitted her into a few more white dresses but Stefania just looked at herself in the mirror with a worried look.

"Sorry, Renata. I'm not usually this picky."

"Yes, you are," her brother called over the curtain.

"Can it, George," she retorted. "This is important."

Renata intervened. "You want to make sure to get the right dress for your special day."

"Whatever you pick will be a trend-setter," Giorgio predicted. What a nice brother—her own brothers would be loudly pitying whatever poor idiot Renata had suckered into marrying her.

"Yeah, I know." Stefania still looked glum. And pale, which was odd considering her beautiful warm skin tone.

"How often do you wear white?" she asked.

Stefania twirled back and forth, her eyes glued to the mirror. "I have a nice winter-white cashmere coat, and some ivory turtlenecks. Oh, and an eggshell silk short-sleeved blouse with the cutest tie at the neck. Dieter loves me in that," she confided. "He thinks it makes me look sexy."

A loud groan startled them. "*Dio mio,* Stefania, save the racy stories for your bachelorette party, will you?"

They both snickered at the typical brotherly response. But Renata returned to the dress subject quickly. "All of those whites you like to wear are actually not pure white. With your lovely coloring, you're attracted to ivories and off-whites. I think this pure white is washing you out."

"Oh. I thought it was the lighting."

"Nope, it's the fabric color." Renata had actually paid one of her lighting designer friends to install the most flattering light possible. "Wait here."

She ducked out of the cubicle. Giorgio looked up from his phone. Renata thought his interest would drop when he saw it was just her, but instead his gaze sharpened. "And which one of your dresses did you pick out for yourself?"

"For me?" She was flustered for a second. "I like all of them, but I've never needed one, I mean…"

"Your boyfriend hasn't, how do they say, popped the question?"

Exhilaration roared through her. "Boyfriend? What boyfriend?" She strutted into the stockroom, making sure her wiggle skirt lived up to its name.

3

Giorgio fought to keep the drool from shorting out his phone. Renata Pavoni was the sexiest woman he'd met in a long time, her dark blue eyes gleaming in a knowing manner. Even the tiny diamond decorating the side of her lovely straight nose turned him on. Like any real man, he loved curvy women instead of the unhealthy string-bean look. And the way she worked that round ass of hers under the tight skirt—*che bella ragazza*—what a beautiful girl. Like those old black-and-white movies his *nonna* liked, where the women's sultry eyes promised untold delights once their men removed their formfitting, low-cut dresses.

Removing Renata's clothing—opening her sheer black blouse, button by button. Peeling down—no, pushing up her tight red skirt to discover for himself if she was vintage down to the garter belt and hose.

The image of Renata's rich red hair spread out on his pillow as he kneeled over her was too much for his lonely, deprived cock, which immediately sprang to life.

Giorgio muttered a curse under his breath. Poor timing, to lose control in the middle of a wedding boutique with his sister only meters away. He peeled off his suit jacket and draped it over his lap, but then his phone buzzed—his assistant, Alessandro. *"Pronto,"* he answered.

"*Signor,* the investigator sent me a preliminary report on the person you requested."

"Ah, yes." Giorgio darted a guilty look at the dressing room, half expecting Stefania to come roaring out. "*Un momento,* Alessandro. I am going to step outside to talk." He leaped to his feet and headed for the front door, his jacket slung over his forearm. "Okay, give me the highlights and then send a copy to my phone."

"According to the report, the princess's fiancé, Dieter von Thalberg, was born to Graf Hans and Grafin Maria von Thalberg, Count and Countess of Thalberg, thirty years ago in Bavaria. He is heir to a large brewery on his mother's side as well as to the ancestral holdings on his father's."

"So he has money as long as the Germans drink beer—forever, I would think. Excellent." He'd heard enough horror stories from acquaintances about freeloaders marrying their sisters, breaking their hearts and then demanding large sums of money in exchange for not writing a sleazy tell-all book.

"Dieter von Thalberg is also the star forward for a big German football club." Alessandro's voice grew animated. "I didn't realize it was the same person—he uses a shortened version of his family name as a player. Three years ago he set the league record for goals scored. But since he turned thirty, he has not had as much playing time and was heavily recruited to come play for a team in New York, probably where he met the princess— *Signor,* why do the Americans call it soccer? I have always wondered. Anyway, the investigator will continue to look for any items in his past that would cause difficulties—previous marriages, illegitimate offspring, personal encounters with, um, professional ladies, videorecordings of a sexual nature, that sort of thing."

Giorgio winced. Stefania would kill him for sure if she found out he was investigating Dieter for prostitutes and sex tapes, but so be it. If the man had something to hide, better she knew sooner than later.

Renata opened the door and poked her head out. "Stefania wants you."

"Okay." He got off the phone and returned to the boutique.

"Sit." Renata pointed to the sofa and he complied. She could boss him around anytime. "Here comes the bride!" She swung the curtain aside and a glorious woman emerged. This couldn't be his baby sister. This young goddess glowed in a golden nimbus of light, her hair a dark cloud around her radiant face.

His jaw dropped. "Stefania?" he asked, as if Renata had exchanged her for another woman.

The vision giggled and broke the spell. "Of course, *stupido*—who else?"

"Wow, Stefania, you look—you look—" He was stammering now.

"Amazing," Renata supplied. "Perfect. Wonderful."

"Yes, yes, all of those." He rubbed a hand over his face. *Mamma mia,* when had she grown into such a beautiful woman? And he would be walking her down the Vinciguerra cathedral aisle to give her hand in holy matrimony to a thug footballer. He desperately wished his *nonna* were here, that his parents were still here on earth, but all he could do was muddle along on his own.

Renata seemed to sense his turmoil and glided toward his sister. "This is a tea-length satin dress with a portrait neckline and ruching down the front." He understood the satin dress part but that was about it.

"Look at all these cool petticoats, George." Stefania lifted her skirt and he winced, but all he saw was layers of fluffy fabric.

"Yes, um, very nice."

"Renata is going to edge a couple petticoats in gold satin ribbon so they catch the light when I turn. And she says her aunt is absolutely fabulous at embroidery and can decorate one with my and Dieter's initials. Don't you just love the color? Renata calls it *champagne*."

"But—it's not white." Giorgio was still thunderstruck by Stefania's womanly transformation and couldn't think of anything to say but the obvious.

His sister shrugged. "Princess Diana didn't wear a white dress, either—hers was ivory." Renata circled her, pulling at the fabric to check the fit.

"Yes, and *Nonna* always said look what happened to *that* marriage."

She stabbed a slender finger at him. "Stop it, Giorgio! The Princess was very kind to me at Mamma and Papa's funeral."

Renata dropped a handful of satin and stared at them. "Wait—Princess Diana came to your parents' funeral?"

Giorgio and Stefania exchanged glances and faced her. Giorgio spoke first. "Yes, she did, and you're right, Stefania. She was kind to both of us."

"I didn't tell Renata about our family, George." Stefania blinked rapidly. "I just wanted to be a regular bride looking at dresses without any fanfare or fuss."

"Tell me what?" Renata folded her arms across her magnificent chest.

"We should introduce ourselves again, Stefania, don't you think?" Giorgio bowed again, hoping that the truth wouldn't send the woman screaming out the door or straight to the tabloids. "May I present my sister Stefania Maria

Cristina Angela Martelli di Leone, *principessa di* Vinciguerra and I am Giorgio Alphonso Paolo Martelli di Leone, *il principe* di Vinciguerra."

"Come on, every bride is a princess on her wedding day, but you—you're a real princess?"

His sister nodded. "But it's a small country, really. Giorgio hardly needs to do anything to keep it running."

He glared at his sister—now Renata would think he was a brainless dilettante. She wore a peculiar expression as it was. "So you're a prince? Correct me if I'm wrong, but Italy is a republic now."

"Our grandmother, Giorgio and I make up the royal family of Vinciguerra, which is one of only two principalities on the Italian peninsula that wasn't taken over when Italy unified in the 1800s," Stefania explained glibly, having given the history lecture many times before. "The rest of the small duchies and kingdoms were absorbed into the greater Italian republic—but not ours. Our father was the Crown Prince, and now Giorgio's got the gig."

His slacker-prince/do-nothing gig. "Yes, I do my best. I do apologize, Signorina Renata, if we have not been up front with you from the beginning, but it is difficult to know if someone will call the infernal paparazzi. They can be very unpleasant."

"Like when Mamma and Papa died."

Giorgio's face hardened into grim lines, remembering the brokenhearted little girl who had sobbed into his chest for years after the awful loss. "So far those jackals do not know about Stefania's engagement, but they will find out eventually."

"Not from me, they won't!" Renata's eyes snapped, her New York accent thickening.

"Of course not," Stefania defended her. "But once they know that I am getting my wedding dress from you, they will not give you a moment's rest. It will be good for your business, though," she added quickly. "Lots of publicity."

"Oh." Renata obviously hadn't considered that aspect, and he appreciated it. "I never blab about our clients and I'll make sure my aunt doesn't, either."

"We appreciate it, Renata." Stefania hugged her, and Giorgio wished he could do the same.

"So this is the dress you want, Stefania?"

His sister turned to him, her eyes shining. "Oh, yes, George, I love it. I know it's shorter than what Vinciguerran brides usually wear, but won't it look lovely in the cathedral with its marble and gold decorations?"

"You will look lovely." He cupped her shoulders and kissed her on the forehead. His eyes watered a bit—had to be the Brooklyn air. He faced Renata, who wore a knowing smile on her red lips. "We'd like to get this dress—perfect for a princess."

"Absolutely." Renata hustled Stefania over to the trifold mirror and they baffled Giorgio with their discussion of fabric options, cuts and embellishments. His only contribution was his credit card once Stefania went to change into her regular clothing.

He blinked at the total on the slip—surely all that fine custom work had to cost more. He glanced up at Renata. "That's all?"

She put her hands on her hips. "Did you expect me to mark it up just because you're this, this royalty thing?"

"Yes," he answered truthfully.

"Then those other shop owners are scumbags. You should find someplace better."

He pushed the signed slip toward her. "I believe we have."

A faint flush crept up her neckline into her cheeks. She

busied herself by shutting down the computer and fussing with a stack of papers.

"You are finished for the day?"

She glanced over her shoulder at a black cat clock with a swinging tail. "I'm meeting my friend at the art school to see a new student exhibit."

Stefania burst out of the dressing room. "And I have class in an hour, George. Can you take me back to Manhattan?"

"Of course." Stefania inexplicably refused to use the car service most of the time in favor of the subway but she was in a hurry. "And, Signorina Renata, are you going to Manhattan, as well?"

"Well, yes, but I don't want to inconvenience you."

"No inconvenience." Stefania tugged on her short wool coat and belted it. "Come on, it'll be fun." Her merry gaze darted between her brother and her dress designer.

Giorgio gave her a neutral smile. So his little sister had picked up on his attraction to Renata and was playing matchmaker. She was in love, ergo, the whole world should be in love. He was a grown man—he knew better. Love was for fresh young girls and foolish young men.

"If you're sure." Renata wrapped herself in a black trench coat, her red lips and hair heating him up. She looked like a sensual spy from a war movie—the brave secret agent who arrives at her contact's apartment one foggy night, wearing her trench coat and nothing else. Or maybe in a corset and that black garter belt he'd imagined earlier…

"George? George!" Stefania was already at the door. "Renata's waiting for you so she can set the alarm."

Grateful he still carried his suit coat in front of him, Giorgio hurried to the door. Paolo must have been watching because he pulled the black limo up to the curb within seconds, coming around to open the doors for them.

"Renata, you sit in back with George. I want to visit with

Paolo since I haven't seen him in months." Stefania again, with part two of her plot. Visit with Paolo? The man put lie to the stereotype that all Italians were chatty. Giorgio would be surprised if Paolo spoke a dozen words a day.

Renata of course didn't know this and slid into the leather backseat and the big car fought its way through traffic to the Brooklyn Bridge, one of his favorite New York landmarks.

Renata tucked her shapely legs to the side as she stared up at the stone towers and steel cables. "It's amazing how well built the bridge is for being so old."

Giorgio smiled. His country still had remnants of ancient Roman bridges, but the Brooklyn Bridge was old by American standards.

Renata's phone buzzed and she reached into her handbag to check the text display. "Oh, darn. My friend Flick had some bad Thai food last night and can't make it to the gallery." She replied to the text and put away the phone.

"Flick?"

Renata grinned. "Her real name is Felicity, but it wasn't edgy enough for her as an up-and-coming artist with turquoise streaks in her hair. She told me to go ahead and she'd catch the exhibit some other time."

Giorgio mentally consigned all the business activities he had planned to the trash heap. "I would be happy to take you to the exhibit. I have no plans for the afternoon."

"Are you sure?" Her lips pursed thoughtfully.

He sneaked a look at Stefania, who was chattering away in Italian to Paolo, who nodded occasionally. He didn't want to let her know that he was going along with her scheming. "I would enjoy doing so."

"In that case, Giorgio, I'd be happy to show you around."

"My pleasure." It was the pleasure of spending time

with her, but he didn't want to come on too strong. "I am Vinciguerran—we love beautiful works of art. All kinds." Especially the one sitting next to him.

4

GIORGIO HATED THE ART—if he even thought of it as art. Renata wasn't convinced from the sideways glance out of the corner of her eye. Scary how well she could read him after only meeting him this morning. He had sent his beefy driver back to their hotel.

"And this signifies..." He gestured elegantly at the smelly mess of vegetation on the floor.

She peered at the information tag. "The broken cornstalks and soybean plants tell the plight of the family farmer in the ever-growing domination of industrial agriculture."

He blinked. "Ah." Giorgio was a good sport, though, examining what looked like his *nonna's* compost heap.

"Let's see the next." She slipped her hand into the crook of his elbow to tug him to another dubious installation. Lovely. A tangle of rusty barbed wire. Her heel caught on the rough concrete floor and he steadied her.

"Careful, Renata. I do not want to take you for a tetanus shot." He smiled down at her and she forgot for a second that he was an honest-to-God prince of someplace in Italy and his suit cost more than she made in a year. No, when he smiled at her, he was just Mr. Hot Guy who made her want to shred that expensive suit off him with her teeth.

Her breathing sped up, pressing her breasts into the nice bodice of her black blouse.

He noticed, his fingers tightening on hers. Not so cool on the inside, then. "And this represents the tangle of modern life?"

"No, the plight of refugees."

Giorgio nodded. "Stefania is patroness of a charity for women and children that often works with refugee and displaced families."

"At her age?" Stefania wasn't much younger than Renata.

"Since she was thirteen." His tone was full of love and admiration. "She testified in front of the United Nations High Commissioner for Refugees when she was nineteen. Stefania has become a better strategist since then. Perhaps I should have discouraged her from studying political science, but when a twelve-year-old reads Machiavelli's *The Prince* so she can pass political tips on to her older brother, what else would I expect?"

Renata let him guide her along to the next exhibit. It was a video installation with a variety of blurry faces grimacing in turn as loud static played in the background. Giorgio regarded it with the same pleasant expression he'd pasted on his face as soon as they'd walked in. He really was a polished man.

Renata went up on tiptoe to whisper in his ear. "This is just awful. Do you mind if we leave now?"

"Aren't you enjoying yourself." His eyes twinkled.

"You'll know when I'm enjoying myself," she assured him.

"Indeed?" He turned his head slowly so their faces were almost touching. Renata swallowed hard. She thought he was going to kiss her but he clenched his jaw instead. Perhaps public displays of affection were against the Vinciguerran Royal Book of Etiquette. "I will call Paolo to pick us up."

"No, don't." She didn't want anyone intruding in what was turning out to be a very intriguing afternoon. "It's a nice day—let's walk."

"Where?"

"A surprise." She tugged him out of the gallery and onto the sidewalk, tipping her face up. "Ah, sun. Makes up for a long and gloomy winter."

"An Italian girl like you should always get plenty of sun."

She patted her jaw. "Bad for the complexion. The rest of my family has the typical dark hair and olive skin like you, but I only burn."

"No wonder you have such lovely skin. You must be careful when you travel to Italy the next time. You know our sun can be very strong."

"The next time? I've never been to Italy before."

He stopped and stared down at her. "Your name is Renata Pavoni and you've never visited Italy? How can that be?"

She laughed and led him along the busy street. "My parents have five of us. You've never priced out airfare to Europe for seven, but my mother did once. We heard her scream of shock down the street."

Giorgio looked momentarily startled—budget concerns didn't cross his radar. He nodded thoughtfully. "What part of Italy did your family come from?"

"After the war, my grandparents on my mom's side came from a little village on the Italian Riviera called Corniglia. My *nonna* says the town is perched on a huge rock surrounded by grapevines. They make this special kind of wine found nowhere else in the world."

"Scciachetrà."

"Yeah, that's right. We crack open a bottle every New Year's Eve to toast the old country." Renata shivered in remembrance. "Boy, is that stuff strong. Made of raisins, so the sugar is very concentrated."

"I've never tried it, although we have something similar in Vinciguerra, called Bocca di Leone—The Lion's Mouth. We serve it in thimble-size glasses and no one can drink more than a few without falling over." He sighed. "I'll have to make sure we have enough for Stefania's wedding. It's the traditional toast for weddings, especially royal weddings."

"And you are the di Leone family, after all."

"Our ancestors invented it." He grinned down at her. "I may need a couple stiff drinks before I walk Stefania down the aisle."

"Buck up, Giorgio." She patted his arm. "Everyone gets a bit misty-eyed when they give the bride away. Which sword and medals will you be wearing?"

Giorgio gave her a sidelong look. "Sometimes I cannot tell if you are joking with me or not."

"That's because you are much too serious." She gestured. "Look at the beautiful day! Here we are in the most fabulous city in the world, we have lovely Central Park over there, the sun is shining, your sister has her wedding dress and you didn't have a nervous breakdown trying to shop for one. Do you know how rare it is to keep good mental health shopping for a bridal gown?"

"Um, no."

"When I worked at a regular bridal salon, fits of hysteria, therapeutic slapping and tranquilizers of dubious legality were an everyday occurrence."

"It seems I've dodged the bullet."

"You sure have. Hey, let's cut through the park."

HE TOOK A DEEP BREATH of the spring-scented air, the pale green leaves on the trees unfolding from their winter's rest.

The tension started to leave his muscles, although they were still mighty buff.

"See? All you needed was a nice little nature walk. I bet it's been a long time since you got outdoors for some fresh air. A guy like you isn't meant to be cooped up indoors pushing paperwork all day. Maybe you should get yourself a yacht—I mean if you don't already have one—"

"We have my father's yacht. We loan it out to people for field trips and marine science expeditions."

"Weddings, proms and bar mitzvahs."

He grinned. "Probably, if anybody requested it."

"Don't you or your sister ever use it?"

"Stefania does for her charity fundraisers." They passed near a tree and he held a branch back that might have scratched her face.

"Not for that, but for your personal use."

He shook his head. "Not since she started at the university and I took over more duties from my grandmother."

"All work and no play makes Giorgio a dull boy," she quoted the old saying. Imagine owning a yacht and being too busy to use it. Running even a small country must take an enormous amount of time.

"Then I should stop being so dull."

He pulled her to the side of the path underneath a big oak tree. "Is that red lipstick smudge-proof?"

"Yeah, pretty much. It actually has a sealant clear gloss that—"

"Good," he cut her off. Wow, for a prince he needed some work on conversational manners.

He kissed her.

And he did *not* need some work on his kissing. Renata's mouth fell open in shock and he took advantage, slipping his tongue between her hopefully smudge-proof lips. She clutched his broad shoulders as he caressed her mouth with his, gently nibbling and sucking at her lips.

Renata had never been kissed like this, with passion and lust but tenderness, too. Her previous boyfriends had been younger than Giorgio, in their early or mid-twenties, and had either been tentative in their kisses or overly aggressive, mashing her lips as if to prove their desire. Now Giorgio was planting kisses across her jaw and holy crap—he licked her neck's equivalent of a G-spot and she nearly screamed with pleasure.

His hot breath quickened against her skin and she knew he was as on fire as she was. "Mmm, Renata." He lifted his head.

Renata's eyes fluttered open when she realized he wasn't kissing her anymore. "Wow."

He wore a dazed look on his face, as well. At least she wasn't the only one. She probably would have socked him if he'd been gloating. "I am sorry, Renata."

"Sorry for kissing me?" She shoved him away and plopped her hands on her hips.

"Never. Sorry for pushing you against a tree and kissing you in public." His lips were plump from kisses but her lipstick had lived up to its promise.

She wanted to taste his mouth again—hell, taste him all over. "You'd rather kiss me in private?" She traced her finger up his golden silk tie.

Giorgio caught her hand in his and pressed a kiss to the palm. "I would like nothing more."

A handful of female runners clattered along the path next to them, all of them ogling Giorgio. He turned away, not wanting to be recognized.

He rubbed his face. "Much as I'd like to invite you to my suite at the Plaza—"

"You have a suite at the Plaza?" she interrupted. "Is it as fancy as in the movies? I've only been in the lobby once."

"I don't know about the movies, my rooms are very nice. But…"

"Too fast, isn't it?" she asked ruefully. Despite her brassy attitude, Renata didn't want to hop into bed with a guy an hour after she met him. Well, she did, but she wouldn't.

He nodded solemnly. "Paolo hasn't had time to do a background check on you."

She squawked in indignation and socked him in the arm.

"Ow!" He clutched his arm and laughed. "Renata, I'm just kidding. It's too fast because I want to get to know you better."

"Good answer." She stood on her tiptoes and kissed his cheek. And although she wanted Giorgio pretty badly, he came with miles and miles of strings attached—business, money and the fact that he had his own country. Maybe it would be best to leave it at a quick kiss. A hot, wet, tongue-tangling kiss on a romantic spring afternoon in the most romantic park in New York City.

Renata mentally slapped herself before she dragged Giorgio back behind that tree and did something to the man that started with *public* and ended with *indecency*. "What's next?" It was a bigger question than it seemed.

He took her hand again. "What would a beautiful New Yorker like to do on an unexpected afternoon away from work?"

Renata spotted a white gleam from beyond the leafy green trees. "How about the real art museum?"

"Whatever you'd like."

That wasn't an option. She dabbed at her mouth with a handkerchief. "How's my lipstick?"

"Lovely." He smiled down at her. "But I could make it smudge if I had enough time."

"I bet you could," she breathed. Darn it, he wasn't making this easy for her. "Come on, let's go."

RENATA LED GIORGIO UP the marble steps to the main entrance of the Metropolitan Museum of Art. He gazed up at the impressive multi-story facade along Fifth Avenue. "Stefania and I came here at least once a month while she was growing up. I haven't been since the cleaning and restoration several years ago. It's quite a dramatic change."

"The gray stone actually turned out to be white after all." The tall marble columns with elaborately carved tops and arched high windows looked like a Greek temple—a temple of art. "Are you sure you don't mind coming along for the historical costume exhibit? Most men aren't terribly interested in women's clothing—just how to undo them." She felt a flush rise in her cheeks.

He laughed at her bluntness and held out his elbow for her to take. She accepted and they started to climb the steep stairs. "But I am terribly interested in women's clothing. Didn't I prove that by flying all the way to New York to look at wedding dresses?"

"It was very sweet of you to come." She impulsively squeezed his upper arm. No give at all. His expensive Italian suit was covering an equally nice body.

"I try to do what Stefania tells me." Giorgio smiled at her. "The children's book where the brother and sister run away to live in this museum was her favorite as a girl. I was quite terrified she might try the same thing, so I brought her here whenever she asked me. If I couldn't, then my friends Jack and Frank did."

He held the door for Renata and they went to the ticket counter. "Two tickets for the museum and the costume exhibit," she told the museum employee, reaching into her purse for the money.

Giorgio put his hand over hers. "My treat, I insist." He reached for his slim wallet tucked into his jacket pocket.

"No, no, you're my guest." She went for her purse again.

"No." He gave a credit card to the employee who hastily swiped it through the reader before they could cause any more delay in her line.

Renata clamped her lips together and accepted her ticket. They went into the museum foyer and she pulled him aside. "Look, just because you are a prince and all doesn't mean I can't afford to pay for museum tickets."

He gave her a considering look. "You think I paid because I have much more money than you?"

"Yes."

"No." He took her hand. "I would pay for your ticket with the last money I owned because I'm a man and you're a beautiful woman who makes me laugh and enjoy myself. Unfortunately, that is a rare occurence for me."

"Oh, please." She made a dismissive gesture with her free hand.

"No, thank you." He caught her other hand. "I know I've had many advantages in my life, but free time isn't one of them."

"Same here." She squeezed his hands. He had said she was beautiful, so she'd cut him some slack. Well, a lot of slack.

"Let's not waste any of our precious time. Shall we go to the costume exhibit?"

"Absolutely. Then we can see whatever you'd like," she offered.

He offered her his arm again, and they followed the signs to the gallery. "I've already seen most of the regular collection, so your special exhibit sounds just fine."

"How about the arms and armor collection? Men always like that."

He sniffed disdainfully. “We have a much better collection at home.”

“What? Better than the museum?”

“I’m just kidding.” He nudged her playfully and she snorted.

“But you do have some arms and armor at your house.”

“At the local museum,” he clarified. “But the armor used to be at my house.”

“You got tired of peasants wandering through looking at it?”

“If all peasants were as lovely as you, I would have no problem with that.” She raised her eyebrows. “I’m only joking, Renata. I’m priviledged to serve my people, not the other way around.”

“All right, then.” She let him off the hook. For a prince, he wasn’t very arrogant. Not that she knew very many. Or any.

He wrapped his arm around her shoulder and pointed to the gallery entrance. “Here we are.”

Renata gave a gasp as she and Giorgio entered the darkened, dramatically lit hall. “Now this is what I call a real art exhibit.” Strategically placed spotlights illuminated mannequins in elegant 1890’s ballgowns.

“Very elegant,” Giorgio agreed. “And little danger of tetanus.”

Renata went as close to the mannequins as she could without getting tossed out of the museum and peered at the fine details of the gowns. They were satin, velvet and silk. The silhouette was a tight bodice flowing out to a small bustle and then fabric draping down to the floor in a small train. The embroidery was elaborately done with crystals, pearls and jet accents. Butterflies and flowers, swirls and loops. “Maybe I haven’t been taking enough advantage of Aunt Barbara’s skills. She could do this in her sleep.”

"The lady who is going to embroider Stefania and Dieter's initials on her, um, underskirt?"

Renata laughed. Typical brother. "That's her. She'll be disappointed she missed you." The overwhelming understatement of the century. A real live prince and princess came to out-of-the-way Peacock Designs and Aunt Barbara was sitting in the gastroenterologist's waiting room. She'd at least get to meet Stefania when she came for her fittings.

The next rooms had sports clothing, a revolutionary idea in the late nineteenth century. Although playing tennis in a floor-length dress or riding a bicycle in a wool skirt and suitjacket didn't appeal to Renata, she saw the historical importance of the broadening of women's activities.

Ah, more ball gowns, but this time they were a flowing, turn-of-the-century style with Asian-influenced fasteners and draping tunic silhouettes. Another set of new ideas for her.

"Art Nouveau, one of my favourite eras." Giorgio gazed at the Tiffany stained-glass windows and classic Italian opera posters.

"Oh, my God, me, too! I just love Gustav Klimt's painting with the man and woman embracing surrounded by all that gold and jewel tones."

"The Kiss." His gaze dropped to her lips.

She licked her mouth, suddenly dry. "Yes, it's called *The Kiss*."

"Have you been to Vienna to see it?" he asked.

She laughed and the spell was broken—at least temporarily. "No, I haven't made it to Vienna yet." Or anywhere east of the Atlantic Ocean.

"You should go."

With what money? She caught his hand and pulled him along. He was a sweet guy, but there was a world of difference—and money—between them. "Maybe someday. Oh, look at the suffragettes' uniforms. Very masculine."

Giorgio stood patiently next to her, not fidgeting a bit or checking his phone as she examined the clothing in the remaining rooms. She wished she could take photos, but the light was too low to get any of the details. They exited into a gift shop with several reproduction jewelry items and books on art and fashion of the time period covered.

Giorgio picked up the hardcover, full-color photo book that accompanied the exhibit. "Would you allow me to buy you a small gift, a souvenir of our afternoon together?"

"That book's not exactly small." But she was dying to get her hands on it, especially to look at the beading and embroidery in close detail.

"I'll carry it for you if it's too heavy." His green eyes twinkled.

She paused for a second and then decided her self-reliance could take a backseat to graciousness for once. "That would be lovely. Thank you."

Giorgio seemed surprised, as if he'd expected her to tussle with him over it. "You're welcome." He hastened to the cash register to pay for it before she changed her mind, probably.

Renata busied herself by examining the jewelry. It was a bit elaborate for her tastes, with filigree and crystals and jet beads galore. Aunt Barbara would love it.

"Do you see anything you like here?" he asked.

She shook her head. "I was just thinking my aunt would like some of this. She likes more…elaborate things than I do."

He eyed her up and down. "A woman who looks like a forties' movie star doesn't think that counts as elaborate?"

"I suppose silk stockings with seams up the back can't be considered plain."

"Not at all." His voice sounded husky for a second. "But authentic, right?"

"Absolutely." Renata had to clear her own throat. "Maybe I'll bring Aunt Barbara to see the exhibit. I've encouraged her to branch out a bit with some designs of her own."

"With you as her mentor, I'm sure it would be a success."

"That's kind of you."

Giorgio shrugged. "Only the truth. You're a self-made woman, whereas I'm the royal caretaker, making sure everything stays intact for the next generation." He sounded a bit dejected.

"But that's important, too. You have thousands of families depending on you to make sure everything runs smoothly, that parents can give their children the opportunities to succeed that they might not have had themselves."

He grinned. "You've very smart, you know that?"

"Of course. And now, if you'll call for that slick car of yours we can tour around for a bit before you meet your sister for dinner."

He immediately texted his driver who showed up in an impossibly short period of time. Giorgio helped her into the limo. "Drive downtown, Paolo."

Paolo nodded and they slid away from the curb. Renata settled back into the luxurious seats. She didn't know where the royal ride was going, but she was sure it would be memorable.

"THANK YOU FOR DINNER, Renata." Giorgio relaxed back into the limo seat. "I have to admit I am not used to ladies paying for me."

"Don't be silly, it was just a chili dog," she chided him. She hadn't been in a limo since one of her brothers' weddings, and this was much nicer than being stuffed into the back with several giddy bridesmaids in poufy dresses. "I'll add it onto the alterations bill for your sister's dress if you insist."

He leaned toward her. "I do."

Stefania had called to cancel dinner since she had a term paper due soon and her fiancé was fogged in at Heathrow airport anyway.

Giorgio had called his driver to come get them and they had cruised the city as best as they could with a giant limo. But it was getting late, and Renata had reluctantly told Giorgio to head for Brooklyn.

"Tell me when you are free again." Giorgio twined his fingers between hers.

"Free for what?"

"Free to see me again. I'll take you to the Plaza for dinner."

She rested her head on his shoulder. "Only if they serve chili dogs."

"I'll make sure they do." He ran the back of his hand along her cheek. "I want to see you again."

Oh, so did she. "Would you like to see my neighborhood?"

"What?" He looked out the window at the identical row houses stretching as far as they could see.

"Tell your driver to cruise around in this area for a little while. I'll give you a private tour." She was practically crawling out of her skin with lust and finally gave in.

He pressed an intercom button and gave instructions in Italian. "There. He will drive around until I tell him to stop. He cannot see or hear anything in the back so you can feel free to say whatever you want." He pressed a button that turned on hidden dim lighting. "I want to see you while we talk. You are the sexiest woman I have ever met."

She snorted.

"What?" He furrowed his black brows. "You do not think you are sexy?"

"Oh, I know I am." And that had been hard-won self-knowledge. "But I'm no six-foot, one-hundred-pound supermodel."

"Thank God," he said fervently. "I'm not a man who likes women with more muscle than me." He caressed her cheek. "A real man wants a real woman, soft and smooth." He trailed his hand down her neck to her shoulder. "Round and ripe, like a juicy peach plucked from the tree."

Renata was ready to be plucked, backseat of the car or not. Her nipples were as hard as peach pits inches from where his fingers stroked the base of her neck and her "fruit juices" were definitely ready for sampling. "And you are a real man, Giorgio," she purred.

"You know I am, Renata."

"Tell me what you think of me—all real, by the way." She sat back and slowly unbuttoned her blouse, her eyes never leaving his. He swallowed hard as her black lace bra appeared.

"Bella, che bella." Still he hesitated, so she shrugged the blouse off her shoulders.

"All for you, Giorgio." She unfastened her French twist and shook her red hair loose like a pinup girl. "I've been waiting all day for your touch. Don't make me wait anymore. You don't want to get a reputation for a tease, do you?"

He groaned, his cock stretching his Italian wool pants in a way the designers never intended. She crawled over to him and cupped his erection. His green eyes practically rolled back into his head. He was huge even through the cloth, his plump head firm and round under her fingers. The thought of all that Italian goodness inside her made her shiver. She started to unzip him.

The next second she was flat on her back on the seat, her bra gone and her breasts bare. His mouth was firmly fastened to one nipple, his fingers playing with the other. He sucked on her as if he were starving for her, and she was starving for him. She arched her back, pushing her breast up for his easier access.

He switched to the other breast, leaving her nipple moist and swollen in the cool air. She shivered and hardened even further.

So did he, his cock pressing against her inner thigh. She wiggled under him and he lifted his glossy black head. "You make me crazy."

"Then go crazy with me."

"Not yet." He slid his hand up her thigh and stopped. "Ah, *Dio mio,* you are wearing *giarretterre*—I do not know the word in English."

"Garters," she supplied. "I'm glad you like them."

"I love them," he said hoarsely. He caressed the slice of thigh between her panties and stockings and cupped her bare ass. "A thong? You are going to set me off like a rocket and I have not even seen you yet."

He shimmied her skirt up around her waist and stared down at her in rapture. "Look at you. So beautiful."

Renata looked down at herself. Her lower half could be described charitably as curvy and fat by several skinny bitches she'd run into over the years.

He kissed her soft belly and she jumped at the ticklish sensation. He grinned up at her. "You give up another secret to me, Renata. You are ticklish."

"You just startled me," she informed him loftily and jumped a second time when he darted his tongue into her navel.

"And again?" He made circular tracks with his tongue,

widening out from her belly button and down to the tiny black ribbon at the top of her thong.

"Well, yes."

As he nuzzled the ribbon, his breath was hot on her belly. He hooked the front panel of her thong and pulled it free. "Are you ticklish here?" He slid his finger between her folds and zoomed in on her clit.

Her back bowed as he lazily circled that greedy bit of flesh and all she could do was groan.

"If you don't like it, I can stop."

Renata smiled at his blather and her eyes rolled back in her head as he lowered his mouth to her thong. With his tongue he caressed her clit, soft and wet at first and then harder as he pressed her with its tip. Her legs fell apart and she gave herself up to his tongue. His big hands had gone right where he wanted, cupping and molding her ass with fervor and appreciation.

Then her mind shut off and her body took over. Or Giorgio took over her body. His five o'clock shadow rasped her inner thighs but his lips were gentle as he drew her clit into his mouth and sucked.

Her fingernails left marks in the soft leather upholstery. Anticipation raced up her belly into her breasts, tightening her nipples even further. She rolled them between her fingers, earning a groan of approval from Giorgio as he raised his head to watch her.

Her brazenness inspired him and he dived back down—this time slipping a finger inside her as he licked her. She immediately clamped down around him. He slid in and out, adding a second finger and flicking her clit hard with his tongue.

Renata propped herself up on her elbows to get a better look at Giorgio. Seeing him even added to her arousal. She was dying, panting, sweating—and loved it. Spread open wide in the backseat of a limo with a man she'd met less than twelve hours earlier going to town on her, his face slick with her juices and his Egyptian cotton shirt damp with sweat.

He pulled his fingers out and stuck his tongue inside her. She collapsed back on the seat, her insides pulsing around his tongue in some dimly remembered but familiar feeling. "Oh, yes, Giorgio. Oh, just like that…" She slapped her hand over her mouth as her moans increased in volume.

He held her tight despite her body's frantic movements, knowing she was very close. He moved his mouth back to her clit and that was enough for her. Pleasure from his mouth shot all through her body, her head whipping back and forth as she fought back a scream of pure delight.

On and on the sweet torture went until she was too limp to do anything but finally put a hand on his head. He lifted his face and gave a satisfied smirk. "What, no more?"

"I am all done, and you know it." Renata was glad the limo driver didn't hit any potholes because she would have slid bonelessly off the seat. On the other hand, she was so floppy she wouldn't be injured. She struggled to her elbows. "My God, Giorgio, where did you learn to do that?"

He moved to sit back on the seat, sighing in relief as he stretched out his back and shoulders. He pulled her to his lap and she noticed he was just as aroused as before. "A trip through the fleshpots of Europe, of course," he enunciated with a perfect upper-crust British accent.

She cracked up. He sounded like the leading man of a Masterpiece Theatre miniseries but was probably telling her the truth. "Sounds like a fun trip to me."

"This trip is much better," he assured her, caressing her bare breasts. They both sighed in pleasure as he cupped the heavy weight, lazily brushing her nipple with his thumb. "Renata, you have the most perfect body. *Le tette bellissimas.*"

She gasped in mock horror. "Why, Prince Giorgio! Such slang from your royal lips." He had told her she had beautiful tits.

"You understand that slang? Then how about this? *Ti voglio fare l'amore questa notte.*"

"You want to make love to me tonight."

"There is always the Plaza," he offered.

Renata glanced at the small digital clock in the back of the partition and almost cried with disappointment. "Is it so late already?"

Giorgio stroked her knee. "Is that a problem?"

She nodded. "I have an appointment at seven tomorrow morning."

He groaned. "Why so early?"

"The bride has a last-minute business trip and it's the week before her wedding. These high-powered brides can be a lot of work."

"Lucky for Stefania that you are so conscientious." He raised her hand to his lips and kissed her knuckles. "Tell me when you are free and I will be waiting on your doorstep."

"How about now?" She certainly hadn't minded the backseat atmosphere.

He looked tempted for a second but shook his head. "I am selfish. What I have in mind will take more time than Paolo has gas in the tank. And if I let you touch me, we will be parked at the side of the road making the limo rock while Paolo walks to a gas station."

She didn't doubt for one second that Giorgio could go for hours, judging from what was poking her through his pants. But, oh, what was she missing tonight? Stupid high-powered bride.

It took all of her willpower to decline his offer but she needed to be alert for her appointment since that bride was a live wire at best and out-of-control crazy at worst. "I'm sorry I can't go to the hotel with you, but I have to get at least a few hours' sleep. My client is difficult and I need my wits about me."

He flopped back onto the car seat. "Duty first. Unfortunately I understand."

"Thank you." She cupped his jaw and kissed him slowly and passionately until they were both breathing hard again.

He suddenly jerked away from her. "Stop that. Or else I will not wait until tomorrow."

Renata grinned. "It is tomorrow. Almost one-thirty."

"Ah, better. Then I will see you later today. That sounds much better." He programmed his number into her phone and took her number. "That is my private line. Only my family and my personal assistant have that number."

"Wow." She checked her phone's display and he had programmed his name in as *G*.

He smiled at her. "We try to guard our privacy but it doesn't always work out."

"I won't let this fall into the wrong hands," she promised.

"I know you won't." He kissed the tip of her nose, surprising Renata with the pure affection behind the gesture.

Her surroundings finally caught her eye. "Oh, we're a block from my place. Turn left at the next light." She directed Giorgio and he relayed the directions to his driver.

"I'm going to ask you to park here around the corner. Many of my neighbors are elderly insomniacs and me pulling up in a limo this time of night will only further convince them I'm a woman of dubious morals."

"I will testify on your behalf that your morals are not nearly as dubious as I would prefer."

She choked with laughter and slapped him in the chest. "Somehow I don't think they would believe you." He looked dangerously sexy with his shirt yanked out of his waistband, his hair mussed and a glittering look of barely suppressed lust in his green eyes.

"Pity." The limo stopped and he handed her out of the door. "I will walk you to your door."

Her neighborhood was fairly safe but she wanted to drag out every moment with him that she could. He constantly glanced around them and inspected her dark exterior basement entrance for any stray wino or mugger. The only man she wanted to take advantage of her was standing beside her. "All clear."

She unlocked her door and was struck by a weird wave of awkwardness. "Well…thank you for everything." That should cover it. Wedding dresses, art museums, chili dogs, heavy petting in the limo backseat—what a wild day.

He drew her into his arms. "Don't thank me, Renata. I owe you much more than a dinner. Your dress has made Stefania extremely happy and meeting you has made me extremely happy, as well." He lowered his head and kissed her lips softly. "Until later, Renata. I'll call you later in the morning after your appointment."

She hated to leave him but a big yawn escaped her mouth.

Giorgio smiled and shooed her into her place. "Go, get some sleep. I can take a hint."

"Fine." She floated into the tiny entryway and locked the door behind her. Once he was sure she was tucked away, he gave a wave and took the steps two at a time up to street level.

Renata glided to her bathroom and gazed at her reflection. Her hair was tousled, her blouse was buttoned crookedly and her face was flushed. So was her mouth, her lipstick smeared.

She grinned. Giorgio was a man who kept his promises. Given enough time and effort, he had smeared her smear-proof lipstick.

5

GIORGIO WET HIS HANDKERCHIEF and cleaned his mouth of traces of Renata's lipstick, a wide smile reflected in the small mirror in the backseat. The day certainly hadn't turned out the way he'd expected, but he took pride in the fact that he had been smart enough to take the opportunity of getting to know Renata.

Especially since Stefania had accused him of being a, what was the American expression? Ah, yes, a stuffed shirt. The girl certainly had a way with words, much to his chagrin. Perhaps his day-to-day duties had encouraged a certain amount of rigidity—and not the good kind.

He laughed out loud. Oh, the tabloids would laugh if they saw what his true life was like. The Crown Prince sneaking around and making out in the backseat of a car like some teenager, stopping his pursuit of passion because of his archaic ideas of proper behavior. He already went further than he intended with the lovely Renata, but her words and body had urged him on past his good sense.

Stuffed shirt, hah! He rubbed his chest—no stuffing needed thanks to dutiful workouts, but maybe a bit sore. He took a deep breath and his muscles loosened a bit.

The Brooklyn Bridge loomed overhead and they sped

over it for the second time in a day. It was impressive, young or not. These Americans had an eye for design, he admitted to himself. Whether it was the bridge or Stefania's dress, New Yorkers knew how to make things work.

He patted his chest again—heartburn from that damned chili dog? He pressed a button to roll down the partition. "Have any antacids, Paolo?"

"You are ill, *signore?*"

"No, I don't think so." He chewed the chalky discs Paolo found for him and chased it down with a bottle of water. He closed his eyes, feeling Paolo's worried gaze on him. Not to worry, the worst thing he had going was a bit of indigestion and a massive case of blue balls. And yes, he'd known that American phrase all on his own.

They weaved through Manhattan traffic toward the hotel and Giorgio felt every bump. This was not good. The antacids hadn't helped a bit and he was starting to sweat.

Agonizing pain ripped through his chest up into his shoulder and down his arm. Dear God, was he having a heart attack? His sister's face flashed to mind, strangely followed by Renata's. Stevie he understood, but Renata? Stevie needed him—her only brother. And Renata—he needed her and he'd only met her.

It felt like a fist was squeezing his heart. He couldn't help groaning.

"Signor! Signor! Are you all right?"

Giorgio looked up at Paolo's panicked face and spoke with a calmness he didn't feel. "I don't think so, Paolo. Get me to the hospital."

"MR. MARTELLI? I'M DR. WEISS." Young and skinny with glasses, the E.R. physician was in need of a shave but looked awake enough.

Giorgio extended his hand, IV tubing dangling from his arm. "I am George and this is my friend Paul."

Dr. Weiss laughed. "And where are John and Ringo?"

Ah, a jokester. Giorgio suppressed a sigh. He guessed working in a New York City emergency department was grim enough that even the doctors tried to lighten things up.

"*Chè dice?* What is he saying?" Paolo asked in Italian.

"*Niente*—nothing. A Beatles joke," Giorgio replied in the same language.

"A joke? He dares joke with the Crown Prince of Vinciguerra when he is ill?" Paolo had no sense of humor under normal circumstances, and a doctor who thought he was a comedian was not helping.

Giorgio gestured for him to calm down. "This place is sad enough, Paolo. It is harmless."

Paolo subsided, but stared hard at the doc, who cleared his throat and got down to business.

"Okay, Mr. Martelli, I got your lab and EKG results back. The good news is, you're not having a heart attack. We think you had a major attack of indigestion, probably from those chili dogs you mentioned."

Giorgio blew out a sigh of relief. He had avoided the one thing he feared for himself. He quickly translated for Paolo, who crossed himself in thanks.

Dr. Weiss continued, "But the bad news is, I don't know why you haven't had one already. You look like a sixty-year-old man on paper. A sick sixty-year-old man."

His stomach churned. He was only thirty years old—what the hell was going on?

"You have a family history of heart disease?"

Oh, no, not that. He blinked rapidly. "Yes, my father."

"Okay." The doctor nodded. "It can run in the family. Your good cholesterol is down, your bad cholesterol is sky-high, your entire body is in a state of silent inflammation and your blood pressure when you got here about blew the top of your head off. It's minimally improved since we got your pain under control."

He muttered to Paolo what the doctor said. Paolo drew in a shocked breath. "So what do you recommend?"

"I don't know what you do for a living but you need to take some time off to get your health under control. Get to your primary care doctor and get a note if your boss gives you any grief. You have a primary care doctor?"

Giorgio nodded. "Yes, yes, I will see him as soon as I get home." He had been neglectful—it had been over three years since his last checkup.

"I mean it. I see young, strong guys like you all the time roll in here grabbing their chests. Sometimes they only roll out in a box, *capeesh?*" His Italian accent was straight out of *The Godfather,* but Giorgio understood all too well.

"I understand."

"Good." Dr. Weiss extended a hand and Giorgio shook it. "Watch your diet—more fruits, vegetables, lean meats and a splash of olive oil. Cut back on the pasta, bread and sweets. A glass or two a day of red wine is actually good for you, but no more than that. You don't want to rev up your liver on top of everything. Any questions?"

He had a million questions—like how fate could be so cruel as to start him along the same path as his father, but Dr. Weiss had no answer for that—no one did. "No, and thank you."

The doc left and Giorgio dropped his head back onto the hard gurney, covering his eyes with his forearm. He didn't want to be in the hospital, didn't want to have this sword hanging over his head. What if he hadn't eaten those damned chili dogs with Renata and instead had gone along his blissfully ignorant way until he dropped dead on the street, his office or God forbid, driving along the mountainous roads of Vinciguerra?

What would happen to Stefania if he died? She would have to run Vinciguerra alone once their grandmother passed away.

He swallowed hard and felt a beefy hand on his shoulder. "*Signore.* You will be all right—I promise."

"*Grazie,* Paolo." He removed his hand and sat up. A prince of Vinciguerra did not swoon and cry like a Victorian maiden. "We leave out the back door. I don't want anyone to know about this, especially the princess."

Paolo nodded. "I will bring the car to a side door."

Giorgio changed into his own clothing and met Paolo at the agreed-upon door. He slid into the backseat of the limo and closed his eyes. "Back to the hotel, Paolo."

He would make himself healthy again so that he could walk Stevie down the aisle, hand her off to that German footballer and watch his nieces and nephews come along. She had always wanted a large family after being so lonely as a child.

He had been lonely, too—a nineteen-year-old university student in New York raising an eleven-year-old girl. He had wanted to set a good example for her and spent much of his time with her instead of freely dating like other men his age. And despite what his sister had told Renata, running Vinciguerra did take a good deal of time. Was he still lonely?

Yes, but not when he was with Renata. He'd met her less than twelve hours ago and aside from his terror-filled medical emergency, she had occupied his thoughts ever since. Her sarcastic New York wit, her talent for handling his sister. And more personal memories, like how her mouth opened under his, how her breasts filled his hands, how her thighs softened for him as he discovered her tender flesh.

He shifted uneasily at his arousal, cautious after the doctor's warning. But the doctor hadn't told him to avoid sex—just bread, pasta and sweets. He'd rather have sex than spaghetti, anyway. And the doctor told him to take a vacation. Giorgio remembered how Renata had talked about her ancestral homeland—Cinque Terre—the Five Lands, a beautiful curve of beach on the Italian Riviera. Relatively quiet this time of year and perfect for a holiday. A holiday for two? She had wanted him as much as he wanted her.

Before he could second-guess the wisdom of inviting a woman he barely knew to visit Europe with him, he found her number on his phone and pressed Send. For once, he would put his own needs before his country's. He would put aside his princely duties this once, and instead just be a man pleasing a woman.

RENATA FUMBLED FOR HER ringing phone and managed to answer it. She'd just fallen asleep after mentally reliving her tumultuous day.

"Renata? It's Giorgio."

"Giorgio?" She yawned. "Are you okay?"

"No."

She sat up in bed, alarmed at the roughness of his voice. "What's wrong? Do you need help?"

"I need you."

"Oh." She looked at the clock. A 4:00 a.m. booty call was not something she'd ever answered. "It's very late and I have to go to work soon." How disappointing he would pull a stunt like this.

"No, not now, I realize that." He exhaled harshly. "I am making an ass of myself. Let me try again. Renata, I can't stop thinking about you. Ever since I dropped you off, all I see is the smile on your face, your hair falling around your shoulders, the scent of you, the taste of your skin..."

She gulped. If this was a booty call, it was a very poetic and arousing one. Maybe she should reconsider her policy…

But he was continuing. "I do need you. I want to know you better, know what you think about things, what you like to read, see at the movies, do for fun. And I want to show you your family's ancestral village on the coast. Come with me to Italy."

Renata patted herself on the cheek to make sure she was really awake having this conversation and not just a really weird dream. If it was a dream about Giorgio, wouldn't she come up with something a little more erotic like actually having sex with the man instead of receiving odd phone calls inviting her to Europe?

"Renata? Will you come?"

Oh, yes, she was awake after all and therefore had to decide what to do. "But, my business—"

"Your assistant you mentioned or your artist friend Flick can manage, can't they? I will pay for a temp if you need one. You have a passport?"

"Yes, I suppose they could manage for a few days."

"A week?"

Her eyebrows shot up. "A week? And I have a passport." She'd gone to Montreal for a short vacation last year. Enough of this beating around the bush. "But, Giorgio, why me? We just met this—well, yesterday morning. Why should I upend my life and take off to Italy with you like some royalty groupie?"

"You know why." His voice deepened to a seductive growl. "Because you *want* me. Me, the man, not the prince. You want what I can give you, but not at the boutique or the jewelry store. You want what I can give you in the bedroom."

Oh, he had her there. The man wasn't even in the same borough with her and was making her crazy for him.

"Remember how I sucked on your nipples last night?

Remember how I touched your silky thighs and hot, sweet center?"

She let out a moan in remembrance.

"That was just a taste of how it could be." Triumph tinged his voice. "I may be a prince in public, but I would be your slave in the bedroom."

A whimper escaped her lips. With talk like that, he could take her to bed anywhere and she'd be more than happy. "Yes."

"Wonderful. I will make arrangements and send them to you tomorrow."

"This morning," she corrected.

He gave a startled laugh. "I'm sorry I hadn't waited until a reasonable time to call you."

"That's fine with me," she reassured him. He'd promised to be her sex slave and she was going to hold him to it.

"Good." His voice dropped into the purr again. "Now think of all the things you want to see in Italy and I will do my utmost to fulfill your wishes."

Number one—see his naked body. Number two—see the bedroom ceiling. Number three—see the bed's headboard. Well, she could maybe come up with some tourist activities. Or not.

"Good night, Giorgio."

"*Ciao, bella* Renata. My only thoughts are of you until I see you again."

She waited until she'd hung up to whimper again. She had a feeling she was going to be just as much a sex slave as he was. Did she mind?

She gave a very New York shrug in the darkness of her bedroom. Nah, of course not.

"SO A REAL-LIFE SEXY PRINCE wants to whisk you off to Italy, have his royal wicked way with you and you are hesitating *why?*" The next morning, Flick put her hands on her hips and blew a long turquoise hunk of hair out of her eyes, spoiling the punk persona she cultivated. She wore ripped-up jeans, a holey lime-green T-shirt and safety pins decorating both. A black military surplus jacket and black combat boots with chrome hardware-store chain strung around like tinsel made her look like a scary Christmas tree.

"I'm not that kind of girl," Renata replied virtuously, crossing her legs primly on her elevated desk chair. She made a face at Flick's raucous laughter. "Oh, knock it off. I'm not that kind of girl *anymore*."

Her friend snorted. "That's only because it's been years since you've had a decent opportunity to be 'that kind of girl.' What's with the cold feet?"

"Oh, all right," she said tersely. "Let's say I do go. What do I tell my aunt?"

"Tell her the truth—you're going on an extended European hookup with one of the tabloids' most eligible bachelors."

"Eeeww, is he really on that list?" Not that Renata wanted Giorgio to have a wife and four kids, but holy crap, was that cheesy.

"Hand to God." Flick cleared a stack of files onto the floor and flopped in the small chair across from Renata's drawing table. "After you called me to come over, I looked him up on my phone. 'Prince Giorgio Armani Ferragamo Versace Gucci Pucci is the crown prince of Vinciguerra—'"

"That is not his name," Renata interrupted.

Flick gave her a sly look. "What is his full name, Miss How-Do-You-Say-Torrid-Vacation-Fling-In-Italian?"

Renata pursed her lips. "Giorgio di Leone. And no, I don't know his middle name."

"Middle names, plural. He has about five. But you only have to know the first. 'Oh, yes, Giorgio. Oh, just like that,

Giorgio.' Et cetera." She ducked out of the way as Renata flung a fat illustration marker at her head, having uttered those very words last night in his limo. "Don't waste your energy on me—save it for Prince Loverboy."

Deciding she didn't want to pay for a replacement desk lamp if it broke when she hurled it at Flick, Renata restrained herself. "Speaking of names, *Felicity,* you really are annoying sometimes. I thought your name meant happiness and joy."

Flick, who had the hide of an elephant, blew her a kiss. "I'm the annoyance who's going to watch your shop while you go happily and joyfully off to Italy. And if you promise me a nice souvenir, I'll even lie to your aunt so she doesn't find out how sex-crazed you really are."

Renata repressed a shudder. If her aunt found out, that meant her whole family found out. "Just what would you tell her?"

"What does your aunt want to sew more than anything?"

"Big poufy dresses," she replied promptly.

"Exactly. So you are going to Europe on a buying trip for lace, ribbons, beads—"

"Sequins and pearls." Renata got the picture. "But I don't want to shop for all that stuff."

"Dumbass, what do princes have secretaries for? Tell the man you need to take some Italian fabric and notions samples home and he will get his staff to pull together a nice portfolio while you romance the hours away."

"Hmm." She tapped her teeth with an unflung marker. "And what do I do when Aunt Barbara asks me about actually making a dress with that? I won't use most of it."

"Have that geeky cousin of yours set up a website for her. She can advertise traditional Italian-American wedding gowns and call it Gowns of Amore or something."

"Not bad, Flick. You put the 'genius' in 'evil genius.'"

"I aim to please. Now if I'm going to be babysitting your biz for the next ten days, you need to get me up to speed."

Renata emailed Flick's phone a copy of her schedule. "Open the file and I'll go over it with you."

"Fine, but don't forget that souvenir you promised me. No airport gift shop crap—you'll have to drag yourself out of the boudoir and actually buy me something nice."

"Sorry, I don't think an Italian gigolo would fit in my suitcase."

"I think your prince Giorgio would be able to make arrangements. Young, hot and stupid are my top requirements."

Renata had to laugh. "I love you, Flick."

Her friend made a noise like a cat with a hair ball. "My God, the prospect of illicit nooky is making you absolutely maudlin. Put a sock in it and tell me about your crowd of Bridezillas. And don't think I won't text you if they give me any crap—loverboy or not."

"I still love you, anyway."

"Arrgh! Get laid already, will you?"

6

AND THAT WAS HOW Renata Pavoni of Brooklyn, New York, U.S.A., found herself ensconced in a first-class seat on Air Italia flying in to Genoa, Italy. Christopher Columbus's hometown and the start of her own adventure. From what she'd read online Genoa was still a busy port town, the biggest city on the Italian Riviera. The coastline of the Riviera curved in a half-moon along the blue Ligurian Sea, stretching from France in the east almost two hundred miles to Tuscany on the west.

The plane touched down with barely a blip and Renata stared out at the early-morning skies, the ugly industrial views of the Genovese airport looking like any other modern airport.

Giorgio's driver-bodyguard, Paolo, stood at the gate as planned. *"Buona sera, signorina."* He relieved her of her carry-on bag. After claiming her luggage, he hustled her to a nondescript beige sedan.

So Giorgio didn't even come along for the ride to the airport. Hmmph. She slid in the back and Paolo got in the driver's seat, accelerating out of the lot as if he were in a Ferrari Testarossa. How much English did this guy speak, anyway? She decided to try out her American Italian. *"Dov'è il principe?"* Just where the hell was that prince?

"Ah, *nell'albergo.* The hotel," he pronounced carefully, the *h* sound foreign to the Italian language. "He wait for you there. At the airport, sometimes paparazzi. Photos." He made noises like the clicking of a camera.

Oh-kay. Needless to say, Renata had never dated anyone who would have been even remotely interesting to a paparazzo photographer. She did hope they'd be able to go out in public without too much obnoxiousness.

Paolo silently drove through the city to a dock at the waterfront. "We need to take boat. No road to Vernazza—the village where we stay in Cinque Terre. Trains not here until morning."

"Oh, okay." Maybe they would have some privacy there if it was only accessible by boat and train.

He carried her luggage down to a medium-size cabin cruiser and nodded to the captain with curly salt-and-pepper hair and a navy blue short-sleeved shirt. After settling her in a lounge-type room, he disappeared upstairs to the bridge. Renata spotted a mini fridge and liberated a water bottle. Flick had warned her about dehydration on long flights and Renata wanted to be dewy-skinned and bright-eyed when she met Giorgio again.

After slugging back a full bottle, she stretched out on the long sofa and covered herself with her travel wrap, a giant pashmina-lookalike shawl she'd spotted at a Brooklyn resale shop. Get the sleep stuff out of the way so they could move directly to the bed part.

It felt as if she had just dozed off when she heard Paolo's voice rumble through the salon. "Signorina Renata? We are here." They had stopped at another dock. Paolo helped her off the boat. "Only a little more." He took off up the hill past several square-looking buildings fastened somehow into a very steep cliff. Well, they hadn't fallen into the sea yet. Glad she had worn sensible shoes for once, Renata followed him to a three-story house a few blocks from the ocean. Paolo showed her a narrow set of stone steps leading to a dark wooden door. "Up the steps, *signorina*."

Renata gripped the handrail as she climbed the stairs. Butterflies hatched in her stomach. What if things had changed between them since their last meeting? Did he still feel the same heat, the same longing she'd fought to keep in check?

Giorgio appeared at the top. She climbed faster but he couldn't wait and clattered down to meet her. "Renata *mia*." *My Renata.*

He pulled her into his arms and firmly dispelled her worries with his kiss. Her neck was cricked up and the handrail poked her in the butt, but who cared? She grabbed his nape and ground her mouth into his. She eagerly accepted his tongue and sucked him deep.

He groaned and dragged her up the rest of the stairs, kicking the door shut behind him. She kept her mouth locked on his and dropped her purse and tote bag on the floor. His shirt was the next to fall as she shoved it off his shoulders, followed by her cropped travel cardigan and wrinkle-resistant linen-look blouse.

Giorgio paused for a second to gaze reverently at her breasts, this time wearing a white satin bra trimmed with matching lace. He didn't say anything, but his eyes darkened to jade and his pupils dilated. As if breaking a trance, he leaped back into action and fumbled with the snap to her capri pants, stripping them down her legs in such haste he took her bikini panties with them—no thongs for her on an eleven-hour flight, complete with plane change in Rome.

She kicked off her white sandals and freed her legs until she stood before him in nothing but her bra. Giorgio scooped her up and carried her through a small living room down the narrow hallway leading to a medium-size bedroom. The dark wooden four-poster bed dominated the room, but there was space for a small table and a floral-upholstered chaise longue.

The matching floral bedspread was pulled back, showing snowy-white linens. He set her carefully on the cushiony mattress and stood back. She rested on her elbows, her ankles crossed. His eyes were hungry, his breathing quick.

"Renata, tu sei la donna più bella del mondo."

That was a promising start. Being called the most beautiful woman in the world was always a plus. Not that she'd ever been called that before, especially in Giorgio's lustfully raspy Italian voice, so different than his normally smooth tones.

"Grazie." She sat up and unfastened her bra, letting her heavy breasts dangle freely.

Her complete nudity was too much for him and his pants and bikini briefs hit the floor. So did her jaw.

Giorgio was regally built in every sense of the word. No wonder his ancestors had held power for several hundred years, being fruitful and multiplying successive generations of princes.

He grinned at her, his physique perfect in the morning light. His broad chest was dusted with black hair that narrowed into a sexy trail down his flat belly, widening into a thick patch showcasing his impressive royal assets.

"That's right—I forgot we did not get this far in the confines of the limo. But now I have plenty of time to make it up to you."

"Please do." His cock was long and thick, toasty brown with a plump head. He knelt next to her on the bed and she couldn't help herself, wrapping her hand around his shaft. He had lovely smooth skin, hot and soft over a core of steel.

She moved up and down and he groaned, tossing his head back. A silvery sheen seeped from the tip, and she spread the moisture around with her thumb.

He grabbed her wrist as if to stop her but she cupped his heavy sac with her other hand and he hissed out a sharp breath. “Renata,” he moaned, his hips jerking into her caresses.

“Giorgio,” she replied, an answering warmth between her thighs.

“Stop.” His hand closed over hers. “I have been dreaming about you for days, waking up like this. Give me a second to regain some control so I can properly make love to you.”

“This seems pretty proper to me.” She moved underneath him and let her knees fall open. “You’re not the only one with hot, nasty dreams, Giorgio.”

He shuddered with desire and quickly protected himself. No little illegitimate princes running around for them.

“Are you sure?” He moved between her legs and stared down at her, his green eyes hot but tender.

She hooked her ankles around his calves. “Absolutely.”

He glided into her as if they had been lovers for a thousand years, locking himself to her. She gasped at the feel of him—hot and thick, stretching her very core. She couldn’t help squeezing down on him and he jerked inside her. “Ah, Renata.” He began moving, almost against his will.

She arched her back and raised her hips at him. If she thought the full heft of his cock was heavenly standing still, his thrusting was amazing. Lovely pressure alternating with a sense of emptiness. She wrapped her legs around his waist, pulling him close.

He buried his face in her neck, kissing the tender skin and murmuring to her in raw, raunchy Italian exactly how she made him feel and how he was going to make her come like she’d never come before.

Giorgio had that part right, especially when he reached between their legs and thumbed her clit. She dug her short, red nails into his shoulders and nearly bucked him off her.

He lowered more of his weight to settle on her, pinning her firmly to the bed. She was going nuts, gasping and writhing under him as his skilled fingers plucked at her as if she were a fine musical instrument. His body clung and pulled at her, his lovely olive skin glistening with sweat.

Heat roiled up from where they joined, making her shake and burn. "Giorgio." She gasped out his name, not wanting to climax so quickly.

"*Si, cara mia.* Let yourself go," he coaxed. "Let me take you where you long to be." He hooked her legs over his shoulders and rose up on his knees. He was deep and hard, his hands free to caress her breasts and clitoris.

"Ahh..." She couldn't help moaning as he pinched her nipples, stroked her clit, all the while pounding into her. It was brash and wild, his domination of her. She couldn't move her hips back up at him, and to her surprise, she loved it.

His lips curved into a knowing smile. "You like this, don't you? Oh, wicked, wicked Renata."

She shook her head, not in denial but in her rising passion. Giorgio was relentless, plundering her body. She sucked in a deep breath as the exquisite pleasure built and shattered her, up from her belly into her breasts and out her mouth in a loud scream of ecstasy. Make that several loud screams of ecstasy. If anyone had wondered what the new guests at the villa were up to, she had thoroughly dispelled any false impressions.

He left her weak and trembling under him as he slowed his pace, lowering her legs to the bed. "More?"

She shook her head. She was absolutely wrung out. "I can't even think."

"Good. Just feel." And there he went again, bending to her breasts as he took her again. His slick mouth sucked and nipped at her breasts, coaxing the throbbing peaks to a rosy pink.

Believe it or not, she wasn't done. This time she could move her hips and she did with a vengeance, rising up to meet his driving thrusts. He tossed his head back, a matching groan escaping from him. She reached up and fastened her mouth on his shoulder, salty and slick under her tongue.

"I'll do that to your cock next time," she promised, tremors building again.

He flinched and jerked inside her, hitting her G-spot. She dug her heels into the mattress and her fingers into his ass. "Do it, now!" She felt her control slipping away and disintegrated into a screaming mass of nerves. He let out a shout and followed her, his neck pulling into cords as every muscle in his body tensed.

Giorgio's climax was as long and impressive as he was. She held tight to him, kissing the slick skin of his chest and shoulders wherever she could reach. He finally stopped and smiled down at her, sweat making little black curls at his temples and the nape of his neck. "Give me a second to start breathing again."

"You can have two."

He laughed and kissed her, his body sliding over hers. They were both sticky and wet, and her hair had to be a fright, but who cared?

After a quick bathroom detour, he collapsed at her side, still gasping for air. She went up on one elbow and looked down at him. "Wow."

He grinned at her. "Yes, as you say, 'wow.'" He pulled her down for a quick kiss.

She rolled onto her back. "I mean, geez, I knew it would be something but that was *something*."

It was his turn to lean over her. "I knew we would be like this together. I had to hide my desire for you with a suit jacket in the first minutes we met."

"Really?" Smooth, suave Giorgio had had an unexpected hard-on for the dress designer? "I'm flattered."

"No, I am flattered that you would be here with me. So beautiful." He ran a tender hand over her cheek, her breasts and hips. "Give me a little while and I will show you how flattered I am."

She smiled and touched his face. "We won't let that one go to waste."

He kissed her hand and pulled her into a spooning position. Even soft, his cock was impressive against her bottom. She wiggled experimentally and he groaned. "Insatiable woman. I can see I will have my hands full with you." To emphasize his words, he cupped her breast in his hand.

She giggled. "Your hands, your mouth, your cock..." She giggled again as he snorted in surprise. "What? Do I shock you?"

"Only in the best way possible. I had forgotten how blunt New Yorkers can be."

The New Yorker yawned. "It's been about sixteen hours since I left there, but I am perfectly willing to boss you around in bed once I get my second wind."

"You say that, but I knew what you wanted." He tongued her earlobe and she shivered. He lowered his voice to a honeyed purr. "You loved it when I pinned you down—your sweet little pussy tightened even more on me. Your body will tell me what you want."

She swallowed hard. Dammit, he was right. She yawned elaborately again and he immediately pulled a soft cotton sheet over their naked forms. "Rest, *mia bella.* I do not want to wear you out the first day."

His breathing quickly fell into the slow, regular pattern

of sleep, but to her annoyance, she was still awake and thinking about what he had said. Yes, he had possessed her in the most elemental sense of the world, pinned her down and taken her like the lord of the manor and the local lovely virgin peasant girl.

On the other hand, the lord of the manor wouldn't have bothered to make the peasant girl come screaming twice in five minutes.

Renata was a modern girl, used to taking charge in her life and in the bedroom, as well, if need be. But what if she didn't need to take charge? It was an interesting idea. Not that she wanted to bring out any weird leather accoutrements that were ho-hum among certain friends of Flick's, but if she were going to do the deed with an honest-to-goodness prince, she may as well try new things. The man was born and bred to be bossy.

And if she wanted some turnabout…she smiled in satisfaction, remembering how he'd crumbled like a cracker when she'd grabbed his erection. A well-placed hand—or mouth—and he'd be putty in her hands. Well, not really putty—she wanted him firmer than that.

7

THE NEXT MORNING, GIORGIO stood on the apartment's terrace and gazed at the bright blue sea dotted with white sails. A fresh breeze ruffled his hair, and he couldn't stop grinning. So much so, his face was starting to hurt.

So this was what freedom felt like. Freedom to wear a battered football shirt—not that Dieter's team, of course—and battered cargo shorts and just stare at the water. Freedom to spend time with a wonderful woman without prying eyes wondering who she was, how long they had been dating and whether or not she would be the next Princess of Vinciguerra.

He didn't have to worry about weddings, deepwater port negotiations or the price of coffee in Vinciguerra. Alessandro was ably manning the fortress and had been providing daily email briefs with strict instructions to call only if absolutely necessary. Even Paolo'd made himself scarce.

He slipped on a pair of sandals, a baseball hat and sunglasses. Once he hid his distinctive green eyes, he pretty much looked like any other young Italian man going to buy coffee and rolls for his sleeping girlfriend.

The café down the street was narrow but fragrant with the scents of coffee beans, cream, vanilla and sugar. He purposely put on a thick Roman accent when ordering, just in case the counter girl enjoyed flipping through *People* magazine. World's Most Eligible Bachelor, pah! Jack and Frank had busted a gut laughing, as the Americans said, and he wouldn't have put it past his sister to have been the person who nominated him. They had had a tiff last winter when she had wanted to drop out of grad school to follow Jack's merry men of medicine to Ulaan Baator or Timbuktu or Bora Bora.

Fortunately Jack had declined her offer since a background in international politics was of little use in treating infections and parasites. Although several international politicians he'd met somehow brought parasites and infection to mind.

He accepted the caffe lattes and pastries with a smile of anticipation at waking Renata. She'd roll over in bed, smile sweetly up at him—maybe even beckon him to her as the coffee grew cold and the pastries grew stale. Yes, a sweet morning wake-up for both of them.

RENATA SQUINTED AS A BAND of dreaded sunlight crossed her eyelids. She wrapped the sheet tighter around her naked body. After their long, exciting night she hadn't bothered pulling on a sexy negligee or cotton T-shirt, her normal sleepwear.

"Rise and shine, Sleeping Beauty," a husky male voice crooned. "I know you have jet lag but it's almost ten o'clock. Come get some sun and you'll feel better."

"No, I won't." Renata rolled onto her stomach and buried her head under a pillow.

"I have coffee, *cara mia,*" Giorgio coaxed. "Lots of cream and sugar and fresh pastries. Just the thing to wake you up."

She pried open a gritty eye to stare at him. He sounded

entirely too perky for her liking. But she did like how the thin soccer T-shirt outlined his chest muscles nicely and his shorts showed strong brown legs. He obviously got more exercise than pushing a pencil across his desk and cracking the whip over peasants. "Giorgio, it's five o'clock in the morning New York time and I'm achy from that long flight."

"Okay, Renata." He set the tray onto the dresser and crossed the room. "Let me loosen you up."

The mattress dipped as he moved onto the bed next to her. Warm hands moved over her shoulders, massaging and loosening them. She sighed as he found all the knotted muscles. "Where'd you learn to do that?"

"I took classes as a massage therapist in case the prince thing didn't work out for me."

A snort escaped her.

"What? You don't believe me? Europe can be a very volatile place and it is always good to have a backup plan."

With that sexy five o'clock shadow, his backup plan ought to be a new career as a male underwear model. Somehow she doubted the massage school. "What's your degree in?"

"International finance. If you ever have trouble sleeping some night, I will tell you all about the Mundell-Fleming model, the optimal currency area theory and the purchasing power parity theory."

It made her yawn just to hear their names. "Good Lord, are those for real?"

He leaned forward and whispered in her ear, "The purchasing power parity theory originated in Spain in the sixteenth century and was modernized by Gustav Cassel in the early twentieth."

"Oh, don't stop, don't stop," she teased him. "Keep talking finance to me, Giorgio."

He laughed. "Will emerging market economies ever become decoupled from developed market economies?"

"Oooh, coupling. Now that sounds kinky."

He brushed her hair to the side and rubbed her neck. "Glad to hear that. There are many more theories where those came from."

He pulled the sheet away and did long strokes down her back to her ass, kneading each cheek with strong hands. She gasped as wetness grew between her thighs. "Oh, so tense here. You will need plenty of massage to loosen such a delicate area."

Somehow his massage had passed from therapeutic to intimate when he stopped massaging and bent to kiss his handiwork. He murmured in between kisses. She squirmed against his mouth. "Soft and round. I have wanted to do this since I saw you walking away from me in that tight black skirt. I almost drooled right there."

Oh, yes, Giorgio liked traditional Italian butts.

He circled his tongue around the base of her spine and rubbed his cheek across, well, *her* cheek. The stubble prickled her skin and she pushed her hips into the bed, futilely trying to ease the ache.

She looked to see why he had stopped and saw him pulling his clothes off and popping on a condom. Sunlight played across his naked body, with nary a flaw to be seen. If he hadn't literally drooled all over her butt just now, she'd have quite the inferiority complex.

He urged her onto her hands and knees. "Oh, yes," she breathed as he knelt behind her, his tip brushing her as he nudged her knees wider.

"Open for me, lovely Renata." He circled her clit with his finger, spreading her folds wide. He slid back and forth between them, his head nudging her clit with every stroke. But she still ached inside for him to fill her.

She arched her back, tipping up for him. He accepted her invitation as he slid inside with a single deep thrust.

She screamed in shocked satisfaction. "Yes, Giorgio, ohh..."

He grunted and kept pushing in and out of her. No more pretty words from him. Her butt ground against his flat belly, his balls swinging into her. His fingers dug into her hips as he pounded her. She clutched the headboard for support and he cupped her breasts with his big hands. She shuddered and tightened on him.

"Ah, Renata, *si,* that's it." He was relentless in his ravishing, the headboard knocking the wall with his thrusts. Her hair stuck to the nape of her neck as he sucked on her earlobe. She started to shake and gasp, wanting to pull away from his intensity but loving it at the same time.

He reached between her thighs to massage her hard, swollen clit and that was it for her. She arched backward, resting her head on his shoulder as he ruthlessly dragged her to amazing peaks of pleasure. His arm tightened over her breasts and he nipped at her neck while she screamed his name. He followed her over the edge, coming so hard she thought they'd break the bed.

He moaned in her ear, and she twisted to look at him and he captured her mouth with his, plunging his tongue deep between her lips, mimicking his cock below. He gave one last shudder and wrenched his mouth from hers, gasping for air. "Ah...*Dio mio,* Renata."

She dropped her head, amazed at the explosive, raunchy sex. A couple minutes of massage foreplay, a couple minutes of thrusting and she was purring like a kitten.

He eased from her and she gladly collapsed back onto the mattress, covering her eyes with her arm.

"Renata?" he asked cautiously, easing down next to her. "Are you all right?"

She stared up at him. "I want you to be honest with me, Giorgio."

"Yes?" He raised a black eyebrow.

"I know this is a personal question, but we're getting pretty personal here so I'll ask anyway. Is sex always like this with you?"

He made kind of a choking noise but didn't say anything.

She continued, "I mean, I figured you and I would be hot together after that limo incident, and you've got the biggest, best cock I've ever seen, but this—" she gestured to their naked, sweaty, sticky bodies "—this is past hot. It's positively nuclear."

"Nuclear," he echoed. "And you say I have the biggest—" Words failed him again.

"Biggest, best, hottest, thickest cock I or any other woman in New York has ever seen. And before Parsons, I went to art school where we drew lots of naked men, so I've seen a bunch."

"And you say I have the best?" He had gotten over his shock and his masculine pride was kicking in, a proud smile spreading over his face.

"Oh, please. Surely some woman already told you that."

"Not in such detail. And since you want me to be honest, I have never been…nuclear…like this with any other woman."

"Oh, come on," she scoffed. "You've probably dated some of the most beautiful women in the world."

He paused for a second, as if to think back. "I've been photographed with many beautiful women. I've kissed some of them, but there's a big difference between publicity and reality. None of them have the same spark, the same joy of living that you bring to everything you do."

"Everything?" His words thrilled her as much as his body did.

"Oh, definitely. Designing dresses, eating chili dogs, making love to me..."

He rolled her against him so they were breast-to-chest, belly-to-belly and nuclear parts-to-nuclear parts. Even after detonation, his rocket was still in launch position. "I can only give you all the credit. You, with your beautiful ivory face and thick red hair like a beautiful Renaissance painting by Titian. And your ripe, lush body." He skimmed his hand over her curves. "You have a body made for pleasure. And I am incredibly flattered you would share it with me. There has not been any woman like you before." He kissed her again, this time softly and sweetly.

"Wow," she said weakly after the kiss had ended. "Do they teach you all that poetic stuff in prince school?"

"No, I find that you are quite the inspiration." He kissed the tip of her nose and pushed up out of bed. "Stay there. Our coffee may still be warm." He grabbed his clothes and hurried into the bathroom. Renata wrapped the sheets around her again. No sense in tempting fate with nudity and hot coffee.

He quickly reappeared in the same casual outfit and brought the tray over to the bed. *"Un caffe latte per la Signorina."* He carefully took the lid off the to-go cup and she sipped at the coffee.

"Yep, you're right—still warm."

"And a fresh almond pastry." He handed her a soft square sprinkled with toasted almonds and drizzled with white sugar glazing.

"Mmm, delicious." Crumbs flaked off the pastry. "Look, I'm making a mess of the bed."

Giorgio grinned, and Renata took a good look at the bed. Pastry crumbs were the least of it. One pillow was in the hallway, the top sheet was wrapped around her like a toga, and the bottom sheet had been totally wrenched free by their frantic couplings. Even the headboard stood in danger of bashing a hole in the wall. Short of dumping the coffee over the bedding, it was a total wreck.

He cleared his throat delicately. “Did I mention maid service comes with the villa rental?”

“Good thing.” She raised her cup in a toast and they ate a surprisingly companionable breakfast among the cheerful mess. Giorgio was turning out to be lots of fun, and not just in bed. This was going to be a great vacation.

And after? The unwelcome thought popped up. Well, Giorgio would need to come to New York sometime, and maybe she would see him then. A friends-with-benefits thing?

Renata must have grimaced because Giorgio asked if she wanted more sugar in her coffee.

She decided to enjoy the moment and stop worrying about the future. “No, it’s perfect. Everything is just perfect.”

RENATA SMILED AT HER reflection in the compact bathroom. Although it had obviously been added after the original construction of the ancient house, it managed to hold all the necessities, plus the ubiquitous European bidet. She stared down at that white porcelain fixture. She’d never tried one before and the sunny Italian Riviera would freeze over before she asked Giorgio how to use it.

Bidets aside, the shower had actually had pretty good water pressure, which was necessary to repair the red wreckage of her hair. She ran a brush through her hair and pulled it into a twist, fastening it with a black lacquer clip.

She slipped on a V-neck sapphire silk blouse and a black circle skirt that poufed around her knees thanks to a hidden tulle crinoline. Both were amazingly wrinkle-free despite how she’d seen the baggage handlers treat her luggage.

A matching small sapphire stud went into the side of her

nose. She owned an assortment of different studs except for ruby—no sense in looking like she had an acne breakout. Red lips to match her nails completed the look, and she smacked them to set the color. Dressy, but casual enough for a seaside dinner at a local restaurant.

She stopped briefly to grab her pashmina wrap out of the closet, not sure how cool the breeze became, and then swanned out of the bedroom into the living room.

Giorgio was standing in front of one of the tall, narrow windows that lined the living room at the front of the apartment. The sun had set a few minutes ago, and twilight illuminated his profile as he looked out over the sea. His strong but straight nose, his full lips and determined chin. He was so beautiful she felt a painful thump in her chest. But he was hers, at least for now.

Giorgio turned as she approached. Hopefully the dim light hid her face as she mooned over him. "There you are, Renata." He flipped on a small table lamp and brought her back to reality.

Reaching for her hand, he inspected her from head to toe. "I didn't want to hurry you, and I see that my wait has been more than worthwhile. You are as lovely as always."

"Thank you." She returned the inspection. "You look great, too." He wore a short-sleeved black silk button-down shirt over loose linen trousers and leather sandals, a summer uniform for many European men, but he made it look like the cover of Italian *GQ*.

"I'm glad you approve." He said it seriously, as if there were some miniscule chance in this universe that she wouldn't. Short of donning a seventies' leisure suit and fifteen gold chains, Giorgio could never look bad. And even then, the clothing's ugliness would just highlight his good looks.

"Who picks out your clothes?" she asked.

"My clothes?" He looked confused and then glanced at his pants and shirt.

"Yeah, do you go shopping, or do they bring items for you to try?"

"I have a personal shopped in Rome," he admitted, as if it were a deep, shameful secret. "Unfortunately I don't have much time for shopping but have many outings and functions to attend, so Antonio has my measurements and brings me new outfits every month or so."

Renata whistled under her breath. That would be a cool gig for a menswear salesman. "He does a nice job," she reassured him. "You look very distinguished." She had another thought. "So when we go out for dinner, do we need to do a perp walk?"

"A what?"

She pulled her pashmina over her head to hide her face. "When the FBI arrests gangsters, they always pull their suit jackets over their head and scuttle by the reporters on the way back to the jail. Of course it's not like there aren't a million pictures of them floating around there anyway." She popped her head free and patted her hair.

He was staring at her in amazement.

"Seriously, you lived in New York for all of your college years and you never heard of the perp walk?"

He nodded. "Must have missed it."

"Another trick is to drape your jacket over your wrists so it hides the handcuffs. But who carries their suit coat that way? Who do they think they're fooling?"

"Not you, obviously."

"Not me. Two of my brothers are cops and two are firefighters. They know all the good dirt."

"I see."

Well, maybe he did. But he'd probably lived in a swanky flat on the Upper East Side, a world away from mobsters in federal court. And a world away from Renata, her four brothers and two parents sandwiched into a Brooklyn bungalow.

"No, Renata, we don't need to do a perp walk to go out in public. I've never been here before and have managed to keep my face out of most of the tabloids."

"Except for *People* magazine's most eligible bachelor list," she needled him.

The pained expression on his face was priceless. "If I ever meet who nominated me for that damned list I will have very harsh words for them. Stefania made me autograph several dozen copies of the magazine so she could auction them for her charity. And then she wanted to sell *me* for charity in a bachelor auction."

"A bachelor auction?"

He winced again. "Yeah, that—like a gigolo hanging around a bar."

"That reminds me—Flick wants you to send her an Italian gigolo. Young, hot and stupid."

He choked with laughter. "Let me call my assistant and have him start looking."

"If he's handsome, just send him instead. I'm sure Flick would give him a good time."

"You New York girls are too bold—I think she would frighten poor Alessandro."

Renata walked over to the floral-print couch that could have been in any working-class Brooklyn living room and posed herself. "And are you frightened of this New York girl, poor little Giorgio?" Honey was sour compared to her voice. "Little Giorgio" was looking not frightened at all, instead rather pleased as it tried to escape his linen trousers.

"As always, I live to serve." He watched avidly as she slowly drew her hemline upward, revealing the sheer black stockings and matching garters he'd loved the first day they met.

"Good," she purred, beckoning him with one red-tipped finger. "Serve *me*."

8

MUCH LATER THAN THEY had planned, Giorgio and Renata sat down to dinner. “See? Dinner out and no perp walk necessary.” Giorgio gestured to the busy restaurant. It was obviously a family place with the waiters and waitresses wearing T-shirts decorated with sports team logos. Most of the tables were lined up in rows almost cafeteria style, but Giorgio had finagled himself a table set apart on the corner of the stone terrace. They sipped a fantastic white wine as they sat overlooking the ocean.

“Someday I’ll see what this place looks like in daylight.” It was fantastic anyway at night, the sky purple against the Ligurian Sea while an ivory pillar candle flickered on the table. Soft Italian pop music played in the background, dimming the clink of silverware and cheerful conversations nearby.

“And whose fault is that? If it weren’t for the landlady stocking the kitchen before we arrived, I would have starved for food.” He rubbed his thumb across the back of her hand. “But not starved for you, Renata *mia.* I think you have taken care of that for now.”

She gave him a goofy grin and he smiled back at her.

"The candlelight becomes you, Renata. Fiery to match your hair—and your passion."

"Shh." She pressed her finger against his mouth. "This isn't exactly a fortress of solitude, you know."

"Fiery to match your blush." He smooched her finger.

"Must be the reflection." Her cheeks were heating. Wow, she'd thought that autonomic nervous reaction had been permanently deactivated years ago from lack of use. Leave it to Giorgio to trip all sorts of triggers.

"If you say so." A mischievous gleam danced in his eyes. He was really loosening up.

The waiter arrived with a plate of antipasti for them to sample, marinated olives, steamed mussels and fried odds and ends of fresh anchovies and other seafood. Of course there was focaccia—a savory flatbread common to the area—with olive oil for dipping. She pulled a hunk from the bread and swirled it through the oil, dotted with hunks of chopped garlic cloves and minced basil leaves. Totally delish. They couldn't be more than an hour out of the oven. "You should really have some." She held it up to his mouth and he took a small bite.

"Tasty."

"Have some more." She gestured at the large disc. If she ate all that bread herself, her snugly tailored skirts would split down the seams.

He picked up an olive. "Thank you, but I will just enjoy watching you eat."

"You're not on a low-carb diet, are you? I thought that was against the law in Italy."

He shrugged. "I have a taste for these olives tonight. Have you tried the green ones? Very good, and probably grown not too far from here." He dished a few onto her plate, and she had to agree they were very good, especially wrapped up in focaccia.

The waiter set a platter of pasta lavished in rich green pesto sauce in front of them. It had an unusual aroma. The waiter chatted with Giorgio for a minute as he dished up two servings. Giorgio thanked him and they were left alone again.

"He says this pasta is called *trofie* and is made from chestnut flour. The pesto sauce was of course invented in this region and has the typical basil leaf base, mixed with pecorino cheese and pine nuts."

"Don't forget the marjoram." Renata smiled at his look of surprise. "My grandmother taught me how to make pesto. Fortunately we have a food processor now and don't need to grind everything in her old marble mortar and pestle."

"My mamma's specialty was desserts. She was an assistant pastry chef when she met my father. He had an amazing sweet tooth and ordered tiramisu at the hotel where she was working. He asked to meet the chef, and—" he spread his hands wide "—the rest is Vinciguerran history.

Renata's heart tugged at his wistful smile. "What was your favourite dessert she made?"

He looked startled briefly, as if he'd been far away in memory. "Lemon cookies. Lemon bars. Lemon cake."

"Lemon anything." She laughed.

"Oh, yes, especially at the end of a long, gloomy winter. Her lemon cookies were a snap of springtime in my mouth."

Renata wondered if anyone made him lemon cookies anymore. Probably wouldn't be the same if he had to ask. Something so powerful as that was made freely and spontaneously, out of love. Did his grandmother or sister have the recipe? Maybe it wasn't too complicated.

"Hopefully our pesto will live up to your grandmother's high standards." Giorgio offered her a forkful of pasta and she moaned with delight. The nutty flavor of the pasta balanced the tang of the cheese and pine nuts in the pesto. He watched her in satisfaction. "I thought I was the only one who made you sound like that."

She winked. "What can I say? I'm a hedonist at heart."

"You are in the right place." He gestured at the vista in front of them. "Food, wine, song and passion. Even though you were not born here, you belong here. The land and the sea are calling you."

Renata stopped midbite. The land and the sea. Yes, she did feel a connection to this slice of Italy perched between the sea and the mountains. But she thought it was more because of Giorgio's presence. He was the lens through which she had focused so intensely. But she couldn't stay in the Cinque Terre forever.

"And your country, does it call to you?" She hoped so, because he couldn't exactly give two weeks' notice and pack up.

"Yes, but in a different way. I hear the call of my father and my mother, the call of my ancestors who ruled Vinciguerra and fought for her people. I know it's my solemn duty to protect them and make sure they thrive in a modern world while preserving our national heritage."

"That's a big job. No wonder you're so serious." Their main course arrived, a whole fish that had been wandering around in the Ligurian Sea that morning.

Giorgio served them each a portion, the fish flaking enticingly under his fork. "Eh, too serious according to my sister. She thinks I need to lighten up. Be sure to drink your wine with the fish. The waiter says if you drink water with fish, it will start swimming around in your stomach." He grinned at her.

Renata sipped some wine. No reanimated fish for her. "Maybe Stefania should cut you some slack since she's not the one in charge of a country and several thousand people." Renata winced after that. Criticizing his sister was probably a dumb idea. He loved her very much. She stuffed some fish into her mouth to shut herself up. Holy cow, were they all geniuses in the kitchen here or just this restaurant? She'd have to get the recipe for her mother.

But he wasn't offended. "No, you are both correct. I do need to lighten up and yes, I am the one in charge of a country. However, do not let my people hear you say I am in charge of them. They are even more stiff-necked than I am and do not hesitate to point out my errors. I don't know why I ever introduced technology like the internet and email to Vinciguerra." He stopped to dip some fish into the garlicky olive oil and hummed in appreciation.

"Before, they had to buy the newspaper, read it and then either call the palazzo or mail me a letter to complain. Now all they have to do is read electronic news on their phones and immediately text me to tell me what exactly I am doing wrong. I should have left them in the twentieth century." But he was grinning as he said this. "I even had to hire a nineteen-year-old email assistant to decipher the acronyms and lack of vowels. I can tell you I wasn't LOL-ing."

Renata did LOL—laugh out loud. His affection for his country and his subjects—if they even considered themselves as such—was evident. "They boss you around terribly, don't they?"

"It's like I have thousands of nosy but well-meaning aunts and uncles." He raised his wineglass and gestured to the terrace. "Which is why we are here and not in Vinciguerra. No privacy there whatsoever."

"What a pair we are. I have to fly across the Atlantic and you have to sneak out of your country for any time together."

He brushed the corner of her mouth with his thumb. "I would have swum the Mediterranean Sea to be with you."

"How sweet." An unfamiliar wave of mushy sentiment

swirled up into her throat as she heard herself practically coo at the man. But she couldn't help it. Large helpings of delicious food, romantic settings and of course hot sex with a capital *H* and a capital *S*.

"How true." He slid his arm around her shoulder. "When I'm with you, you are my only responsibility. I've let my duties deprive me of the normal pleasures of being a man. I'm grateful you reminded me."

Renata played with the fish with her fork. "I've been working like a madwoman for the past several years. I was full-time at the traditional bridal salon and spent evenings and days off designing fun dresses and writing my business plan. I finally opened Peacock Designs two years ago and work even harder than ever."

"We are two of a kind. Driven, ambitious and determined."

"I hate being beholden to anyone," she admitted. "Just so you know, our trip is the first time I've ever accepted anything like this."

He nuzzled her neck. "Renata, Renata, please don't worry. If you were only interested in my money and status, you would have tripled the charges for Stefania's dress, accepted my offer to the hotel immediately and then dragged me to the nearest jeweler for a 'little remembrance' of our time together. And I would have realized what kind of person you were, and extricated myself with a polite excuse."

Jealousy swelled in her stomach and she pointed her fork at him. "Been in that situation before?"

Giorgio kissed her cheek. "Yes, a couple times when I was young and *stupido*. Not in the last several years, of course." His free hand came to rest on her knee, stroking her thigh. "I have become a much better judge of character, but I have never been so impulsive as this."

"Me, neither." She set down her fork. "And since we're being impulsive, why don't we order dessert to go?"

"I impulsively agree." He sat up and signaled the waiter, his hand still on her knee. "Dessert is best eaten in private."

THE NEXT MORNING, Giorgio slipped from their bed and pulled on a pair of shorts. Renata murmured in her sleep and rolled over, a lock of red hair falling over her round white breast to curl around her coral-pink nipple. He nearly changed his mind and slipped back into bed, but realized they had only fallen asleep a few hours earlier and he hated to wake her.

He contented himself with staring at her for a minute, something he couldn't do while she was awake. She reminded him of an Andrew Wyeth painting he had seen at a museum in New York during college—a beautiful redhead sleeping, the sheets falling to her waist to bare her breasts.

Something about the painting had intrigued him, and it wasn't just the sight of a naked woman. The sheer peacefulness of the painting, pale linens, pale skin and a dark window behind, the only color from her hair and the crests of her nipples.

Giorgio realized why he'd been so struck by both the painted woman and Renata, the real woman—it was the sheer trust exhibited to be vulnerable to a man in sleep.

He gazed at her for a minute longer and gave a deep sigh of contentment before walking into the living room. After a quick call, the café across the street was happy to send over a carafe of coffee and platter of pastries. He thought for a second and added an assortment of fruit for him. His doctor had made him promise to eat better. He had wanted Giorgio to stay for more tests and not leave Vinciguerra at all, but once he learned Giorgio was taking a vacation, he stopped protesting.

He tipped the delivery boy and checked on Renata again. She'd rolled onto her back, a round arm slung above her head in sleeping abandon. He couldn't get enough of her, but she'd had enough of him—at least until she woke again.

Some grapes, melon and a small pastry were enough to tide him over and he realized he hadn't checked his phone. Although he almost never turned it off, his time with Renata was an exception. The palazzo had Paolo's number and would notify him if there were a serious problem.

A text from Stefania, inviting him to Germany to have a meet-the-parents dinner with Dieter's family. Lovely, beer and brats for everyone—oh, and maybe sauerkraut and some of those lead ingots that masqueraded as German dumplings. He'd have to check his schedule with Alessandro for the week after his vacation, since hell would freeze over before he cut short his time with Renata.

Mmm, a text from Frank, asking him how New York was and if the German footballer was a suitable match for Stefania. Too complicated to text back.

Frank answered on the second ring. "Hey, George! How's New York?"

"I'm actually back in Italy."

"So quickly? Did they drag you back for the grand opening of an orphanage? Senior citizen center? School for wayward girls?"

"Not exactly," he said cagily.

"Ah," Frank said understandingly. "The Royal Vinciguerran Society for Unwanted Puppies and Kitties?"

Giorgio laughed.

"Ah, you think I'm kidding, but put aside your dislike for animal fur on those expensive suits and think of the possibilities. Prince Giorgio surrounded by frolicking baby animals. Prince Giorgio petting a kitten. Prince Giorgio having his royal face licked by a white fluffy puppy. I tell you, George, the women would fall all over you in a heartbeat."

"Frank, I don't need women falling all over me."

Something in his voice alerted Frank. "Because you already have one?"

Giorgio protested but Frank went charging ahead. "George! You never mentioned this to me when you called about Stevie's engagement. Is it because you didn't want to distract from her news?"

"No, Frank, it's because I didn't know her then."

Well, that got Frank to put a sock in it. But not for long. "My, my, *my!* Aren't you the fast worker. Someone we know?"

"You may meet her—she's designing Stevie's wedding dress."

"So you just met her last Wednesday?"

"Yes," Giorgio muttered.

"So why aren't you back in New York with her? You may have a lot of advantages over us non-princes, but sometimes out of sight means out of mind."

Giorgio rolled his eyes. Francisco Emiliano José Duarte das Aguas Santas was the duke of one of the largest estates in Portugal plus a whole island in the Portuguese Azores and wasn't exactly hurting for female interest. He also happened to know that Frank hadn't always been one to talk about "out of sight, out of mind" when it came to women, one in particular, but that was his business. And Giorgio's business was apparently Frank's business, as well.

"Go back to New York, George. You deserve to have a private life, too."

"You know, I couldn't agree more. That's why I am on the Italian Riviera—and not all by myself."

Another silence—that had to be a record. Then Frank

started to laugh. "You must have swept her off her feet, George. Good job."

"I think she likes me, yes." Giorgio started to wonder how Renata did feel about him, thanks to Frank's line of questioning.

"Obviously, if you convinced her to go to Europe with you after only a few days."

Only a few hours, but that *wasn't* Frank's business.

"Any progress on planning Stevie's wedding?" That would distract Frank for a second.

"Yes, but I asked my mother for some advice and she laughed, George. When I told her one day of a wedding was simple compared to a lifetime of running our estates, she laughed even more."

Giorgio rolled his eyes as Frank continued, "And that was not a nice laugh, George. She told me not to be stupid, that men didn't know anything about weddings except how to get stinking drunk at them."

"We *are* bachelors, Frank."

"Since she wasn't in the mood to be helpful, I ordered a wedding planner notebook from the bookstore and Stevie and I have been emailing back and forth. Her wedding colors will be gold and ivory, and she and Dieter are looking at their calendar to set a date at the Cathedral of Vinciguerra. We'll work on the guest list later."

Wow, Frank needed a different hobby. Or more likely, a woman. Another thought struck him. "About my trip here on the Riviera, Frank…Stevie doesn't know I'm here and doesn't know I'm here with Renata, okay?"

"Renata Pavoni, the dress designer? Stevie emailed me a photo of her dress so I could see the style."

"Right. But keep it quiet, Frank. As far as Stevie knows, I'm back in Vinciguerra."

"Cutting ribbons for dog pounds, right?" Frank laughed

again. "Don't worry, I won't say anything. I told you last week you were burning the candle at both ends, eh? A nice vacation with a pretty girl is just what you need."

"Thank you. Speaking of burning the candle at both ends, have you heard from Jack?" Dr. Jacques needed to write himself a prescription for some R & R.

"He sent me a quick email from his satellite laptop that said he was going upriver and would be incommunicado for a few days. The news service says the flood casualties are even worse than originally reported."

Giorgio shook his head. "He won't be happy until he's come down with some previously unknown dread tropical disease that medical science can name after him." *Jacques stupidii.*

"Or being chased by pirates," Frank agreed. "Talk about a man who needs to relax, huh?"

"If he makes it that long. Especially since we have a wedding to pull off." Not that Jack knew anything about that sort of task, either.

"Right, George. Don't worry about a thing. Stevie and I have it all well in hand, so you enjoy your vacation, okay?"

"And not a word to her about where I am, right?"

"Right. We're just emailing and texting, so she can't tell if I am lying or not." Frank was a terrible liar.

"Good. I'll let you know when I am back in Vinciguerra."

"Take your time—and give that pretty *signorina* a kiss from ol' Frank, okay?"

"Not okay, Frank. Find your own. You should settle down and make little dukes for your mother to spoil."

"Right." His voice was cool for the first time. "What's the American phrase? 'Always the bridesmaid, never the bride.' Well, I am happy to be the wedding planner and never the groom."

Giorgio winced. "Frank—"

"*Tchau,* Giorgio."

"*Ciao,* Franco," he replied, but to an empty line. Ah, he'd touched a nerve there with his offhand comment. As if Giorgio ever talked seriously about settling down. He'd apologize later when Frank had regained his normally sunny mood.

He stared at his phone. Frank was more of a homebody than any of them, preferring to work in the fields or build some new and elaborate project for his estate. Giorgio was the dutiful one, working in the palazzo like some CEO, and Jack had been bitten by the travel bug, probably the least harmful than the rest he'd encountered, and put more stamps in his passport saving the world than the Dalai Lama.

But none of them had had more than short-term relationships that fizzled instead of sizzled. He knew about Frank's unhappy foray into first love only because of a late-night, wine-soaked confession of misery. Giorgio had poured Frank back into his bed that night right before the start of their second year at the university.

Jack had an aloof vibe that drove the girls crazy to learn what was behind the charming, but remote French facade. He'd preferred to go out with the cool, brainy types he met in his premed classes, and once he started medical school, dating fell by the wayside.

And Giorgio had had several girlfriends but had always put Stefania, his grandmother and his country before them—in that exact order. If he'd been his ruthless medieval ancestor, the original Giorgio Martelli di Leone, the Hammer of the Lion, who had carved out a principality from the rugged Italian hills, he would have put country first and women relatives a distant last. He would have sold Stefania off to a husband who offered the most advantage for him, chucked his grandmother in a nunnery if she gave him any grief and would have married the woman with the best dowry, regardless of looks or appeal. That original Giorgio had done pretty much the same thing, additionally fathering roughly a dozen children with nearly as many women. He'd often met other green-eyed Vinciguerran men who looked enough like him to be a cousin, if not a brother.

An odd thing, the fortuitous circumstances of his birth. He'd never thought much about it, traveling through his life like a swimmer in a river, constantly moving and dealing with rocks as they popped up. But if his great-something grandfather had been the son of the dairymaid instead of the son of the lady of the manor, Giorgio would be another tall, green-eyed Vinciguerran man reading the morning paper at his breakfast table and wondering aloud at great volume what that idiot prince of theirs was up to again.

He sipped his coffee thoughtfully. In that cozy Vinciguerran flat, his beautiful Italian wife, a redhead from the Cinque Terre, would shrug at the mysteries of foreigners as she poured him a caffe latte and kissed the nape of his neck.

He brought himself up short. That humble, sweet life that happened every day in his country was not his life. His flat was a gigantic palazzo and his life was not conducive to a normal marriage.

But while he and Renata were here in this lovely town along a lovely sea, he would make little memories like that imaginary breakfast and newspaper. And maybe when he was back at his immense desk arguing over traffic crossings and fishing rights, he would think back to how her hair curled over her breast as she slept on a sunny spring morning.

He set his cup down forcefully, awkwardly so the handle cracked off. Memories. Scraps of life. He was a man who had almost everything, could get almost anything with the snap of his fingers or the ring of his phone—and he was jealously hoarding mental snapshots to remember like an old widow staring at family photos.

Giorgio jumped to his feet, strangely disconcerted. Who was he to live like this? Had he not been living like this since his parents had died? Remembering how they had been happy and whole, Papa, Mamma, brother and sister. Making Stevie's life happy and whole again seemed to have left a hole in his.

He stalked toward the bedroom. Well, if he was to be a man of memories, he was damn well going to make more.

Slipping off his robe, he slid into bed with Renata. She turned toward him in her sleep, wrapping her soft white arms around him. He swallowed hard and kissed the top of her head. Another memory for Prince Giorgio, rich in worldly goods but a pauper in the things that really mattered.

9

DESPITE HIS BEST EFFORTS to delegate work back to his assistants, Giorgio had to set aside a couple hours to attend to business. Renata did the same but since she was running a shop and not a country, finished sooner. Despite her decidedly antinuptial tendencies, Flick was a smart cookie and had no trouble managing the shop.

Renata closed the app on her phone and went looking for Giorgio. He was sitting on the couch, leaning over a tablet PC while talking to his assistant in rapid Italian. She waited until he paused for breath and then waved to him.

"*Momento,* Alessandro." He pressed mute on the phone. "Renata, sweetheart, I am so sorry. An issue about the new seaport came up. Something about how deep the water must be. I'm in a conference call with our consultants—retired American Naval officers as a matter of fact."

She saluted him and smiled.

"Are you bored? I can have Paolo take you somewhere."

She gestured dismissively. Vernazza wasn't exactly New York, and there she didn't need a bodyguard, either. "I thought I'd take a walk and do some shopping. I need to buy Flick a gift and a little something for my parents and

Aunt Barbara. Maybe a bottle or two of Scciachetrà for a special occasion."

Giorgio peeled several large-denomination euro bills from his clip. "Buy one for us. I can think of several special occasions we can create."

Renata raised an eyebrow. "That's way too much money for a bottle of wine."

"Then buy something for yourself." He pressed the money into her hand. "I know how independent you are, but let me treat you. Something small even."

"Oh, all right." Renata still had mixed feelings about accepting his money but after accepting a whole luxury trip, what was some spending money for wine? He'd drink it, too.

But she had one more favor to ask him. "While you have your assistant on the phone, don't forget, I have to have some fabric samples to take back to New York, or else my cover is blown."

"I've already put Alessandro to work." He kissed the back of her hand. "He tells me the samples from Milan will arrive in a few days."

"Thank you, Giorgio."

"You are very welcome." He reached for the phone. "We can go out for dinner later or else have something brought in."

"Either sounds good."

He nodded and returned to his previous conference call.

Renata stared at him, realizing all his focus was back on business. Well, he was a prince after all. What did she expect? He certainly had more responsibilities than the junior executives she saw running around New York with a phone attached to their ear and several other devices attached to their belts. It would be negligent of him to avoid his country's business, even for a week.

She remembered how easily her own place was running despite her being gone. Of course Flick was doing sales and management only, not design. If Giorgio thought some of her wedding dresses were wild, she could only imagine Flick's ideas. Knowing what her friend thought of holy matrimony, it would probably have an embroidered panel of Edvard Munch's *The Scream* over the bodice and tiny handcuffs stitched in metallic steel gray over the skirt.

Renata stifled a giggle but Giorgio heard her. He winked at her and grinned.

It was like when one of her brothers elbowed her in the solar plexus and knocked the breath out of her. She actually had to suck in air before she swooned off her wedge sandals at His Sexy Highness.

Giorgio had been drawn back into his princely duties and didn't realize what he'd done to her. Since when did a casual smile make her give goo-goo eyes to a man who wasn't paying her a bit of attention?

On the other hand, maybe that was a good thing. She was sure if she looked into a mirror she would be absolutely mortified at her mushy expression.

She mentally slapped herself and escaped with some shred of dignity before she tossed his phone over the balcony and shoved herself into his arms.

She stepped carefully down the narrow stone stairway from their little apartment. The fresh air outside was a welcome relief to her overheated self.

As if summoned by a genie rubbing a lamp, Paolo appeared across from the foot of the steps, trying to look inconspicuous in a village of six hundred people who were probably all related to each other.

"Paolo?" She beckoned to him and he looked around as if she were talking to some other giant security man named Paolo. *Who, me?*

She huffed in frustration and strode over to him. "Honestly, Paolo, you don't need to follow me. Nobody's going to mess with me in a tiny town like this."

He just stared at her. She tried again in Italian. "I will be fine. *No problema.* Go check on *him.*" She waved her hand in the direction of the villa.

"*Signorina, he* is fine. On the phone much time, not go out. But you are here. With me, *no problema* for you."

Paolo was dead serious. Good Lord, a few days of nooky with His Royal Highness and she needed a bodyguard? Besides Giorgio, of course, who was jealously guarding her body whenever he could.

But what possible trouble could she find in a quiet morning of shopping in a small Italian town? "Paparazzi?" she asked.

He nodded seriously.

"You know if anyone bothers me I'll brain them with a bottle of Scciachetrà." She mimed whacking somebody over the head, and his mouth turned up a millimeter or two. Positively a guffaw from anyone else. "Oh, all right." She sighed and rolled her eyes like the worst teenage drama queen. "Let's go." She silently vowed to take him into the pharmacy and spend twenty minutes in the "feminine protection" aisle.

But off they went, Paolo hanging fairly far behind her so she at least didn't have to try to converse with the man in her Brooklyn Italian, which consisted mainly of curses and food items.

She bought herself a nice cappuccino at a café where the barista sketched a heart into the foam with chocolate syrup or something. Paolo, apparently not needing to eat and drink like a normal human being, declined. Then it was off to the stores. Renata found a boutique that had items from all over the Riviera. A length of lace from Portofino for Aunt Barbara, a small model of Christopher Columbus's ship *La Santa Maria* for her father, who had been in the U.S. Navy. A carved wooden Madonna and Child for her mother, who was still asking the Holy Mother to find Renata a husband, and a bottle of *limoncello* lemon liquor for her grandmother, who had given up on Renata and turned to drink. Actually her grandmother had always loved anything with lemon.

She considered buying jars of the famous Ligurian anchovies in olive oil for her brothers, but the idea of carrying four glass jars of oily fish home in her luggage was enough to make her quail. So they each got a miniature wooden version of a ship's figurehead—long-haired and bare-breasted, of course, so all the guys at the police and fire stations could get a yuk out of it.

By then she was famished and collared Paolo. "I'm hungry and these are heavy. You carry the packages, and let's eat."

She picked a quiet trattoria on a side street that had great smells coming from it and dragged him in. *"Mangia, mangia."* Paolo stood awkwardly next to her tiny table, blocking the waiter who was lugging a big tray of soup and antipasti.

"Come, sit." She motioned him into a chair. He hesitated but seemed to acknowledge he was drawing more attention standing like a Roman statue in the middle of the restaurant.

"Grazie, signorina," he muttered.

"You are most welcome. What is good to eat?"

"Here, the fish."

"Ah, of course." No concerns here that the fish had sat in the back of a delivery truck for a dangerous amount of time. "You like *pulpo?*"

His eyes lit up and he nodded. A fellow octopus devotee.

She loved it, too, but hadn't wanted to order it in front of Giorgio since eating the chewy seafood was less than sexy.

"Okay, why don't you order *pulpo* and whatever else you think is good."

The octopus was cut into rounds and deep fried. Renata and Paolo chewed their way through an order. Really, she didn't understand why people hated octopus. When it was fresh, it was almost tender.

"Good octopus, right, Paolo?"

He nodded.

"Does your boss like octopus?"

He finished chewing and gave her a considering look. Probably he'd been pumped for information before about Giorgio, but decided his master's preference for invertebrate seafood was not a state secret and nodded. The few days she'd spent with Giorgio were much more juicy than his eating habits but she wouldn't be one to blab.

The soup was tomato based with seafood and herbs with fresh garlic toast rounds plopped right on top and the main course was a whole fish cooked with white wine, lemon and herbs.

"He like this soup," Paolo offered. "We make this at home."

"It's very good." She noticed how Paolo never mentioned Giorgio or Vinciguerra by name and figured it was part of security. "What else do you eat at home?"

"Our part is more *del nord*—north. We like polenta, sausage, much butter and *crema.* Meat roasts and risotto. Good food."

It was the longest speech she'd ever heard. Food was close to his heart. "You should write a cookbook for recipes from—" She'd almost slipped and mentioned Vinciguerra. "From your home."

He made a self-deprecating sound. "Nobody need a cookbook. Everybody know how to cook."

"Oh, no, we don't." Renata had to be the only Italian-American girl in New York who could goof up a pot of pasta. "Think about it. Everybody thinks Italian food is spaghetti and meatballs. You could do something different."

"Okay, *signorina*." He was humoring her.

"Look at me, Paolo. Does New York need another dress designer?"

He shrugged in puzzlement.

"I'll tell you—it doesn't. But I didn't care. And now the, um, other signorina has a nice dress and is very happy."

"Yes, is true. She tell me so. And tell me, and tell me."

Renata snorted with laughter. Ol' Paolo had a sense of humor after all. "I'm glad to hear it. A beautiful girl."

"Si, si." They smiled at each other at their mutual fondness for Stefania.

Renata took a sip of coffee but declined dessert, having filled up on the delicious focaccia in addition to the rest of her meal. If she stayed in Italy much longer, she was going to get a shape like her grandmother, who resembled a Magic 8-Ball in her black dresses.

Ah, well, all the walking and romping around with Giorgio would help. He'd shown no signs of slowing his pace, so she was running out of new lingerie to show him. She'd passed a pricey boutique earlier—maybe that was the place to go.

She set down her cup. "One more stop and then we can go back."

Paolo nodded placidly, as if it were his life's dream to follow her around Vernazza like some giant shopping cart with arms. There was a brief tussle when she tried to pay for lunch but apparently having a woman pay for his meal was more humiliating than carrying her packages. Renata gave in, figuring Giorgio would reimburse him.

She found the place she was looking for a couple blocks away. Paolo gave the display of bras and panties in the window a wary look.

"Don't worry. You don't have to go in."

"Grazie, signorina." He parked himself against a wall across the way where he could see the entrance.

Renata walked into the shop and immediately saw a bunch of possibilities. Racy, demure, corsets, nightgowns, garters, lace, satin…she pulled out her phone. "Hey, Flick, I'm standing here in a lingerie store and don't know what to buy."

"Something sexy, of course."

"Well, duh, but what?"

"What did you bring with you?"

"A bunch of fancy bras, all my garter belts and a corset."

"Okay, so you've got the slutty look covered, let me think."

Renata made a sound of protest at the "slutty" bit but in the end had to agree.

"How about the total opposite?"

"They don't sell flannel nighties here, Flick."

"Not that. You'd sweat to death. How about a nice demure pure white nightgown, as in the 'please be gentle with me, it's my first time' look."

"Ah, the virginal wedding night, but isn't that a bit cliché?"

"No more so than running off to Europe with a hot Italian guy. Trust me, 'Virgin Princess' is the way to go."

Renata snorted. "Guys do love that, even if they know better."

"It lets them pretend they're breaking new ground, so to speak."

"Okay." Renata moved to a billowy rack of white garments. She pulled one off the rack. "Honestly, Flick, this first one here looks like I should be fleeing the manor on the moors in gothic-y terror as the brooding lord chases me."

"That's the idea, dummy. If the gothic-y chick has any sense, she'll pretend to twist her ankle on a rock and let Lord Longmember catch her."

"Really, Flick. Lord Longmember?" she muttered into the phone.

"Or Laird Lang-member, if you prefer the Scottish fantasy. What's under his kilt gives new meaning to the phrase *auld lang syne*."

Renata groaned and reached for another gown. "Hey, this looks promising."

"Send me a pic."

Renata hung it back on the rack and took a quick picture and emailed it to Flick. "What do you think?"

"Positively diaphanous."

"Yep." The nightgown was a sheer white silk with blousy three-quarter sleeves and a satin ribbon fastening the neckline. The gown was cut on the full side but that didn't matter since it was practically see-through.

"You *have* to buy it. 'Oh, milord, I do not understand all these strange new feelings in my forbidden places. Are you ill? You have the strangest swelling in your trousers. Ooooohh.'" Flick made a noise as if she were about to swoon.

Renata cracked up. Her aunt Barbara loved books like that, and Renata had "borrowed" them when she was younger just to read the racy parts. Hmm, maybe that was where she got her taste for hot, dark and handsome upper-crust men. On the other hand, Giorgio would be to any woman's taste. Yum. "Okay, I'll get it. Never hurts to change things up a bit."

"Wear your hair down with some hanging in your face so you can peep from behind it like that blonde starlet. What was her name?"

"Veronica Lake," Renata answered promptly. "Cool, Flick." She'd enjoy this—and of course so would Giorgio.

"Thank you," her friend said smugly. "And about my gigolo? What flight does he arrive on?"

"Sorry, I can't in good conscience send a poor innocent like that into your clutches. How about a nice ceramic vase?"

Flick's response would have shocked a real gigolo but only made Renata laugh. "Okay, no vase. I'll find you something else." Renata spotted the saleswoman who had been lurking nearby straightening piles of panties. "I'll let you know how it goes."

"And in excruciating detail," Flick warned her. They said their goodbyes and Renata carried the nightgown to the counter to pay for it. After mentally calculating the euro-to-dollar rate, she winced but put it on her credit card. She probably had enough cash from Giorgio, but that was her present to him.

The saleslady wrapped it in a white box with matching white satin ribbon. Renata supposed that made sense since it looked like a wedding present. She tucked it under her arm and rejoined Paolo outside. "Ready?"

"Of course, *signorina*."

She sighed. "You can call me Renata, Paolo."

The look of horror on his face made her fight back a smile. It was practically the first real emotion she'd seen from the man since they'd met.

"I cannot do that, *signorina*. Much disrespect for you and disgrace for me."

"Really?" She tipped her head to the side as they started down the narrow cobblestone street. "But I am not exactly in a position of respect here—traveling with the, um, boss." She'd almost forgotten and said "prince" in public.

Paolo shook his head. "He say I will serve you as I serve him. *Molto rispetto* for him—and you."

Renata nodded. Feudalism was alive and well in the Italian culture, even in her own watered-down New York version. What the guy in charge said, went. If you showed disrespect for someone the boss approved of, you showed disrespect for the boss. She got it.

"Do you think the boss will be finished with his business now?" She had something in mind for an afternoon siesta.

"Si, signorina." Paolo turned a corner through narrow houses and led her back up several narrow sets of stairs.

She was pretending not to gasp for breath when she heard an annoying male voice with a thick Italian accent catcalling. "Eh, *bella ragazza!* Give me a kiss, red-hair girl."

Renata looked around, pissed off. She had enough hooting and hollering at her living in New York, and the Italian version was just as bad.

"Come up here, pretty lady, and I show you good time, huh?" That was followed by several loud smooching sounds.

She tipped her head back and was about to give the man an international gesture when she saw Giorgio grinning down at her from the terrace. "What do you say, gorgeous?"

"I say, 'Okay!'" She opened the door and climbed the stairs to the second-floor living room. She gave Giorgio a quick kiss and made a beeline for the bedroom. Renata the Innocent Virginal Maiden was about to make an improbable and unprecedented return.

10

"IS THE SIGNORINA ALL RIGHT, Paolo?" Renata had disappeared into the bedroom with an armful of packages and hadn't reappeared yet. Maybe she'd gotten a bit of sun or was unpacking her finds.

"She seemed fine, *signor.* Although she did ask me to call her by her first name." Paolo looked as if that request were enough to doubt her mental capacity.

"And you complied with her request?"

"Signor!" Paolo appeared torn, as Giorgio knew he would. His natural formality and knowledge of what was proper conflicted with obeying a request from his prince's current lady friend.

Giorgio let him stew for a second before letting him off the hook. "You of course told her why that was not possible."

"*Si, si,* I did." Paolo would never slump with relief but relaxed slightly.

"Americans are very informal, as you know. It can be quite appalling how much personal information they share with each other on merely a short acquaintance."

He nodded eagerly. "That is so true, *signor.* The other drivers I met in New York…" He winced. "I am not a *dottore, signor.* Why do they think I want to know about their prostate problems?"

Giorgio winced, as well. "Paolo, you've had a busy day. Why don't you have a glass of wine at the trattoria across the street? The *signorina* and I will be staying in this afternoon."

Paolo nodded and left. Giorgio headed to the bedroom. He wasn't sure what awaited him on the other side of the door, but was eager to find out.

He tapped on the door. "It's me. May I come in?"

"Of course." Her voice was sweet and soft, and he grinned in anticipation as he twisted the doorknob.

"Mamma mia!" The exclamation escaped him just before his jaw dropped.

Renata stood next to the four-poster bed wearing something that looked like it had floated down on a cloud. She raised her hand to delicately stroke a post and the thin white silk outlined the curve of her breasts, the thrust of her nipples. He could see nothing but was seeing everything. And that up-and-down stroking was enough to drive him mad.

"Do you like it, Giorgio?" She tipped her head and gave him a coy look from behind the curtain of her luxurious auburn hair.

"What do you think?" He stripped off his shirt and yanked his belt loose.

She ducked behind the other side of the bed before he could finish undressing. He moved opposite her once he was naked except for his boxer shorts, ready to dive across if need be. "Why don't you come here and let me show you how much I love it?"

She gave him a wide-eyed look. "I need you to show me so many things."

"Ohhhh." He nodded in understanding. She was taking things in a different direction, aiming for a little role-playing with her in the lead role as Innocent Virgin. Although the droit de seigneur, or right of the lord to deflower local lasses, never existed in Vinciguerra and was largely mythical elsewhere, the blood of his conquesting ancestors surged in his veins, his cock hardening even further at the bawdy suggestion.

"I am Giorgio Alphonso Franco Martelli di Leone, Hammer of the Lion and Prince of Vinciguerra," he informed her, using his formal family name and all his royal hauteur. "Your duty is to please your prince—and obey whatever he orders you to do."

Her eyes flashed at the obedience part but she lowered her head. "Yes, Prince Giorgio."

"Come here." He thought about snapping his fingers but figured he was pressing his luck.

She glided to him. The afternoon sun slipping in through the shutters totally illuminated her body. Her breasts swayed over a narrow waist and round hips.

"I should rip this gown down the front for you daring to wear it in front of me. It is against the law to appear in the Prince's bedroom with clothing on."

She muffled a snicker.

"But since it is so sheer, I will make an exception for you." How far was she willing to go for this mutual fantasy? If she balked, he'd stop, but if she didn't… "Put your hands behind your back."

Renata complied but her expression was confused. He grabbed a necktie from the back of the chair and wrapped it loosely around her wrists, then to the bedpost. Her eyes widened, although she didn't protest. In fact, her breathing quickened and her nipples hardened against the silk.

He moved close so her gown brushed his body, the silk resting on his erection. Oh so close to shoving up the nightgown and taking her how his ancestor would, with thoughts only for his own pleasure, the smoothness of her thighs, the hot, wet tightness of her flesh enveloping him as he pounded deep inside her. And to do it again whenever he felt like, to have her ready and willing at any time of the day or night. The good old days…he bit back a groan.

"What are you going to do, Prince Giorgio?" Her words held a challenge and he answered it.

"Whatever I want." He smoothed his hands over her breasts, admiring the plump weight as he stared at the dark round nipples showing through the fabric. "And before long, you will beg your master for his touch, his mouth, his cock." She inhaled sharply at his promise.

He covered a nipple with his mouth and she pushed her head against the bedpost, arching her back. "Oh, Giorgio."

He worked the tight nub with his tongue and teeth, the silk a flimsy barrier to his determination. She gave a little gasp and he smiled in pleasure. Her breast felt different under his mouth, cool and wet at first but then hot as his breath and her skin heated the fabric.

He moved from one breast to the other, leisurely exploring their curves through the intriguing veil. Renata wiggled in his embrace, a bead of sweat trickling down her neck between her breasts. He licked the salty trail until it fell below her neckline.

Giorgio sat back on his haunches. What would his ancestor do? He gave her a long, slow grin and put his hands on her neckline. "I will buy you another."

"Another what?" Her dazed eyes widened and she squealed as he ripped the nightgown right down the middle. "Giorgio! Do you know how much this cost? The dollar-to-euro conversion is terrible this week!"

"I will buy you, ten, twenty of them," he swore as he followed that intriguing droplet of sweat down her belly to where it pooled in her navel. Ah, just right for his tongue.

"And I thought bodice ripping was the stuff of myth and legend," she quipped, breaking off into a long sigh as he licked her belly.

He had no idea what she was talking about since he was dizzy from her scent, intoxicated from the feminine musk rising from her arousal. He gently spread her folds and dabbed his tongue onto her clit.

She stopped a scream and sagged against the bedpost.

"Here." Not wanting her to fall, he lifted her onto the mattress, and raising first one leg over his shoulder and then the other, supporting her weight. Her hands were caught loosely enough to take any pressure off her shoulders.

Once she was comfortable, it was time to go to work pleasuring her. He returned to his previous position and opened her wide to him. She had an attack of uncharacteristic shyness and brought her legs together.

"None of that." He stroked her breasts until her knees fell apart.

"Giorgio," she sighed his name. "This is so…so…" She stopped, unable to find the words for her thoughts.

"Arousing? Sexy? Incredibly hot?"

She swallowed hard. "Yes. This is amazingly erotic. I feel like the lord of the manor is preparing to ravish me."

"Good. Then you have the right idea. You will be ravished." He bit her smooth neck, careful not to mark her white skin. "Totally." He suckled one nipple to a plump red peak, pleased at her moans. "Completely." He nipped the other, tugging until it swelled to match. "And quite thoroughly." He dipped his tongue into her soft, sweet belly button, so glad she had pale, lush feminine curves instead of a stringy boyish build.

She raised her hips in invitation, which he accepted, staring at her again. She was beautiful in her feminine secrets, medium pink like the inside of a conch seashell, her hidden pearl peeping out as it swelled with arousal.

He inhaled her musky scent eagerly. He couldn't stop remembering how she had gone up in flames under his mouth in his limo and had been eager to see if she would respond like that again. Her thighs quivered in anticipation.

"Do you know how pretty you are here?" He traced his finger around one petal, then the other, purposely avoiding her clitoris.

"No, I never thought much about it," she panted. "But you can show me your appreciation in one very special way."

"Oh, I will." He kept up his lazy tracing, spreading her juices freely. She plumped up even more under his touch, darkening to a deep rose. "In many special ways."

He slid a finger inside her passage, smugly noting how she instantly pulsed around him. He leisurely thrust in and withdrew, mimicking what he would do later with his cock.

A second finger joined the first.

He rubbed a slightly raised slick spot and she gave a short scream. "Oh, my God, Giorgio! What is that?"

Thrilled that he was teaching her new ways of pleasure, he kept fucking her with his fingers. She attempted to move him along faster by wiggling her bottom, but that made him stop, increasing her frustration.

"Gently, sweetheart. You are always so impatient. Must be that New York temperament of yours."

She strained at her soft bonds. "You can't just tie me up and tease me like this. I want you to make me come now."

He inspected her carefully. She was frustrated but not frightened by their sex play, and he had noticed her pussy dampen and her nipples tighten with lust every time he mentioned the neckties.

"Dammit, Giorgio."

"Careful, my innocent maid. I may tire of your complaints and decide to quiet you."

"What with? Another one of your fancy silk ties? Why did you bring so many on a vacation?" Her breath was coming faster and harder the deeper they fell into the fantasy.

He laughed. "Why would I use a silk tie? There are much more pleasurable ways to fill your mouth." He deliberately rubbed his cock along her leg.

She stared at him, wide-eyed, a fresh slick of moisture running over his fingers. An answering drop soaked into his boxers. He desperately wanted to open his shorts and show her exactly how he could fill her mouth, her hands, her pussy…having her tied up and screaming with pleasure as he took her until his cock exploded.

Merda! His civilized veneer was paper-thin around this woman. With her hair falling down over her magnificent breasts and her nightgown in shreds, she was arousing his previously dormant pillaging and ravaging urges. The Princes of Vinciguerra had long been a hard-fighting, hard-loving lot but he thought modern life had stamped those characteristics out over the past several decades.

Apparently not. He counted to twenty in Latin and calmed down enough to move back between her thighs.

This time, he didn't stop once he'd rediscovered her G-spot with two fingers and watched with strained satisfaction as she climaxed quickly, pulling at the ties in ecstasy. Red-faced, sweaty and gasping, she was the most beautiful woman he had ever seen.

He knew she had more response left, so he stroked her clit experimentally. Plump and swollen from her powerful orgasm, it quivered under his touch.

And under his tongue.

He inhaled her scent greedily as he buried his face deep.

Her clit rolled easily in his mouth, pulsing as he sucked her gently. She sobbed his name when he rolled his tongue around her passage, dipping inside it as if it were filled with sweet nectar.

"Oh, Giorgio, yes!" Her hips bucked under him, and he scooped his hands under her round ass to hold her still for his mouth. His cock was twitching and jerking like mad; a flick of the wrist and one quick thrust and he could possess her lush, moist pussy with it. She would eagerly submit to him and probably immediately climax, squeezing him in her hot depths as he pulsed within her.

But he would wait. Just a little longer. He gave a long groan of frustration and she pushed against his face, crying out as he rubbed his lips over her. Her legs trembled and she sucked in a deep breath. He sucked hard on her clit and she shrieked her release, thrashing into him as he penetrated her with his tongue, aching to do the same with his cock.

He held on to her until she stopped shaking and sobbing.

"Giorgio," she whispered.

He raised his head and gazed up at her, worried that it had been too much for her.

But then she smiled at him, and a wave of affection passed between the two of them.

"Renata, are you all right?"

"Fantastic." She rolled her shoulders and he quickly undid the ties.

"Are you sure?" he asked anxiously, trying not to get distracted by her satiated nudity.

"Absolutely. You high-handed princes know how to show a maiden a good time." She stood and ran her finger down his chest, swirled it into his belly button and then stopped right above his waistband. "And now it's time for the maiden to show the prince." She snapped his waistband.

He gulped. For the first time in known history, a Vinciguerran prince would be the one getting ravished. Thank God for modern times.

RENATA STIFLED A GIGGLE at the look that passed over Giorgio's face, half relief and half nervousness. "Sit." She pushed him toward the upholstered chaise and he sat like a king on his throne.

His black silk boxers were strained to the limit in the front. A quick flick of her finger and his erection popped free. Wow, that was sexy-looking, his desire too much for even his clothing to contain. His pupils dilated and then contracted as he stared at her in silent anticipation.

She dropped to her knees in front of him. "Let your loyal subject please you, Your Highness." She deliberately put her hands behind her back as if she were still bound.

His mouth opened in shock at her submissive posture. "Renata, no." *No,* her ass. He'd been fighting his desire to dominate, take her, penetrate her, so much he'd been shaking.

She brushed her lips over his cock and then he wasn't protesting anymore. He dropped his head back against the upholstery, his mouth opening in a groan. "Ah, *si, si...*"

She lifted her head. "Your Highness, I want to please you. Show me what to do."

His eyes blazed green and she could tell he was at the edge of his formidable control. Considering what he had done to her while she was tied to a bedpost, she figured that was an even exchange. She deliberately ran her tongue around her mouth and he cracked, tangling his fingers in her hair.

"Take me in your mouth. Now."

She opened her lips and he thrust inside. She meekly accepted him, waiting for him to instruct her further. He moved her head up and down on him, his cock growing hotter and tighter. She fought the instinct to participate more actively but the juicy, fat head slipping along her tongue was starting to turn her on, too.

"Harder," he gritted out. "Suck on me."

His wish was her command. She immediately applied suction and he went wild, digging his strong feet into the carpet and boosting himself deeper. She relaxed her throat and flicked her tongue along the base of his shaft, humming in appreciation.

His skin was hot and taut under her lips and tongue, a salty drop coating his flesh. Renata sucked hard and felt him harden further.

"Ah, Renata, more, more…" He relaxed his hands and she lifted her mouth off him.

"Tell me, Your Hardness, who's in charge now?"

His gaze was blurry with desire. "You are, Renata. You always have been." Before she could blink, he pulled her onto his lap and shoved her nightgown up to her waist. She automatically spread her legs for better balance and he prodded her slick passage with his erection. "Release me from my misery, sweet Renata."

She sighed with satisfaction and sank onto his cock, moving up and down on him. His hands tightened on her ass and a flash of brilliance popped to her sex-soaked mind. "Spank me."

His eyes flew open. "What?"

"You heard me. Just a tap, okay? I don't want to have trouble sitting tomorrow. Don't you think it would be hot?"

"Si." His voice was raspy, as if his mouth were dry. "Very hot."

He lifted his hand slowly and smacked her bottom.

She let go with a shocked puff of air. He looked at

her anxiously until she smiled. "I'm not going to break, Giorgio."

"I would never hurt you, Renata," he promised.

"This is for fun, not hurt."

He did it again and this time, she was ready, moving up and down him as his hand landed on her. She shuddered, this time with naughty arousal.

Giorgio grinned. "You just tightened down on me. What a bad girl you are, Renata, darling. I should take my cock out of you and put you over my lap for a good spanking."

"Sorry, Prince Giorgio," she said in a falsely meek voice, knowing that she'd just spasmed around him again at the image of her spread over his lap, his dick pressing up into her breasts as he reddened her bottom.

"For punishment, play with your nipples. I like to see them pink and plump—just like your pussy." He punctuated that with another light slap.

She cupped her breasts, teasing herself with light and then firm touches until her nipples were hard and red as rubies.

From his answering groan, it was punishment for him, too. His eyes were heavy with lust as he watched her avidly. "Very, very risqué, darling. You like to touch yourself, don't you?"

"Mmm." She was having a hard time catching her breath.

"Of course you do. Next time, I want you to sit in this chair and show me how you like to play with yourself. Maybe I will do the same. After we met and I was waiting for you to arrive, I couldn't stop remembering your naked wet body under mine."

"What did you do?" she whispered.

"Wrapped my hand around my cock and thought of you. Many times. In the shower. In the morning. At night. You stripped my self-control. And now it is not any better." He sounded almost angry. "I smell your perfume, see the curve of your neck and can't think of anything but ripping your clothes off and fucking you."

He stopped talking and put action to words. She thought he'd wrung every bit of pleasure out of her earlier, but she was wrong. He reached down to play with her clit as she lifted herself up and down on him.

Oh, he felt so good, inside and under her. She closed her eyes to revel in the sensations he was building in her but he called her name.

"Open your beautiful blue eyes. I want you to look at me when you come."

She gulped. That seemed even more intimate than some of their previous activities.

He stopped caressing her. "I mean it. No dress-up or games. Just Giorgio and Renata, together."

She bit her lip and nodded.

"Good." He sat forward and wrapped his arm around her waist. "Move on me, lovely Renata."

She did, her breasts brushing his face until he captured one in his mouth, his fingers toying with her clit. The delicious pressure built again. Her back bowed and he let go of her nipple.

"Look at me!"

She forced her eyes open to see his fierce expression. He was barely restraining himself and that made her even hotter. She wiggled on top of him and he pinched her nipple, rolling it under his thumb.

She clamped down on his erection and he let go with a stream of very slangy Italian telling her exactly how she was tormenting his cock and how his balls were about to explode. He also threatened to spank her again and she involuntarily spasmed around him.

He began to laugh. "Eh, so you understood that." He

gave her a little slap on the ass and it was all over for her. She crumbled to pieces. Her climax overtook her.

He dug his fingers into her hair. "Look at me," he gritted.

She did, gasping, sweating, captured by his cock and his hands even more effectively than when she'd been tied to the bedpost.

His nostrils flared at her capitulation. "Oh, yes, that's it." He heaved a sigh and she saw how he surrendered to his own orgasm as easy as stepping off a diving board into a pool.

He clenched his jaw and pounded into her, his groans growing louder and louder as his seed jetted from him. His gaze was locked onto hers like a laser and she instinctively knew this was a part of him he had never shared with another woman before.

She wrapped her arms around him and rocked back and forth in time with his movements until he slowed. Before he could say anything, she pushed forward and caught his mouth with hers. Their lips clung for what seemed like forever and then he broke the kiss, resting his forehead on hers as they caught their breath.

"Oh, Renata *mia,* just when I think this cannot get any better, you prove me wrong."

"I thought you'd like that nightgown."

They both looked at the remnants of that poor abused garment, bunched around her waist and covering his like a see-through loincloth.

"I will have to buy you many more."

"For a modern monarch, you sure do have archaic tastes in the bedroom," she teased him. "Tying up an innocent maiden, forcing her to satisfy your debauched lusts and beating her when she was too frightened…"

He eased out of her. "You call that a beating?" He stood

and scooped her into his arms. "I think milady doth protest too much, as the playwright said. I think she just protests because she liked it *too* much."

Renata flushed and hid her face in his shoulder. He was right. She never would have even tolerated a spanking from any other man, much less enjoyed it so much. He laughed uproariously and set her on the fresh, cool sheets of the bed.

"Giorgio, I'm a mess!"

"A lovely, well-satisfied mess." He tugged the nightgown down her legs and tossed it on the chair. "Your monarch needs *un reposo* and will be very cross if his favorite maiden doesn't join him for some sleep. I plan to stay up for a late dinner and an even later bedtime." He crawled into bed next to her. "You Americans should try an afternoon rest. It does wonders for your disposition." He pulled her back to him so they were spooning and draped an arm over her waist.

"You do wonders for my disposition," she admitted. "You may not believe this, but some people think I can be difficult."

"No!" He spoke the denial with such shocked sincerity that she looked over her shoulder in suspicion. He quickly hid his expression by kissing the nape of her neck.

"Hmmph." She muffled a snicker, which turned into a yawn. "As punishment for your sarcasm, you can take me out to the nicest restaurant you can find."

"Only the best for you, *principessa mia*." He yawned, as well, but Renata's eyes flew open. He'd just called her his princess. From a regular guy, that wouldn't mean a thing, but from him?

She slowly shifted to face him but he was fast asleep already. A slip of the tongue, no doubt. It wasn't as if he were offering her the job. She sighed. That was how things got sticky—the girl started imagining herself in a hip, yet lovely wedding gown while she doodled *I HEART PRNZ GIORGIO 4EVR* or *PRNCS RENATA RULEZ.* Literally.

Well, no more of that. Despite how hot, sexy, sweet, kind and wonderful Giorgio was, Renata would not fall in love with the man. Giorgio might like her adventurous Brooklyn personality for a fun vacation, but not permanently. No, when he finally settled down, he would want a sweet, delicate woman who could bake him lemon cookies, wave at crowds and never think of wearing a diamond in her nose or embroidering tiny skulls on a wedding dress. Renata wasn't princess material. Her heart was still packed away in acid-free tissue and a big fancy box, just like one of her vintage wedding gowns.

LATER THAT EVENING, Renata poked her head out of the bedroom. She could hear men's voices in the living room. Many men. She followed the voices.

She clutched her robe around her when she saw how many guys there actually were. Giorgio glanced up at her from an intense photo conversation and lifted his finger in a "wait a minute" gesture.

She turned to the beefy guy standing next to her. "What's going on?" she whispered.

He turned his head to stare at her with blank brown eyes but didn't answer. Maybe he didn't speak English, or maybe he wasn't paid to speak.

She retreated into the bedroom and dressed hastily in a button-up white blouse and denim capri pants, slipping her feet into plain white sneakers. The sexpot look was inappropriate for a serious situation.

She returned to the living room and sat in the floral armchair. Giorgio continued speaking in rapid Italian on the phone, gesturing emphatically. She understood that he was asking about the safety of his sister and grandmother and started to get alarmed.

For once, though, she kept quiet, realizing that she would only at best be a distraction and at worst a nuisance if she pestered him in the middle of his conversation.

He paused to bark orders at Paolo, who pulled out his own phone and made a call as well.

Renata forced herself to stay calm—until the night exploded with noise. A two-hundred-fifty-pound man was pulling her to the ground and covering her with his bulk.

The clattering noise continued in bursts for several seconds. Was some nutjob shooting at Giorgio? They still assassinated princes and prime ministers. She pushed at her own bodyguard but it was as futile as pushing on the wall. She yelled Giorgio's name but the other men were drowning her out as they called information to each other.

Renata slowed her breaths. Finally the noise stopped and she thought Paolo shouted something. Her bodyguard heaved a sigh of relief and eased off her. *"Petardi,"* he said.

"What?"

"Like American Fourth July. Pop, pop, pop." He imitated a string of fireworks.

"Oh, firecrackers." She started to sit up, but he pulled her back down and shook his shaved head. "Well, if we're going to get horizontal together, I should atleast know your name." It was a feeble attempt, but at least it gave her something to think about besides the adrenaline shakes starting up.

He gave her a puzzled look.

"Never mind."

"Okay!" Paolo shouted. "All clear!"

Renata sat up this time and spotted Giorgio across the room. His bodyguards had dumped over the couch and coffee table, sandwiching him between two of them as well as the furniture. He sat up looking mussed but not particularly upset. This must have happened before—maybe even with real bullets instead of firecrackers.

"You okay, Renata?" he called.

"Fine." She lifted a hand to wave at him, and her shakes made it wave on its own. She quickly dropped it.

He looked concerned but lifted his phone again. *"Pronto? Pronto? Si, petardi."* He laughed about how firecrackers could send them all into a state of siege.

Renata wasn't. She didn't think she could stand yet. She scooted so her back rested against the bottom of the chair and pulled her knees up.

Giorgio talked on the phone for another minute and then passed it to Paolo.

Giorgio came over to her. "Are you okay? Giuseppe there is a pretty big guy so I hope he didn't hurt you when he pulled you down." He extended a hand. "Come here."

She took his hand and only wobbled a bit getting to her feet. He guided her to the couch, which was back on its feet as well.

"Giorgio." Her voice quivered a bit. "Giorgio, what is going on?"

He sighed and gestured at the front windows. "That was firecrackers. Probably the local football team won a match, or someone got married, or just teenagers fooling around."

"You have eight huge guys standing in the living room on the remote chance firecrackers go off and they need to hurl you to the floor?"

"No, of course not. These men are the rest of Paolo's team. They've been staying nearby in case of incident."

"What incident brought them all out here? Is your family all right?"

"Yes, and thank you for asking." He lifted her hand to his

mouth and kissed the back. He kept hold of it, his warmth starting to ease her chills. "But there was a bomb threat at home. At the palazzo."

"A bomb threat? Where your grandmother lives?"

Giorgio nodded. "Of course the anti-terrorism squad was deployed immediately with the bomb-sniffing dogs. They did not find anything. But when one member of the royal family is threatened, it is standard protocol to deploy extra protection to the other members in case of muliple points of attack."

"So Stefania has her own team swarming her in New York."

He gave her a sad smile. "Yes, this doesn't happen often, but this is not the first time. My grandmother is probably more annoyed than frightened. She has seen Vinciguerra through worse."

"Worse than bomb threats?"

"She was a girl there during World War II, and during my grandfather's reign many different factions wanted control of the country. We have a natural deep-water port and the original palazzo is a heavily fortified citadel. Violence was not rare."

"Oh." Renata had imagined his country as sort of an Italianate theme park, untouched by darkness or pain. However, one glance at the serious men around her told her that violence was not part of the past. "Who called in the bomb threat?"

Giorgio snapped his fingers and Paolo immediately came to his side. Renata blinked. She didn't think she'd like Giorgio snapping his fingers at her, but the bodyguard wasn't offended by the princely gesture. "Paolo, who did this?"

Paolo replied at length. Giorgio signed at the end of his explanation and turned to Renata. "He says the Vinciguerran police have arrested a local group with anarchist affiliations. Their landlady overheard part of their phone call and put two and two together. They had been acting strangely—even more strangely than usual—the past couple days."

"Anarchists?"

He smiled, which startled her. "One advantage of dealing with anarchists is that they're pretty disorganized. No one is in charge, after all."

"Giorgio!" His gallows humor was disconcerting.

"Sorry, sorry." He put his arm around her. "I know you aren't used to this. We try our best to stay safe, but we have to live our lives without fear."

"You're not scared?" Renata was terrified, disorganized would-be terrorists or not.

He shrugged. "Not for myself, but for Stefania, my grandmother. And you."

"Me?"

"Of course." He kissed her forehead. "I am responsible for your safety. Anyone who tries to harm you will have to come through me."

"And Paolo and the rest of his guys."

"That goes without saying." His eyes filled with pride as he surveyed his team. "They'd do anything to protect us, and I hope to God they never need to."

Renata shivered. Assassination attempts and squads of bodyguards were something from the nightly newscast, not something she'd ever expected to experience. "What do we do now, Giorgio?" she whispered. She meant it as a rhetorical question, but he took her literally.

"Pour us each a glass of wine. Your nerves don't need any caffeine." His phone rang and he snatched it up. *"Pronto. Si."* He listened and gave her a wry smile. "Stefania is safe. Apparently the security team, uh…startled her and Dieter."

Poor Giorgio. Renata was sure he would have rather pretended Stefania and her fiancé spent their time pining for each other, but such was obviously not the case.

Renata hid a grin, but sobered quickly. Not much to smile about. She found a nice red wine in the rack and popped it open. That puppy wasn't getting the chance to breathe—one glass was going straight down the hatch.

11

"WHERE ARE WE GOING TODAY?" Renata was intrigued. Giorgio had told her to pack an overnight bag with swim gear. "To the beach?" She had worn a white peasant blouse over a snug denim skirt and high-heeled slingback sandals with a cork wedge and red snakeskin embossed leather upper.

"In a way." Giorgio, carrying both of their bags, led her down to the pier a block away from the hotel.

"Ooh, a boat ride." A good-size yacht was docked at the end of the long pier. She was glad she'd popped on a wide-brimmed white straw beach hat and oversize Jackie O sunglasses. Sun rays bounced off the water like crazy. And she could always pretend to be Jackie O reading a very serious book on Onassis's yacht. Except she didn't have any serious books and Giorgio was infinitely more interesting than one anyway.

"A yacht. You once suggested I should try it for relaxation. And I wanted to make it up to you for the commotion last night."

She waved a hand at him. "That wasn't your fault."

"If I were a regular man, it would have never happened."

He handed the luggage to a sailor wearing a bright blue polo shirt and helped her up the gangplank.

She recognized that shade of blue. “I think this is the same boat we came on from Genoa.”

“Yes, you’re right. We’re going on a private overnight cruise.”

Her eyes widened. “We have the whole yacht to ourselves?”

“Us, plus the captain and a couple crew members, including a chef.”

She climbed a set of stairs to the upper deck. He made an appreciative noise and gave her a quick pinch on the butt as he followed her. High heels plus a tight skirt were a killer combo since she’d thrown a bit of extra wiggle into her step.

They emerged on deck where they got a kick-ass view of the harbor with the ocean behind it. “Well, you just dodged a bullet by not having me cook.”

“An Italian girl who doesn’t know how to cook?” He shook his head in mock dismay and slipped his arm around her waist as they leaned on the rail. “What would your mamma say?”

“She’d say I’d never get a man without knowing how to keep him happy in the kitchen, but…”

He raised his eyebrows. “What?”

“My grandmother would say it’s more important to keep him happy in the bedroom.” Unless she was baking lemon cookies.

He threw his head back and roared with laughter. “Not to disparage your mamma, Renata *mia,* but I think your *nonna* is correct in this instance.” The yacht began to move away from the dock and the salty breeze picked up.

“I agree. It’s socially acceptable to order out for meals, but not the other.”

“That depends on who you hang out with,” he told her.

She screwed up her face. “Yuck!”

"No, not me," he assured her. "Perhaps it comes from having a little sister, but that kind of girl never appealed to me. They are always somebody's daughter—or sister."

"Good for you." She reached up to kiss him. Of course Giorgio wouldn't need to pay for sex, but he probably knew men who did. From what she'd seen on tabloid TV, some girls flocked around rich guys like skimpily dressed moths to a flame.

She had an unwelcome thought. What was the difference between them and her? She was here on Giorgio's dime and had only paid a fraction of what had to be extensive expenses. On the other hand, she had gone out with him in New York because he was gorgeous and fascinating and had never asked him, never even considered hinting that he should take her to Europe. That was *his* idea. She had never been a gold digger and she wasn't about to start now. Besides, he knew she wanted him for sex, not money, and had said so when he called to ask her on the trip.

Maybe that would salve her conscience. She was here because she couldn't get enough of him the man, not him the prince with a royal treasury bankrolling their activities. She would have gladly spent a week in New York doing the same thing they were doing, minus the sightseeing. Logistics and nosy people had made that location impossible.

Renata sighed and looked over the beautiful blue water, the seabirds wheeling above the waves. It was too fine a day to worry. Giorgio knew she wasn't like that, and so did she.

A steward in a white dinner jacket handed them each a glass flute and disappeared. "Ooh, champagne."

"Prosecco," he corrected her. "They grow Prosecco grapes north of Venice in the foothills of the Alps, not too far from Vinciguerra."

"I'm sure I'll love it."

He surprised her by reaching under her hat and gently taking off her sunglasses. "I want to see your lovely blue eyes."

Renata blinked her lovely blue eyes in the dazzling light. Giorgio lifted his flute and she did the same.

"To us."

"To us?" Was there an "us"? At least for the next week or so.

"And our cruise on the lovely Italian Riviera."

Ah, a little bon voyage toast. "To our cruise." She lifted her glass to clink his and then drank. The sparkling wine was fruity and dry with a hint of peach.

Giorgio certainly was showing her the lifestyles of the rich and famous on their trip. She'd been slightly concerned she wouldn't see anything of Italy but the bedroom, but Giorgio, probably realizing she wouldn't be jet-setting back to Europe anytime soon, was being so considerate in arranging typically tourist opportunities.

The yacht slowly began to move away from the dock with a low humming of the engines. "This is really lovely, Giorgio." Her arms settled around his waist as if they belonged there and she clung to him.

He smiled down at her. "Nicest bon voyage I've ever had."

"Me, too." She'd have to get an extra-long bon voyage kiss before she hopped a plane for New York.

"What's wrong?"

Her expression must have reflected her dismay at leaving him in only a handful of days. "Oh, um, the sunlight bouncing off the waves got me for a second."

"Then you need these back. I'd hate for you to get a headache from the sun. It often bothers visitors who aren't used to it." He slipped her sunglasses back onto her nose, and she was glad for the concealment. He put his own pair on. They stared out over the water, each safe from revealing too much thanks to their shatter-resistant dark lenses.

"Where is the trip taking us?"

"Another surprise, but it will involve lots of sun, fun and food."

"Three out of four of my favorite things."

He pursed his lips into an air kiss. "I'm sure we can make time for your other favorite thing."

"What, swimming?"

He laughed. He slid his hand down her waist so it rested on the curve of her hip. "The captain will be down in a minute to give us a tour of the towns as we pass them, but I think after that I will give you a tour of our stateroom. You will have had a bit too much late-morning sun and retire there for a nap—with me, of course."

"Wow, how decadent. A nap already?" She rolled her hip slightly so he caressed her bottom.

"Everyone knows redheads are susceptible to heat," he told her with a serious expression.

She wiggled her eyebrows. "Only to your heat," she whispered as the captain arrived, maritime-spiffy in his white shirt with black-and-gold epaulets. He had sunburned crow's-feet at the corners of his snapping black eyes.

"Ah, Capitano Galletti," Giorgio greeted him warmly.

"*Signor, signorina,* welcome to my ship, *La Bella Maria,* named after my lovely wife, Maria. *Benvenuto!*" He bobbed his head in a respectful nod. "A pleasure to have you join us as we cruise the Cinque Terre. If there is anything we can do to make your trip the most enjoyable possible, please do not hesitate to ask."

"*Grazie, Capitano.* Signorina Renata's great-grandparents came from Corniglia and she would like to learn more about that village."

"Ah, from Corniglia!" His face crinkled into a mass of

wrinkles, his smile the widest one. "I should have known from your beauty. *Signore,* the most beautiful women in Italy are from Corniglia. But do not tell my wife I said so—she is from Manarola." They laughed. That was the village next to Corniglia. He gestured extravagantly at the panorama behind him. "They are so beautiful because of the sun, the sea, the fresh air and the *fish,*" he said in a significant tone of voice.

"The fish?" Renata asked, wondering how a love of seafood contributed to beauty.

"We always knew fish made you healthy and strong. And now the rest of the world knows—but they take fish in pills." Capitano Galletti shook his head at that foolishness. "Pills, pah."

"Indeed," Giorgio said with grave respect. "We are looking forward to some fresh fish. You have an excellent reputation for your seafood dishes."

"But, of course! The cook will prepare grilled swordfish for you tonight—fresh caught just this morning while we were still in bed."

Renata suppressed a grin. They had indeed been in bed, but probably not asleep. For spending so much time in bed, she was awfully tired. A nap like Giorgio had suggested sounded great.

The captain had other ideas, though. "Come, more Prosecco." He topped off their glasses. "I show you the most beautiful coast in the world."

He was as good as his word. After they left the inlet at Vernazza, he showed them a picturesque view of the hills and cliffs studded with coral, white and yellow houses leading down to the pebbly beach.

"And now, Corniglia!" the captain announced like a proud father. "The first Roman farmer here named it after his mother, Cornelia. What a good son, eh?"

Renata stared at the tiny hilltop town, amazed that her great-grandparents had summoned the nerve to leave it for the wilds of New York City. They must have had the mother of all culture shock when they arrived in America early in the twentieth century. She had friends who lived in apartment buildings with more people than the entire village.

Giorgio leaned in close. "It is only a few kilometers' hike from our flat. We will visit before you go."

She nodded, noting how he'd said "our flat" and then followed that up by reminding her she was leaving. Mixed messages? "I'm not looking forward to leaving."

"Me, neither," he admitted. "This has been a little slice of heaven."

"Heaven indeed! Beautiful wine country," crowed Capitano Galletti. "Jugs at Pompeii had ads for white wine from Corniglia. I have a friend there who makes her own wine—*delizioso!* I can get you a nice, nice discount." He winked at Giorgio, who smiled in return.

Renata wondered what Giorgio might have said if the captain hadn't inserted the ad for his friend's wine. She just had to get up her nerve and ask him again when they were alone.

Renata scanned the coastline and stood up straight. "Look, that guy is jumping off the cliff."

"Crazy, eh? Cliff diving." Something in Giorgio's slightly nostalgic tone made her narrow her eyes.

"So crazy you've never tried it?"

"Well..." He shrugged, a mischievous look in his eyes. "I seem to recall trying it once or twice while vacationing with Jack and Frank in the Spanish Riviera when we were in college. I have to confess my wits and judgment were dulled by major quantities of sangria but we all managed to survive without significant injury. Think Frank sprained an ankle."

"Giorgio! I can't believe you did that." Her jaw dropped. The captain suddenly realized he had to be somewhere else and hastily departed.

"I have to admit cliff-diving was my idea."

"Yours? Were you crazy as well as drunk?"

"Frank was both. He was coming off a bad breakup and wanted to jump off a cliff, minus the ocean below. So I told him if he was going to jump off a cliff, he had to take us with him. Jack calculated the angle and velocity to avoid smashing onto the rocks. We all made it into the water, although Frank moved his foot at the last second and wound up spraining it. Water is very hard when you hit it incorrectly."

"Anything for a friend, huh?" That poor guy Frank had been so down he didn't care, his friend Jack had put some scientific method to the madness and Giorgio had coordinated the whole thing like the leader he was born to be.

Considering how Giorgio was the only male heir to the throne and taking care of Stefania, the risk he'd taken was shocking. "I never knew you had that reckless side."

He raised one black eyebrow. "Didn't you?" His tone was low and seductive.

Oh, yes, she did know about his reckless side. He buried it well under fancy Italian suits and perfect royal manners, but it did exist, simmering away like a pot of pasta water until someone turned it up to boil over. She had been the one to heat him up.

He placed a fingertip beneath her chin and leaned over to kiss her lightly with closed lips, thanks to the presence of the crew, who were probably peeping at them. Renata closed her eyes, the sweet, warm pressure promising sensual delights later.

He moved his finger up her jawline. "We men are all reckless, especially where beautiful women are concerned."

"And why is that?"

"The same reason we dive off perfectly good cliffs. The danger. Do we dare to approach the edge? Once we decide to make a move, it is anticipation followed by pure exhilaration. And what will the finish be? Successful, or—"

"Or a sprained ankle or cracked-open head," she finished dryly.

He grinned and raised his Prosecco again. "Ah, but that only gives us war wounds and battle scars that we can brag about. Almost like breaking a leg on the slopes in Gstaad and then sitting in the lodge while ski beauties bring you brandy."

Renata rolled her eyes. And this was why they were destined to be a vacation fling—just another example of their different worlds. He was a Verdi grand opera singer and she was a Frank Sinatra impersonator. He was a fancy five-star restaurant and she like a mom-and-pop hole-in-the-wall hangout complete with red-checked tablecloth and wax-covered Chianti bottle candlestick.

LUNCH WAS A BUFFET of antipasti, sausages and salami, Italian cheese and fresh-baked focaccia dotted with garlic. One dish Renata had never seen before was the Cinque Terre version of potato salad with small red potatoes, green beans and pesto sauce, but it was delicious. Wouldn't her mother be surprised when Renata brought back a new recipe?

After a dessert of lemon gelato, Renata stretched out on a deck chair facing the ocean. "Ah, this is the life." She was so full she was considering taking a real nap.

Giorgio sat in the adjoining chair and took her hand. "I'm glad you are enjoying yourself. Although Cinque Terre can be the quietest area of the Italian Riviera, being on the water is even more so."

The crewman finished clearing away lunch with the

captain looking down from the bridge in an avuncular manner. He gave them a friendly wave and they waved back.

"Does he know who you are?" she asked in a low voice.

"Probably." He shrugged his shoulders. "Paolo made the arrangements, and he can be very persuasive in convincing businessmen to maintain their confidentiality standards."

She giggled. With his size and intense demeanor, Paolo could convince anyone to do anything. "Well, the captain seems like a good guy, unlikely to alert the paparazzi. You don't want to wind up on the front of the tabloids, do you?"

"I'm used to it. They've been publishing my pictures since my mother carried me out onto the palazzo balcony after my baptism."

"Since you were a baby?"

He preened. "I was very photogenic. Bald, but photogenic."

"I don't like having my picture taken." She shuddered. "Probably a holdover from my overweight Goth days. I used to hide behind my brothers during family photos. Good thing they're all big guys—"

"Stop. I'm sure you were too hard on yourself. Most girls go through an awkward phase. Stefania wore braces for a couple years and spent hours in the bathroom checking for spots on her skin."

"But to live your life in that fishbowl?"

He stretched out his legs. "But we don't live our lives in the fishbowl. At home, when I was young, my mother would bake cookies and dig in the garden and my father would build model airplane kits with me and go fishing in the nearby river. We were just a normal family, except with fancier clothes and more job titles than most."

"You must have had a happy childhood."

"Happier than the latter part of Stefania's." He caught

Renata's hand. "But what could I do about that?" he asked philosophically.

"You did your best, which was better than most young men would have done." Would her brothers have taken her in under the same circumstances. Of course, she decided. They drove her nuts but they were fiercely loyal.

"I did threaten to punch out a photographer once," Giorgio reminisced with a fond air. "He cordered Stefania in a boutique when I was taking her shopping for a prom dress. We had him thrown out of the store."

Renata made a face. Following a teenage girl dress shopping—a career to be proud of. "If I see one of those camera jerks, I won't threaten to punch him—I'll just go ahead and do it."

He gave her a considering glance. "I believe you. But so far on our ocean trip we haven't done anything worthy of the tabloids."

"What a shame." She smiled at him. "When do we start?"

"How does *now* sound?" He gracefully got to his feet and extended his hand to her. "I would carry you to our stateroom but the stairs are too narrow. You will have to settle for holding hands."

She wiggled her finger at him. "All right, but we'll do better than that once we get in there."

"Of course."

He guided her into the stateroom and she was suitably impressed. Bigger than their bedroom in the villa, it had a king-size mahogany bed with a champagne-colored brocade coverlet and ivory sheets. Little gold sconces were hung over the matching nightstands, and a wide dresser stood off to the side. A big, full-length gilt mirror hung on the wall opposite the foot of the bed. It was classic and lush.

"What would you like to do?" she asked him.

"This." He started to undo the peasant style laces on her top and pulled her bodice open. "*Mamma mia,* what is this?" he asked with delight.

"A bustier." White satin to go under her white top. "You like?"

"I love."

Her heart flipped, even though she knew he was just talking about her lingerie. "Good." She yanked her blouse over her head and unbuttoned her denim skirt. It fell to the floor and she kicked it away.

He actually bit his knuckles and groaned. "Why did we bother eating lunch? If I had known this, you wouldn't have seen anything but this room."

She smiled in sly satisfaction. Her second surprise had been the matching white satin thong. When those paired with the bustier and red high heels, it was no wonder Giorgio was already moaning.

He made a grab for her and she ducked away. "No, no, no." She wiggled her finger at him. "You have to take off your clothes, too."

"Fine." He popped a couple buttons on his shirt, making her laugh.

"And then, I want you to sit at the foot of the bed."

He quickly stripped and sat, beckoning to her. "Come here, baby. Giorgio will make you feel so good."

She shivered, knowing he spoke the truth. He was the most generous lover, making sure she came first every time—sometimes more than once. But she wanted to give him a special thank-you for the surprise cruise and if he had to wait a little bit, then too bad.

"Tell me, Giorgio, were you one of those wild princes when you were younger? Did you and your friends Jack and

Frank blow money watching half-naked girls strut around on stage?"

He laughed. "We were amazingly dull. Which is why I think you are so exciting, Renata."

That gave her just the opening she was looking for. "Let me make it up to you. Sit back and enjoy the show." She found a small radio on the nightstand and tuned it to a hard-beating Italian pop song.

"Come here, Renata. I have something for you." It was more a plea than a command. He spread his knees and showed her what he wanted to give her. He was plenty aroused, his cock large and toasty brown like a sweet-tasting pastry and his sac was full almost to bursting. As she watched, a drop rose on his plump tip, begging her to lick him clean. She almost gave in because she loved the taste and feel of him in her mouth, soft skin over hard flesh, slippery but firm. He loved it, too.

She shook her head and started swaying her hips, trying not to giggle. Two-to-one odds she'd fall on her ass if she tried anything too complicated since dance had never been her strong suit and being on high heels was another mark against her.

Giorgio didn't seem to notice her less-than-professional skills, his gaze hungry as she slowly swiveled her butt. She turned her back to him and wiggled more, pleased at his intake of breath.

"Tell me what you like, Prince Giorgio."

"I want that pretty ass in front of me as I pump into it."

She staggered on her heels, the image hard-driving and graphic. Her thong was immediately sopping wet. "What else do you want?" She turned to face him.

"I want your tits in my mouth so I can suck on them while I fuck you with my fingers."

"These tits?" She slowly lowered the satin cups on the

bustier and folded them down. Her breasts were supported by the corseting but totally naked. Her own breath was coming as hard as his. "Like this?" She sucked on her index finger and slowly rubbed the saliva across the tips. Her nipples hardened and deepened in color to a shiny deep rose.

Giorgio groaned and cupped his cock. "Look at what you are doing to me, Renata." His shaft bulged with veins, the head darkened to a rich plum. "Show me some mercy."

She shook her head. "Show me how you touched yourself when you thought of me. Before I got here and you were hot, hard and horny."

He swallowed hard but he obeyed her for once and stroked himself up and down from base to tip, using his own moisture for lubricant.

Her clit was pounding at a crazy pace so she slipped a finger under her thong.

"Stop." His nostrils flared, his pupils dilating with desire. "Come here."

She obeyed him this time, shaking with desire as she stood in front of him.

"You are quite the little tease, Renata, with your bottom and breasts bared for me but not allowing me to touch you."

She grinned and he lifted an eyebrow. "You need to be disciplined for your disrespect."

"Oh, yeah? Whaddaya have in mind?" she asked in her broadest Brooklyn accent.

"This." He gestured to his lap and for a second she thought he meant the obvious, which wasn't a punishment for either one of them. Instead he actually eased her down so she was lying facedown across his lap. She couldn't believe how turned on she was with her bare breasts falling free on one side of his thighs, her bare ass sunny side up on the other and his long cock smack dab in the middle of her stomach.

Her face burned, and not just from being gravitationally challenged. It was so exciting and so shameful, but way more exciting than shameful because it was Giorgio, after all, and she wouldn't be caught dead doing this with any other man. "Have you ever done this before?"

"No," he rasped. "But I can't help wanting to do all sorts of crazy things to you. You are driving me mad. I only think with my cock when you are with me. When you are not with me I only think of how I can please you."

"Enough talk—more action." She rubbed her satin-covered belly over his cock and he groaned.

"Deal."

Their sexual bargain agreed upon, he set out to consummate it. Her breasts were easy targets as they swayed like ripe fruit for the picking. He brushed her nipples, one and then the other, with the lightest of touches. Then firmer passes, more and more until he was rolling her nipples between his fingers. She let out a moan as he unexpectedly pinched her, bearing the weight of her breasts in his hand.

"I would like to make you come by just playing with your tits." His tone was casual, but the way his cock throbbed against her was anything but casual as he continued to play with her. "But to do that, I want to use my mouth on you. You will lie on top of me and dangle your pretty pink nipples against my lips until I decide which one I want to suck first."

Renata couldn't keep her hips from grinding.

"Oh, none of that." He rubbed his hand over her quivering butt cheeks and then suddenly smacked them. She jerked her head back in surprise but not pain. It was more of a tap than anything. "Stay still and you will get a reward."

"You know I will anyway," she retorted. Her "reward" was currently making its presence known against her belly.

"Minx." He tapped her butt again.

"Ooh, when you call me that, I…I…"

He sighed. "I can see this is not arousing enough to sufficiently distract you from side commentary. Perhaps we should stop…"

"Please don't, Your Highness. I promise to be ever so submissive."

His cough sounded suspiciously like a muffled laugh. "See that you are." He stroked her bottom again to the tops of her thighs and pulled her thong aside.

She arched her back again. "Oh, Giorgio." He had slipped his thumb inside her pussy and was rotating it lazily, stretching her sensitive opening. He bumped her G-spot again and she cried out. It was torture, the constant circular pressure, never in the same place for very long and slow enough to drive her crazy.

His other hand found her breasts and he rubbed his hard palm over both nipples at once. She tried to push them against him harder but he was tormenting her with his light sexy touches.

She started gasping for breath. It was all too much, but not enough. She ground frantically against his hand. "Make me come, Giorgio. I need it now."

"Do you?" he asked lazily. "And what will you do for me in return?" He gave her a quick tap on the ass.

"Anything…anything."

"Tell me. I want to hear you say it."

"I'll take you in my mouth. Suck you until you come. Open my body to you and let you do whatever you want."

"Good." He found her clit with his long index finger and flicked it back and forth. He rolled her nipples between his fingers, pulling them to impossibly long peaks. She started to writhe on his lap, burning hot and cold at the same time.

Her tremors grew harder and closer together as he played her with his hands. She was vulnerable but safe, knowing he had ironclad control over himself—and her. "Hurry, Renata," he crooned. "Hurry to your first climax so I can give you another with my cock."

She groaned and succumbed, arching and crying as she came. Her thong was soaking wet and pressing up into her pussy, her breasts throbbing and full.

She barely had a minute to catch her breath before he was helping her up. "Now it is your turn."

He stood and turned to the side. "Look, Renata." He gestured to the long mirror opposite them.

They were perfect contrasts, her soft body white with red, red nipples and a red shadow under her thong. He was tanned and muscular, his erection strong and dark.

She swallowed hard. "What do you want to do, Giorgio?"

"What you offered me. Your mouth and your body. And we both get to watch."

She'd never done that before but her pussy throbbed at the thought. She eased to kneel in front of him.

"There, Renata. Watch the mirror as I take your mouth. As you wrap your pouty lips around me." He turned his head so he could see her reflection.

She did as he asked, her eyes widening as she saw and felt his pulsing cock enter her mouth. She was stretched into the perfect O around him and felt utterly possessed.

He hissed out a long breath as she automatically applied suction. *"Si, si, mia bella."*

Who was that wanton redhead, dressed in red heels and satin lingerie, on her knees watching herself in a mirror as she hungrily sucked on a man's cock? It was beyond raunchy and she loved it—because it was Giorgio.

His gaze met hers in the mirror. "Touch yourself."

She raised her eyebrows.

"I know how insatiable you are, no? You are close to coming already."

He was right. She slid her hand inside her thong and strummed her clit. Her moans excited him even more, and he cupped her head as he thrust into her willing, wet mouth.

Her breath came in short, choppy bursts and she climaxed again, careful not to scrape him. She thought for sure he'd come, too, but he pulled out of her mouth and helped her kneel on the bed, facing the mirror. He quickly moved behind her, even as she was still coming.

He parted her knees and shoved inside. Her moan turned into a scream of pleasure as his cock stretched her pulsing body. She dropped to her hands and knees and panted, but he pulled her upright.

"Watch us," he commanded. "Watch my dick slip in and out of your body." He covered her bare breasts with his hard, hot hands. "Watch me play with your big, round tits."

She did. She watched helplessly as he drove her to the edge of sexual insanity. He thrust quickly, then slowly, pinched her and then stroked her with a featherlight touch.

"Spread yourself open. I want you to see *everything*."

She whipped her head to the side to meet his hard gaze.

He stopped moving inside her and stopped touching her tits. "Do it, Renata." He snapped the back elastic of her thong and tossed the whole garment aside. "Now you can see."

She slowly spread her folds wide and gasped. Her clit was round and hard as a pearl, her pussy dark rose with arousal. Most of his penis was hidden inside her, his heavy balls resting against her ass. As she stared, he withdrew from her slowly, until his shaft sat between her folds and his head rested right below her clit.

He thrust slowly along that groove, his slick tip brushing

her clit. Renata clamped her legs around him and shuddered.

Giorgio cupped her breasts again, moving leisurely without entering her. The purple head of his cock peeped coyly between her legs with every thrust.

"Who do you belong to, Renata?" he commanded, thumbing her nipples. "Tell me. Who does your body belong to?"

"You, Giorgio," she sobbed. "Only you."

"Mine." He nipped her earlobe. "All mine." Those were the magic words because he slid into her, his tip settling deep inside her.

A few more thrusts and she started to shake. "Yes, yes," he hissed. "Come now, but *watch.* Open your eyes. See the wild woman I make you—the wild woman you are."

She was sweaty and messy—but ripe and fabulous at the same time, her eyes hazy and her mouth red from sucking on him. No wonder Giorgio was so turned on by watching her. Together they were incredibly erotic, his thighs bulging with muscle as he pumped into her.

He held a breast in each hand as if offering himself a present, his hands tanned and strong against her soft white flesh. "Touch yourself."

In a daze, she moved her hand down to her swollen clit and plucked the knot of nerves. Her moans grew in volume and intensity until she exploded. She collapsed but he held her upright, one strong arm across her breasts while he played with her clit. She tossed her head back and forth as he licked and sucked on her neck.

Her world shrank to the three of them—her, Giorgio and the mirror.

She'd never tried watching herself climax before and was mildly chagrined at her goofy expressions, but the one expression she couldn't get enough of was Giorgio's.

Hungry and lustful, sure, but tender and affectionate, as well. And when she'd hit the absolute peak, he wore a look of satisfaction and masculine pride, that yeah, he'd been the guy to do that for her.

And she wanted to be the woman to do that for him. She looked over her shoulder and gave him her best come-hither. "Come on, big boy. Your turn."

He sighed happily and pounded into her, grunting with every thrust. It was hard and wild and full and tight. "Look," she reminded him. "Look at how you take me."

He opened his eyes wider and stared at their bodies locked together in untamed passion. *"Che bella, la cosa più bella del mondo..."*

Good, he thought it was the most beautiful thing in the world. So did she.

He stiffened and started to come, trying valiantly to keep his eyes open to see them. He gave up after a couple earthshaking shocks and buried his face in her shoulder, his breath hot and wet on her skin.

Renata stared at herself in the mirror. Who was she, that she could bring a powerful man to such a shuddering climax just by being herself?

It was a disturbing idea that she had such power over him—and he had such power over her. He lifted his head suddenly and their gazes locked. "Ah, Renata." He looked like he wanted to say more but was at a loss for words.

"Giorgio," she whispered, at an equal loss.

He eased from her and kissed her cheek. "Let's rest. Then you can show me whatever amazing swimsuit you packed."

She smiled back, more at ease again. "You've got a deal."

12

RENATA CAME OUT of the bathroom in her brand-new bathing suit she'd bought last summer from a pinup girl clothing website based in L.A. It was a pure vintage look with bright red cherries dotting the white fabric. The bottoms were high-waisted with enough coverage for her ample tush, and the bikini top was halter-style, a knot between her breasts that hiked up the girls quite nicely. It made her look ripe and lush, and she thought it was the cat's meow.

Giorgio obviously agreed. "Swimming is canceled. We're staying in."

"Oh, no we aren't." She skipped by him, neatly dodging his grab. "If we wait much longer, it will be too dark to swim."

He frowned. "All right. But don't you have a robe or cover-up you can wear?"

She raised an eyebrow in puzzlement. "It's not exactly chilly out there." Then she understood his disgruntlement. "You don't want the sailors whistling at me. Don't worry, the captain runs too tight a ship for that."

"Tight ship or not, they are men. And a man would have to be dead not to notice you—the good captain included."

"Aren't you sweet." She went up on tiptoe to kiss him.

"Relax, and help me put on some sunblock." She handed him a bottle.

"You reject my advances and now want me to rub lotion all over you in the privacy of our lovely bedroom? Cruel woman." But he opened the lid and squirted some into his palm.

"Do it here, or else the sailors can watch you slick me up." She pulled her hair into a quick French twist and clipped it into place.

He grumbled at her flip suggestion but did as she asked him. "You do need this sun lotion with your white skin. How did a redhead like you avoid freckles?"

She laughed. "Have you ever heard of Goths?"

"Somehow I do not think you are not talking about the Germanic tribes that invaded Rome during the Dark Ages?"

"No." She grinned, bending slightly so he could rub some into the small of her back. "I used to be a Goth girl. Sad, gloomy rock music, white makeup and lots of black eyeliner. Oh, and black hair."

He spun her around to face him. Wow, he really had something against the Goths. "You…you dyed your beautiful red hair…black?"

Her grin broke in laughter. "Black as yours, but not as nice and shiny since it was from a bottle."

He still stared at her. "But you are perfect the way you are."

She stifled a snort. She had many good qualities but perfection wasn't one of them. "I wasn't very happy when I was a teenager. I didn't want to take the college prep classes that my father wanted me to take and I didn't want to take the secretarial classes my mother wanted me to take. I just daydreamed and doodled outfits in my notebooks all day long."

Since it was *True Confessions* time, she told him the rest. "My mother was always nagging me to lose weight."

He lifted a questioning eyebrow but prudently didn't comment.

"Although I'm not exactly skinny right now—"

"Again, you are perfect. Round and smooth and…and… voluptuous," he announced, triumphant at remembering the precise English word.

"I had about sixty pounds of extra perfection back then. I looked like a black olive, short and fat."

"I love olives." Giorgio folded his arms over his chest.

"So do I. And I loved pasta, cannoli, lasagna, veal parmesan and all the Italian home-cooking that I ate three times a day." She shook her head and laughed. "Come on, three-cheese lasagna for dinner and they expected me to lose weight? My brothers could eat like that because they were either cops or firefighters or training to be cops or firefighters. I was sitting in school all day and sitting listening to Goth rock on my CD player at night."

"So what did you do?"

"I just got sick of black." He gave her a puzzled look. "Seriously, I wore all black every single day. Even Christmas. Some of my black clothes got worn-out and my mother refused to buy me any more. She told me to wear my grandmother's dresses if I was going to dress like an old Italian widow."

He groaned.

"Yeah, I know. Tact has never been her thing, but she had a point. So I took some money and went to the thrift store. And on the mannequin, there was this absolutely gorgeous dress. It was this stunning grayish-blue silk with a tiny waist and fitted bodice and full skirt—the kind of dress you'd wear if your boyfriend got front row seats to a Sinatra concert. Nineteen-fifties," she added in case he didn't realize what era she was describing.

"And you wanted that dress."

"Desperately. I fell in love with the dress and fell in love with vintage fashion. But I quickly learned a couple things—if I wanted to fit into the originals, I would need to lose some weight. And if I wanted to make copies, I would need to learn how to sew. My aunt Barbara was thrilled to teach me, and I lost enough weight to where I felt better physically, stopped wearing so much makeup and let my hair grow out. It was two-toned for a while, avant-garde for Brooklyn back then, but it's now actually stylish among some kids."

He nodded. "Stefania had blue streaks in her hair as a teenager."

"It's practically a requirement when you attend art school."

"Well, my grandmother didn't care for it. I barely kept her from getting a tattoo or body piercings."

Renata touched the small diamond in her nose. "She probably wouldn't like this. My mother hates it but my grandmother thinks it's great—mostly because it annoys my mother."

"Your grandmother sounds like fun."

"She's a real pistol—she's reached that age where Italian women just let it rip. Whatever they think comes out of their mouth. She horrifies my mother and Aunt Barbara because they never know what she'll say next."

"If only you were an older woman, Renata. That way you could say what you really mean instead of holding back your true thoughts." He couldn't even finish his sentence without cracking into a wide grin.

She swiped at him, but he easily ducked away.

"If only you could speak your mind—I never know what you are thinking." He was guffawing by then.

She grabbed him in a bear hug, her lotioned arms sliding around his waist. "You are a terrible tease."

"Who, me?" He put on an innocent look. "Do I ever arouse your sexy body and then leave you unsatisfied?"

"Not that kind of a tease." She huffed in mock indignation.

He gave her a quick peck on the lips. "If you are not satisfied, Renata, you are sure fooling me."

"Giorgio!" she squawked and pushed him away. "You're making me blush." The heat was creeping up into her cheeks.

"All right, all right. Let me show you the surprise the captain and I have planned for this afternoon."

"You can't possibly have any more surprises for me. I think I'm all surprised out." The past day had been the culmination of an astonishing trip.

"One more, if you promise you won't faint from shock. On the other hand, I could loosen your garments to make sure you're breathing properly…" He leered cheerfully at her.

She rolled her eyes. Considering she was wearing a two-piece swimsuit, the outcome would be less than altruistic. "Is the surprise up on deck?"

"In a way." He grabbed their robes and a couple towels, so it looked like they were going for a swim. She hoped the water wasn't too cold.

They climbed up to the deck and the boat slowed as it passed a rocky outcrop. "Here we are—are you ready to swim?"

"Oh, okay." She was a pretty good swimmer—all the padding in her boobs and ass made her a champion floater.

Giorgio went into the water first and then helped her

down the boat ladder. She flinched slightly at the water temperature, but it was pretty good considering there were probably icebergs floating somewhere outside New York Harbor this time of year.

Giorgio noticed her wince. "How's the water?" He seemed to notice everything about her, even the small things.

"Brisk, I'll get used to it." She moved her arms and legs experimentally.

"Let's swim over to that rock. The captain tells me you can sometimes see interesting fish there."

"Sure." It had been a long time since she'd swum in salt water and she really enjoyed the increased buoyancy. "This is nice, Giorgio." She fell into an easy crawl. He did a lazy backstroke, his long arms and legs holding back so he could stay with her.

"Glad you like it."

"I've never gone swimming off the side of a boat in deeper water like this." It was kind of spooky to imagine a hundred feet of open water below her. Anything could be swimming down there, looking up. *Oh, look, what kind of new snack is that, flailing around in the water? Yum, wonder how that tastes?*

"Giorgio!" She squealed and slapped at the water's surface, splashing him with droplets. "Stop that!"

"Stop what?" he asked.

"Tickling my feet with yours."

"Renata, *cara,* I am a couple meters away from you. How can I reach your feet?"

She yelped at the sensation of something smooth brushing her ankle. "There it is again." She launched herself at Giorgio at the glimpse of a dorsal fin below them. "Oh, my God! Are there sharks here?"

He caught her easily and glanced over at the yacht. The

deckhands were pointing to them out in the water but were smiling instead of screaming in horror.

Renata took a closer look at what was going for a swim with them. “Dolphins,” she breathed. A herd, or pod, or squad of dolphins had come upon them and circled around them, their slick bodies gleaming silver under the clear water.

She’d seen her share of dolphins at the zoo and aquarium, but they were a performing poodle version of this wild animal. Moving at incredible speeds crisscrossing each other, they never faltered.

Renata relaxed her grip on Giorgio’s arm, doubly glad they weren’t sharks because she had probably dug her fingers in hard enough to draw blood. “Have you ever seen them in the wild?”

He shook his head. “Only in the distance from a boat—never to swim with them.”

“What do we do?”

“Since we don’t resemble a school of anchovies, I think we are safe.”

“Safe,” Renata echoed. She always felt safe with Giorgio—everything but her heart. “I don’t want to be safe.”

“No?” He grinned at her. “How did I guess that about you? Come on.” He grabbed her hand and took a deep breath. She only had a split second to do the same before he tugged her under the blue water.

Instantly they were in a different realm that muffled their vision and hearing but heightened touch. Despite his assurances, Renata clutched Giorgio as several hundred pounds of marine carnivore slid by, her gasp coming out in a soundless stream of bubbles. He patted her arm and pointed. A mother dolphin and her baby nodded their sleek, round heads at her, their wide mouths silently laughing at the gangly mammals who’d stumbled into their home turf.

The mother nudged Baby toward them, but Renata was running out of air. She and Giorgio surfaced and so did Baby, spraying them with a fine plume from his tiny blowhole. Mamma Dolphin popped up a second later, clicking and squeaking at them.

"Is it okay to touch them?" She'd seen wildlife documentaries where it could cost a limb to mess with a baby and his mother.

"Let me see." Giorgio held his arms open wide and crooned to them in sweet Italian, almost as if he were talking to a human baby. Renata's heart melted as the baby swam to him, chittering at ultrasonic pitches.

"Okay, so now you're the Dolphin Whisperer?"

He laced his fingers through hers and pulled her close. "Italian dolphins like to hear their native tongue. Here, you try."

Holding her wrist with his as if she were a small child petting a dog, he glided their hands along the dolphin's skin. It was slick and rubbery but warm and vital. She let out some chirps and her whole upper body vibrated like the lid of a grand piano during a powerful chord.

Mamma dolphin bumped Giorgio, his testosterone obviously undiluted by the seawater. He grabbed her dorsal fin and she sped away with him, Giorgio's delighted laughter echoing back to her.

The sailors hooted, as well, talking excitedly among themselves. "Giorgio!" she yelled, panicking before she remembered that baby was still with her.

Giorgio looked like a Greek god, frolicking with the dolphin. He was perfectly at ease with the female dolphin, splashing and smiling as she towed him around the cove. He was young and carefree, much as he probably looked before the weight of substitute fatherhood and ruling a whole country fell onto his shoulders.

"Renata!" he yelled gleefully. "Have you ever seen anything like this?"

She shook her head. No, she sure hadn't. Of all the wonderful things she had seen since coming to Italy, he was the most wonderful. In a fancy suit, swimming, or naked, she loved it all. Her heart gave a funny thump that had nothing to do with the baby dolphin butting her in the chest for attention.

Her smile faded into more of a grimace. She was in big trouble. She'd known he was someone special since laying her lustful little eyes on him, but his fine qualities went deeper than his smooth, tan skin.

He blew her a kiss and her heart thumped even faster before sinking. Three more days and she would be winging her way back to New York as—what was that musical theater song? Oh, yes, as the proverbial sadder but wiser girl. Well, she needed to wise up and fast. Starting to fall for one of the world's most reputed eligible bachelors was definitely one of her stupider ideas.

He came whizzing back to her, towed by the dolphin. He glided to a halt, still laughing with joy as the dolphin bumped him in salute before gathering her baby to follow the rest of the pod.

"Ah, Renata! That was so amazing. It was like flying. I've never felt anything like that." He pulled her into his arms for a thorough kiss that earned more catcalls from the crew. He laughed and waved to them before turning back to her. "Okay, I have felt that way with you. Free and happy, without any worries. But not with anyone else."

Oh man, was she sunk. She pasted a smile on her face.

He didn't notice her strained expression as he wiped the water off his face. "I think the baby liked you, too. Did you have a good time with him?"

"He was very sweet, but I thought for a second his mom might drag you out to sea without me."

He wrapped his arm around her waist, his eyelashes clumped together to frame his sparkling green eyes. "Renata *mia,* I would never leave you. I would swim all the way back from Sicily if I had to."

"You're such a charmer," she scoffed. "My mother warned me about men like you."

"I'm not this charmer you think I am. I spend too much time at my desk worrying about work. The rest of the time I am cutting ribbons for grand openings of senior citizens centers and dog pounds." He laughed. "My friend Frank says I should get dog fur and slobber all over my good suit so I can appeal to women."

He needed more sex appeal like the sun needed a flashlight. "Your buddy Frank doesn't know much about women, then."

"I leave that up to him. He can keep his puppy paw prints and I will stick with you." He kissed the tip of her nose. "And you are turning a bit pink right here. Shall we head back to the yacht? I don't want you to get too tired out here in the water."

"I'd hate for you to have to give me mouth-to-mouth resuscitation." She kissed him back.

"That's for later, not in front of the help." His tone was aristocratically arch, the effect spoiled by his quick grin.

She swam toward the boat, her arms and legs heavy from the unaccustomed exercise. Giorgio kept to her pace, making sure she got back safely.

He climbed the ladder first and helped her up, wrapping her in a big towel warmed by the sun.

"All right." She padded along the hall with him. He opened the door to their stateroom and bowed her inside like a fancy restaurant's maître d'.

She gave in to an impulse and caught him around the waist. He held her in his arms and rested his chin on her head. They were a perfect fit together. It was just a hug, but it was at the same time much more than a hug as his heart beat under her ear, his chest hair tickling her cheek.

They stood there contentedly for what seemed like minutes. Renata wished it would never end, but she shivered involuntarily.

He pulled away, his face serious. "Come, Renata *mia,*" he murmured in her ear. "Let me wash the salt from your beautiful hair. Then we will rest."

She followed him quietly into the bathroom, where he helped her into a hot shower. He shampooed her hair, his strong fingers rubbing the salt out of her hair. She tried to think of some snappy comment about high-class shampoo boys, but her smart mouth failed her.

It was sensual without being blatantly sexy, and Renata was afraid she would break the quiet companionship that came from Giorgio just taking care of her. Not so he could grope her, because he wasn't. But just because he had noticed she was getting tired and sunburned swimming in the ocean. Because he had noticed she was cold and shivering and needed to wash her hair.

He quickly washed his own hair and got out first, wrapping himself in one of the white terry cloth robes. He grabbed a thick towel and held her hand as she stepped out, as if she were alighting from a carriage.

Renata stood passively as he squeezed the water out of her hair, buffing her body dry until she was glowing. He finished and tucked her into a matching robe. "One last drop." He rubbed his thumb across her cheek.

"No one's ever done that for me." Made her feel so safe and secure, as if she were fragile and precious.

"Taking care of you is my pleasure. Always."

She yawned suddenly, overcome with fatigue from their swim and a bit heavy in the head from a day of the strong Mediterranean sun bouncing off the waves. "Oh, sorry."

"Come to bed. It's time to rest anyway." He straightened the rumpled sheets and tucked her in, kissing her forehead.

"What about you?" He didn't make a move toward the other side of the bed.

He shook his head. "I'm not tired. I need to check with Alessandro if anything needs my attention. Later, you will get my whole attention."

"Good." She took his hand and squeezed it. "Go take care of *your* business now so you can take care of *mine* later."

He threw his head back and laughed, his solemn mood disappearing. "Ah, Renata. I cannot believe how much you make me laugh."

"It's good for you."

"You are good for me." He kissed her fingers. "Look at you, yawning again. Don't worry, I'll wake you up so you don't miss dinner. I will always take good care of you." He slipped his hand free and closed the door quietly behind him.

Renata tried to think about what his unusual mood earlier in the shower meant, but her mind kept wandering to what he meant when he said he would always take good care of her. That *always* was only for a few days more, wasn't it?

13

Renata hopped out of bed after another late night and pulled her robe around her naked body. It had been a couple days since they returned from their cruise and she was scheduled to leave the day after tomorrow.

She didn't want to think about it. She shoved her hands through her hair and padded out of the bedroom to look for Giorgio. It was almost an automatic thing, needing to find him, wanting to know where he was. Not exactly the cool, detached Brooklyn girl she'd always prided herself in being.

Mooning over a guy—Flick would laugh to see Renata right now.

She shook her head. "Giorgio?" she called.

The apartment was silent. She poked her head into the living room and small kitchen, but she was alone.

Suddenly the walls pressed in on her. Since coming to Italy, she'd developed a real fondness for being outdoors, even if it was only to sit at the trattoria and eat focaccia while she and Giorgio watched the sunset.

She opened the door to the terrace and flopped down on the canvas-covered chaise lounge. The terrace was private on three sides due to the curve of the hill and had a wooden arbor over the top covered in lush flowering vines. Not much of a difference from lying in bed, but the air was fresh with all sorts of different scents—the salty, fishy ocean, the explosion of red, pink and yellow flowers from baskets and window boxes, and…coffee?

"Giorgio!" She jumped off the chaise and ran to him.

He waved a white bag and a cup holder with two white carryout cups. She ignored the food for the time being and tossed her arms around his neck.

"Hey, hey." He laughed, spreading his own arms to avoid spilling on her. She gave him a big smooch and his mouth quickly changed focus from laughter to sex. No, not sex, more like…affection?

She broke the kiss as quickly as she'd initiated it. "Good morning!" she said cheerfully.

He staggered back slightly as her weight came off him. "And *buon giorno* to you, too. I have to admit, I didn't think I'd get quite this welcome just by bringing our morning meal. Come sit. Eat." He made sure she was comfortable again on the chaise lounge before passing her a caffe latte and pastry. Fresh as always.

"You know, I'll miss this when I go back."

"They are good." He licked a smear of sugar off his finely shaped lips, which distracted her from her thoughts for a second. "But I am done." He set his half-eaten pastry to the side and ate a slice of cantaloupe instead.

"I'll take that if you don't want it." He handed her the pastry and it was just as good as hers had been. "I mean, I won't just miss the food." She gestured to their terraced surroundings as they relaxed on side-by-side lounge chairs. "The whole atmosphere—*la dolce vita,*" she announced. "The sweet life."

"And if I remember correctly, New York does not have *la dolce vita.*"

"New York is more of a *vida loca* place. It's crazy. I get up, grab a granola bar and a cup of instant microwave coffee."

He winced. "Not even a caffe latte from one of those chains?"

"Stop running down coffee chains. I buy one of their overpriced drinks when I can afford it. I drink it on the way to work then switch to water there so I don't spill on the fabric. For lunch I eat a cup of ramen noodles or peanut butter crackers. For dinner I microwave a frozen entrée and try to figure out the bookkeeping and financial software. I work at the shop every day except Sunday when I work at home drawing up new designs or sewing sample dresses for display. Aside from a couple days off at Christmas and Thanksgiving, this is my first vacation in three or four years." She wound down, embarrassed at both her outburst and at how grim her life sounded. More like *la vita suckola.*

"I am sorry you are always so busy. I am not the man to ask about how to slow down and lighten the load. You and I both need to stop and smell the coffee, eh?"

She smiled and made a production of lifting her coffee to under her nose. "Ah, *delizioso.*"

He reached over and took her hand which had been holding the pastry. "Ah, *dolce.*" He raised her fingers to his lips and sucked the glaze off them. She wiggled her eyebrows at him as he nibbled at her.

Dropping her hand from his mouth, he laced his fingers through hers. "I know I speak for Stefania when I say she would not begrudge you any extra advertising or publicity in regards to having her as a client. I believe she wants to keep everything a secret until she and Dieter make an official announcement. They haven't set a wedding date yet, although she'll likely choose June next year. The gardens at the cathedral are in full bloom then, and she loves the roses there. After that, you'd be welcome to promote your business as an official vendor to the Royal House of Vinciguerra. It may not mean as much to your American clients as it would to some Europeans, but perhaps it would help increase your sales."

"I think Americans are more impressed with royals than the countries that actually have them."

He snorted.

"Oh, I didn't mean it like that."

"No, it's true. In Vinciguerra my so-called subjects treat me as a nephew who needs to be watched closely and talked to sternly whenever necessary." He rolled his eyes. "Don't ever tell anybody this, but my nickname in Vinciguerra was Giò-Giò."

"Jo-Jo?" This tall, elegant prince was called "Jo-Jo"? She fought back a snicker.

"Yes. With a *g*." He spelled it out for her. "Apparently I had trouble saying *r*'s when I was quite small and the local papers picked up on it. It lasted much too long and my father finally made an announcement on my thirteenth birthday that the Crown Prince would be going by his given name in order to preserve the dignity of Vinciguerra. Nobody wants a grown man named Giò-Giò running a country."

"A circus, maybe."

He grinned. "Look at the politics of any small country and tell me it's not a circus. I am the ringmaster."

"Do you enjoy it? I mean, it's not like anybody ever asked you what you wanted to be when you grew up."

"No, that is true. Fortunately, running Vinciguerra is what I'm born to do. Although some people tell me I'm bossy."

"You don't say."

"And certain redheaded ladies enjoy my bossy side."

"Do tell."

She got an attack of the giggles and flopped back on the lounge chair. Quick as a wildcat, he pounced on top of her, nibbling her neck and pulling open the lapels of her robe. "I thought so. Nothing on underneath?"

"No."

"Good. How about *una sveltina?*"

"A what?"

"*La sveltina.* You never heard of that fine Italian custom before? Along with afternoon naps and evening walks, *la sveltina* is practically a national institution. As you Americans call it, a quickie."

"Geez, Giorgio. Well, come on—you know where the bedroom is." She pulled her robe together so they could walk back inside.

"I want to take you right now." He undid his shorts, releasing his erection from the fabric. He held his penis in his hand. "To continue your Italian vocabulary lesson, this is my *cazzo.* My *cazzo* likes you very much and is often a *cazzone* when you are near—a nice, big *cazzo.*"

She giggled but squeaked, "Here?" and glanced around. "We're outdoors."

"No one can see us. We're back away from the railing and at one of the highest points in the village. And we have a roof over us." He rubbed his cock on her bare thigh. "I've wanted to do this outdoors ever since we kissed in Central Park."

"Oh, me, too." She quickly opened her legs to cradle him.

"This is your *fica.*" He ran a finger over her already-wet folds. "I can tell your *fica* likes me because it is always *succulenta* around me—nice and juicy. And this is your *grilletto.*" He rolled her clit between his finger and thumb. "That means 'little trigger' in Italian. I can make your little trigger fire easily, don't you think, Renata?"

"*Si,* Giorgio." Her head lolled back on the chaise as he thumbed her clit and slid his fingers into her pussy—or *fica,* if today was Authentic Italian Sex Day. Seemed like every day should be that day.

He slid down her body and opened her robe with his strong, white teeth. They did have good royal dentists.

"Ah, *molto bene.*" He gazed raptly at her breasts, but then he was a breast man as well as an ass man. She was one lucky girl, having plenty of both.

"What do you call them, *signore?*" she asked coyly.

"Bellissimas." He nuzzled between one and then the other, his hand still working her *fica.* "*Ti voglio succhiar le tette.* I want to suck your tits." He captured a nipple between his lips, tugging gently.

She clutched his head to her breast, running her fingers through the silky black hair. It curled slightly over his ears and felt like heaven against her skin and especially between her thighs. His eyes were closed as he sampled her, licking and sucking one nipple then the other leisurely until she closed her eyes, too.

He sighed against her skin and moved back up. Adding protection, he slid into her without any more foreplay, but she was ready and more than willing.

"Ah, Renata. You feel so good around me." He started moving inside her, resting his elbows on either side of her head.

She hooked her ankles around his calves. "Just…because no one can see any body parts…doesn't mean they can't… tell what we're doing."

"I know. Doesn't that make you hotter?" He laughed as her body agreed, clamping down on him. "It does, you little exhibitionist."

She couldn't help blushing.

He laughed again. "Even your pretty tits are pink now. Oh, poor Renata. So shy—but your *fica* is in charge now."

She couldn't disagree. Her body was totally the boss of her, but who cared?

He dug his legs into the chaise for better leverage and thrust in and out, sweat running down his temple. His body was taking over for him, too.

She lifted her knees to allow him even deeper access. He grunted with pleasure and fitted himself to the hilt, filling her completely.

For a second, he stopped and gazed up into her eyes. "Renata, this is perfect. I never want to leave you."

She wrapped her arms around his broad, strong shoulders. "Then don't."

He groaned and buried his face between her neck and shoulder. "No, no, I won't."

Renata clung tighter. If only that were true. But enough time later to wonder why she wished for that so much. Falling into his embrace, she kissed his cheek, his earlobe, wherever she could reach as he made her his, really his.

The sun filtered through the green vines, turning their veranda into a secret bower that sheltered the two of them, hiding them from everyone but each other. She was utterly safe in the circle of his arms—but then she wasn't. She had the sensation of standing on the edge of a precipice, safe for the time being, but on the brink of danger.

He lifted his head and stared at her. "You feel it, too, don't you?"

"What?" He couldn't read her thoughts—could he?

"It's never been like this—not with anyone."

"No." She shook her head, her voice failing her after that one syllable. She didn't know if she was agreeing with him or trying to deny it. Taking a deep breath, she closed her eyes and just concentrated on the physical sensations, blocking out the messy emotional ones.

Her fingers pressed into his butt as a signal and he went along with her silent request, starting to move inside her again.

"Oh, Renata, Renata." It came out a long groan. He pounded into her and she wrapped her legs around his waist. Her sensitive nipples brushed over his silk shirt, and she wished he was totally naked. Wished she was naked, too, right out in the open, the sun beating down on them. Where anyone could see them, could see how perfect their bodies fit together, how big and hard and thick he was—and he was all hers.

The exhibitionistic image made her moan.

"What are you thinking?"

She told him what she'd been fantasizing.

He jerked inside her. "You would?"

"Yeah." She blushed again.

He withdrew from her and stripped off his shirt and then his shorts. Totally naked, where anyone with a long-range camera could see him. And they would need a panoramic lens to capture his cock, wet and glistening from where it had just been welcomed inside her burning, throbbing body.

"Giorgio!" She reached for his hand to pull him down.

"Ah, let them see." He tugged her to a standing position and shoved the robe off her arms so she was totally naked herself.

He sat on the chaise where she had been and pulled her on top of him, sliding easily up into her. "Now they can see. They can see your naked body taking your pleasure on top of me—using me as your sex toy, a tool to make you come and nothing more."

She shuddered, lust rushing through her trembling body.

"The world is watching, Renata," he taunted. "The

women want to be you and the men would kill to take my place."

She fingered her clit, brushing his shaft as he ground into her. Faster and faster, she raised and lowered herself. Shivering and crumbling, her breath came in pants. Unlike Giorgio, who wore none.

"Oh, Renata, what a *fichetta* you are." He shook his head in mock sorrow. She knew that one—he was calling her a hot piece of ass. "What if they saw me spanking you?"

She lifted her ass slightly in invitation and his nostrils flared with arousal. He gave her a quick rap. "You asked for it."

She had, and he gave it to her, pounding into her. His hands fell from her breasts and he gripped her butt, playing and squeezing her cheeks as she touched herself. He spanked her lightly. Pressure built up deep inside her, radiating from her nipples down to where his shaft filled her and around to her stinging buttocks.

His face was strained and dark. "Come now, Renata. Show them how a real woman fucks a prince."

His provocative taunt pushed her over the edge and she came hard. Her orgasm triggered his and he gave a loud shout before exploding into her.

Locked together, they clutched each other as Renata writhed on his pulsating cock. He suddenly let go of her butt and stroked her clit. "Go again. I *command* you."

"No, no," she whimpered. He ignored her and circled the throbbing knot, pulling and teasing at it until she sobbed. Leaning forward, he cupped her breast and flicked its peak with his tongue, sucking and nipping at her until she couldn't stand it anymore and threw her head back in a climax more powerful than the first.

Wild, almost animalistic noises came from her throat, startling her with their ferocity. But this was who she was with him—anything he wanted to do to her, she would let him. Her naked body on top of him outdoors was proof of that. If anybody was watching them…she shuddered again a third time, her pussy jerking and quivering around him.

He threw his head back and laughed in sheer masculine triumph. "Ah, if only I could come three times in ten minutes!"

"Shh," she managed before collapsing on his chest.

"I mean it. The only sights of Italy you would have seen would have been your view out the window as I fucked you all day and night."

"You mean you haven't been?" She lifted an eyebrow.

"I cannot help it." He shrugged. "My appetite for you is insatiable, my thirst unquenchable." He kissed the top of her head and eased out of her.

The ocean breeze cooled her overheated nether regions and was quite chilly, in fact. She reached for her robe but Giorgio insisted on walking around the terrace buck naked as he gathered his clothing.

"Geez, who's the exhibitionist now? Won't you be embarrassed if any naked pictures of you get out?"

He straightened from where he picked up his shorts. "I am not particularly vain, Renata, but I have nothing to be embarrassed about concerning my body."

She had to agree, drinking in the sight of him.

He waggled a finger at her. "Ah, ah, ah. You keep looking at me like that and we're back to noisy, naked public acts of indecency."

She fought to restrain herself. "What about your subjects? Wouldn't they be embarrassed?"

Now he was really laughing. "We are an earthy bunch, like the Italians. If there were photos, I would get a round of raunchy jokes emailed to the palazzo, but they would take pride in their ruler's masculinity, so to speak." He stalked toward her, his cock actually hardening again. "The di Leone princes have always had reputations for being, ah, well equipped and well versed in using it."

OKAY, SO THE REST OF THE morning had been taken up by discovering the capacity of the hot water heater—not so much hot water, but plenty of heat.

She had managed to dress in something besides a robe, choosing a frilly teal-green blouse over a white tank top and khaki capris. She was wolfing down a ham-and-cheese toasted panini sandwich that Giorgio had bought from the breakfast pastry café. He was eating an *insalata caprese* made of fresh basil leaves, tomatoes and slices of fresh mozzarella. He'd tossed it with only a little olive oil vinaigrette and had given her several slices of the cheese. The man certainly took his healthy eating seriously. She, on the other hand, was on vacation and would just deal with extra poundage by returning to her ramen and cracker diet.

She set down her water bottle and brushed the crumbs off her blouse and pants. "Did you want to go out this afternoon? We could take a guided tour of the castle or sit on the waterfront drinking *vino.*"

"I had something else in mind. Do you have any sensible shoes?"

"You want me to wear sensible shoes? Out where everyone can see me?" She'd been more embarrassed at their bout of semipublic, raunchy sex. She drew her bare feet up on the couch and admired her dark red pedicure. Taking care of her feet was one thing she didn't skimp on. Healthy food, yes, cute feet, no. Maybe she needed better priorities?

He shook his head. "No more of those sexy high heels. You need to wear good walking shoes today."

"I can walk fine in high heels, even on these cobblestone streets." Even if the wine hit her a little hard, she'd just clutch Giorgio's nicely muscled arm.

He shook his head. "Today, we are hiking."

"Hiking?" She raised her eyebrows. Walking, sure. She walked most everywhere since she didn't own a car. Did he mean in those really high hills behind the town? Even the vineyard workers took a special elevator/train up to the grapes. "I'm more of a pavement girl."

He burst out laughing. "What is the American saying? You can take the woman out of New York City, but you can't take the New York City out of the woman. The people I talked with assured me that some of it is pavement. You did not bring walking shoes?"

She wrinkled her nose. "Yes, but…" She almost hadn't, but had feared her feet swelling on the airplane.

He lifted an eyebrow and waited silently.

She couldn't help herself. "They're ugly, okay? I only bought them last year when my brother stepped on my toe with his heavy cop shoes and broke it."

He held up his hand. "I promise not to think the less of you because you are wearing less-than-fashionable footwear. I have a nice collection of Italian leather shoes myself."

"I noticed your shoes when you came to my shop. I admire good footwear in a man."

"How lucky for me." He pulled her close. "I also have many excellent suits, Egyptian cotton shirts and Vinciguerra's largest collection of ties." He nuzzled her neck. "As you well know, they are sewn of finest silk that slips over your skin yet still holds a firm knot. Perhaps you would like a closer look at them."

She glanced over her shoulder at the bedroom and gulped. The idea of him tying her hand and foot to the bed was wildly arousing, to put it mildly. She wet her lips and he groaned. "Enough. We need some fresh air." He turned her away from him. "Go put on your walking shoes. I promise I won't tell anyone."

Renata dug down to the bottom of her suitcase and pulled out the boxy white leather sneakers and a pair of white ankle socks. Her feet settled into the unaccustomed padding and actually felt good.

Not that she would wear gym shoes with her work clothing like a suburban commuter, but maybe on weekends…

"All right, here I am."

"Lovely. Now I don't have to worry about your twisting an ankle. The path to Corniglia can be steep."

"Corniglia? We're walking to Corniglia?" He had to be kidding. From what she'd seen on their boat trip, Corniglia was straight up a cliff. She'd even wondered in amazement that the whole town hadn't plunged into the Mediterranean drink aeons ago.

"You cannot come to Cinque Terre and not go to your ancestral village. It would be a terrible disgrace."

"But that sucker is vertical. They probably have to bring supplies in by rope and pulley," she whined.

He was implacable, and Renata shortly found herself wearing a floppy sun hat and carrying a backpack filled with sunblock, water and snacks. Giorgio wore matching gear but of course he didn't react to the sun like she did. He was even more of a bronzed god after a few days of sun exposure.

"All right, where to?"

"The trail starts up by the train station." He grabbed her hand and guided her toward the top of the town.

"No train going up there?" she asked wistfully.

"Not for us."

She gave up, but not before one last parting shot as they

started uphill. "If all my muscles cramp up, you're carrying me on your back."

He laughed. "Come on, city girl. You should see the hills in Vinciguerra."

"So that's why you have such nice legs." She leered at his strong calf muscles and tight glutes.

"Stop buttering me up and walk."

The trail wound around the base of the watchtower of what used to be the castle. It had crumbled away over the years and now was just a stretch of grass overlooking the harbor.

The watchtower was still impressive—perfectly round and made of dark gray, flat, rectangular stone. "The lookout for when Turkish and North African pirates came raiding for slaves in the Middle Ages. They would build fires to warn the other villages along the coasts."

Renata shivered. To be living in a sleepy Italian village where you never went anywhere else or met anyone else, and then to be kidnapped and sold into slavery in a Middle Eastern slave market. It was a horrifying thought. "Did they ever go home?"

"Some of them." He gave her a gentle smile. "Others would have adapted as best as they could to a new life."

She snorted. "You would have been bought by a lonely old widow and kept in the male version of the harem."

"As long as there was a sexy redheaded maidservant who could sneak in, I would be content." He wrapped his arm around her waist. "Now come—let me take your picture. How about there?" Giorgio pointed to a section of trail with a great view of the harbor.

"Okay." She faced him and smiled as he took several pictures.

"That looks great with the boats behind you."

A young couple came around the corner and oohed and ahhed at the view. They spotted Giorgio and Renata.

"Hey, y'all speak English?" the pretty blonde woman asked. Her dark-haired boyfriend wore a University of Texas shirt, so no bonus points for guessing where they were from.

Not quite like she did, but close enough. "Sure, I'm from New York."

Apparently, from the amused glance between them, her accent was just as entertaining. Giorgio didn't say anything.

"This is such a super spot—we could take y'all's picture and then if you didn't mind, you could take ours," the woman offered.

"Oh, sure. You want to go first?"

The blonde handed her a pink cell phone. "Sure! Chase and I are on our honeymoon..." She stopped to gaze adoringly at Texas Longhorn Man. "And we're updating our Facebook as we go."

"Every ten minutes, Mandy?" the groom grumbled.

The happy couple posed in front of the Vernazza harbor and Renata fired off several shots, feeling rather like a prom photographer when Mandy turned Chase so she could gaze into his eyes and looped her arms around his neck as if they were slow dancing.

"Thanks!" Mandy bounded back up toward them. "Now your turn!" She accepted Giorgio's camera. Renata decided to hang on to Mandy's pink one so she couldn't accidentally take Giorgio's photo and plaster it on her Facebook wall.

"Come on, George, let's get our picture taken." Renata thought she heard Giorgio sigh but he followed her to the scenic spot.

He slipped his arm around her waist. "All right, *Renée.*" She winced. She'd been mistakenly called that since she was a kid.

"Snuggle in so I can get a great shot." Mandy aimed Giorgio's digital camera and took a few pictures. "How romantic! Don't they look sweet together, honey-bun?"

Chase grunted, either in agreement or disgust at being called "honey-bun" in public. Renata wasn't sure which.

Giorgio was shaking with silent laughter by then. "Do not ever call me 'honey-bun,'" he muttered.

"Don't worry," she spoke out of the corner of her mouth. "I'd wear black socks with tennis shoes before I do that."

Mandy finished, and she and Renata traded equipment. "It's so neat to meet other honeymooners, isn't it, Chase? We're staying in Manarolo at the cute little hotel above the Dionysus wine bar, so stop by if you want to hang out."

"Thank you." Giorgio gave her his most gracious nod, turning his green gaze full wattage on her. "Have a wonderful time here in Cinque Terre."

"Oh, my." She stared up at him in wonder. "You have the cutest accent, doesn't he, Chase?"

Chase was understandably less enthused. "Him and every other guy here in Italy."

Sensing a potential brouhaha in Honeymoon-Land, Renata pulled Giorgio down the trail. "Congrats! Happy honeymoon!" she called over her shoulder.

He hurried after her. "Ah, Texans certainly are friendly. I expect meeting fellow honeymooners George and Renée will make her next posting. If only you New Yorkers were as easygoing."

"Hey, we have things to do—we can't run around after cattle all day."

He laughed. "I'd pay a thousand euros to see you in cowboy boots running after a cow. Red boots, to match your hair."

She groaned. "I barely do hiking trails—I definitely do not do cow pastures."

"How do you do with vineyards?"

"Can I get some wine?"

"Once we get to the top," he promised.

She took a deep breath. Never let it be said New York girls lacked grit. "Let's go."

The trail was steep but green with lush vineyards, and despite Giorgio's initial whip-cracking, he stopped often to admire the scenery and gallantly ignored the loud wheezing noises emanating from her lungs. They hit a wider point on the trail next to a nasty-looking cactus plant.

"Wow, I didn't know it was warm enough for cactuses up here."

A grizzled old vineyard worker came over to greet them. He and Giorgio chatted in Italian. "Ah." Giorgio nodded. "He says these are called *fichi d'india*—figs from India. I think the English name for them is prickly pear cactus fruit. I had some in California once."

The old guy told Giorgio something else.

"He says he is sorry you are not here in late summer. They are a beautiful golden-yellow and so sweet and juicy. You will have to return to try them. He promises you will love them."

Giorgio gestured to Renata and told him that her ancestors came from Corniglia, which inspired an excited exchange.

"He said, of course you are from Corniglia because you are a beautiful girl and everyone knows the girls from Corniglia are the most beautiful in Italy. I told him the most beautiful in Europe."

"Aww." She smiled up at him.

"Well, anyway…" Giorgio reddened slightly under his tan. "He says to visit his cousin's wine shop on the main square and tell him Carlo sent us."

"Sounds great. And maybe something to eat."

"Of course." They shook hands all around and headed uphill again. "Carlo also said we passed the nudist beach a while back."

"Really? I don't remember that."

"No, I didn't see any nudists, either. It must not be nudist tourist season yet."

Renata shuddered at the idea of full-frontal sunbathing. All the money in the world couldn't make her risk sunburned breasts and even worse…a sunburned…no, that would never happen.

"Carlo said that back in the seventies, the locals, not being fond of nudist tourists, stormed the main beach and gave them the boot to that smaller beach farther away."

"Tourists without anywhere to carry their wallets are never welcome," she informed him.

"Apparently the national park service may buy the current beach and kick them out again."

"Oh, those poor nudists. Whatever will they do?"

"Go to one of several hundred other clothing-optional beaches around the Mediterranean." He shrugged. "I know you Americans think they are full of centerfold models, but really, they are not that interesting. Imagine people your parents' age, your grandparents' age, lying naked on towels and you can see how it is very far from arousing."

Renata made a horrified face. "I'm gonna have to drink a *lot* of Corniglian wine to get that image out of my head."

"Poor, sheltered girl." He grabbed her hand to help her up a particularly narrow stretch of trail. "Let's go get you some wine."

A while later, Renata straggled into Corniglia. "This is so pretty." A wide town square with some sort of war memorial in the middle overlooked an old stone church and that all-important Italian village institution, the soccer field. A bright yellow school building stood to their left, and she realized it had been turned into a hostel. Right now, she just wanted to get off her feet. "Let's find Carlo's cousin." Sensible shoes or no, the dogs were barking.

"You did a good job." Giorgio pulled her in close and kissed her. "As a special treat, we will take the train back."

She sagged against him. "Oh, thank goodness."

They found a table at the local wine bar in the main square, the Largo Taragio, under the shadow of an ancient gray-and-white stone church. It looked almost like a bird-house with its round dark window above a tall narrow pair of dark doors. A curiously modern verdigris bronze statue of a boy looked over the square. Renata tried to figure out what he was supposed to be and gave up under the mental strain.

Giorgio quickly ordered a bottle of water, a bottle of the famous local white wine and the fixed-menu lunch for both of them. Renata closed her eyes and drank a glass of water. "Ah, that tastes good." She picked up her wineglass and sniffed the fresh aroma. "But that will taste better." Had her ancestors made similar wine? Maybe even using fruit from the same vines, since the plants could live hundreds of years.

Giorgio raised his own glass. "To Renata—on this very special occasion of her return to Corniglia."

She leaned over to kiss him. "Thank you, Giorgio. That was lovely."

"This visit, everything, has always been for you. I want you to remember this day always."

"I will," she promised. Every day with Giorgio would be burned into her memory.

The waiter quickly brought them an *antipasto misto,* a mixed appetizer plate consisting of delicious mussels stuffed with buttered breadcrumbs and saffron, sweet prawns in lemon juice and a ringlike dish that Renata couldn't quite identify.

Giorgio asked the waiter. "He says it is *una insalata,* a chilled squid salad with olives and tomatoes."

"Really." She jabbed one of the rings, and boy, the tines of her fork bounced back like she'd poked a rubber ball.

"Do you dare?" he teased her.

"What the hell," she muttered, forking a tentacle segment into her mouth. Couldn't be that much different from octopus, could it?

Several minutes of chewing later, she realized cold squid was a bit tougher to eat than warm, cooked octopus. At least it was tasty, the olives, superfresh tomatoes and hint of capers and oregano jazzing it up.

She abandoned the squid when her pasta came, a mix of steamed mussels, clams and prawns tossed in a tomato-parsley sauce.

Giorgio went for the local fresh anchovies over pasta. "Want one?" He offered her one of the tiny fish.

She accepted, eating it with gusto. "I can't believe I'm eating anchovies. My brothers would laugh their asses off if they saw me. I used to gag when they'd get them on a pizza."

"Ah, but this was swimming in the sea last night. Those that make it to New York are processed in unmentionable ways before they are shipped—mashed into a tin can and handled roughly."

"Ah, kind of like my flight out of Genoa the day after tomorrow." She meant it as a joke but it came out flat. That was the one topic they had avoided discussing—her leaving.

He cleared his throat. "Yes, I have had flights like that." He changed the subject back to food and she went along with him, not wanting to spoil their afternoon, either.

They passed on a main course but Renata couldn't resist the homemade gelato, flavored with honey from local bees. It was so creamy and sweet she had a hard time resisting the urge to lick out the bowl. Giorgio didn't order any dessert but consented to her feeding him a couple spoonfuls.

After finishing her dish, she leaned back in her chair. "Listen, Giorgio, I won't need a train ticket. You can just roll me down the hill."

"No rolling. Time to walk it off." He left money for the tab and pulled her to her feet.

Despite his threat to walk off her lunch, he set a leisurely pace hand in hand through the town, stopping to peer into various small shops. They also strolled into the surprisingly bright birdhouse church, which was actually something called the Oratory of St. Catherine, a meeting place for various Catholic groups in the village, but not specifically a church.

The ceiling above the white-and-gold altar was painted a cool sky blue with white clouds. Right below the main dome was a large round oil painting of a cheerful woman sitting on a green throne and surrounded by fat blond cherubs. Presumably St. Catherine, if her memories from Catholic school didn't fail her.

Just standing in the not-quite-a-church took some of the buzzing thoughts out of her head. She would figure out what to do about her growing feelings for Giorgio later. They had each other for the time being, and she wouldn't sandbag her last couple days with worry.

She sighed out a big breath of relief. Giorgio looked down curiously at her. "Are you all right?"

She smiled up at him. "Great. Now this is art, isn't it?"

He laughed, obviously remembering the barbed wire and cornstalk mess that passed for art in some circles. "It's beautiful. We have a similar chapel in Vinciguerra. My ancestor built it in penance for sacking a neighboring principality. Unfortunately that prince was the Pope's cousin."

"Oops!" Feudal Europe certainly had been a different world.

"Yes, that particular ancestor was more a man of action than a man of thought. And he kept half of what he had looted, figuring the other prince got off lightly."

"And in the meantime, my ancestors were making wine in their huts and trying to avoid being sold in a Turkish slave market. That is, if the slavers could even make it up the hill without collapsing."

"Probably easier to go elsewhere, I imagine." They drifted out of the oratory and around the village. Renata tried to imagine living here all her life, marrying a local boy and raising a crop of kids along with the grapes.

There was something about Italy that made her think of fertility. The fruit of the land, the fish in the sea, the bright sky. She sneaked a look at Giorgio. And of course, Mr. Sex God in person. Everything about him spoke of potency and reproduction. He would make some beautiful babies, dark-haired with pretty green eyes. A little girl with beautiful black curls that would look great with a gold satin headband…

Whoa. That was a weird thought. Yes, of course she knew the connection between sex and babies, but aside from an occasional chill down her spine, the idea of small, adorable children did not cross her mind at all.

Was she looking at Giorgio as a possible baby-maker? She stopped dead in her tracks. So did he. "Are you all right?"

Hell, no! She'd taken the batteries out of her biological clock as soon as she hit puberty. That sucker had never ticked in her life. It wouldn't start now. Would it?

"Renata?" He gently brushed a sweaty lock of hair off her face as if she were all fancied up for a formal ball.

She stared at him. "Yes, yes, I'm fine. Maybe a bit thirsty."

"We'll find a drink for you. How about a bottle of lemonade?"

"Sounds good." She shoved her disturbing thoughts deep down and smiled. "Lead the way as we sack Corniglia for its lemonade."

14

THE NEXT DAY, Renata had only dressed and made it out to the terrace after a couple pain relievers, a hot shower that strained the goodwill of an Italian water heater and two pastries with coffee. Giorgio had offered to give her a massage, but she had put him off until later when she could hopefully enjoy it more.

Giorgio had gone out to check if her packet of sample Italian fabrics and laces had arrived from his assistant yet, so Renata had some time to laze around the apartment on her own.

She was enjoying an Italian soap opera that seemed to involve evil twins, secret babies and husbands returning from the dead when her phone rang. She answered it. "Hey, Flick."

"Hey, yourself. How goes sunny Italy?"

"It's going, going, gone—just like me the day after tomorrow."

"Well, yeah. All vacations come to an end. Otherwise we'd be living on the beach in a cardboard box."

Renata grunted.

"Don't bail on me now, Renata. I've been smiling at these brides so long my mouth's dried out. Any more time here and I'll have to grease my teeth with Vaseline like those Amazon beauty queens."

That momentarily distracted her. "Really? That's what they do in beauty pageants?"

"Gross, isn't it? I saw it on the reality TV channel. They also use double-stick tape to keep their dresses and swimsuits in place."

"Holy crap. I would think a flash of skin would get extra points."

"A wardrobe malfunction is a dangerous thing, Renata. It's been known to topple entire civilizations."

They both had a good laugh, but Renata quickly fell silent.

"Aren't you going to ask me how your precious business is doing while you bop your brains out?"

"How is my business doing?" she asked dutifully, but her heart wasn't in it. How nuts was that? She'd worked eighty-hour weeks the past several years to make it a raging hipster success and now she couldn't even remember to ask about it.

"You don't want to come back, do you?"

"What? That's crazy. Why wouldn't I want to come back to New York? Everything important is there, after all." Not Giorgio, though.

"Not your prince," Flick uncannily echoed her thoughts.

"His sister lives there. He'll be in New York sometimes."

"If they're planning a big hometown wedding, it'll be more likely for her to go back to Vinciguerra to work on things instead."

"Oh. I guess." She'd never considered that possibility, and it was an unpleasant one. "Wow. Well…" Her eyes started to fill and she brushed them with displeased amazement. Really…what was wrong with her?

Flick, perceptive as she was, had an answer. "Babe, I

hate to be the one to tell you this, but you know what I think?"

"What?" Renata forced out between dry lips.

Flick cleared her throat, her usually flip mood totally absent. "I think you went and fell in love with the guy, Renata."

"No," her mouth said, while her head and her heart said *Nyah, nyah, yes, you did!* "No," she repeated loudly. "No, I didn't! People don't fall in love like this after only a week. This is a vacation fling. The real world doesn't come into play. I came to Italy for a lighthearted, fun vacation and, dammit, I am having lighthearted fricking fun!" She realized she was shouting absurdities into the phone but couldn't help herself.

"Okay, okay," Flick said soothingly as if Renata were the crazy lady who lived in a box across from their subway stop and was starting to see purple aliens pop up from the sidewalk. "You're right. Of course you're right. Nobody falls in love like that. It takes weeks, months, years. Hell, some people never fall in love—like you and me, right, Renata?"

"That's right, Flick!"

Flick blew out a loud sigh that she probably didn't mean to carry quite so well over the phone lines. Great, Flick thought she was a basket case and was probably already blocking out time in her schedule to buy wine—non-Italian, of course—to commiserate with her as she bawled into her wine, and then hold her hair back as she barfed up her overindulgence in wine. And a good time was had by all—not!

Renata took a deep breath. Her mental whine/wine scenario was frighteningly possible. And why would that be? Why, perchance, would a former Goth girl turned hard-nosed New York entrepreneur need alcohol and sympathy on her parting from a guy she'd only met eight days earlier?

Because she'd fallen in love with the jerk! "Shit."

"What?" Flick asked cautiously.

"You know damn well," she said crossly. "I did. I did go and fall in love with him." Her stomach churned. "I think I'm going to puke." How stupid could she have been? She flopped back onto the bed and banged her head on the pillows a couple times.

"Renata, are you there?"

"Yeah," she muttered sullenly.

"If it makes you feel any better…" Renata rolled her eyes. She'd never heard a good ending to a sentence that started with that phrase, but Flick continued bravely, "If it makes you feel any better, you really had the deck stacked against you. Your prince is good-looking, swept you off your feet to a wonderful seaside resort and is fabulous in the sack from what I can read between the lines, since you never did tell me the really good parts, Renata!" Flick sounded pissed for a second and then laughed. "That should have been a clue right there for you."

"What?"

"You didn't want to spill any details because you were starting to care for him and didn't want to giggle with me over your sweet lovin'."

"Don't be silly. That doesn't mean anything."

"Okay, what position does he like best? How big does he get? What's his personal record for rocking your world?"

Renata clamped her lips together before she realized what she was doing.

"Oh, ho, ho!" Flick crowed. "I never got one good story out of you—not even from the first day you met, and I bet that was a doozy."

She couldn't help grinning at her memory of a certain

limo ride. "But wait—does that mean I loved him even then?"

"Love at first sight—who ever heard of such a thing? Oh, yeah, every single goober who ever wrote any poem about love."

Renata's eyes began to sting and she bit her lip. "Promise me you won't tell him, Flick."

"You think I'd rat you out? Call up the Royal Palace in Vinciguerra and leave a message with his secretary?"

"No, of course not."

"You need to rat yourself out."

"What?" Renata jumped to her feet. "Tell him? Oh, no, oh, no."

"Oh, yes, oh, yes. Tell the man how you feel and you too can be saying that, only under much pleasanter conditions."

Renata clutched the phone and sank back onto the chair. "Flick, he's a *prince*. I'm a dress designer."

"Hey, it worked pretty well for Cinderella, didn't it? And besides, what are you, a stupid peasant girl, bowing down before royalty? Or are you a strong, Italian-American girl from Brooklyn who bows to no one? Grow a pair and tell him how you feel."

Renata sat up straight. "Yeah. But what if he says, 'I'm flattered but here's your ticket back to New York'?"

She sighed. "Do I have to spell out everything? Then say thanks for the trip and come home, Renata. Sheesh. I think you've been out in the sun too long."

"Oh, Flick."

"Go on. Stop whining to me and move it. Where did Prince Charming go, anyway?"

"He said he had to run some errands, so he just left a few minutes ago."

"Go after him, Renata."

Renata jumped to her feet. "Chase after a man? I have my pride."

"Great. I'll see you at the airport tomorrow. Be sure to pack up your pride nice and snug so the baggage handlers don't damage it on your return trip."

Renata grimaced. Flick was right, dammit. She'd never been a coward, and it was embarrassing to admit she might chicken out. "All right, Flick. Off I go. There's only a small shopping area so I can find him easily."

"Get going. Text me when you can."

A CROWD WAS GATHERED around the newsstand talking excitedly and waving their hands. Renata craned her neck to see what was going on. Had someone been caught passing off bad fish? Did the local team lose a major soccer match? Had Italy declared war against Vinciguerra?

Renata didn't really care, but an older woman at the edge of the crowd spotted her and jabbed her neighbor in the ribs, both falling silent. A few more jabbed ribs and quickly hushed conversations, and the whole crowd of locals was staring at her.

"Ah. *Buon giorno.*" She waved awkwardly at them. Maybe the cat was out of the bag about Giorgio's celebrity status and she was being eyeballed as the companion *du jour.* Well, fair enough. It was none of their business anyway.

One of the older gents pointed at her and said loudly, *"Si, è lei."*

Yes, it's her? Renata looked around but she was the only one standing there.

As if by some prearranged signal, the crowd parted and she saw a rack of garish-looking tabloids. Her stomach flipped as she slowly approached the rags, her knees stiff.

No way! The Italian *and* the British ones both had front page shots of Giorgio as he'd swum with the dolphins.

Judging from the angle, probably one of those sailors had taken the photos. If she found out which one, she'd toss him overboard and let the fish nibble him to death.

So why did the locals recognize her? She picked up the British one, even tackier than American tabloids if that were possible, and flipped to the inside story.

Yep, there she was climbing up the boat ladder, wet red hair and white bikini with the cherries looking like polka dots.

She forced her eyes to read the text. Usual stuff about sexy prince and mysterious redhead frolicking in the sunny Italian Riviera, etc, etc. Thankfully she was too pasty to go topless and they hadn't gotten any shots while she and Giorgio "frolicked" on the apartment terrace.

But then—now her stomach was really cramping—the part she hadn't known.

> Prince Giorgio of Vinciguerra is lucky to be cavorting in the sea after a recent fright for his life at a New York hospital. According to insiders at Manhattan Medical Center, the bachelor prince arrived suffering chest pains.

Chest pains?" she muttered. Giorgio acted as healthy as a horse.

Renata read further.

> Too much work and not enough play was the diagnosis. The prescription? Rest and relaxation, and it seems the magnificent monarch has found both in the arms—and charms—of his sexy redheaded gal pal.

She wrinkled up her mouth. "'Gal pal,' my ass." And what was that crap about a prescription for R & R? She'd known he'd needed a vacation, but it had been medically necessary?

"Signorina?" the old lady running the newsstand asked cautiously. Renata could feel a flush creeping up her neck.

"Here." She tossed a handful of euros onto the counter and took a copy of each colorful publication. She spun on her heel and stalked back to their apartment, the villagers watching her with wide eyes.

She crashed the door open. "Giorgio!"

"Ah, Renata." He came toward her with open arms, slowly dropping them to his side as she clutched the tabloids to her chest. "What is wrong? What do you have there?"

She shook the papers at him. "One of those sailors sold photos of us to this British magazine. And this Italian one, too, although I couldn't read the story. God only knows what *that* one says."

"Renata *mia,* I am so sorry. I thought we might avoid their notice by coming to such a small town before the busy season started."

"That's not the point. Read the article." She shoved the British one at him.

He read the article, his face darkening.

"Is that true? You went to the emergency room with chest pains?" Her own chest hurt at the thought of what must have been his pain and fear.

"Yes. Yes, I did."

"When?"

For the first time, he looked embarrassed and unsure of himself. "The day we met."

"Before or after we met?"

"After," he admitted.

Her eyebrows shot up into her hair. "So after our wonderful day in New York and some heavy-duty stuff at night, you dropped me off and Paolo rushed you to the emergency room."

"Yes."

"With chest pains."

"Yes. But not a heart attack, fortunately."

"Fortunately," she echoed. "So what was it?"

"Chili dogs."

"Indigestion? And anything else?" She wanted to see if the tabloid report of his overwork and stress was true.

"Not really."

"Why did you go to the E.R.? Certainly you've had indigestion before?"

"Paolo was worried."

"And after you left the E.R., you called me to invite me to Italy with you. Were you even home by then or did you call me from the car?"

He shifted. "The car."

She was getting mighty sick of his short answers. "Giorgio, something's not adding up here. God knows these magazines are not the fount of truth, but they say the E.R. doc told you the chest pains were partly caused by too much work and not enough play."

He winced again. "Renata, I am a busy man. I do have much work and I haven't had a vacation in several years."

"That's not what I mean!" She threw the papers on the floor. "We met and had a great time. Then you decided to invite me to Italy to blow off some steam and I accepted because we really hit it off. But I'm missing something here. You never told me anything about your hospital trip. You never said the doctors told you to take it easy. That's why you wouldn't eat much bread or pasta, right? They even put you on a diet." She started to tear up. "We never took it easy. All that hiking, swimming and sex. I could have killed you."

"Ah, but what a way to go." He gave her a devilish grin.

"Jerk!"

He looked confused. "The doctor never told me not to have sex."

"Not that, *stupido!* You lied to get me here to Italy. You never mentioned any of this medical crisis. I thought you wanted me here so we could spend time with each other, have some fun..." *Fall in love.* She angrily brushed away that thought.

"I regret my actions have caused you distress."

"Ah." She stared at him, but he didn't say anything more. And why did he need to explain anything to her?

He never pretended to be someone he wasn't, had never spoken of undying love for her in an attempt to get her in the sack. But something wasn't jibing. Even if he had told her ninety-nine percent of the truth, he was still hiding something. She could read it in the way he had put on his formal manners instead of just being plain Giorgio, the man she had come to care for over the past week. "What else is going on, Giorgio?"

"Nothing." His face closed down, his expression as lively as an emperor's profile carved on an ancient coin.

She narrowed her eyes. "I may only be a dressmaker from the backstreets of Brooklyn but I know when some guy is blowing smoke up my skirt."

"I am not, as you say, blowing smoke anywhere. I wanted to be with you and took the opportunity to invite you here. Do you regret coming?"

She stared at him. How could she answer that? She'd loved every minute she spent with him, both in New York and Italy. That was the problem. The more time she spent with him, the more she longed for him—and the less she wanted to leave him. "I...I don't know."

He grew even more remote. "I see."

No, he didn't, but telling him she had done something incredibly stupid like fall in love with him would make things even more awkward and awful. "I need to get back to New York." That was part of the truth. "My business needs me, and I'm sure your country needs you." She sounded like a military recruiting poster. Vinciguerra needs *You,* Prince Giorgio.

"Yes, of course." He pulled his phone off his belt clip with a smooth move. She hid her trembling hands in the folds of her skirt. He tapped a few commands into his phone. "I've changed your flight to an earlier one. Paolo will make arrangements with Captain Galletti to get you to Genoa in plenty of time. You can leave within the hour."

Her nails bit into her palms. "Fine. Good. I will go pack."

He gave her a brusque nod. "I will leave you to it. In the meantime, I need to run an errand." He replaced his phone and disappeared out the door.

Renata swallowed hard, a bitter taste in her mouth. Was he even bothering to come back to say goodbye or was it another of Paolo's job requirements to clean up messy romantic entanglements, as well?

She looked at the clock over the small dining table. Well, screw Prince Giorgio and his minion. She'd get her own butt back to Genoa and they could take a flying leap. Spinning on her heel, she blew through the bedroom and bath, stuffing her belongings willy-nilly into a suitcase. Forget the bottles of Scciachetrà, forget the frilly lingerie. The wine would sour in her stomach and the sight of the undergarments would make her cry. If she had time, she'd burn them in the outdoor fireplace, but she didn't.

All Renata wanted to do was to get home to New York, where she could make wedding dresses for girls stupid enough to believe in happy endings. There would be none for her.

GIORGIO KNEW HIS LEGS were moving because he was descending, but the rest of him was numb. He arrived at the street level somehow and his feet slowly picked a path along the cobbled streets.

Renata was leaving him, going back to her real life in New York City. She hadn't told him never to call her again, but she hadn't left the door open for him, either, telling him she partially regretted coming to Italy with him.

What had he done that was so terrible she had to leave him even sooner than anticipated? He had given her a fairy-tale vacation, complete with seaside cruise, romantic hikes and a cozy villa for their lovemaking.

Images of her face lit with passion flashed to his mind and his breath left him with a whoosh. She had been like no other woman—and no other would ever measure up to her.

He stared at the brightly painted houses and shops. He knew he would never return to Vernazza, could never stand to return to the Cinque Terre again in his life. The café where they ate breakfast, the trattoria where they ate dinner. The gift store where she'd bought the inexpensive souvenirs for her family. And the lingerie store with a sheer, flowing nightgown in the window. He stumbled slightly on a raised stone and caught himself before falling.

The worst thing is that he probably would have to see Renata again in the course of the wedding events. It was not unusual for designers to help the bride dress for the wedding ceremony in case of last-minute mishaps or alterations.

If he told Stevie the truth about what had happened between Renata and him, she would cancel her gown out of misguided loyalty, the gown that she loved and that made her look like an angel descending to earth. All three of them could be miserable: him for losing Renata, Renata for losing her commission and Stevie for losing her gown.

Hopefully by then the pain of missing her would lessen from the current hot coal sitting in his chest. If he hadn't recently been assured of at least marginal good health in that aspect, he would have sworn his heart was literally breaking.

Again memories of her threatened to flood his self-control. Renata giving him the eye as she flirted with him in her shop. Renata sleeping so innocently tangled up in their sheets. Renata laughing with the dolphins.

Giorgio stopped at the window of a small jewelry store. Diamonds, rubies, gold and platinum. None shone as bright as she did.

If only he were plain George di Leone, New York businessman. He would date Renata for the minimally acceptable amount of time, give her a diamond ring and then have her design the most beautiful gown in the world for the most beautiful bride.

If only.

But no, he was Prince Giorgio, ruler of his very own country in the back reaches of the Italian peninsula. What woman would want to give up her New York address, her New York business for a position, royal though it may be, that sucked away most of your privacy and tied you to duty for the good part of your life?

There would have to be a very good reason. Giorgio stopped in his tracks. He knew her well enough to know that riches and power would never sway her, not even the most expensive item in the jewelry store.

He saw a small heart-shaped pendant made of diamonds. That heart. Her heart. His heart. His heart that he worried about so, worried at every minor twinge—he worried about it stopping when he should have been worried about it breaking.

He pressed a hand to his chest. It thumped strongly, but for what? An empty heart could live a long time, but for what? No Renata to listen to it as she rested in his arms, no Renata to fill it with her smiles and her…love?

It was almost a blow, that realization. Was she so upset because she loved him?

A gasp escaped his lips. And he had done what to deserve her love? Nothing. In fact, he had kicked it away like a football in a World Cup tournament.

Moron! He clenched his fist. He needed to find her. Would she believe him…believe that he loved her? Because he did. How would he convince her?

By giving her this heart of his, this unquenchable burning that she had set aflame since the first smile of her ruby lips. It was the only thing he had to offer her that she might accept.

He immediately ran back to the villa, cursing his previous stupidity with every step. How had he not realized he loved her?

He arrived at the stairs leading up and stopped short. Instead of a beautiful redhead waiting for him to come to his senses, Paolo stood there.

"Where? Where is she?" He pushed past Paolo, but his driver put a beefy hand on his shoulder.

"*Signore,* she is gone before I get here."

"Gone? How?" He searched wildly up and down the street.

Paolo jerked his head up the hill. "I think she must have taken the train. It left only a few minutes ago—the train to Genoa."

He clutched at his head. "Paolo, I love her. I can't stand to lose her. What do I do?"

"Cancel her plane ticket."

Always the practical one. "Right." He grabbed his phone and called the airline, his face contorting as he listened to the ticket agent. He hung up. "Paolo, she already canceled her ticket and bought herself a new one—I can't cancel that." Renata and her stubborn pride. He didn't know whether to admire or curse her independence.

"Capitano Galletti is waiting for us at the dock. We can intercept her before she gets to Genoa."

Giorgio was already running. "Let's go." He'd already made a terrible mistake by letting her go once—he wouldn't make that mistake twice.

RENATA STARED GLASSY-EYED out the window of the train as it jolted along the tracks. All she had to do was get to the airport, get on the plane and then get home. Once she was back in New York, she could fall apart, cry all she wanted and generally act like a lovelorn maniac without involving airport security, customs or Interpol.

She had passed the point of beating herself up for falling in love with Giorgio and was just trying to numb herself for the next several hours. Would several airport cocktails help with that or turn her into a sniveling mess? Hard to say. She tried but failed to suppress a sigh.

The older woman sitting next to her took that as a signal to chat. She offered her a strawberry, delicious and fresh from her garden.

Renata shook her head and told her no thank you. She would choke if she tried to swallow anything.

"*Signorina,* you sick?" Her seatmate furrowed her sun-weathered brow. Her eyes were dark and kind, her graying hair pulled back into a bun. She was the quintessential Italian mamma, and that made Renata feel even more homesick.

"No, um, sad." Her tears started to well up despite her

efforts at ice-maidenhood. Damn that Giorgio! For someone so wonderful, he sure was making her miserable.

"Oh, bad. *La famiglia sta bene?*"

"Yes, my family is fine. A man—*un uomo.*"

"Bah!" Her face lit up in knowing disgust. She turned to the other women and explained Renata's distress, wrapping a heavy, comforting arm around her shoulder.

A white-haired woman with the face of a dried apple waved her hands. "Pah!" She spit on the train's floor and shook her head. The other women made noises of sympathy.

Her new friend patted her hand with her work-roughened one. "*Si,* you find new man. A girl so *bella*—easy. *Bella figura, bella faccia.* The men all chase you. My son—he very 'ansome. He own a boat for fish," she said enticingly.

Renata smiled politely. Even a fisherman who probably lived with his mamma sounded better than Giorgio.

The train slowed to a stop. From the loud protests and big gestures, it wasn't a planned stop. Hmm, who had the clout to stop a train? It had better be some stray animal on the tracks, or else.

The women were worked up into a frenzied pitch by the time the door slid open and the conductor came in. He cringed at the noisy imprecations and protests aimed his way. Making a placating gesture, he stepped to the side and there *he* was.

Renata groaned and jumped to her feet. "Get lost, Giorgio!"

He extended a hand to her. "Renata, please. Listen to me."

"You aren't the boss here—this isn't even your country."

Her seatmate turned her glare to Giorgio. "He the man you cry for?"

Renata turned her puffy, sore gaze at him. "Yes."

"Oh, Renata." Giorgio's face sagged and he tried to say something to her.

Renata's new protectress shouted something to the other women and in the blink of an eye, she pulled a ripe tomato from her sack.

"Wait, no..." Renata tugged at the woman's arm but she shook her off and chucked it straight at him.

That was the signal to the other women and Giorgio's immaculate white linen shirt soon looked like the canvas of a Jackson Pollock splatter painting. He twisted and tried to get out of the way, but the railroad car was narrow and he was pinned down.

She gasped and laughed at the same time, but then the farm-fresh eggs came out. Even the hens were on her side in this female battle. "No more!" she shouted in Italian. "Enough!" Eggshells were sharp. She should know; she'd walked on them often enough.

The women grumbled and gave Giorgio the *malocchio,* the Italian version of the stink eye.

Giorgio wiped tomato pulp off his face and plucked an anchovy off his shoulder. "Your new friends certainly look after you, Renata."

"Yes, well..." She'd definitely won the pity vote on her unexpectedly short train ride. "What do you want, Giorgio?"

After a wary look around, he approached her. She stood, arms folded across her chest. "Renata, I want you—"

"Yeah, I already knew that." He wanted her, all right. Wanted her as the sexual equivalent of a stress reliever. "You could have told me the truth, you know. You could have said, 'Hey, Renata, I need a vacation or my doctor says I'll keel over. Feel like having sex with me in Italy? I'll find a nice hotel.'"

The women muttered angrily, getting the gist of her

accusation. She continued, "Instead, you have to go and lie and tell me all that crap about how you can't stop thinking of me."

"All of it true." He glanced warily at the women. "Please. Step outside with me for a minute—only a minute, I promise."

She pursed her lips but consented. Giorgio helped her down the train car's iron steps to a small stone terraced wall with grapevines dangling above it. "Please sit with me." He waited until she grudgingly sat, a good foot and a half away from him.

"I don't even want to look at you," she informed him, not quite telling the truth. He was so beautiful he made her eyes hurt, even with the equivalent of a spaghetti dinner for five on his shirt.

"Don't, then. Listen to me."

She fought a quivering lip but nodded.

"Renata, I am sorry."

She made a hurry-it-up motion with her hand. He already said that and she still didn't believe him.

"I know you are hurt and I would give anything to prevent that. The magazine article, part of it is true. I was in the hospital after that chili dog and I thought it was a heart attack."

"Why? You're so young."

"My father, I told you how he and my mother died in a car accident in Vinciguerra when I was just starting at the university."

"Yes." She hoped he wasn't aiming for sympathy, cuz she was fresh out.

"My parents had gone away for a quiet weekend at the house in the country and were driving back to the city when my father had a massive heart attack. He dropped dead at the wheel. They were on a hilly road and the auto went over the edge of a ravine, landing about thirty meters down."

Renata whipped her head around in shock. He was as pale as his tan would let him be and his lips were bracketed in white lines. Oh, yes, he was telling her the truth now. "How terrible."

"My mother was of course alive at the time of impact and had severe internal and head injuries. Although they flew her to the trauma center immediately, they could do nothing for her and she died five days later."

Renata's eyes began to sting.

"So you see, that is how Stefania came to live with me. She was inconsolable in Vinciguerra and screamed for our mamma every night. My grandmother was afraid she would have a nervous breakdown so she sent Stevie to me in New York for a change of scenery. We were always close and I was the only one who could calm her."

Renata sniffled. Damn him, she did not want to feel one iota of sympathy for the man.

"When I thought I was having a heart attack, I thought of Stefania, of course. But I also thought of you."

"Me?"

"Yes, you. The woman I had only met that afternoon, the woman who was so kind to my sister, the woman who had made me crazy with her red lips and red hair and soft skin. I thought of you when I thought I was dying, and I bitterly regretted that I hadn't met you five years ago."

"Really?" Now her stinging eyes had decided to move directly to watery.

"Ten years ago. Forever ago." He dropped to his knees on the rocky ground and grabbed her hands. "Renata, *mia bella,* I don't want any more regrets. I have been entirely stupid but I am a poor, broken man without you." He took a deep breath. "I love you. *Ti amo,*" he repeated in Italian in case she hadn't gotten it the first time.

"Oh, Giorgio." She bit her lip.

"Tell me you feel the same," he pleaded, and he was not a man who pleaded. He mistook her hesitation for denial and his shoulders slumped. "I will not bother you any longer. If you do not want to take the train, I will have Paolo take you back to Genoa and get you a first-class ticket back to New York."

"Great, so I can sob my way back to the Big Apple like I was crying on the train? How considerate of you, Giorgio. First you tell me you love me, and then you want to get rid of me."

His head snapped up. "I do not want to be rid of you." He took a good look at her face. "It is your turn to tell the truth about how you feel, Renata. Don't be a sissy."

"A sissy? You think I'm a sissy because I haven't told you how much I love you?"

"You haven't," he goaded her. "I thought New Yorkers always spoke their minds. How much do you love me?"

"A ton. I fell in love with you days ago but was afraid—" Her lips turned downward as his turned up. Man, he'd tricked her not only into admitting she loved him but that she was scared about it. "I mean, I was…oh, all right, I love you, too, Giorgio. Now what the hell are we going to do?"

"We do what people in love do." His face split into a grin and he launched himself from his knees to wrap his arms around her. She shrieked as tomato pulp and fish guts smeared her clothing. "My shirt!" Her shriek was cut off by his kiss. It was a familiar kiss, but different, deeper, knowing the love behind it.

He finally lifted his head. "Now we are a matched set. I'll take you shopping for a new shirt anywhere you like."

"Oh, that's right—you're a prince. I forgot."

"Thank you for forgetting. For you, I am plain George di Leone, hapless brother of the bride."

"And don't forget, my love slave." She giggled, giddy.

"And you will be my princess."

She laughed. "Every Italian girl in New York is already a princess."

"No, Renata." Back to his knees again before she could blink. "Will you marry me and be my bride?"

She gaped at him. He was honest-to-God proposing to her? "Marry you?"

"*Si,* marry me. The prince and princess duties can be dull, but I apologize in advance. In important matters such as love, I am the same as any other man longing for his girl."

"Oh, no you're not. You are the sexiest, most wonderful man I've ever met. You're kind to your sister, loyal to your friends and I can't believe I met you." She impatiently swiped tears off her cheeks. She'd just cried in misery, now she was crying in joy? Her eyes were pink and her nose was red.

Fortunately Giorgio didn't care as he cupped her jaw in both hands, cradling her face as if she were a precious work of art. "I have been single for a long time and never met anyone like you. It is difficult for people to see beyond the trappings of my position and obligations to see the man. I always thought I would have plenty of time before I took my father's responsibilities, but that was not to be."

Renata caressed his hand, knowing the hole their deaths had left in his life.

"But I am not telling you this for pity. I want you to know that you will always be first for me—like my mother was for my father."

She didn't know what to say. The downside was immense. Become princess of Vinciguerra? Leave New York and her business and her family? "Giorgio, that's crazy. How long have we known each other? A week, that's how long. What will people think?"

He shook his head before she finished her protest. "Who cares? I am a grown man who knows his own mind. And don't tell me you care what other people think. I know you better than that." He kissed her nose and sat back, wrapping his arm around her waist.

She stared at him. Her life as a princess in Vinciguerra was almost unimaginable. But her life with Giorgio would be to wake up with him every morning, to kiss him every night, to watch his dark hair gradually lighten to gray, his green eyes undimmed by age.

A man she loved, who loved her back.

Oh, that would be enough upside for any woman.

His fingers tightened on her knee as he waited for her answer, tension radiating from him. She covered his hand with hers.

"Yes, Giorgio, I will marry you. I have no clue about this princess stuff but I do know about loving you and wanting to be with you forever." They'd work out the details later.

He crushed her into his tomatoed chest again, but his lips immediately distracted her, until her heart overflowed. She began to laugh at the wild improbability that her tough New York heart had been so easily turned to mush by a chivalrous Vinciguerran prince.

He lifted his mouth from hers and grinned, resting his forehead on hers. "We have a very interested audience."

Renata blinked slowly and turned her head toward the train. They sure did. Every single passenger was goggling at them from the windows, and her seatmate even stood on the metal steps for a better view. She gave a small sigh, but what did she expect, making out with a prince at the side of the railway?

"Ah, hello." She figured, what the hell, and sat up straight, giving them a wave to rival the Queen of England. "*Grazie!* Thank you for coming. You've been great! Read all about it in the next issue of *Today's Paparazzi!*"

Giorgio muffled a snort. "You are picking up on this very quickly."

The conductor approached them cautiously and Giorgio made quick arrangements to remove her suitcase. "For you will not go to Genoa today. I will come back to New York with you and meet your family, like a proper Vinciguerran man meets the family of his wife-to-be."

Hmm. Renata waited for the anticipated figure of Edvard Munch's *The Scream* to run across her mental landscape. Nope, the Italian birds were still chirping, the bright sun was still shining, and she had agreed to marry Giorgio Something Something Something di Leone. She didn't remember all his names. No more "Galaxy's Most Eligible Bachelor" for him. Maybe they could invite Mandy and Chase from Texas to their wedding. That would knock their socks off.

The train slowly pulled away, the passengers waving like crazy while some of the younger ones took their photos with their phones. Ah, well, welcome to life in the fishbowl.

She linked her arm with Giorgio's and carefully picked her way down the trail leading to where Paolo and the captain had anchored the boat. He was rock-steady, on the path and in her life. "You know, Giorgio, if we're going to have this big royal foo-foo wedding at some point, I'm going to have to remember your full name. I'd hate to look like a jerk on international television."

"Giorgio Alphonso Giuseppe Franco Martelli di Leone," he said slowly for her to catch all of his names.

"Good Lord, no wonder your friends call you George."

"*Si.*" He laughed. "But you may call me anything you

like, especially if it is 'my love,' *'amore mio,'* 'my heart,' *'mio cuore.'*"

She stopped. "And what will you call me?"

"The most wonderful woman in the world," he promptly answered. "The woman who has made my every dream come true, even when I did not know what I was dreaming for."

"Oh, Giorgio." She threw her arms around his waist and rested her head against his chest, her eyes filling again.

He set her suitcase down. "I know, I know. My heart is full, also."

"Just for a minute. Then we need to get down the hill so we can get out of these terrible clothes." The odor of tomatoes and anchovies was getting very strong.

He laughed, his chest rumbling under her ear. "Ah, I knew we were of like minds. You are a woman after my own heart."

She laughed and he joined in, her lighter giggles mixing with his warm masculine tones ringing through the countryside like a clear, strong bell announcing his joy. It was the finest, happiest sound she had ever heard, and joy welled in her, too.

A day of joy to start the rest of their joyful life together.

Epilogue

"I HAVE TO HAND IT TO YOU, George. How many men can go shopping for a wedding dress and wind up picking out a bride?" Frank's tone was admiring, after more than mild disbelief when Giorgio had called him from New York to announce his own engagement.

His face stretched into yet another love-struck grin. It was a good thing Frank couldn't see what had to be the most cow-eyed expression ever. "Not many, I suppose."

"You know, I went to the bridal salon when my sister got married." Frank definitely sounded disgruntled. "And do you know who was there? Women old enough to be my mother—my grandmother, even. Oh, and a couple flower girls who couldn't have been older than eight. But you, you find an Italian girl who looks like a redheaded Sophia Loren from that picture you emailed me. Where is the justice in the world?"

"There is none, Frank. I am amazed she's agreed to marry me."

"Me, too."

"Hey, you don't have to agree so quickly."

"Oh, knock off the false modesty, George. You know you're a great guy and I'm just kidding you. Tell me when the wedding is so I can dry-clean the formal wear."

"After Stefania's wedding. She deserves all the focus on her." Renata was definitely happy to leave the "big foo-foo royal wedding" to her sister-in-law to be.

"Don't get between a bride and her perfect day, eh? Good plan." Frank cleared his throat. "I heard from Jack. Not to rain on your parade, but he did pick up some bizarre ailment and they flew him to the hospital in Bangkok."

Giorgio winced. "Is he going to be all right?"

"Yes, yes," Frank soothed him. "Lost a few kilos he couldn't afford to lose but he claims he's much better."

"Frank, why doesn't he accept that professorship in tropical medicine they offered him at the Pasteur Institute last year?"

"Me, I do not understand it, either. I don't have the travel bug and all the bugs that come with it. But if I had a fiancée like his, I would move to Antarctica."

"And study tropical medicine there?" Giorgio asked dryly.

"It *is* very far south, George. Ah, poor Jack—he would rather get dysentery than be on the same continent as that awful Nadine."

Giorgio snorted but couldn't disagree. "Nothing is set in stone. Until I see them standing at the altar of that chapel on the family estate, I have to believe he may change his mind."

"But you won't!" Frank said gleefully. "Renata has caught you, line, sinker and hook. Bring her to meet me so I can see how the mighty have fallen."

Giorgio perked up his ears as several locks opened. They were in New York, after all, even if it was at a nice flat on the Upper West Side they'd chosen together.

Renata's family had been shocked to learn she was engaged, much less to a prince from a place they'd never even heard of. Her brothers had made him show them the official website of Vinciguerra before they believed it was a real country. He'd even had a hard time convincing them he wasn't a Eurotrash con man until he pulled up his online bio and official photo.

Her mother had quickly broken down into happy tears after that, and her grandmother had the unsettling habit of leering at him and then giving Renata a knowing wink.

Renata's Aunt Barbara and her friend Flick were going to run the bridal salon once Renata joined him full-time in Vinciguerra. She would design from a workshop in the palazzo and send them her creations. He couldn't wait for her to marry him and move there. His palazzo had all sorts of interesting nooks and crannies they could explore together. Naked.

"Giorgio, I'm home," the sweetest voice in the world called.

"Gotta go, Frank. Renata's back from work." He was already shutting down his laptop.

"Two's company, three's a crowd. I know when I'm not wanted—"

He laughed and hung up.

Renata appeared from the foyer, a sexy pout on her face—and a white box in her hands. "Look, Giorgio, my new shoes got wet. That stupid weather forecast never said anything about rain."

"I will buy you a thousand pairs if you come here and kiss me."

"Bribery, sex and shoes. I could get used to this." She sauntered over to him, purposely swaying her hips from side to side. Bright red toenails peeped out from the black high-heeled sandals. Today she wore one of his white dress shirts knotted at the waist over skintight dark denim capri pants. *Molto* sexy. She looked like a fifties starlet with one thing on her mind.

Lucky for him, he was of a like mind. "Come here."

"Wait a second, Giorgio." She shoved the white box at him. "This is for you."

He accepted it and lifted the lid. "What?" He inhaled the sweet fragrance in awe and pleasure. "No, these can't be." He picked up a delicate lemon cookie dusted in powdered sugar.

"Try it," she urged. "Stefania sent me your mother's recipe and my mom and grandma have been teaching me how to bake her cookies for you."

Giorgio was stunned. "You learned how to bake these—for me?"

"Of course. Don't just look at it, eat it."

He popped it into his mouth and springtime burst on his tongue, sunshine on a gloomy day. Just like Renata.

Yes, his mother's recipe, with a dash of Renata thrown in. How lucky a man he was to be loved by such women. His mother, his grandmother, his sister and now his fiancée. "I love you, Renata."

"And I love you, too." Renata puckered her lips into a luscious red pout. "Kiss me, so I know this is all real and not some crazy romantic comedy."

"Your wish is my command." He stood and pulled her into his arms.

She laughed and twined her arms around his neck. "Oh, Giorgio. I love you so much."

His heart flipped again, but this time it only made him smile instead of worry. He wordlessly scooped her up, wet shoes and all, and carried her off to bed where he proceeded to show her just how much he loved her, too.

* * * * *

THE ENGLISH LORD'S SECRET SON

MARGARET WAY

CHAPTER ONE

SEVEN-YEAR-OLD Jules slapped a fist into his palm as Cate nosed the Beemer into the parking space vacated by a run-about so compact it could fit into the owner's pocket.

"Good one, Mum," he whooped.

"Talk about perfect timing!" Cate Hamilton had come to rely on her parking skills. At times like this they proved invaluable.

"That was ace!"

Ace had taken over from the battered *awesome*. Jules always liked to keep a pace ahead.

"Noah really looks up to you, Mum." It was a source of pride to him. Noah, his best friend, was seriously impressed by Cate's driving. Noah's mother, a nice lady, had the really scary knack of either side swiping vehicles or on occasions reversing into them. She should have had a number plate bearing the warning: WATCH OUT. There were always scrapes and dents on their silver Volvo. Repairs were carried out. Back to Square One. It was a pattern pretty well set. Noah said his mother didn't know *how* to explain it. His father had a hard time understanding it as well.

So did Cate. She often had coffee with Noah's mother, who was a bright, intelligent woman, right on the ball, apart from her driving habits. She switched off the ignition, eyeing the busy road. At this time of the morning there were cars everywhere, causing a worrying amount of chaos. There didn't appear to be any order on the part of the drivers. She had even begun to question the safety of the pedestrian crossing. People appeared to be in such a desperate hurry these days. Where were they going? What was so important every nanosecond counted? Surely nothing could be more important than the safety of a child? The difficulty was, parking spots were at a premium for the junior school. Small children, even big children, didn't leg it to school these days. They didn't even bus it. They were driven to and fro by their parents. Different times, worrying times. Or maybe that perception was a beat up by a media who seized on anything when there was a dearth of stories.

A recent coverage featured an attempted snatching of a thirteen-year-old schoolgirl. Even the police had been sucked in for a while until a child psychologist in their ranks pointed out thirteen-year-old girls were known to have a burgeoning need for attention. Some were more demanding and more inventive than others. That particular young lady had a future writing fiction.

Cate glanced at her son's glowing face. The most beautiful face in the whole wide world to her. Not only beautiful, Jules was *smart*, really smart. Her one and only child. Pure and innocent. Her sun, moon and stars. Cate relished the moment of real joy, lifting a hand to acknowledge a departing driver, another mother, who fluttered curling, separated fingers in response.

It was a beautiful day, so bright and full of promise. A great time to be alive. Scent of trees. Scent of flowers, the heat amplifying the myriad scents to incense. Tangy taste of salt off Sydney Harbour. The Harbour, the most beautiful natural harbour in the world, made a splendid contribution to Sydney's scenic beauty. No wonder Sydney was regularly featured as one of the world's most beautiful and liveable cities. Few cities could boast such a glorious environment, a dazzling blue and gold world, with hundreds of bays and beaches of white sands, magical coves and waterways for its citizens to enjoy. To Sydneysiders it was a privilege to live within easy distance of the sparkling Pacific Ocean. Even the trip to school was a heart-lifting experience.

The great jacaranda trees that lined Kingsley Avenue on both sides were in full bloom. She recalled as a student it was a superstition among them that if a jacaranda blossom fell on one's head, one would pass one's exams. A fanciful notion and, like all fanciful notions, not one to count on. Nothing in life was as simple as that. Blossoms fell indiscriminately on heads all the time. This morning there were circular lavender carpets around the trunks, with spent blossoms fanning out across the pavement and the road.

Cate turned off the ignition. Only a short time to go now before term was over. The long Christmas vacation lay ahead.

Christmas.

Out of the blue her mind gave way to memories. She could never predict when they would invade her consciousness, frame by frame, unstoppable now, near obscuring her vision. A moment before she had been celebrating life. Now was not the time to allow dark thoughts to kick in. Yet inexorably she found herself going back in time to a place she knew from bitter experience was no place to go. Christmas across the world where it snowed instead of rained mauve blossom; where snow blanketed roofs and gardens, and frosted the trees, their skeletal branches outlined in white. For all the frigid air it was a world transformed. A fairy land.

Another time. Another place…

She had turned eighteen, an innocent at large, at the happiest, most exciting time of her young life, when the road ahead offered nothing but promise. She had thought at the time her guardian angel had to be watching over her, because it was then she fell helplessly, hopelessly, in love. The miracle of Destiny. She had revelled in the magic for long dreamlike months before all her happiness had been cruelly snatched away.

Overnight.

How *was* one supposed to respond to having one's heart broken? Not just broken, *trampled* on with feet that came down hard. What had been required of her was to absorb the terrible loss and disappear like a puff of smoke.

A Housman poem had run continuously in her head for years.

Give crowns and pounds and guineas
But not your heart away.

She had come to think of it as her theme song. She had given her heart away and given it in vain. She had learned a hard lesson—were there any better?—there were never guarantees when two people fell in love. What was love anyway between a man and a woman? A period of mesmerising madness? A period of lust, a desperation to assuage a physical hunger, without a single thought as to looking deeper for longer-lasting qualities? Just how many people were blessed with the sort of love that endured? Love for *life*. Was that too much to expect given the fickleness and limited attention span of human nature? Far too many suffered the sort of love that vanished as suddenly as it arrived. A case of love running out.

Or in my case, without warning, a changing course.

These days she was back to loving Christmas, indeed the whole festive season. The arrival of Jules had miraculously put her world to rights. She could see the big picture as she had never done before. From the instant he had been placed on her breast, he had become the most important person in the world to her. No love like a mother's love. No passion as strong. His impact on her very existence was profound. She no longer focused on herself and her pain. She had a *son* to focus on. She knew from experience children raised by a single parent, usually the mother, needed that parent to play dual roles, mother and father. She had read publications from eminent people in the field that had arrived at the conclusion children from the nuclear middle-class family, mum and dad, with a bit of money, fared much better in life than children raised by single parents. While she respected the findings she had seen plenty of kids from affluent homes with both parents to care for them run off the rails. On the other hand, she had seen many success stories of people who had grown up in single-parent homes with very little money to spare. Wanting something better was a great driving force. So as far as she was concerned there were two sides to the issue. She was definitely on the side of the single parents and their difficult, challenging role.

She and Julian had a very special relationship in the best and brightest way. She couldn't really say she'd had to work at it. They had loved one another on sight, neither wanting to offer the least little bit of hurt or upset to the other. It might have been a support programme between mother and son. It had worked beautifully.

Other cars were cruising the avenue, looking for a parking spot. A late-model Mercedes shamelessly double parked to take advantage of the fact she might soon be leaving. They were a few metres from the gates of one of the country's top-ranked boys' schools, Kingsley College. The school buildings of dressed stone were regarded by all as exceptionally fine. The grounds were meticulously maintained with great sweeps of emerald green lawn, and a meld of magnificent shade trees. Parents were proud to be able to send their sons there, even if in some cases the fees almost broke the bank.

Thankfully they had found their parking spot when she was really pressed for time. She had received a text message to the effect a meeting with a potential client had been called for first thing in the morning. No name was mentioned.

Briskly Cate bent over to kiss the top of her son's blond head, taking enormous pleasure in the scent of him. His hair was so thick and soft it cushioned her lips. "Love you, darling," she said from the depths of her heart. Ah, the passage of time! She had visions of Jules as the most adorable baby in the world. Jules as a toddler. It seemed only the other day since he had taken his first steps. Wonder of wonders it had been a Sunday and she was at home. She was convinced he had delayed the momentous event so she could witness it; so she could be there for him to half run, half stumble into her waiting arms. Surely it wasn't that long since he had turned four and she had put on a big birthday party with clowns and rides on a darling little Shetland pony in the grounds? It had to be only a few *months* since he had lost his first baby tooth heralding the arrival of the tooth fairy? Time was so precious and Time was passing far too quickly. Her son was being shaped and developed before her eyes. He was rapidly turning into a questioning child, looking at the world from his own perspective.

"Love you too, Mum," Jules answered. It was their daily ritual. The "Jules" had started the very first day of school when his best friend, Noah, had hit on it in preference to the mouthful Julian. Now he was Jules to everyone, his wide circle of friends, classmates, even teachers. He took overlong unfastening his seat belt. He even hesitated a moment before opening out the passenger door.

"Everything okay, sweetheart?" Her mother's antennae picked up on his inaction.

For a moment he didn't answer, as though weighing up the effect his answer might have on her. Jules was super protective. Then it all came out in a rush. "Why can't I have a dad like everyone else?" He spoke in a half mumble, head down, when Jules never mumbled. He was a very clever, confident little boy, much loved and cared for with all the warmth that was vital for the growth of his young body and soul. Jules was no solitary child.

At his words, Cate's heart gave a painful lunge. Deep down, no matter how much he was loved by her, his mother, it seemed Jules longed for a dad; the glory of having a dad, a male figure to identify with. Clearly she couldn't cover both roles. Her mouth went dry.

Haven't you always known you'd have to address this? The dark cloud over your head, the constant psychological weight.

Adept at masking her emotions, her voice broke halfway. "It's biologically impossible not to have a dad, Jules." A pathetic stopgap, unworthy. Jules was at the age of reason. Everything changed as a child grew to the age of reason. Jules, her baby, was pushing forward. Questions were about to be asked. Answers sought. Her fears would be revealed as secrets became unlocked. This was an area she had to confront.

Now.

"Be serious, Mum," Jules implored. He turned back to her, pinning her with his matchless blue eyes. Everyone commented on the resemblance between them. Except for the eyes. "You don't know what it's like. The kids are starting to ask me all sorts of questions. They never did it before. Who my dad is? Where is he? Why isn't he with us?"

She put it as matter-of-factly as she could. "I told you, Jules. He lives in England. He couldn't be with us."

God, he doesn't even know there's an "us". What would he do if he did? Acknowledge paternity? Easy enough to prove. Let it all go? Not enough room in his life for an ille-

gitimate child? Surely the term illegitimate wasn't used any more? What would he do? Would he act, acknowledge his child? That was the potentially threatening question. Only no one was going to take her son from her. She had reared him. She had shouldered the burden of being a single mother. If it came down to it—a fight for custody—she would fight like a lioness.

Except her case could be unwinnable. No wonder she had woken up that morning feeling jittery. It was as though she was being given a warning.

"Doesn't he love us?" Jules' question snapped her back to attention. "Why didn't he want to be with us? The kids think you're super cool." They did indeed. Jules' mother was right up there in the attention stakes.

Julian's young life had been woman oriented, sublimely peaceful. He lived with his mother, and his grandmother Stella, who had always looked after him, especially when Cate was at work or delayed with endless long meetings. Jules had lots of honorary "aunts"—friends and colleagues of hers. They lived in a rather grand hillside house with a view of the harbour. It was a five-minute drive down to a blue sparkling marina and a park where kids could play. The city, surrounded by beautiful beaches, offered any number of places to go for a swim. Jules was already a strong swimmer for his age. He lived the good life, stable and secure. Jules wanted for nothing.

Except a father.

"Why couldn't you get married, Mum?" Her son's young voice combined protectiveness for her and unmistakable hostility for the man who had fathered him. This was a new development, emotionally and socially. Jules was clearly reviewing his position in his world.

"We were going to, Jules," Cate told him very gently. To think she had actually *believed* it. "We were deeply in love, starting to make plans." Their romance had been close to sublime until they had started making plans. Plans did them in. "And then something rather momentous happened. Your father came into an important inheritance called a peerage. That meant he would never leave England." *Didn't want to leave England.* "I was desperate to come back to Australia. My family was here. His people were there. His *life* was there. It was as simple and disruptive as a grand inheritance. Your father's mother had someone in mind for her only son. She was the daughter of an earl. Born to the purple, as it were." Even now the breath rushed out of her chest.

Your paternal grandmother, with her silk knickers in a twist. Alicia, the patrician-faced hatchet woman who expected Cate to do the right thing and go home.

"Didn't she like you?" Jules sounded incredulous. His mother was perfect in his eyes.

Cate had to acknowledge she still bore the scars of that last confrontation with Alicia, the icy determination of the woman, the breathtaking arrogance of the English upper class. "Well, she did at first," she managed after a moment. It was true enough. Alicia had been supremely confident this young woman was going back to Australia. It was no more than a holiday flirtation, a passing fancy for a pretty girl. But there were strict limits to the friendship. The question of succession had finally been settled. "Later I was made very aware there was no question of a marriage between us."

"None at all, my dear. How could you think otherwise? My son will marry one of us." Alicia had been adamant. Here was a woman with a deep understanding of *noblesse oblige.*

She must have muttered aloud, because Jules asked with a flash to his beautiful eyes, "Who's *us*?"

"Oh, I soon discovered that!" She gave a brief laugh. "People of the same background. The English aristocracy and the like. It's still a class system no matter what they say."

"Class system?" Jules was getting het up.

That wouldn't do. "It's different from here, Jules," she said soothingly. "Don't worry about it. I'll explain it to you this evening."

"So he married someone else, the *us*?" Anger simmered in Jules' clear voice. Another stage in his development.

"I expect so. I never followed through. I left him and England behind, my darling. My life is here, Jules. With you and Nan. You're happy, aren't you?"

Jules rallied. He wasn't going to upset his mother any further. "Sure I'm happy, Mum," he declared, though it was obvious to Cate he was grappling with this fresh information. He leant over to give her a kiss. "I can take care of the boys at school. What's his name, my father's name?"

"Ashton." She suddenly realised she had not spoken his name *aloud* for years. *Ashe. Julian Ashton Carlisle, Fifth Baron Wyndham.*

"That's a funny name," Jules said. "Bit like Julian. I expect he named me. English, you see. I'm glad everyone calls me Jules. Better go, Mum. See you tonight."

"Take care, my darling."

"I will." Jules gave her a quick hug. Mercifully Jules wasn't one of those kids who were embarrassed by public displays of affection. Noah, on the other hand, had forbidden his mother to kiss him when any of the other kids were about. Jules made short work of heaving up his satchel then hopping out of the car. Noah was racing towards him both arms outstretched, one up, one down, dipping and rising mimicking a plane's wings. He was calling out in delight, "Jules…Jules…"

Cate watched a moment longer, her heart torn. *May joy fill your days.* Both boys turned back to wave to her. She responded, putting a big carefree smile on her face.

This is only the start of it all, my girl. Her inner voice broke up the moment, weighing in with a warning.

At twenty-six she was well on the way to becoming a high flyer in the corporate world. She knew she appeared to others to have it all. Only one person, Stella, the person closest to her, knew the whole story. She could never have managed without Stella's selfless support. It was Stella who had taken charge of her baby when she was at university. She needed a career. They had both agreed on that. She had a son to rear.

Stella was the guardian angel for her and her son. Stella, her adoptive mother.

It had taken well over twenty years for her to find out who her biological mother was. And that only came about because her biological mother had thought it prudent to make a deathbed confession before she met her Maker.

A sad way to clean the slate; devastating for an unacknowledged daughter to find out the truth. Sometimes she thought she would never forgive Stella for not having told her. Over the years she had met "Aunty Annabel" perhaps a half dozen times when she visited Stella, her older sister in Australia. Cate realised then, as never before, one should not keep secrets from a child. Inevitably at some stage it would all come out causing confusion and conflict and often estrangement. She'd had her own experience as an adult. She couldn't delay all that much longer discussing her past with her child. What choice did she have? Questions would be repeated over and over if the issue wasn't addressed. She couldn't allow her old emotions to get in the way.

"Good morning, Cate." It was the attractive young brunette behind the reception desk.

"Morning, Lara."

Lara was busy appraising Cate's smart appearance. "Mr

Saunders and the others are waiting for you in the boardroom. Some bigwig is coming in."

"Have you got a name for me?" Cate paused to enquire.

"Actually, no." Lara sent her a look of mild surprise. "The appointment is for nine-fifteen. Love your outfit." Lara had learned a great deal about grooming, hair, make-up, clothes accessories, simply from studying Cate Hamilton. Cate had such style. She was wonderfully approachable too. No unbearable airs of superiority, unlike Cate's female colleague, the terrifying Murphy Stiller, who held herself aloof from everyone not on the command chain. Stiller was supremely indifferent to office perceptions of her. Cate Hamilton appeared to know instinctively office alliances were important.

"Thanks, Lara." Cate moved off. In her own spacious office she swiftly divested herself of her classic, quilted lambskin black handbag, and then checked her appearance in the long mirror she'd had fixed inside the door of one of the tall cabinets. She always dressed with great care. It was important to look good. It was expected of her. It went with the job. She was wearing a recent buy, a designer two-piece outfit with a slim black pencil skirt and a white jacket banded in black. Her long blonde hair—the definitive Leo's mane—she always wore pulled back into various updated arrangements for work. Looking good was mandatory. All-out glamour wasn't on the agenda. Too distracting to the clients. Even so she'd been told she was considered pretty hot stuff.

They were all seated around the boardroom table—big as any two ping-pong tables shoved together—when she entered the room.

"Good morning, everyone," she greeted them pleasantly, and received suave nods that hid a variety of feelings. Downright lecherous on the part of Geoff Bartz, their resident environmentalist and a very unattractive man. The hierarchy was still men, though not as inflexible as it once had been. The richest person in Australia was in fact a woman, the late mining magnate Lang Hancock's daughter, Gina Rinehart, worth around twenty billion and counting. All of the men were Italian suited, Ferragamo shod, the one woman at the table as impeccably turned out as ever, cream silk blouse, Armani power suit. No one reached a position near the top of the tree without being exceptionally well dressed. Lord knew they were paid enough to buy the best even if they rarely strayed from imported labels. Cate trusted her own instincts, giving Australian designers a go. They were so good she stuck to them.

"Ah, Cate," Hugh Saunders, CEO and chairman of the board of Inter-Austral Resources, oil, minerals, chemicals, properties etc. sat at the head of the table. He was credited with almost single-handedly turning a small sleeping mining company into a multibillion-dollar corporation. On Cate's entry he exhaled an audible sigh of pleasure. A lean, handsome, very stylish man turning sixty, he had personally recruited Cate Hamilton some three years previously. He considered himself her mentor. If he were only ten years younger he privately considered he would have qualified as a whole lot more, sublimely unaware Cate had never entertained such a thought. "Come take a seat. There's one here by me." He gestured towards the empty seat to his right.

Territorial display if there ever was one, Murphy Stiller thought with a tightening of her lips and a knitting of her jet-black brows of one. Murphy Stiller was brilliant, abrasive, ferociously competitive. Murphy's sole aspiration was to move into Hugh Saunders' padded chair while it was still warm. The great pity was he was such a stayer! Before Hamilton had arrived on the scene she had been Queen of the Heap, able to command attention and a seat at the CEO's right hand without saying a word. Then the newcomer she had mentally labelled *upstart* had from the outset started producing results. Corporate politics, balance sheets, marketing plans, impromptu presentations, refinancing. It could have been familiar territory. Hamilton was up for the challenge. A compulsive over-achiever, of course. Murphy knew the type. A multitasker, always up to speed. Saunders seemed mesmerised by her. Certainly he had carefully mapped out her career. But that was what men spent a lot of time thinking about, wasn't it? Sex. Whether they were getting it. Or more often missing out. When Murphy had entered the boardroom she had naturally made for the seat on the CEO's right—she never jockeyed, jockeying was beneath her—only to be forestalled by Saunders' upraised hand smoothly directing her to a seat on his left, as though oblivious to her chagrin. Time to hot up her nightly prayers her young rival would get her comeuppance. Flunk something. Take a fall. Get married. Go into politics. Fall under a bus. Anything.

Murphy forced herself to stop daydreaming. It wasn't going to happen.

All were now seated. All faces were turned to the chairman, who had glanced at his watch to check what time they had. "What we do and say here before our prospective client arrives is extremely important," he announced with great earnestness. "This is a man used to meeting people at the highest level. I believe he even talks to the Prince of Wales on a first-name basis."

Cate pretended to be lost in envy. She had her own understanding of the English upper classes, though the Prince was said to be a genuine egalitarian.

"He's already acquired a small empire in different parts of the world," the CEO was saying. "He's now looking at our mineral wealth. Overseas the news is Australia is being driven by mining and resource. Not surprising their top entrepreneurs want in. We're going to prove extremely helpful." He paused as another project came to mind. "He's also interested in acquiring a property in the Whitsundays. Virgin territory as it were, far away from the usual haunts of jetsetters and the current hot spots, the Caribbean and such. You all know the late George Harrison bought up there. Had a holiday home on our far-flung shores, then a virtual outpost. George knew what he was about. I know we can help our prospective client. Perhaps you, Cate. You're very good at dealing with people. You might even be able to persuade Lady McCready to finally sell Isla Bella. She trusts you. Aren't many places left in the world as pristine as Isla Bella."

"Sure our prospective client doesn't want to turn it into a resort?" Cate asked. "Lady McCready is totally against any such project."

"Goodness me, no!" Saunders vehemently shook his head as though he'd had it straight from the horse's mouth. "This is a man who shuns glitz. He wants a private sanctuary for him, his family and close friends. He will want to visit, of course, if Lady McCready is agreeable. She must be a great age now. Only the other day someone told me she had passed away."

"Still very much alive, sir," Cate said, watching the CEO hold up a staying hand as the mobile on the table rang. He listened for a moment, said a few words, then put the receiver down. "Ah, he's arrived."

It was delivered with such reverence the prospective client could equally well have been Prince Charles or even President Obama. The Clintons had made the great escape to North Queensland and the Great Barrier Reef islands, pronouncing the whole area an idyllic destination. Perhaps it was Bill Clinton or some retired American senator, who just wanted to sit around all day without anyone taking cheap shots at him as political enemies tended to do.

Lara entered the boardroom cheeks glowing, her mouth curved up in a smile. After her came an extremely handsome man in a hawkish kind of way: aquiline nose—perfect to look down on people—finely chiselled aristocratic features, thick jet-black hair with a natural wave, extraordinary eyes, the colour of blue flame; immediate impact that would linger for a long time. He stood well over six feet, very elegantly dressed. Not Zenga; Savile Row made to measure. A tailor's dream. Snow-white shirt, striped silk tie no doubt denoting something elitist, tied just so. So sophisticated was his appearance it held them all speechless for a while.

But none more transfixed than Cate.

Time collapsed. How vivid was memory; how powerful was the past!

For a fleeting moment she felt her breathing had stopped. Then as air came back into her lungs she knew such fright she thought she had actually fainted while still remaining conscious. Her whole body was shaking, her mind sliding out of kilter. Thank God she didn't have a glass of mineral water in her trembling hand for everyone would have watched her drop it to the ground where it probably would have shattered.

This is it, she thought. The heavens had shifted. She knew he had taken her in at once.

Lord Julian Ashton Carlisle, Fifth Baron Wyndham.

The father of her child.

She had come to him a virgin, the man who had devastated her life. So this was the way Karma worked? Action, effect, fate. She was trapped in the same room as the man she had never succeeded in erasing from her mind or her heart and hated him for it. He was indelibly fixed there by lost love, sorrow and humiliation. She had tried with every atom of her being to put the past behind her, but the past had had its effect on all of her subsequent relationships. No other man measured up.

Now her brain was signalling warnings.

The Day of Reckoning is at hand.

Over the past years she had almost succeeded in convincing herself Jules was solely *hers*. A virgin birth as it were. She knew now she had lost all touch with reality. Jules at some point in his life was going to want to meet his father. Jules' father might very well want to meet the son he had hitherto known nothing about. The only way she could avert such a thing happening was to keep them far apart. At least until Jules was of an age to undertake his own search for his biological father, who probably by now had children with his aristocratic wife. Impeccable breeding, of course. It was expected, after all. Someone had to inherit the baronetcy, keep up tradition. Social status was something to be cherished.

Cate made a massive effort to calm herself by focusing on how appalling things had been for her. Alicia, steely eyed, tall, rail-thin body vibrating as she told her to go away and not come back. All Alicia had ever been up to then had been no more than a bit on the snobbish side—a woman with a mindset stuck in the early twentieth century, very patronising to a young woman from the colonies, but pleasant enough. Then everything had abruptly changed. It had been crisis time, with Ashe away for a few days in London on family business. It had all been stunningly, shockingly sudden.

"There's simply no place for you here, Catrina." Alicia had spoken with a gleam of triumph in her slate-grey eyes. *"My son has acknowledged that. I am sorry for you, my dear, but you allowed yourself false hopes. You made a terrible mistake, but then you're so very young. So ignorant of the ways of the world. Frankly I did try to warn you. There are unwritten rules to our way of life. We all understand them. You don't. You would never have fitted in. Marina was born for the role. Julian may have thought you special for a time, but now he knows he has to take a step back. Life is all about doing one's duty, assuming one's responsibilities."*

Cate hadn't accepted that blindly. She had fought back claiming all were equal under the sun, her expression so combative any other woman but Alicia might have ducked for cover. She'd told Alicia she needed to hear it all from Ashe himself.

Ashe, please help me.

Only Ashe wasn't there.

"That's the thing, my dear. Julian is in London," Alicia had countered, trying to sound pitying and only succeeding in sounding chilling. *"He's not there on business. I assumed you would guess that. He went away because he couldn't bear to tell you himself. It was far from an easy decision but I helped him see it was the best way. Indeed the only way. You are both far too young. Julian simply didn't realise you were taking him so utterly seriously. Holiday romances tend to fade pretty quickly, my dear. You'll find that out when you get back to Australia. You have your own life. My son has his."*

And so she had vanished. It took her a couple of months more to come to the devastating realisation she was pregnant. *Hello, pregnant?* When they had practised safe sex. She had never trusted safe sex from there on. She was pregnant to a young man, to a family, who didn't want her. Moreover would not be eager to know her child even if it had their blood. She wasn't good enough. It was a grave situation and one of her own making. She had turned to the only mother she had ever known to help her.

Stella.

CHAPTER TWO

England, 2005

CATE HAD BEEN driving for miles through the picture-perfect English countryside, a patchwork of emerald-green fields bordered by woods, lovely towering trees and wondrously neat hedges. Miraculously it had stopped raining. She had only been in England a couple of weeks, and the rain had been falling without end. And, Lord, was it *cold!* The European winter was fast setting in. But for now the sun shone, however briefly, and what lay before her was a pastoral idyll, a symphony of soft misty colours. It made her feel good to be alive. On her own at last. Freedom! Was there anything so good? *Freedom.* She sang it aloud. No one to hear her anyway but the woolly white sheep that dotted the enchanting landscape. It was simply wonderful to be footloose and fancy free.

Her base for her gap year was the great historic city of London, squeezed into a *teeny* flat with two of her university-going pals. Not that they noticed the lack of life's little luxuries to which all of them had long been accustomed. They were too busy enjoying themselves and exploring the cultural wonders the great city had to offer. This was to be a great year for them, their Grand Tour. Afterwards all three would embark on their chosen careers. Josh came from a long line of medical doctors, so it was Medicine for Josh. Sarah with her legal family would read Law. Cate had decided on the high-flying world of Big Business, maybe along the track of an MBA from Harvard? So that had meant an Economics degree. At school her brilliance at Maths had set her apart. That didn't bother her. She had been something of an oddity all her life.

Why wouldn't she have been, given her history? She had been raised not knowing who her biological parents were. That alone put a girl at a severe psychological disadvantage. But at least she had been adopted as a baby by a beautiful young Englishwoman who to her great sadness couldn't carry a baby beyond a couple of months without suffering a miscarriage. She had come by all accounts as a gift from God, albeit a giveaway baby to the right couple. Stella and Arnold certainly were. She knew they loved her. She loved them. They were good people, kindness itself, encouraging her in every way. But she had never truly felt she *belonged.* Forever a step away. Despite all their efforts—and she had been a difficult child she had to admit—she was and remained, in her own mind at least, an *outsider.*

Stella had had no idea when Cate left Australia that her adopted daughter fully intended tracking down the Cotswold manor house where Stella and her sister, Annabel, had grown up. "Lady" Annabel, her ravishing adoptive *aunt*, had only visited her sister in Australia a mere handful of times in the last two decades. A true and loving sister. Annabel had remained in England where she married one Nigel Warren, knighted by the Queen for something or other and a seriously rich man many years her senior. Stella, on the other hand, had married someone her own age. The great mystery was Stella and her new husband had abandoned their gracious lives in England to migrate to the opposite end of the earth: *Australia.* An extraordinary move, one would have thought.

They hadn't arrived penniless, however. Quite the reverse, which surely had some significance? With private funds they had settled into a new life on the oldest continent on earth.

Surely though they had to be missing all this? Cate thought. Even the softly falling rain had its own enchantment. Home was Home, wasn't it? This part of the world somewhat to her surprise—used as she was to a brilliant, eternally shining sun and vast open spaces—she found truly beautiful. Comforting. *Oddly* familiar. It was as though she had stepped into a wonderful English landscape painting by Constable. One with which she identified. That mystified her. Such a landscape couldn't be further removed from where she had grown up. There the sun dominated. The rain when it came didn't require one to keep a raincoat forever handy—often it required a boat.

For now she was intent on catching a glimpse of the manor house that had been in Stella's family for many years. Yet Stella had chosen to abandon the country of her birth and what had to be a gracious heritage for the comparative wilderness. Cate had to think it was love. Arnold was as English as Stella. Both, even after twenty years, retained their upper-class English accents. A few of her schoolmates in the early days had dared to call her a "Pom". They hadn't done it twice. At least not to her face. But even she knew her accent was more English than English-Australian. Why wouldn't it be the way she had grown up?

She had arrived in the village now, with no idea her life was poised for dramatic change. She pulled to the side of the street, then switched off the ignition of her little hire car, looking keenly around her. The village was so small but very pretty, dominated by what had to be original Tudor buildings with a handful of speciality shops. Glorious hanging baskets featured a spilling profusion of brightly coloured and scented flowers. She spotted a tea room, a picturesque old pub, The

Four Swans, and a post office. There was a central park that had a lovely large pond. Over the green glassy surface glided the said four snow-white graceful swans. Her heart lifted. She stepped out of the car, rounding the bonnet, to enter the post office. Graceful in body and movement, she walked fast with a long confident stride.

A pleasant-faced woman carrying too much weight was behind the counter deep into a romance novel. A bodice ripper by the look of it. The woman glanced up with a welcoming smile as Cate entered. "Lost yourself, love?" She inserted a bookmark to mind her place.

Cate had to laugh. She had an excellent sense of direction. "Not really. I was enjoying this very beautiful part of the world."

"So it is. So it is. I'm the postmistress among other things. Aussie, love?"

Cate's smile widened. "At home more often than not I'm mistaken for a Pom."

The woman nodded sagely. "Not the accent, love." Upper-class English, but not *quite*, Joyce Bailey thought. "Something about your easy manner, the confident stride, the attitude."

"Now that is flattery at its finest." Cate gave a little mock bow.

The postmistress leant heavily on the counter. "I have family in Australia. Been out there a couple of times. Ah, life in the sun! The family, especially the kids, won't come back now. They're fair dinkum Aussies. So how can I help you?'

"Radclyffe Hall," Cate said, moving closer. "Which way is it? I'm keen to take a glimpse."

The postmistress abruptly sobered. "Great white elephant of a house. Lots of tragedy in that family. Sons that served in the army. Lost in all sorts of battles. Crimean, Balkan, First and Second World Wars, the Falklands. Enormous devastation, wars! The present Lord Wyndham who inherited when his older brother was killed doesn't entertain much. Not like the old days. But the whole village has learned the historic gardens and the parklands are being restored. Be quite a challenge, I reckon. A famous landscape gardener has been working there for months. His aim is to bring the estate back to its former glory. Best of luck, we all say. We'll have the tourists back in no time. The hall's rose gardens used to be ever so famous. You won't be able to get in, love. But you can enjoy the view. The manor house—it's built out of our lovely honey-coloured Cotswold stone—stands on the top of the hill. Keep driving north out of town, no more than three miles on. Can't miss it. All of them rolling acres belong to Lord Wyndham. Only had daughters. No surviving son. The estate is entailed so it will pass to another male member of the Radclyffe family once Lord Wyndham is gone."

Cate absorbed all this information in utter silence. In truth she was poleaxed. Stella had rarely spoken of her former life. Stella had made secrecy an art form. Cate hadn't even known the house where Stella and her younger sister, Annabel, had grown up was called Radclyffe Hall until fairly recently when she had overheard a conversation between Stella and Arnold. So this all came as a revelation. Lord Wyndham was Stella's father. My God! Wasn't Stella a woman for burying the past? Cate felt incensed but shook it off.

"What's lunch like at the pub?" she asked, swiftly changing the subject. It would take time to absorb it all. Lots of time. Quietness to reflect.

"Second to none!" the postmistress declared stoutly.

"Think they can put me up for a few days?"

"I'd say so, love. Me and my hubby, Jack, run it. Shall I book you in?"

"If you would. My name is Cate Hamilton, by the way. I have ID in the car." She half turned to go out and get it.

"Won't be necessary, love," the woman stayed her. "We'll get the particulars when you return from your sightseeing jaunt. I'll have your room prepared."

"Thank you. You're very kind, Mrs—"

"Bailey. Joyce Bailey."

"Pleasure to meet you, Mrs Bailey." Cate put out her hand. It was heart-lifting to be so warmly received.

Joyce Bailey took it. She just loved that radiant smile. Funny thing was the girl—she couldn't have been more than eighteen—reminded her of someone. She tried to think who. No one who lived in the village. She was absolutely sure of that. She knew every last soul. But the smile, the girl's beauty, struck some sort of chord. Maybe it would come to her some time. Never an oil painting, she suddenly remembered the beautiful Radclyffe girls, Stella and Annabel. Dark-haired both, with lovely melting dark eyes; Annabel had been considered the more beautiful of the two. The whole district had been stunned when Stella and her husband had taken off for Australia. Annabel had gone with them at the time. But Annabel had returned almost a year later to marry a baronet who carried her off to London.

It had taken little time for Lord and Lady Wyndham to adapt to losing their beautiful daughters. The loss of their son, the heir, in infancy was the big tragedy. Everything else rated far below the line. The death of the son had come as the great blow of their lives. Other losses could be sustained. It was well known in the village the Radclyffes were a dysfunctional family.

After Lady Wyndham died, her husband retreated from the world, seeing few visitors. The Australian girl had no chance of getting a glimpse inside the hall. She could get as far as the garden. Beautiful girls had a way of getting in where the ants couldn't.

* * *

So her objective Radclyffe Hall was only a few miles away. Cate couldn't help feeling a quickening excitement. She slipped back behind the wheel with a parting wave to Mrs Bailey who, intrigued, had come to the post office door to see her off. Cate was really looking forward to this excursion. Lunch too for that matter. She was hungry. Back on the road there was a continuation of the chequered green landscape, a tapestry with all its different textures. It had the most potent charm. She had the window wound down so she could feel the breeze against her cheek. This was a muted world of soft pastel shades, and a totally different quality of light. Even the underlying colour schemes were different. She was used to such a flamboyant palette.

Just when she thought it was all plain sailing, the engine of the little hire car gave a cough, then a splutter. She urged it onto the verge where it quietly died.

"Blast!" Cate hit the wheel with both hands. Clever she might be at maths, but a car mechanic she was not. She looked ahead, then back. Nothing coming. She could lock the car, then proceed on foot. She couldn't be that far off her objective. But what about getting back again? She got out of the car, setting about lifting the bonnet to have a peer inside. Perhaps the car had overheated and she could restart it after a while. She heard a vehicle coming along the country road behind her. She didn't turn around, trusting whoever it was would stop. Help out a young lady in distress. The English were mannerly helpful people. Or so she'd been told.

The resonant male voice when it came wasn't in the least solicitous. It was unmistakably a young man's voice, but it proclaimed the legendary public-school accent—Eton? Harrow? Maybe modernised a bit.

"Think you can handle it?"

She found herself bridling at the tone. It was shocking in

its languidness. "Clear off," she muttered, risking she would be overheard.

He pounced. "I did ask a question."

"Really!" She spun around, shocked by the level of aggression that tone had provoked. "And I'm asking *you* one. What's so funny? Do you want to help or are you just being bloody-minded?" Of course he was. She could spot it.

He gave her an extraordinarily beautiful if condescending smile. Humour the girl. Beautiful white teeth, perfectly even and straight. She felt all her nerve ends clench. "Exaggerating, aren't you?" he asked ever so slowly, at the same time taking her in. "I only enquired if you can handle the problem."

She couldn't mask the irritation his persona engendered. Such feelings had never attacked her before. He was as handsome as the devil. Those *eyes*! She had never seen eyes so intensely blue. Sapphires set in coal-black lashes. A wave of jet-black hair flopped down onto his high forehead. His skin faintly dewed with perspiration was very fine, lightly tanned. He had a nose disagreeable to her. An aquiline *beak*, the bone as straight as a blade. You could get impaled on it. He was using it to good effect looking down it at her. Some girls would really fancy him. Most would actually. "I've never met with a problem up until today," she told him shortly. "A less than efficient hire car, in fact a bit of a rattle trap. Steering a bit wobbly. But it's been okay up to date, which doesn't explain why the engine suddenly died on me."

"Would you allow me to take a look?" he asked, mock super suave. He wafted an elegant hand in the air. The Scarlet Pimpernel dressed like a gardener, square shoulders, narrow hips, tight jeans, navy jersey, a red kerchief tied loosely around his neck for a bit of dash, high muddy boots.

Cate didn't rush to answer. "Know about cars, do you? I didn't catch your name?"

"Nosey Parker," he said, moving to stand beside her. Suddenly she was dwarfed when she wasn't all that short: five-four.

She knew she was being terribly ungracious, but her feelings of hostility were expanding by the minute. "Suits you," she commented.

From peering into the car, he stood to attention running his vivid blue eyes over her flushed face. Eyes that sparkled and snaffled her up. She preferred soft eyes. Gentle, humorous eyes. Brown maybe. "Have you been drinking?" he asked.

She couldn't ignore that. "Right! You can smell the fumes, can you?"

"You could have stopped off at The Four Swans," he answered, continuing to study her keenly.

She might have stepped out of a wrecked space shuttle instead of a beat-up piece of British engineering. Cate's blonde head snapped up. "Ha, ha and ha! Apart from being nosey, you're downright rude."

"No different from you," he returned with the arrogance that had to be bred into him. "Looks like we've rubbed each other up the wrong way."

"You don't stand a chance of rubbing up against me," she said tartly. "So what's wrong with the car, or don't you know? I'd say you were used to leaving all that to the chauffeur. No doubt you're the centre of someone's solar system?"

"Perfectly true. How did you know?" He got into the car, making a business of squirming before cranking back the seat as though the car had previously been driven by a midget. He then switched on the engine, which kicked over briefly, then gave up the ghost. "The reason for your breakdown—tempestuous little Aussie that you are—is you're out of petrol," he announced as he got out.

For a moment Cate was seriously embarrassed. "Nonsense! It was reading a quarter full. Or near enough. And stop staring at me as though I'm from another planet."

He laughed. "To be perfectly honest I didn't know extra-terrestrials came ravishingly pretty."

Had she blushed? Damn it, she had. "Don't feel the need to flatter me."

"I thought it was a plain statement of fact. As for my opinion of your manner? Prickly as a rose bush. Now, the petrol gauge is obviously not reading true. Where are you going anyway?"

She backtracked. "How did you know I'm an Australian?" she asked as though that created a definite barrier.

"I'd rather not say." He shut his mouth firmly. It was a very good mouth, a clean sensual line above his chiselled jaw. The edges were faintly upturned. She found herself noting all the little details. She really had to concentrate on something other than his mouth. She felt in her bones he would be a great kisser. It would be interesting to see what happened if he suddenly grabbed her.

"Why would that be?"

"Maybe I'm frightened you'll attack me." His sapphire eyes were alive with mockery.

Did her heart turn over? Something in her chest did. Even her legs were feeling a bit flimsy. Nevertheless she took a step forward. "You find Australians threatening?"

Instantly he took a step back, holding up his elegant hands in a gesture of appeasement. "On the contrary, I like Australians. Within reason."

Cate gave up. He had a very engaging laugh. It made her want to laugh back. "I was on my way to Radclyffe Hall. You would know it."

"Why exactly?" he asked, with an unexpected frown. "Why Radclyffe Hall?"

Cate's turn to frown. "Look, can't we drop the interrogation? I just want to look at it."

"Then you'll have to do it from afar," he said.

"I never said I wanted to drop in for tea and scones." She tilted her chin. God, he was tall! "What's your name, by the way?"

"Ashe."

"Ash?" She raised a supercilious brow. "Your parents called you Ash?" she asked, feigning incredulity. "I've never met anyone called Ash. I take it that's Ashe with an e?"

"Julian Ashton," he informed her, looking impossibly, unbearably superior. "And you are?"

She considered not telling him. Only she could use his help. "Catrina Hamilton. My family and friends call me Cate."

"Then I shall call you Catrina."

"That's okay. Please do, *Ashe*. So are you going to help me out?"

He shrugged a shoulder. His body was perfectly proportioned, giving the strong impression of superb physical fitness. "How can I? I'm heading in the opposite direction," he retorted carelessly.

Cate didn't know what to make of that. "I understood Englishmen were gentlemen," she said with sudden dismay. "You must be a rare species."

He shook his head, loosening the satiny black wave that had stuck to his forehead. "Our womenfolk are much sweeter and more persuasive than you." He sounded deeply grateful for the fact.

"You must know only quiet, controllable creatures. Does this mean you're going to leave me stranded on a lonely country road?"

He considered a while, looking this way and that. "An apology might be in order," he suggested.

"We take it in turns, do we?" she asked. Goodness, he could only be a handful of years older than she, maybe twenty-three or four, but with an imperiousness well beyond his years.

"Okay then. I'm off." From nonchalance he was energised, turning purposefully towards his parked four-wheel drive.

"So much for being a gentleman, then," she called after him severely. "Go on. Drive away." He looked very much as if he was going to. "All right, *sorry.*" She only said it because that was what he wanted.

Immediately he swung back, beckoning her towards his vehicle, a dusty banged-up Range Rover. "Come along," he called briskly as though it were possible he'd change his mind. "I'll run you up to the hall, then send someone back with a can of petrol to pick up your old bomb. The only thing that surprises me is you didn't finish up in a ditch."

Cate swallowed a put-down. No need to antagonise him further. Maybe his turning up was an omen?

Good or bad she couldn't yet tell.

Courteously he held the door for her. His fingers brushed against hers, setting off such an explosion of sparks it almost had her crying, "Ouch!"

Inside the battered Range Rover, the sparks continued to jump the distance between them. It radiated a heat through her body, to her arm, her breasts, her stomach, working its way lower. Every last nerve ending seemed to be on fire. What she had to do was separate her body from her mind. *Difficult.* She was experiencing the sort of dizziness one had when in the company of someone overwhelmingly attractive. He was definitely *not* gay. She had gay mates. Love was love wherever cupid's arrow fell was her reasoning. This guy was powerfully heterosexual. Married? She found herself hoping he wasn't. He was too young for a start.

* * *

He stopped the Range Rover at a certain point. She could see why. It offered a sublime view of Radclyffe Hall. It sat high on a hill overlooking the beautiful countryside and the rolling hills.

It was an extraordinary moment for Cate. She felt a disconcerting prick of tears, blinking them back before he saw them. Whatever she had been expecting, the postmistress's "great white elephant of a house" in an advanced state of decay, it surely wasn't this. She couldn't remain in the vehicle. She threw open the door and jumped out onto the lush green verge, holding a hand to her sunstruck eyes.

He joined her, staring down at her as though faintly perplexed. "Not what you expected?"

Her tone was soft, almost reverent. "Wow, oh, wow! To be honest I'm a bit in shock."

"Why exactly?" He sounded as though he really wanted to know.

She almost told him why. It was on the tip of her tongue. The moment when she would confide her adoptive mother was Stella Radclyffe that was. Only caution, grounded in childhood, took over. She didn't know it then but her secret history was in the making.

"Well, it's some house, so *grand*. Georgian, I think. The symmetry, the balance, the adherence to classical rules. Chimneys rising to either side of the gabled roof." One-storey wings had been built to the left and right of the imposing central building most probably at a much later date.

"Correct," he said briefly, his eyes glittering. "The hall was built in the late fifteen hundreds by Thomas Willoughby-Radclyffe of Cotswold stone. It's stood for over four hundred years but for a long time now it's been in great need of repair. The house and the estate—it's been reduced to around three hundred acres with tenant cottages—belong to Lord

Wyndham. He hasn't enjoyed good health for some time now. In fact he's quite frail."

Four hundred years?

Shock wasn't too strong a word. Why had it been so important to Stella to cover up her past? "Do you know Lord Wyndham?" she turned to ask, her eyes on his profile. Oddly enough she was getting used to that aquiline beak.

"I'm working on a large project there at the moment," he said by way of a response. An evasion if ever there was one. "The restoration of the hall's once famous gardens, particularly the rose gardens. It had become something of a wilderness, quite a challenge, but Lord Wyndham hired a world-famous landscape designer, David Courtland."

She was fortunate she had grown up with a passionate gardening team, Stella and Arnold, who had passed on their passion to her. "I've heard of him." She nodded. "I'm assuming you're the gardener?"

"You could say that."

"A pretty posh one, if you don't mind my saying so." Her amazing lime-green eyes flashed mockery.

"Don't mind in the least. If you're very good between here and the hall I'll let you see over the garden. It has a number of 'rooms' but Dave has begun a new project. He's in London for a couple of days."

"Leaving you in charge? Call him Dave, do you?" she asked provocatively.

"The first strike against you," he clipped off.

"Ah, come on."

"Get back in the car."

"Certainly, m'lord."

And so it began. The great star-crossed love affair of her life.

CHAPTER THREE

The present.

HUGH SAUNDERS stood up to perform the introductions, a delighted smile on his lean, tanned face. Each member of the team and their specific function was acknowledged. Handshakes all round. Murphy Stiller's habitual glare was replaced by a sunburst. When it came to Cate's turn she actually considered fleeing the room, like a woman teetering on the brink of a major crack-up. For all the little niggles of nameless anxiety the last thing her mind had focused on was this momentous blast from the past. Would he now confound her and say, "But I know you, surely? It's Catrina Hamilton, isn't it?" all the while pinning her with his blazing blue eyes?

He did no such thing. Not a muscle on his striking face moved. He calmly took her hand. God, was she bound to him for ever? Even that brief, cool contact evoked such grief, such remembered pain she almost moaned. This time it seemed he had no mind to be cruel. All that came was the usual rhetorical "how do you do?" requiring no answer. Somehow she was able to resume her seat. She had to cast out her devils. And fast. At least her blood was coursing around her body again. A few fraught moments, then she was able to regain enough composure to not put her job in jeopardy.

As CEO, Hugh Saunders dealt with matters mostly but

when he turned for her input she was able to contribute from a wealth of research. Her brain was on autopilot. Not for the first time in her career but never when she was in such a high emotional state.

"Absolutely right, Cate." Hugh spoke with approval. Always rely on Cate to give clear concise answers, he thought. Nothing routine. Outside the box. She was one classy young woman, with high-grade diplomacy skills. He admired her capacities and shrewd gut instincts. Gut instincts he considered important. They provided an edge. Even more importantly, never once in his experience had she attempted to capitalise on her beauty.

For some reason Murphy Stiller had suffered a collapse of her usual supreme confidence so Cate was invited to speak out more often. It might have been a triumph despite Murphy's periodic grunts. Murphy was looking a bit as if she wanted to kill someone, preferably Cate. Cate for her part was falling back heavily on experience. Wyndham's questions when they came were brusque, very explicit. It was obvious to everyone seated around the table he was well acquainted with big business, Money Business. They all knew it was conducted in a certain way, bland enough on the surface, underneath extremely tough. He wasn't relying on his advisors. He was managing his own negotiations. While the team was taking the fifth Baron Wyndham's measure he was taking theirs. In the course of the meeting it was revealed he had substantial investments in the mining sector of Chile and Canada. Although the vast State of Western Australia was the usual target for their investors, Cate suggested Queensland as an excellent alternative. Mining drove the Queensland economy just as it did W.A. The traditional bases of wealth created over several generations were being overtaken by mining magnates, some of them surprisingly young. These men were fast rising to the top of the Rich List, rubbing shoulders with the multibillionaires.

Eventually the meeting broke up. Discussions had been intense. A follow-up meeting was scheduled for midweek.

Cate was still concerned he was going to expose her. As what, for God's sake? No one on the planet outside Stella knew Lord Wyndham was the father of her child. Not a single soul since dear Arnold had passed away after two very painful years of battling lung cancer. Her adoptive father always had smoked too much.

Hugh's up mood was infectious. They were moving out of the boardroom, when he suddenly brought up Wyndham's other interest. Buying land on some beautiful Whitsunday island.

"Just a moment, Cate." For some reason Cate was moving away too fast.

"Yes, sir." She turned back.

"Cate here might very well have the answer to your Barrier Reef island retreat," he told Wyndham.

"No." Wyndham responded suavely.

"Cate works hard at everything she does," said Hugh. "She has managed to build a very good relationship with a lady, Lady McCready actually, now in her mid-eighties, who owns a small but fabulous Whitsunday island called Isla Bella."

"After one of Italy's great gardens perhaps or simply a beautiful island?" he asked without looking at Cate.

"Lady McCready did confide she and her husband named their island after a trip to Italy," Cate said. "They loved Italy and the wonderful gardens."

Now he looked down his blade of a nose at her. "The island is for sale?"

"Could be. Could be," Hugh broke in, somewhat puzzled

by a certain tension in the atmosphere. He had an instinct for such things.

"You have doubts, Ms Hamilton?" Wyndham asked, his tone faintly brittle.

"Up to a point, yes. Lady McCready is very much against exploitation of her island. No boutique hotels for the rich and their…friends. Certainly no tourist destination. The island has been her home since the death of her husband. She would never be budged on an investment."

Before Hugh could intervene Wyndham pre-empted him. "Let me make it quite clear, Ms Hamilton. It's a private home I wish to build. A tropical retreat for me and my family. Hopefully a few friends will be allowed. I'm a very busy man. Occasionally I like getting away from it all. This is the first trip I've been able to make to Australia. I very much like what I see. The Great Barrier Reef is one of the great wonders of the world. I intend to see it while I'm here."

"Wonderful!" Hugh said, giving Cate the beginnings of a sharpish look. "If you are seriously interested, perhaps Cate could contact Lady McCready. She trusts Cate, you see."

For a fleeting instant Wyndham looked as though he wouldn't trust her for a minute. "Perhaps we could discuss it over dinner this evening," he suggested, as though formalising the matter, making it a business call.

"Cate?" Hugh prompted, his grey gaze turning faintly steely.

Hugh was as near to perturbed as she had seen him. Her behaviour, she knew, wasn't being consistent. She always did what was expected. The intelligent, indeed the only, thing to do.

Her training took over. "Certainly, Lord Wyndham," she said, demonstrating her loyalty to the firm. "That would be lovely. I could in the meantime see if I can contact Lady McCready."

"With that happy thought in mind," he said smoothly, "perhaps you can recommend a restaurant. You know Sydney. I don't."

"C'est Bon!" Cate and Hugh said together.

"I could pick you up at your hotel," Cate said, trying hard to be charming for Hugh's sake. "Shall we say eight o'clock?"

"Are you sure I couldn't pick you up at your home?" Wyndham asked, a glitter in his sapphire eyes. "A limo has been put at my disposal."

"It's quite a drive," said Cate quite untruthfully. "Really, Lord Wyndham, it suits me perfectly to pick you up. No trouble at all."

"Well, that's settled!" Hugh made the emphatic announcement while wondering at the same time what was going on. The fact Cate and Lord Wyndham were antagonistic hadn't been lost on him. It wasn't as though Wyndham didn't approve of career women. He had caught the gleam of respect in his razor-sharp glance as Cate demonstrated her expertise. Perhaps they would settle down over dinner. He sincerely hoped so. This was a big deal for Inter-Austral. Wyndham was prepared to invest a heap of money. Obviously the man was massively rich. Cate was right: Queensland was emerging as *the* hot spot. The state had huge potential expanding on the back of the resources sector. Australia for that matter had one of the highest concentrations of wealth in the world: one super-rich individual per eight thousand or so as opposed to around thirty-seven thousand globally. Lord Wyndham had come to the right place.

Stella, an exceedingly observant woman, saw the upset in Cate's face the moment she walked through the door. It was as still as a marble carving. "Cate, what's up? Are you going to tell me?" Stella, whose whole background had been a gigantic puzzle, perversely demanded she know everything in Cate's life. It had taken Cate many long years to realise Stella in her own quiet way was very controlling.

Cate put her expensive leather handbag down on the marble-topped console in the entrance hall, wondering how best to break the momentous news.

Stella took her silence for refusal and began to walk away, obviously offended.

Cate followed Stella, taking hold of her arm. "Where's Jules?" she asked urgently.

Stella turned to stare at her. "Why, he's in his bedroom playing the video game you bought him. He's done his homework. Never have to tell him. He really is a remarkable child."

"Come into the living room." Cate kept her voice significantly lower. It was their favourite room, furnished with a mix of Asian and Western antiques. Three plush white leather sofas faced the magnificent view across the sparkling blue satin water to the Harbour Bridge and the Opera House. The wide covered deck to the rear was the only major structural change they had made. It had been worth every penny.

"So what is it, then?" Stella set a silk cushion aside as she continued to study the face of her adopted daughter. Both of them had kept Annabel's secret and agreed they would continue to. Cate, however, had stopped calling Stella Mum. Whether she was aware of it or not she had never really thought of Stella as her mum. Jules called Stella Nan. Maybe it wasn't going to stay that way, Cate thought with a funny little stab of premonition.

"Something extraordinary happened today," she announced, collapsing beside Stella. "I have trouble even getting it out."

"You might try," Stella said, a formless anxiety starting to spread through her. "You've lost your job?" She squeezed her eyes shut. Cate lived such a high-powered life. She handled incredible sums of money. Could something have gone wrong? Big mistakes happened.

"That might have been easier." Cate impatiently kicked off her high-heeled shoes. "I can't put off telling you—"

"But you *are*, dear," Stella stressed somewhat impatiently.

Cate had seen that coming. "All right! You have to know. Of all the men in the world—you're not going to believe this, so steel yourself—Julian Carlisle, the present Baron Wyndham, walked into the boardroom this very morning."

Stella threw up her arms as though she were going to dive into water. "For God's sake!" Now she bent over as if in pain, winding her arms tight around her body like some form of shield.

"Exactly," Cate seconded grimly. Since the revelation that Annabel was her mother, not Stella, Stella's penchant for secrecy loomed large in Cate's mind.

"Has he come in search of you?" Stella asked, as though sensing big trouble ahead. "Has he come in search of Jules?"

"How could he? He knows nothing about Jules." Cate was sorry for the way the colour had faded out of Stella's face. In her early fifties, Stella was still a fine-looking woman. She had kept her slim figure; her thick dark hair was stylishly cut. She had excellent skin and lovely dark eyes. There was no physical resemblance between aunt and niece. For that matter, Cate didn't even resemble her biological mother, Annabel. Annabel never had confessed who Cate's father was, but he had to have been blond with light eyes. "He doesn't know Jules exists," Cate said so harshly, she might have been willing it to remain so. "I'm certain he hasn't found out anything in all these years. He had his own life then. He has it now. I've been no part of it. Probably a vaguely unpleasant memory."

"You hardly came from the wrong side of the tracks,"

Stella burst out indignantly. "I never did understand why you didn't tell him about us."

"My God, Stella, that's good coming from you." Cate couldn't help ramming that point home. "How would I have known about *us* when you told me nothing? It was as if it was none of my business."

Stella flushed. The truth was hard to take. "I was trying to protect you."

"Protecting your little sister was your main priority," Cate responded bluntly.

"I loved her." Stella spoke as though Cate was lacking in sensitivity for not understanding. "I looked after her all my life. My mother certainly wasn't interested in us. Neither was my father." Stella's calm face was suddenly bitter. "They mourned the loss of our brother instead." Stella's mind was racing ahead, envisaging a monumental disturbance to her world. "Is Wyndham a potential client?" she asked with faint hope.

Cate nodded, sure a reckoning was in the air. "Apparently he's got truckloads of money. He wants to invest in our mineral resources. Hugh was over the moon."

"I bet," Stella said acidly, struggling to take it all in. "He recognised you, of course." In maturity Cate was even more beautiful than she had been as a ravishingly pretty teenager.

"Of course." Cate reached out to pat Stella's hand. "You know how Hugh likes to put me forward?"

"I've told you before, Cate, the man is in love with you," Stella said with distinct disapproval. Why, Hugh Saunders was even older than she was.

Cate pulled a wry face. "Be that as it may, I have no such interest in Hugh. I'm sure he's got the message."

"They never get the message," said Stella flatly. "Anyway, go on."

"Apparently Lord Wyndham, that relative of yours—"

"And *yours*—" Stella drew her attention to the fact.

"I refuse to acknowledge that," said Cate. "Anyway, he wants to buy or build a tropical hideaway in North Queensland, specifically the Whitsundays. Hugh immediately seized on Lady McCready's retreat, Isla Bella."

"But surely she doesn't want to sell?" Stella asked. "I remember you told me how adamant she was when Keith Munro, the developer, wanted to buy it. She's probably deeded it to a relative. She's a good age."

"Eighty-five. I spoke to her this afternoon." Cate's voice, another of her assets, turned low and ironic. "She's prepared to meet Lord Wyndham."

"Oh, capital!" Stella cried, throwing up her hands. "The *Lord* Wyndham did it, I suppose?"

"Sure helped. After all, your father was the fourth Baron Wyndham, was he not? One would have thought he was a criminal, you kept it so quiet. The thing is Lady McCready doesn't have the right sort of relative to leave Isla Bella to. She believes any one of them would sell it on the spot. So I guess the right buyer thinking of a private retreat might appeal. I'm sure he means what he says. Bring the wife and kids, and some close friends."

"He married her, then?" Both Cate and Stella had fully expected it. "What was her name again?'

"Marina," Cate supplied briefly. She had never felt any bitterness towards Marina. Marina wasn't to blame for anything. Her bitterness was reserved for Ashe and his dreadful snob of a mother who had given Lady Marina the thumbs up.

"So you're expected to arrange a deal?" Stella asked. Hugh Saunders had told her once Cate was going to go to "the very top"!

"That's what Hugh wants," Cate replied. "It would mean a trip to the island. It would mean a day or so in the company of the man who betrayed me."

"See you don't let it happen twice," Stella warned, sharply. "I'd go mental if you did. You've never got over him."

It was a flat-out accusation. "Maybe not," Cate said, wincing at the harshness of Stella's attack, "but I'm over the torment. I'm my own woman. And I have you and my beautiful boy. He mustn't see Jules." Cate heard the fear in her own voice.

"All you have to do is keep calm," Stella urged, though she too had gone white.

"Not that Jules resembles him—"

"Except for the eyes," Stella was swift to point out. "I went to school with a relative of his, Penelope Stewart, as I'm sure I've told you."

"God, that's a breakthrough!" Cate only half joked. "I'm equally sure you haven't. I would have remembered. I have a photographic memory, you might recall. You've always carried your past in your *head*, Stella. Locked it up and threw away the key."

"I'm sure I told you." Stella decided to hold firm, when she knew perfectly well she hadn't. Her past life was deeply private, even from Cate. Let the secret life be the secret life was her motto. "Penelope's brother, Rafe, was another one madly in love with Annabel." She dropped an involuntary snippet, her tone suggesting that was a very bad thing.

"Really?" Cate was taken aback. "Another thing you've never mentioned before. Tell me, Stella, is this a kind of paranoia you have, this difficulty with speaking about the past?"

"Maybe it is." Stella wasn't about to talk it over. "But the past is past. It's no longer important." She shrugged off what could well have been of grave importance.

"Now that's where you've got it all wrong," Cate murmured sadly. "The past is never past. It follows us around like our shadow. We can't hit the delete button and *whoosh* it's gone."

"May I contradict you there?" Stella said with an odd expression.

"I was expecting you to. But my view is, we're never free of the past, Stella. Especially when much of it is desperate to get through."

Stella gave an ironic smile. "You're referring to Annabel."

Cate nodded. "Annabel, my mother. She certainly got around." Cate sounded both sad and deeply disillusioned. "One wonders who my father was…*is*? He could still be alive and well."

Stella said nothing. She was a little tired of Cate's truth seeking. She pressed her two hands together. Jules' beautiful blue eyes always came as a jolt. So did Cate's golden colouring and green eyes. The past was where so many bad things happened. No wonder she had shut it down.

Cate shook off a prickling sensation at her nape. She continued to stare at her aunt. Of the two of them Stella appeared to be more devastated by the news Julian Carlisle was in town, almost on their doorstep as it were. How come? "*Could* it have been this Rafe?" she abruptly asked, feeling an element of shock.

Stella bit hard on her bottom lip, then surprisingly gave a sour laugh. "I have no idea, Cate. Truly. Annabel never breathed a word. I asked her and asked her. All she ever said was, *Please don't, Stell.* After a while I gave up. She never told me even on the day she died."

Many things were starting to occur to Cate. Unanswered questions asserting themselves strongly. "Maybe she didn't *know*?" Her laugh had a tremor in it.

"She never wanted to hurt you, Catrina," Stella said, as though Cate really should get her act together.

"But she hurt *you*. She must have been incredibly selfish, self-centred. She fooled you, about a lot of things. She not only fooled you she practically forced you and Arnold to emigrate. You gave up the life you had known. You sacrificed yourself for your promiscuous little sister."

Stella appeared in no rush to refute it. "It was no great sacrifice," she said. The only trouble was it came out unexpectedly virtuous. "I never thought my parents would say, *Please don't go, Stella,* though they gave me a huge wedding. Expected, you know. But look, Cate, you more than made up for it. Arnold and I took you to our hearts on sight. I was never able to bear a child. I don't think it was my fault, rather poor old Arnold's. But we were happy."

"Were you?" Cate flicked her aunt a sceptical glance.

"Well, not *exactly* happy, but good enough. We left our burdens behind. We loved this country, the freedom and the climate. Most of all we had *you*. Have you any idea what a joy that was? You are my own blood, Cate."

"Well, you jolly well could have told me," Cate said, thinking the hurt would never go away.

Stella had long since formed the habit of shrugging off her sins of omission. "So you're always going to blame me?" she asked, as though questioning Cate's capacity for forgiveness.

Cate shook her head when she wasn't at all sure. "I love you, Stell. Let's not talk blame. Things happen in life. But for now, we both know it's not safe for Wyndham to catch sight of Jules."

"God, no!" Stella shuddered.

"It's possible he'll spot a resemblance."

"Bound to," Stella said, as if that would be the horror of horrors. "Are you thinking what I'm thinking? He could acknowledge him?" Stella's slim body tensed up at the thought. She loved Jules. He could have been her own grandchild.

"How do I know?" Cate exclaimed. "Times have changed. Fathers, even of high social standing, are acknowledging children they never knew they had all the time," she said sharply. "For all I know he might have a couple of daughters. We now know the firstborn to British royalty male or female can inherit the throne. Which I think is as it should be. I don't know about entailed inheritances that always went to the male. There's even a possibility Wyndham and his Marina split up. I could've found out if I'd wanted to."

"But you've never wanted to," Stella said. "And I had my own grief, of course." Grief she had openly expressed. "Only Annabel attended my father's funeral. I was told to keep away. *Don't come. Please don't come, Stell. It's not as though he will know, but questions will be asked.* She pleaded and pleaded with me, my self-centred little sister. She was absolutely terrified. As usual I gave in, coming once more to Annabel's rescue. It wasn't as though I didn't have more pressing concerns. You'd returned home from England sunk in despair, however hard you'd sought to hide it. It hadn't taken all that much longer to be faced with the reason. You were pregnant. Then of course it all came out."

Julian bloody Carlisle! The Radclyffes, the Carlisles and Others.

Cate's voice snapped Stella back to the present.

"I had to turn my back on what had happened to me," Cate was saying. "It was the only way to survive."

Stella's reaction was on the instant. "You had *me*. There's no reason for Carlisle to come near the house?"

"This is going to further amaze you." Cate gave a hollow laugh. "We're having dinner tonight."

Stella tapped her forehead so hard she could have cracked it open. *"Wh-a-a-t?"* Nothing would ever be the same again. She was sure of it. "Is it the anniversary of your split?" she asked, a real bite in her voice. She was terribly perturbed about Julian Carlisle's re-entry into Cate's life. Cate had had to work super hard to take up her life. They had built a life together. They had Jules. They didn't need anyone else. It would be terrible if Cate thought differently. Cate was, after all, a beautiful young woman living without a man. Cate could rebel. That fact wasn't lost on Stella.

Cate rose to her feet, her golden hair and her luminous skin drawing in all the light. "I'm okay, Stella," she said, bending down to kiss Stella's cheek. "Don't worry. Hugh more or less forced this one on me. He doesn't want to lose Wyndham. Dinner is in the nature of a business call. He wanted to pick me up but I assured him it would be easier for me to pick him up at his hotel. I don't want him anywhere near the house."

"Dear, oh, dear!" Stella looked at her in extreme agitation. Her hands were starting to shake. "Hang on a second, would Hugh Saunders have mentioned at any stage you have a son?"

"I don't think he'd want to get tangled up with all that," Cate said, with a sudden frown. "I have to go, Stell. I need to see Jules, then I have to shower and dress."

"Wait, wait, wait," Stella implored, jumping up. "Someone is bound to tell him. That dreadful Murphy Stiller perhaps? You're a single mother and all that." She knew Cate withheld a great deal of information about herself. A well established family trait.

Cate's green eyes were glittering like gems. "If need be I can come up with a convincing story. Anyway, it's none of his business."

"That's where you're wrong, Cate," Stella said, her fine features drawn tight. "You'll see if he ever finds out."

It was a possibility neither of them could afford to ignore.

In the end she chose a dinner staple, the little black dress she felt confident in. She enlivened it with the right jewellery. She wasn't out to make any statement. This wasn't a dinner date. This was business, albeit agonising. He had always loved her hair long and loose so she pulled the mass of it back from her face, arranging it in a modern update of the classic chignon. Her only concession was her satin heels. She had to have her heels. Anyway, he was so tall. Gave him a natural advantage.

"You look beautiful, Mummy," Jules pronounced when she went downstairs for inspection. "How come this man isn't picking *you* up?" His mother's male friends always picked her up at the house, not the other way around.

"Easier this way, darling." She put her hand on his squared little shoulder. No sloping there. "Bedtime nine o'clock. What are you going to do?"

"Watch a video with Nan. *Happy Feet*." Jules looked up at Stella. They were great friends. "This man, he's a lord?" Jules asked with interest. "I bet he's a big snob?"

"Only on his mother's and father's side," Cate replied, ruffling his thick hair.

Both Jules and Stella laughed.

"I'll walk you to the car," Jules said, taking Cate's hand. Cate had left the BMW out on the driveway lined on one side by beautiful flowering hydrangeas.

"Thank you, darling."

"I'll wait up for you," Stella whispered urgently when they reached the front door.

"No need."

"I won't get a wink of sleep if I don't." Stella was in no mood to take no for an answer.

In the car their bodies were very tense. The whole situation felt indescribably dangerous. He didn't say a word other than murmur a taut, "Good evening." She nodded a silent reply. Things went very quiet after that. It all spelled out a kind of fraught hostility. Surely that was entirely reasonable for her, the abandoned one? What on earth was his problem? She was angered by the sheer irrationality, the injustice of it all. She drove on without speaking.

It had to be her day for finding parking. There was just one spot left in the restaurant's private car park beside a very impressive Maserati. She knew who owned it, a very flashy playboy who had taken an awfully long time to take a firm no for an answer.

Inside the elegant dining room with its floor-to-ceiling windows, all was soft opulence, under gleaming down lights. Tonight's palette was palest gold. Floor-skimming gold tablecloths covered the circular tables, with matching steepled napkins. Gold-rimmed wine glasses. A glass vial held a perfect single yellow rose. The comfortable chairs surrounding the tables were upholstered in an aubergine silk velvet that blended in with any number of the colour changes that occurred with the settings. Cate had been to the restaurant countless times before. She was well known to the staff and maître d'.

"*Buona sera*, Ms Hamilton, how lovely to see you."

"Buona sera, Carlo."

Such a lovely smile. A man would do anything to be the recipient of such a smile. A seasoned giver of compliments, the Italian maître d' meant what he said. He wasn't surprised to see Ms Hamilton with an extremely handsome male escort. Unknown to him, which was unusual. He thought he knew just about everyone in society. But such a beautiful woman would naturally be accompanied by a man of distinction. This one he totally approved of. He had a veritable *stile di un principe*. The way he held himself! He stood a full head over Ms Hamilton, who was wearing stunning stilettos. They were an eye-riveting pair: the young woman so blonde, the man, so tall, with a fine head of hair gleaming like jet but with extraordinary blue eyes. Almost the electric blue of the male peacock's plumage, the maître d' thought fancifully. At any rate they looked so arresting they turned heads.

* * *

A bottle of white wine was settled on. No thought of champagne. No lively conversation. This wasn't a celebration. No romantic little interlude. The handsome young Italian waiter in his cropped white jacket sped away.

"So?"

"I do not want to talk about the past, Julian," she said, sounding ultra-controlled. This wasn't the incredibly exciting, incredibly passionate Ashe she had known. Even the beautiful, maddeningly upper-class English voice had hardened into tempered steel. Shades of his dear mother. Even men could turn into their mothers.

"Of course you don't," he conceded. "They tell me you have a child, a boy."

She swallowed down the flare of panic. Surely Hugh hadn't told him that? "Yes I do," she said. Her voice sounded perfectly normal.

"But no husband?"

"I'm fascinated you're interested. What about you? Wife, children, an heir to the title, *noblesse oblige* and all that?"

"My life is *my* business, Catrina." He looked straight at her.

"And so is mine," she said sharply, drawing back a little. "Shall we leave it at that?"

"How old is your boy?" His intense gaze pinned her in place. It didn't make him happy to see she had grown even more beautiful over the years, confident, polished, beautifully dressed, understated, perfect. A very assured woman.

Cate drew breath. There was no option but to lie. "Five," she said, holding his gaze, but a rose glow had entered her cheeks. "He's the love of my life."

"What about the father?" He continued to study her, this enigma that was the girl he had fallen crazily in love with. Love made such fools of people. The great and the good. It ruined careers, damaged lives, sometimes irrevocably. He hadn't really known that girl. Nor the woman. "What was he?" he asked. "Live-in lover?"

She didn't answer.

"Live out, then? With your boy. You had to consider him?"

"Hard to say what he was really." She shrugged a nonchalant shoulder. "He didn't pass the test at any rate. Look, the waiter is returning with the wine." Her gaze shifted over his shoulder.

"That sounds like the truth." He gave a brief laugh. "It's mythology in a way. Suitors being required to pass a series of tests. I've never figured out which one I failed," he said, openly contemptuous. "She's gone, she's gone, she's gone, she's gone!" He crooned it, low voiced, like a melancholy love song.

Her physical reactions were involuntary, unstoppable. Dopamine, she thought. The brain's motivational chemical. The sight and sound of him gave her enormous pleasure, an erotic rush. She wasn't entirely responsible. The man was devastating. Devastatingly handsome, devastatingly charismatic, devastatingly rich and important. Devastation all round. She knew now she had never been healed. What she had to do was push her memories further and further behind her. "Can we drop this?" She looked the picture of perfect confidence, but she was churning inside.

Cool it! her inner voice warned her.

God, she was trying to but she was using up every scrap of control.

"I don't like talking about it either." He was perilously close to bluntness, but at just the right moment he had to turn in his chair to acknowledge the waiter, who made a little business of showing the excellent Australian Riesling. It rated high on a world list. A little was poured for sampling. Cate was never sure if the ritual was absolutely necessary.

Consequently she took no notice. It was a relief to study

the menu, although stress had robbed her of all appetite. Same old lethal sexual attraction; same old primitive physical responses. Could *nothing* kill them? If she knew nothing could—as in outside anyone's control—she might feel a little better about herself.

But her brain decided to kick in. *You're pathetic.* She sought to whip up a degree of self-disgust. One would have thought betrayal would have been a huge incentive. Betrayal killed every time. Only it was impossible for them to be strangers. He was the father of her child. Their lives were mired. Cate turned her face away, acknowledging a female acquaintance who was staring over with avid interest. Dinner dates were a very public matter in city society. No hand-holding with this one. No melting glances across the table.

What, then? Let the curious figure it out.

One course after the other arrived, each looking like a work of art. The Japanese chef was a celebrity. The lobster was superb. It settled her stomach slightly. But it was impossible to relax. She had a life. Her son had anchored her to the earth. She had to shield herself and her little son from all harm. Julian couldn't know about him.

"But, darling girl, why call him Julian?"

It was Stella smoothing the damp hair away from her tear-stained, exhausted face.

"I don't know," she had wailed.

Eventually Stella stopped asking.

But Julian Arnold Hamilton it was.

Coffee. Both declined a liqueur. It was then she finally asked, "Who told you about me?" There was more than a hint of aggression in her voice.

"About you?" he asked, settling his coffee cup onto the saucer. His thick black eyelashes were pointing down towards his prominent cheekbones. Jules had inherited those eyes and lashes. Abruptly he glanced up.

"Please," she said, fighting the urge to get up and run away.

"A devoted colleague." His reply was sardonic. "That Stiller woman. I gather you and she are rivals in the workplace?"

She could barely speak. "The rivalry is all on Murphy's side."

He spread his elegant hands. "Okay. I knew that. I'm not stupid. She's not only jealous of your abilities. She's jealous of your relationship with Saunders."

She was taken aback. "Hugh is my boss," she said icily.

"Fine. But he wants you, you know."

That was a truth she didn't want to know. "Then he's got a big problem," she said, coolly. "Apart from being my boss, he's old enough to be my father. And a married man. Murphy has a sick way with her. When did you see her, anyway?"

His blue eyes glinted. "For a few moments after you took off. Apparently she thought I would find the fact you're a single mother interesting."

"God alone knows why she thought that," she said, shocked by Murphy's enmity towards her. Thank God Murphy had never laid eyes on Jules. None of them had.

"Perhaps she's one of those people who can spot sparks between two people?" he suggested, very smoothly. "Sometimes there's no way of hiding our sparks. And our sorrows. That's of course if one can *feel* sorrow. Can you, Catrina?"

Some note in his voice sent a shiver down her spine. "It's hard for you to accept, isn't it, that I walked away from you?"

"You did better than that." His retort was crisp. "You *flew*. There one moment. Gone the next."

For a moment she forgot where she was. "What else could

I do after that little chat with your mum?" she asked fiercely, instantly regretting her loss of control.

His black brows came together. "What little chat?" His tone bit.

"Nothing to do with *you*," she lied and waved a nonchalant hand.

"I'd like to know."

"Nothing *to* know," she clipped off. "If you're ready, I would like to leave. This was a business dinner, after all. I've told you Lady McCready is happy to meet with you. I need to accompany you but we can handle that. You can take it from there. We're both adults. There's no need whatsoever for her to know we've met before."

"Meet? Is that what we did?" His voice had taken on a decided edge. "You obviously have no trouble burying memories."

"You had no difficulty coming out of it, either," she said. "Lady McCready will be sure to ask you something about yourself and your family. I didn't ask after your mother. How is she?"

His eyes turned as cold as an iceberg. "You're actually interested?"

"Only possibly."

"She was bitterly disappointed in you."

"Blimey!" she said facetiously, gathering up her satin and brass-studded evening clutch. "That's mothers for you. Shall we go?" But there was fear in her. And a sudden confusion. But that was just Alicia protecting herself. Alicia had always had her own agenda.

"Certainly." He put up a hand signalling their waiter, who hurried over.

"I'll pay for this," Cate said, her credit card already in hand. This was business. She could claim.

"You *will* pay, Catrina, but not for dinner," he said. His bluer than blue eyes held her to him.

Captive.

For a moment she damn near crumpled.

Stella was waiting up just as she had promised. Stella was a woman who would go to any lengths to protect her little family. Cate. Jules. Herself. She was a protective person and she had proved it. Hadn't she gone to extraordinary lengths to protect her little sister? She had devoted her life to the interests of others, Annabel, then Cate. Like mother, like daughter, both fallen pregnant though she had avoided sitting in judgment. And there was darling little Jules. Occasionally all her self-sacrifice, her stress on the importance of family, had put easy-going Arnold's nose right out of joint.

I took on this job, Arnold.

Now you're stuck with it. I'm stuck with it. We're stuck with it. Or are you really, Stella?

Always those searching looks from Arnold as if he sought to put a huge dent in her armour but couldn't quite bring it off.

"Give it to me straight." Stella took Cate's arm, leading her into the living room where down lights cast a golden glow. Through the sliding glass doors onto the balcony across the multicoloured sequinned waters Sydney's great landmarks, the Bridge and the Opera House, lit up the night.

"I think I'll have a drink first," Cate said, going in search of one.

"What?"

"I need a drink. Trust me." Cate headed to the kitchen, Stella following, a pleat of concern etched into her forehead. She was wearing a luxurious nightgown with a matching robe, which she pulled tight in a fit of nerves. "Join me?" Cate held up a bottle of cognac.

"I have a feeling I might need to," Stella returned crisply.

"Besides, it will make you sleep better." Cate poured a shot into two crystal balloons. They went back into the living room and settled into two armchairs. Only then did Cate begin to relate economically the events of the evening while Stella sat with folded hands…

"What did that Murphy Stiller think she was gaining telling him you had a son?' Stella rolled out her anger. On the odd occasion Stella was seriously formidable.

"Unsure. Murphy has her own agenda. He did ask how old my son was. Of course I lied. Had to. I said he was five." Cate ran her tongue around her lips, tasting fine brandy.

"And he never said a thing about his own family? I would have thought he would. Are you keeping something from me?"

"Nary a word." Cate shook her blonde head while thinking, *You certainly did.* "His father was always a no-go area with the whole family."

"I can understand that. Much too painful." Geoffrey Carlisle, recruited from Oxford into the British Security Service—MI5 or MI6, no one seemed to know—had been killed by a militant's bullet in the Middle East where he was touring. That was years back. He was a highly intelligent man and a polyglot; the Middle East had been his speciality area. Had he lived it was he who would have inherited the title Baron Wyndham, not his son.

"He told me his life is his business," Cate said. "Our meeting was business, not a rehash of old times. I did, however, ask after his mother."

Stella's expression froze. "Was that wise?"

"Confound them all," said Cate, polishing off her drink. "Don't worry, Stell. I can handle this."

"Surely there's someone else who can go with him, introduce him to Lady McCready?" Stella felt a great surge of anxiety. She wondered if her niece had the strength to resist the man who had ripped her heart out. It didn't feel that way.

Cate gave a crooked smile. "I could suggest Murphy. She took to him at first sight. Turned into a positive sunbeam. Ask anyone." She laughed, then abruptly sobered. "No, Stell, I have to do it. Hugh expects it. Show commitment. Integral part of the team and all that. I just have to get it over with. He'll buy his island retreat. He'll invest in our mineral wealth, then he'll go home. Back to what's important to him." Her eyes frosted over. "I could of course lead him on. What do you think?" Her laugh held black humour. "The physical attraction is still there. Can't kill it. Fact of life. I don't think I'd have all that much trouble coaxing him into the palm of my hand," she said with contempt. "Just think of it!" she crowed.

"I don't *want* to think of it," Stella said, her jaw clenched. "Now is not the time to play with fire. Sacrifice everything we've built up."

Cate waved her brandy balloon in the air, not really hearing. Stella sometimes did set the calm image aside. "I could tell him to get lost. Reverse process if you like. Put *him* on the rack."

"Don't even think of going there," Stella warned, unable to control a shudder. Cate had never been cured of Julian Carlisle. That was at the heart of it all. Cate was only in remission. Stella felt a savage anger.

CHAPTER FOUR

LADY MCCREADY HAD readied herself for their visit. She had made it her business to go around the island in her cute little go-cart, driven by her faithful Davey, who managed just about everything for her. His wife, Mary, did the cooking and the housework. She was well looked after and she looked after her staff, her friends, really.

It was a glorious day, the sky a cloudless azure blue. Bluer yet the sparkling sea. The green lawns were mown to perfection, fringed with alternate borders of agapanthus in blue and white. There were sculptural beds of strelitzias and agaves, numerous types of hibiscus, marvellous tree ferns, pandanus and of course the soaring palms, their fronds swaying gently in the breeze. As they swept past, the scent of ginger blossom and gardenia spiked the air. Davey was a zealous and talented gardener. He had turned the island retreat into a botanical garden with his imaginative mix of exotic and endemic plants.

Lady McCready brushed a snowy strand of hair off her high forehead. "Such a lovely cooling breeze, Davey."

"That it is. I'm looking forward to meeting your guest, a lord and all. Miss Hamilton, of course, I've met. She's a special young lady."

"She is that." Lady McCready had taken an instant liking to Catrina. Not only was she a lovely-looking young woman, but she was kind with a quick intuition. "I know Catrina will have our best interests at heart. You and Mary are very dear to me, Davey. You've always made us proud." As ever Lady McCready included her beloved late husband as though he were still there. She fully intended telling Lord Wyndham part of any deal they might strike would include a clause stating Davey and Mary were to remain on the island for as long as they wished. Isla Bella had been home to them for over twenty years. They would make perfect caretakers. They loved the island as much as she did. She had provided for them in her will. Which was as it should be.

They had taken the morning flight from Sydney to Townsville, then twenty minutes later boarded the launch *Petrel* for the trip to the island. The only access was by boat or helicopter. Wyndham held her hand tightly while she moved rather perilously into the launch that was swinging away from the jetty on the high tide. Again contact was like being plugged into a million volts. She would have to avoid it. He was casually dressed, beige chinos, tan leather belt, short-sleeved, open-necked blue cotton shirt, a wide-brimmed cream straw hat, slouched on one side. Sunglasses in his breast pocket. He looked extremely handsome, perfectly at ease.

She had dressed casually as well. All virgin white. White cotton-denim jeans, white shirt, added a fancy snakeskin belt, leather and canvas bag over her shoulder, Gucci sunglasses on her nose, her long hair tied back with a silk scarf that matched the vibrant yellows and reds in her bag. Both wore sensible albeit stylish shoes.

"No need to be nervous," he mocked. "I wasn't going to let you fall."

"I don't believe you."

"Really?" His tone bit.

"Well, I have caught the odd flicker of hostility. God knows why."

"Catrina, you would have to be joking," he drawled.

She felt caught in the *thrust* of it all, translated the momentary sense of powerlessness into a brilliant smile. "The captain is looking our way."

"Probably wondering what's going on." He nodded to the captain, a good-looking bearded man some forty odd years, as spick and span as his boat. The owner nodded back.

They were under way, heading eastward to Isla Bella, a continental island some six nautical miles from the mainland. She peered down into the water. It had gone from aqua to turquoise, deepening into cobalt the further they moved away from the quay. It wasn't going to be a placid run. The trade wind was chasing them.

"Any sharks around?" he asked after a while.

"Why don't you chance it?" she suggested, almost cheerfully.

"I'd make sure I pulled you in." The look on his dark face was a bit scary.

"You're a prince," she remarked.

"Not I."

"No, you're a lord. I bet you revel in it?'

"Well, it can make one's passage through life a little easier," he admitted. "This is a very beautiful part of the world." He spoke in conversational style, maybe for the captain's benefit. "Of course the Great Barrier Reef is one of the world's natural wonders."

She played her part. She couldn't help but notice the owner of the launch *had* been fixing them with a speculative eye. "It's the great breakwater that protects hundreds of kilometres of our eastern seaboard and the continental islands. Isla Bella is a continental island, as I told you. It has a rather steeply sloping hill cutting down the middle. The house is on the leeward side—"

"Needless to say," he interjected smoothly.

She continued like a tour guide. "There are volcanic islands, coral islands, some with extensive fringing reefs, cays, hundreds of them. I hope you know about our cyclones," she said with a warning in her voice. "Most years they're spawned in the Coral Sea before they eventually cross the Queensland coast. We had horrific Yasi at the beginning of 2011. The largest and most powerful cyclone to hit Queensland in living memory. It wreaked havoc. There was a phenomenal amount of flooding. Thousands left homeless. The whole state was affected. Parts of Brisbane went under."

"It did make world news," he pointed out gently. "From what I've seen and heard you're well into the recovery process."

"True. The entire country got behind Queensland and the areas of Victoria that were flood affected. There was enormous community spirit."

"And Isla Bella?"

"Mercifully it was spared," she said, visualising the old TV flood coverage. "Although a couple of the tourist islands weren't. Lady McCready and her staff actually stayed on the island right through. I believe there's a cyclone-proof bunker."

"That's good to know," he said wryly.

"Not putting you off?" She ventured a sideways glance. She had tried *everything* to forget him. Now she was up to her neck in it again.

"Are you trying to?"

"Simply want you to understand. There are risks to be considered."

"Which I'm well acquainted with. Hurricanes affect the Bahamas as well as many other countries in the world. I could have sworn I told you all about Hurricane Noel in the late nineties when my family was there."

She shrugged. "Don't recall." Why admit to any memories at all? Hadn't Stella perfected it? "Still own property there, do you?"

"Yes, as a matter of fact. But I'm looking for a less accessible holiday retreat. I'm hoping Isla Bella is a good choice."

"How about a little more information? How many children do you have—three or four?"

"To your one?" he said, leaning on the rail and looking out over the deep blue sea mantled with silver pinpoints of light.

"Of course, you're not going to tell me."

"Why should I?" He glanced at her with eyes that luminous electric blue. "I would have thought you'd check up on me."

She had thought of it. Too many times. "Why ever would I do that?"

"Odd, I never checked up on you either," he said. "Of course I knew I was bound to sooner or later."

Prepare yourself.

"Meaning what?" she asked, clear challenge in her voice.

"Then I thought it would be a big mistake," he admitted. "Why would I ever want to hear of you again?"

She hid the tide of anger that swept through her. "Absolutely right. I, for one, am a totally different person these days."

"You were a totally different person *then*," he returned curtly. "At least from the person I thought you were."

"Dangerous to assume you know anyone," she retorted. "We don't even know ourselves. Everything changes, that's the thing."

"Well, I'm resigned to the fact I never knew you."

"Our goals in life weren't the same." She had to breathe in deeply. What would he do, what would he say, if she told him she was the mother of his child? React with rage, toss her overboard? She knew the fact that she had kept that momentous piece of news from him would bring a forceful response. For all she knew he didn't have a son.

The wind had picked up. It suddenly seized her silk scarf, wrenching it from her head. She made a wild grab for it. It was a lovely scarf. Hermes. He lunged for it too, executing some manoeuvre that had him rescuing the scarf while capturing her pivoting body in a powerful one-armed grip. They slammed into one another.

Heat scorched her body. It burnt holes in her character that felt as weak as her arms and her legs. Deep, dark emotions were swirling through her like dangerous debris. The tips of her breasts were against his chest, hard as berries with a physical response she couldn't control. What she felt was desire. Shame and guilt would follow. She thought she had wised up, grown up. Now it appeared she really hadn't.

She jerked away from him violently. She had loved him once. The man who had deceived her. "Thank you," she said, sounding more ferocious than grateful.

"No trouble." He kept watching her like a hawk.

The wind had picked up considerably, making a grab for her hair. The full length of it whipped free, a long column of blonde shining silk. "If I might venture a suggestion, leave it," he said.

For answer she put up her hands, scraping her hair back with her fingers. Long tendrils were escaping but she couldn't help that. Once more she tied the scarf, knotting it twice. "Well?" She found she couldn't bear him staring at her.

"Just for a moment you reminded me of a girl I once knew," he said, for a moment pitched back in time. "Hard to believe it was you."

"I was very young and incredibly foolish. Let's drop it."

"Why not? What the hell!"

His private life had not fared well during the ensuing years. Not that he was about to tell her that. Inevitable she would find out eventually. His public life, his business life, had gone exceedingly well. Losing her—the way she had left—the short, pitiful letter of explanation, if that was what one could call it, had affected him deeply. No one could have been treated worse. The moment his back was turned, she had fled at frightful speed. The final indignity. Maybe she had known what she was doing from the beginning? It was he who had got it all wrong. His mother, appalled by Catrina's behaviour, had done everything in her power to console him, until finally she was forced to stop in despair.

He had chosen his own way to get through. He had used his perfectly good brain to amass a fortune over a few years. On solid evidence he was a great success, a man of property, with many possessions.

He didn't have a wife. He didn't have a son. Marina had hung in there as long as she thought there was hope. Now and again under pressure from the family, especially his mother, he had considered asking Marina to be his wife. Had he not met Catrina Hamilton who knew? He could have married Marina. She was a lovely person, eminently suitable. Marina had deserved better. She had gone on to marry a good friend of his, Simon Bolton. He had in fact been best man at the wedding. They remained close friends.

It was Catrina who had stolen his heart. She had never contacted him again. Simply vanished from his life. Once hope was gone there was only heartbreak to be endured. Women weren't the only ones to suffer that. Men did too. He had missed her. God, how he'd missed her. Hated her too. What she had done he regarded as not only cowardly but cruel. The cruellest, the most demoralising part was, there was hardly a time and a long, long night he hadn't thought of her. He could almost believe destiny had thrown them together again. For a crime there was punishment.

This time she wouldn't get off so easily. An unmarried mother said it. Catrina played games with men's minds and men's bodies. Probably nothing really touched her. Except—and he knew it in his bones—her son. Her son would be her Achilles heel. Meeting the boy might deliver a judgment. Apparently she kept him well hidden. Hugh Saunders hadn't met the boy either. But he knew where she lived. The big mystery was how had the boy's father opted out so easily? Either he had placed little value on being the father of a child, or Catrina hadn't told him.

Simply used him.

It happened. Women were getting better and better at using men.

They sat down on the loggia to a light, delicious lunch served by Lady McCready's housekeeper, Mary, a pleasant, capable woman clearly devoted to her mistress. The loggia with its series of archways faced a cerulean infinity-edged pool. Beyond that, breathtaking views of the Coral Sea. There were comfortable white furnishings set back from the pool, the tables, couches and chairs protected from the dazzling sun by large blue, white fringed umbrellas. Huge terracotta planters framed either side of the arches, filled with blossoming hibiscus in a range of brilliant colours. The house presented the classic Mediterranean style of architecture he was long familiar with.

Over lunch Lady McCready didn't bother him with personal questions. He had asked to speak to her privately regarding possible negotiations. If she was surprised she had hidden it well. Davey would take Catrina on a tour of the gardens while they talked. Catrina, however, was allowed to take him on a tour of what was the large house.

"I'm not as spry as I once was," Lady McCready said with a laugh and a little wave of her beringed hand. Indeed the regal little lady dressed in a gorgeous kaftan looked quite frail, though the years had dealt kindly with her. "I'll wait here for you."

Immediately they were out of earshot and Cate went on the attack. "So you cut me out of the negotiations? That wasn't the plan."

"Plans change," he said briefly, moving ahead of her. "I really don't need *you* to make a business pitch. I would have thought that it was obvious I can handle it myself. Lady McCready and I won't have a problem dealing with each other on what I'm sure is a seven-figure deal. It's a truly beautiful home they've created here, but I haven't yet decided whether it's irresistible to me. It's clear no expense has been spared. Isla Bella is much more than a hideaway. More like an Italianate villa. It must have taken a long time to complete the project?" He suddenly turned to her, caught her out staring at him.

"Five years, I believe." She knew she gave a betraying flush. "They commissioned an Italian architect. Lady McCready loves all things Italian. She was responsible for creating their island home. Surely you can tell me what you think so far?"

He gave an elegant shrug. "The house in the Bahamas is British West Indies style. It's lighter, more airy, minimalistic when compared with this. I suppose this could be called a grand house. It's lavishly decorated. Some might find it overwhelming. Changes would have to be made."

"Many VIPs have stayed here as guests," she pointed out stiffly, thinking he now had reservations. It wasn't what he wanted? Good. "The McCreadys were known for their lavish hospitality. Three prime ministers have stayed here. But then you would have VIP guests of your own. Who knows, even royalty might stay a day or two?"

"Okay, you can show me upstairs now." He ignored her last comment. They had seen the major rooms of the first floor. He had declined entering the housekeeper's domain, the kitchen, which Cate knew had been brought up to state of the art. Perhaps he simply wasn't interested in how kitchens worked.

They walked back into the hallway with its intricately patterned flooring featuring three types of Italian stone before taking the black wrought-iron curving staircase to the upper floor.

"Six double bedrooms all with en suites." She spoke exactly like a Realtor showing a client over a high-end property. "How many family members have you got?" Her voice was remarkably cool when inside she felt terribly unsettled. Sexual radiance came off him in waves. She made certain she didn't stand too close to catch them. Even then, the scent of him was in her nostrils, as powerful an aphrodisiac as it had ever been. She took a deep breath.

This has to stop.

"I don't think you have any right to ask," he answered in a terse, pragmatic fashion. He continued to move ahead of her, as though not caring if she followed, which she did briskly. All the bedrooms were very spacious with a series of white-shuttered French doors opening out onto a covered balcony. The master suite was the most luxurious with a huge canopied bed with white filmy bed hangings. He walked out onto the balcony and looked at the glorious view with the brilliant sun scattering diamond sparkles across the deep blue waters.

"The master suite," Cate said quite unnecessarily when he came back inside. How could she ever cancel out her memories, the two of them in bed together, the weight of his body on hers, the power of his hands, the interlocking limbs, their mouths, their tongues…the high-burning passion of it all. The way of all flesh. She had prayed for someone to come into her life to supplant him. No one had even come close. It was a savage blow, but she had been adjusting to it. She had her son. Not everyone found their soul mate.

Had Cate only known it, Wyndham was thinking much the same thing. The excitement, the heat, the enormous pleasure he had taken even in their clashes, too little time before they had been thrown headlong into love making. She had touched his body, his heart, his mind and his soul. He had thought things would never change. How wrong could a man be? The merry dance she had led him went nowhere? To hell? Even now, God help him, he wanted to bolt the door, throw her down on the bed, make punishing love to her. She had known all about passion. About giving herself to a man. The merest contact with her had brought back the past.

Yet when he spoke his voice was coolly casual. "I think that does it. Enjoy your trip around the garden. They look splendid, by the way. Such a pity you never did get to see the full restoration of Radclyffe Hall's gardens."

"I did what I wanted to do," she said, her tone tight. "I got away."

The question was, what was she going to do now?

Just the sight of him and the years had melted away.

The buggy ride around the gardens was a pleasure. It even shifted her mind off what was going on inside the house. Davey had packed the leeward side of the island with dozens of species of native plants that required minimal watering. An astonishing array of agaves caught her eye, some with pearly marking. There were striking aloes with yellow flowers and millions of hot pink and bright yellow little succulent flowers. Davey seemed to welcome her interest in the garden he had created out of what was once a wilderness.

Wyndham didn't need her. He was the billionaire potential buyer. It hadn't taken her long to see Lady McCready both liked and trusted him. Lord Julian Wyndham was a very charming man. He had certainly made the old lady's eyes twinkle. No problem with an *à deux*, then. Amazing Lady McCready hadn't asked him a single question about his private life. He had acted as if he didn't have one.

When she returned to the house it was obvious the meeting had gone well. Lady McCready's soft powdery cheeks were flushed with pleasure. *Catrina has justified my faith in her,* Lady McCready thought. She had brought her the right person to buy the island. Lord Wyndham would treat it like a second home. Now wasn't that a wonderful outcome? She didn't tell Catrina. Julian—he had insisted she call him Julian—had asked her to give him a little more time before they made their announcement. In return he would allow Catrina to have a contract drawn up. Rather than wanting Davey and Mary off the island, he was delighted they would stay on as caretakers.

The launch returned for them mid-afternoon, with the sun casting a glittery veil of light over water as blue as a precious stone. Cate was glad she didn't suffer from motion sickness because the sea was unusually choppy, more so than on the run over to the island. She started for the shelter of the cabin not long after they boarded, her skin dewed with fine spray. She took a couple of tissues out of her tote bag, gently mopping her face. He was still out braced against the rail. She was reminded he was a good sailor. Or so he had said, though she was sure it was true. They had never got around to the trip to Cornwall they had planned, but he had shown her a photograph of the family yacht, *Calliope IV*, long and sleek as any luxury automobile, all varnished mahogany that gleamed even in the photograph, a golden mast tall enough to reach the cloudy sky.

The rocky passage tested her. The diesel fumes were making her feel sick. She would be glad when they reached the mainland. He had asked her if she was okay before going off to speak to the launch owner. She heard the owner laugh out loud a few times, genuinely amused. Again she remembered he could be really funny, witty and entertaining. He had been spoilt rotten by his mother and his sisters, Olivia and Leonie, both older, both endowed with beauty, who adored him. She supposed his sisters—strangely enough she had got on well with them—were married as well. Probably with children. There had been plenty of young men in their lives. Part of his close-knit family who no doubt would be visitors to Isla Bella if he bought it.

So far no commitment.

The launch slid smooth and easy into dock. An exchange of handshakes with the captain before they moved off.

"Sure you're okay?" For a minute he sounded genuinely concerned. "You've gone very pale." Her satin-smooth skin had lost colour.

"I'm fine," she said testily. "The diesel fumes were getting to me."

"And you haven't found your land legs."

"Don't you believe it." She pulled away from his steadying arm, her body as poised and alert as a dancer's. "We can catch a taxi back to the hotel, or we can walk."

"Up to you." He shrugged. "I'd like to look around. What are those beautiful trees?" he asked, looking towards an avenue of them. "The flowers look like frangipani, but the leaves don't."

"Evergreens," she said. "They're a species of frangipani. As you can see the flowers are a pure white. They grow prolifically up here. I saw a whole grove of them on the island.

Davey is a wonderful gardener. He and Mary have a blissful lifestyle. I believe Lady McCready required a clause in any contract to state they remain on the island for as long as they want."

"I believe so," he said, not to be drawn any further.

CHAPTER FIVE

THE BEDSIDE PHONE rang with a startling shrillness.

"Yes," she said briefly, focusing on pulling the bath robe together. She'd barely had time to get out of the shower.

"Wyndham." His voice was quiet, impassive. "I assume you intend to eat?"

A heart-stopping moment. She gave a tiny cough as though clearing her throat. "I thought I'd have something in my room."

She heard his exasperated sigh. "Don't be so damned ridiculous. I'm told there's an excellent restaurant within walking distance, the Blue Lotus."

"I'm in no mood for dinner. With *you*," she added. Perched on the side of the bed she was feeling all of a sudden stricken. She should complain to God for allowing him back into her life again. How could God be so cruel?

He gave you free will.

"My dear Catrina, you're supposed to keep me happy," he answered smoothly. "Isn't that what your boss told you? We need to keep him happy until he comes on board?"

"So this is blackmail?"

"Blackmail is fine with me. Saunders is your boss. He was speaking to one of his senior staff. He only had praise for you. Don't disappoint him. I'll call for you at seven-thirty." He hung up.

She had two options. Not answer the door. Or get dressed. Hugh had thrown her head first into the thickets. It was a dark picture she had of herself. A sad, permanently love-struck woman. A woman whose whole mission had been to forget one man. And dismally failed.

"We're a crazy lot, aren't we?" She addressed the woman in the bathroom mirror.

Better believe it! her reflection replied.

She could behave very badly, be provocative, try to seduce him. She had hinted as much to Stella, who had been appalled. But there would be some satisfaction in playing that game. Only he was a married man. And after all these years he still had enormous power to hurt her. Besides, the past had a way of repeating itself. She had asked for what she got. She had paid the price. Accepted responsibility.

Wyndham was untouchable.

When she was dressed she knew she looked good. She liked looking good. A woman needed every aid in the arsenal. On impulse she had packed a resort-style maxi dress by a well-known Australian designer famous for her kaftans and resort wear. The floral-printed silk was beautiful, a luscious collection of tropical blooms. The light green tracery of leaves picked up the colour of her eyes. She left her hair long and loose when her intentions had been to pull it back.

Maybe you're just losing it?

Fair enough! A woman was allowed to lose it now and then.

They had a table facing the promenade and the beach beyond. He looked absurdly handsome, absurdly sexy, so tall and lean with his dark hair and intensely blue eyes. He had even picked up a tan. It gave her an involuntary shock of pleasure just looking at him. What she needed was vigilant self-management. He was wearing a teal-coloured open-necked linen shirt with tiny pearly white buttons, the long sleeves turned back, navy jeans. He looked great. The young waitress thought so too. Not even close to hiding it. When he gave her his heart-lurching smile, colour flamed into her cheeks. No question—a great smile was a fantastic weapon.

She heard herself agreeing to an entrée, a tartare of ocean trout garnished with salmon roe, for the mains, steamed Reef Red Emperor served in a banana leaf with a papaya, chilli and coconut salsa. All local products, the seafood caught that very day, the hovering waitress assured them. Cate sat back allowing him to choose a crisp New Zealand sauvignon blanc to go with the meal. The whole thing felt like an exquisite piece of theatre. Two people hostile to each other but maintaining an urbane façade.

The restaurant was a far cry from the elegance of C'est Bon. It was unpretentious, but very clean and attractive, above all welcoming. They were fortunate to get a table because the large open room was near full. She heard a mix of languages from the enthusiastic diners at the other tables: Japanese, Chinese, German and Italian and, she thought, Taiwanese. The colour blue set the tone. Unusual blue lighting, blue and white candy-striped tablecloths, comfortable white painted chairs. A lovely creamy conch-shell centre table held an exquisite blue water lily positioned atop its emerald-green pad.

He glanced up at the lighting over the small bar with real interest. "They did a study fairly recently on colour and the effect it has on us. One of our leading London architects designed the experimental blue lighting in a new restaurant. Far more usual to see red, but the blue worked wonders apparently. Diners came *alive* at around ten p.m. It was as though their body clocks had been reset. They stayed much later into the evening too. Drank more. Never tried it myself."

She had to make a contribution. "They tried much the same experiment with the colour red. Professional footballers were given either a red or a blue jersey to wear in a game. Those wearing the red jerseys not only felt more confident of a win—their own explanation—they did win."

"Well, the theory can be demonstrated tonight," he suggested, the curve of his mouth frankly mocking.

"I can promise you it won't be a late night for me," she answered repressively.

"Why so anxious to get rid of me?" he asked with mock humour. "Surely I'm someone from the old days? A one-time boyfriend? I mean, it wasn't as though you were fixated on me."

She turned her blonde head away, exposing a sculpted jaw line and throat. "That wasn't the plan."

"What was the plan? Two-timing someone at home?" A hardness had entered his voice.

"A variety of reasons," she said.

"All tainted."

"Nothing could have been further from my mind. Can we keep the focus on the present," she said firmly.

"By all means. Why can't you say my name?"

He was exerting far too much pressure. "I don't trust myself to."

"Meaning?" Baffled, he stared into her eyes, not knowing what the hell she was talking about.

Why can't you keep your mouth shut? the voice inside her head cut in.

"It was good to walk away from you, Ashe. Good to walk away from your family, England."

"When my family liked you so much?" Anger hit him. "You just pulled the plug on all of us?"

His sisters had really liked her. She had liked them. They had treated her like a friend, respected her and her opinions. Briefly they had touched her life. His mother? Another story. Memories of Alicia would stay with her for ever. She would always feel that backlash of rejection. It was a wonder Marina had been considered good enough for her son. "Surely it can't be of any importance any more," she said, with no emotion in her voice.

Provoked, he suddenly caught her hand across the table, his fingers very tight on hers. "You claimed you *loved* me."

Denial was impossible. "Oh, for God's sake!"

Betray nothing.

Only he wouldn't let her fingers go. That mystical clasp of their hands! She had to suck in her breath. She was no better at controlling her responses now than she had been years ago.

"You inherited your Gothic pile, the title, Marina, the Earl's daughter, Radclyffe Hall. Wasn't that enough?"

"Not Gothic at all as you very well know," he returned shortly. "What the hell are you hiding, Catrina?" His black brows drew together, making him look extraordinarily formidable.

"And I suppose you're so up front?" she retaliated, still keeping her voice low. "We've been thrown into this situation. I'm not enjoying it any more than you."

"Brave words, but what's the reality?" he challenged. "Your hand is trembling."

"That's because you've got my fingers wedged tight."

"No, I haven't."

"Look," she said in what she hoped was a conciliatory manner. "Don't let's have a spat in public. We'll finish up, then walk back to the hotel." It was much too dangerous to stay within his orbit. "I gather I might become privy to an announcement some time tomorrow so we can head back. No doubt you've told Lady McCready all about yourself and your illustrious family. You can't help looking and acting very grand. Lady McCready would like that. A mega-hero."

"Please, no fake admiration. It's just a waste of time. I have no doubt of your powers, Catrina, and I'm speaking from experience, but it appears all you can offer a man is delusion."

"Takes one to know one."

He had been busy finding his credit card but his dark head shot up. "What did you say?"

"I'm just going with the flow, Ashe." Her green eyes beneath their naturally dark brows were enigmatic.

Sexual attraction was hell, he thought. No way to get rid of it. "Know what I think? You're still playing tricks," he returned with a lick of contempt. "You started out that way as a girl. You've kept going."

She was rattled, but managed coolly, "The short answer is, not with a married man. That's a no-go zone."

"*Is* it? What about the man who fathered your child? I have to say I feel sorry for the guy. Did you even tell him you were pregnant?"

Her control almost slipped. "That's the tricky part," she said, tossing a long lock of her hair over her shoulder. "Write me off, Ashe."

Just like you wrote me.

On the way back to the hotel he had to rescue her again. She had stepped off the pavement precipitously; a second later a car window was wound down and a young male voice bawled at her, "Yoo-hoo, blondie, are you trying to get yourself killed? You can get in if you like."

Heads swivelled everywhere. Wyndham grabbed hold of her and smartly waved the young driver on. She was staggering now under the rush of adrenaline, dry-mouthed with fright. She had stepped off the pavement looking right but not left, the reason being *he* was to her left. She had made it clear she hadn't wanted him to take her arm. The bad news was, she was such a mass of leaping nerves she hadn't been paying sufficient attention to the road or indeed anything much. The traffic was by no means heavy. Couples were strolling arm in arm enjoying the balmy breeze but the beetle-sized vehicle approaching the corner would have come close to collecting her only for Wyndham.

A dead silence lasted for several seconds. "As the kid said, are you trying to get yourself killed?" he snapped. He sounded deeply angry.

"Hey, don't get excited. Nothing happened."

He didn't buy that. "Come on." His retort was sharp. "Your heart is hammering."

He would know. His arm was pressed over it. "Well, you see the problem, don't you? You're manhandling me."

"You *need* manhandling," he said, abruptly releasing her.

She said nothing. She was so shocked she was able to maintain a spurious air of total calm. They set off again, but this time he kept a light hold on her arm. She didn't protest. Her brain wasn't working yet.

Back at the hotel he walked along the empty corridor, stopping first at her door. His room was further down.

This is your chance to self-destruct.

"Goodnight," she said rapidly, her agitation evident. What she had here was a major departure from her rational, ordered life.

"What on earth's the problem?" He stared down into her overwrought face. The first time he had seen vulnerability from the Frost Queen. Oddly enough it hurt him.

"Okay, I feel a bit shaky," she admitted. "If you hadn't pulled me back I could have been injured." It was Jules she was thinking about. She had to stay safe and well for her son.

"*Would* have been," he corrected. "You're pale enough to pass out." Indeed her creamy skin had lost colour. "You want a slug of something. Come to that, I need one too." He felt like a man standing on a cliff with his feet halfway over. She wasn't worth loving. She never had been. But by God she was more of a threat than ever. She still possessed her powerful sexual allure in spades. He didn't *need* her love any more. But he was mad to take her to bed. The surest way to move on. Taking her to bed was a strategy of sorts. Finally get her out of his system.

He took the entry card out of her nerveless hand, opening the door, waiting a moment for her to precede him. She had such grace in her movements. Her lovely subtle perfume was in his nostrils. He even knew it. Chanel. He was the one who had actually introduced her to Chanel, buying her perfume along with a dozen and more Christmas presents all packaged up beautifully, the card bearing her name. Those were the days when he was just Julian Ashton Carlisle with no idea a peerage was waiting for him. That honour should have been for his beloved father, a hero in many people's eyes, not just his family's.

"Ashe, this is—" She broke off, unable to find the right words.

"Madness?" he asked. The black humour of it overtook him and he began to laugh.

"Leave now." She was in near despair.

"It would be a very good idea, but let's have a drink first. Settle the nerves." Settle the feelings that threatened to become overwhelming. He went to where the drinks were kept.

"I'll go splash water on my face," she announced.

"Might as well," he said, as laconic as any Aussie.

She returned after about five minutes, feeling a bit closer to normal.

He on the other hand looked as though he had zipped back into top gear. "You look better," he said casually. She looked exquisite. But she had lost the ultra-control he had seen from her. "Recovered?"

"I didn't actually fall apart, did I?" she shot back.

"You could have fooled me." He passed her a glass containing a small measure of whisky.

"Cheers," she said idiotically and drank it down, shuddering a little as the fiery spirits kicked in. Her capacity for controlling herself was stretched so far it was about to snap. "Thank you for tonight. But time to go," she said with determination, before she was drawn even further into the whirlpool.

"I know that. I know if I were in my right mind I'd have steered clear of you."

"What a relief it is to hear you say that."

You breaker of hearts.

"Only exposure to you has quite clouded my better judgment."

"Well, it hasn't clouded mine. What I told you is true. Married men are in the no-go zone."

"As though I believe it," he scoffed. "You'd have married men falling over one another with insatiable desire. Look at poor old Saunders."

"I'm not happy to hear you call my boss 'poor old Saunders.'"

"I'll be glad to call him 'poor old Hugh Saunders, CEO Inter-Austral' if you like. Give me your hand."

"Sorry. Holding hands with you is way down my list."

"Whatever did you see in me? No, seriously, I want to know."

"It was like a switch was turned. On. Off. You know how it goes."

"Catrina, that's wicked," he condemned her. "Seriously wicked. No one has the right to deliberately break the heart of someone who cares for them."

She stared at him in amazement, then snapped, "Destroyed by grief, were you? How long after did you get married?"

Something was all wrong, he thought. The expression in her crystal-clear green eyes was haunted. How could that be? It was the moment to come clean and tell her he and Marina had never tied the knot. That had been his mother's grand design. But why should he answer head-on and expose himself to even more humiliation? She would find out soon enough.

Cate waved the question off. "Hey, no need to tell me. Wedding of the year, was it?" There was a definite giddiness in her head. "Please go, Ashe." She made an effusive gesture towards the door.

Mockery was in his glittering eyes. "See you for breakfast?"

She laid her palms against her ears. "Never!"

"How about coffee? I'll have Lady McCready's answer by tomorrow afternoon."

"Coffee will be fine," she bit off. "We'll have it at the airport."

She went to move past him, but as she did so his arm encircled her waist. That was the trigger. Immediately she was engulfed in fire as her flesh came into contact with his. She could feel the searing glow on her skin. She could feel the blood pumping in and out of her heart. Surely he could hear the loud beat? For a shocking moment she actually leaned against him, *compelled* to, assailed by memories so vivid they could never be erased.

At a touch, I yield.

"So the seduction scene," he murmured, blatant cynicism in his voice. "Who planned it, you or me?" His arm tightened.

"None of it was ever planned." She twisted her body away from him.

Something inexplicable was in her tone. It frustrated him immensely. He swung her fully into his arms, more roughly than he intended. For all he knew she could be in some way deranged. "Look, I'm not following you at all," he cried with more than a hint of desperation. He stared into her translucent green eyes that hid so much. "Is this your on-and-off stunt? If it is, *stop* it."

"Pray it isn't!" Masses of her long blonde hair had fallen back. At this moment of extreme upset the very worst thing could happen. It lured her as much as frightened her.

The promise of her was too lavish for him.

The rush was headlong.

His mouth on hers. Call him a fool, but this was what he wanted. This helpless, hopeless admission of need.

It blitzed all rational thought. Her full mouth was luscious, a magnet for his. Their tongues flickered briefly, coiled in a dance of love to some hypnotising rhythm. Cate's eyelids fluttered shut. There was no tenderness to their kiss. Rather, raw passion, a kind of anger, like a two-edged sword. What had started off as a moment of shock rapidly turned to intense physical pleasure. But even the extravagant passion of kissing couldn't satisfy the deep hunger, the force of it that shook them. She could never mistake any other man for Ashe. No other man could arouse such feelings. No other man could be so addictive.

She was hooked. Her love-starved body wanted more and more of him.

He hauled her right up against him, his hands slipping down over her, warm and strong, The hardness of his arousal pressing urgently into her cleft. The miraculous feel of her body against his! Would he never stop wanting her? He hadn't been able to erase the memories. She had buried herself deep in his psyche, locking him in with a golden key.

Now they were totally absorbed, the one in the other. The pleasure was ravishing. Cate's body felt full to the brim of it. There had never been anything measured in their lovemaking. It had always been total. She was a one-man woman. That was the reality she had to face. Only she couldn't allow him to see it. This could be written off as an aberration; an overwhelmingly powerful sexual attraction. No more to it than that. She had to make him understand that if she could only control the hunger.

It would be so easy to forget everything. Forget he near mortally wounded you. Forget he's the father of your child. Forget he's a married man. He certainly has. He expects you to lie back, invite him into your yearning body. Enjoy it.

Enjoy was a nothing word.

Once burned she was for ever marked.

The palm of his hand covered her breast. Her nipple was so painfully taut she gave an involuntary gasp as his palm brushed it. Her stomach muscles spasmed. What they were doing was scandalous.

She jerked away in a panic, pressing her hand hard against his chest. "No."

"No? Catrina, you crazy woman, you were loving it. We both want it." His tone was ragged with intimacy.

"I'm too full of pride." Her whole body was shuddering, trying to cope with the assault on her senses.

The past was as yesterday.

He felt driven beyond endurance. "Pride, really?" His hands shot out of their own accord, clenching her shoulders. "What does a treacherous woman like you have to do with pride?" His blue eyes flashed lightning.

She had to force herself to speak. That he could say that! "Go!" She was gripped by a helpless rage. "Go." Before the whole fragile edifice of her self-control collapsed in a cloud of dust.

She sounded as though he intended to harm her. "Just how sane are you?"

"I'm not sane at all." *Not around* you. *The love of my life. The enemy. How I hate you for it.*

There was a harsh mocking edge to his voice. "You're a remarkable woman, Catrina, but critical little bits and pieces have been left out of your genetic code," he said, preparing to leave.

"Not to the extent of yours," she shot back, his opponent. "Goodnight, Ashe, or should I say Lord Wyndham? I remembered you're a married man even if you didn't."

Everything she was saying was hitting him blindside. Fancy *her* taking the high moral ground. He nearly told her then he had never married, only damn her! She was the one who had betrayed him yet she was acting the part of a victim. It didn't make sense. He could hear his mother's voice:

Julian, my darling, the poor girl needed help. Lots of help. She was just using you. Using us. She'll probably spend her time when she gets back home amusing her friends with what was no more to her than an adventure.

His mother had talked and talked until he was drained of all emotion. His mother had never thought his love for Catrina was a fairy story. His sisters had not been so severe, but they too had been shocked and confused.

I had thought you two were madly in love. That from Olivia, shaking her head. *You were the one, Ashe, who was building the dream. I'm so, so sorry.*

She wasn't cut out to be your wife, Julian darling, his mother had lamented. *Perhaps she was frightened of taking on a new way of life? Eighteen is just a baby after all.*

And that was the last he ever heard from her. A pretty destructive "baby".

Cate shut the door on him, promising herself…promising herself…that would never happen again. The urge had been on them to make love, satisfy a physical hunger. That was all it was.

Shame for her own weakness hung over her.

CHAPTER SIX

ON THE FOLLOWING Monday afternoon he drove the car put at his disposal to the house where she lived. He parked in the leafy tree-lined street looking upwards. The house looked pretty impressive from the outside. Built on the side of a hill, it would have a stunning view of the blue marina he had passed along the way. Not that marinas weren't scattered all around the harbour. This was an island continent. People loved their boats. Loved their sailing. He knew the famous Sydney Hobart Yacht Race had become an icon of Australian sport attracting yachts from all around the world as well as a huge international media coverage. So there was sailing, swimming and of course the cricket.

He was a mite surprised at how beautiful Sydney was, how dynamic, very cosmopolitan. It was a world-class city with a harbour that was a splendid asset. Then there was the climate! Day after day of glorious sunshine, beautiful and balmy breezes off the harbour. Catrina had always made jokes about their English "never ending" rain but he had sometimes thought she secretly enjoyed it. Or a certain amount of it anyway. She had certainly enjoyed the snow. She had never seen snow in her entire life or the wonderland it created. So many times over the years he had kept coming back to their walks in the snow.

* * *

Fresh snow had fallen during the night. He had prayed for it. The months of October and November had been unusually warm, but in these days before Christmas the snow had set in. A Godsend! They badly wanted to be alone together. He was amazed at the strength of the bond that had grown so swiftly between them. It was as though they had known and loved one another in another life. Was that possible? Millions of people believed in reincarnation. What he did know was, she was everything...everything...he wanted in a woman: beautiful, glowing, clever, full of curiosity with such a broad range of interests. He knew she was ambitious. She had plans. He knew she was the sort of girl who would have and he approved of that. Only he needed to be a part of her plans. She already was with him. In the deepest caverns of his heart he knew she was the answer to his dream.

He helped her into her warm topcoat, then for extra measure wound a cashmere scarf around her neck. She wore an emerald cap on her head that accentuated the colour of her eyes. He had found a soft pair of gloves for her hands. They were ridiculously big.

"You love looking after me, don't you?" She looked up at him, flipping her thick blonde braid over the collar.

"I want to look after you all our lives." There didn't seem to be any other kind of answer.

"Terrific!" At eighteen she might have been fearful of such an early declaration. No, she embraced it, holding up her face for his kiss. Her face was so radiant he thought he had never seen anything so glorious in his life. "You'll make a wonderful husband, a wonderful father," she told him as soon as her mouth was free. They were too close to the house. They found it restricting with so many eyes on them.

"That shows what an excellent judge of character you are," he joked. Their emotions were so deep, so overwhelming, their falling so passionately in love had transformed

their lives. They hadn't had sex. They had come close. But not yet. It was enough for now for the two of them to be together. He knew he was going to make love to her the way he wanted. He knew he wouldn't be able to help it. All her responses incited him. He knew her flame of desire would fire up to meet his.

Snowflakes fell through the chilly air, landing on their heads and shoulders.

"Angel dust strewn from the heavens," she cried, lifting her lovely face. "God's gift to the world."

"The grounds look even better in midwinter," he told her. "The contrast between dark and snow-white is surreal."

"Like stepping into a dream." She was laughing, hugging him like this was such an adventure. She talked about the way Turner had painted the most sublime and romantic Alpine snowscapes. She told him it had actually snowed in Bethlehem the Christmas before. She told him she could roller skate. She was sure she could perform as well on ice. There was so much they wanted to do together. They had plenty of time. He would make sure of that, although he had to return to Oxford to complete a joint honours degree in Law and Economics. The family retained an apartment in London. He would find somewhere else. Somewhere suitable for just him and Catrina.

To doubt they would always be together was to doubt that destiny had brought them to this moment in time.

At least he had been destined not to die before seeing her again, he thought grimly. Such were the glories and tribulations of life. Breakdowns in relationships brought a lot of stress into lives. People *did* die, some chose to die, of a broken heart. He had responsibilities and his own brand of pride. What he felt now was a deepening need to address the events of the past. So much of it didn't make sense. Or was he only seeing clearly now. As he sat there staring up at the house where she lived memories began tugging at him again. They were so poignant they caught at his heart. She had snared him that very first day; ended by sabotaging his life.

"How many acres to the estate?" she asked, looking around her. The sheen of excitement, almost rapture, had brought a flush of colour to her cheeks.

It was a lovely face, perfectly symmetrical, the eyes a crystalline green, the creamy skin flawless, the mouth with a luscious fullness. She really was a beautiful woman. "Approx two hundred," he said, pretending offhandedness when he was amazed to find things were actually getting pretty heavy. For that matter he had felt a bolt of pleasure the instant his eyes had fallen on her spirited, challenging face. Now she was staring up at the hall as if at a vision, something from a fairy tale. One would have thought she'd travelled halfway around the world just to see it. He couldn't quite grasp the extent of her interest. It seemed a shade extreme.

"How splendid!" she breathed. "Go on, how many rooms?" She had looked to him for the answer.

He obliged. "The reception hall, four reception rooms, I'm not sure how many bedrooms, certainly a dozen. Quite a few bathrooms. No en suites. Housekeeper's accommodation, stables, coach house, tennis court. There's a lake with white swans, a stone bridge over it. Thinking of buying it, are you?" he asked very blandly. It was a defence mechanism. A lot of emotions were stirring in him. He had to slap them down fast. She was reeling him in much too easily for his liking. They'd only just met!

"How do you know I'm not an heiress?" she retorted, sounding amused.

He gave her another appraising glance. She looked back. They went on looking at each other. For much too long. He would have to take care not to run off the road. Or he could sneak glances at her when she was looking the other way. "Heiresses usually travel in their own private limousines," he said crisply.

"Easier to travel incognito," she replied airily. "Do we take the main driveway to the house or do we have to go around the back, the tradesmen entrance?"

"Why not make it an exhilarating experience for you?" he suggested. "How come the English accent, by the way? That's a bit of a puzzle unless your parents are English and migrated."

"For a better life," she said shortly.

For a moment he had thought she was on the verge of saying more but stifled it. "Or they never worked a day in their lives? That's an English public-school accent with a trace of Oz thrown in."

She weighed up what he said with a frown. "You obviously have remarkable powers of deduction."

"Too close for comfort maybe?" he shot off.

"Don't be absurd." There was an edge to her voice. She tossed back her golden head. "My...mother is English."

It was clear she wasn't going to say anything more.

Woman of mystery. She looked exactly the part. It was a great pity his best girl, Marina, didn't look or act a bit more like her. He shouldn't really be comparing the two. Marina certainly didn't lack a very attractive appearance. She was a good friend—he had known her from childhood—a lovely person, but she didn't have what Catrina had. More was the pity. Marina was an earl's daughter, but extraordinarily enough she lacked the cool arrogance of this Australian beauty. Neither did Marina have the sweeping confidence in herself. Their positions could have been reversed. It suddenly struck him it was possible to become obsessed by a woman. He had never understood it before. He'd never had a lot of sympathy for men who allowed it to happen. Now a young goddess with exceptional powers had crossed his path. He was already wondering what it would be like to kiss her. He knew, somehow, he would. He definitely didn't want her to disappear.

Which was exactly what she did. How wicked was that?

He was just about to restart the car, when a silver car looking slightly the worse for wear pulled up at the foot of the incline. A moment later a good-looking, stylishly dressed woman in her late forties-early fifties stepped gracefully out of the back seat followed by a boy around seven, wearing a school uniform. He was a very handsome boy with a shock of thick blond hair that shone in the sun. He was dragging what looked like a too-heavy schoolbag behind him. Another boy seated in the passenger seat wound down his window to throw his friend his school hat.

"See you tomorrow, Jules," he called breezily. "Goodbye, Mrs Hamilton." This time the tone was very respectful.

For a moment he felt his brain seize up. *Jules? Mrs Hamilton?* "God, oh, God," he muttered. "No, it can't be." There was a roaring in his ears; pain in his body as though a car had collected him, throwing him against a brick wall. He was having what was loosely termed an *epiphany.*

Jules? His friend Bill Gascoyne often called him Jules, rather than the preferred Ashe. But he couldn't possibly consider what was before him. Not for a moment. Yet he found himself straining to see the faces of the woman and the boy as they started up the incline. How he needed his binoculars! The driver of the car who had decided against driving up the slope took off with a wave. He knew exactly where the pair was going. To the elegant sandstone house with the delicately ornate cast-iron lace balustrades, decorative posts and valances.

Catrina's home.

The slim, dark-haired woman had to be her mother. The boy was Catrina's son. She had said he was five. A lie. His sister Olivia and her husband, Bram, had a six-year-old boy, Peter. This boy was taller and more developed. He had to be going on seven. He couldn't shake a profoundly disturbing thought. Was it possible this fair-headed boy was his own son? The thought nearly made his head cave in. Even Catrina wouldn't have done such a cruel, cruel thing. His eyes still hadn't left the pair, woman and boy. The boy had his head uplifted, talking in an animated fashion to his grandmother. Probably giving her the news of the day. Clearly they were devoted to each other. There was something about the woman that suggested perhaps he had met her before? Not possible. Yet he felt a very strong reaction inside.

He sat there a little longer. What to do? He was more shaken than he could have imagined. Even the first sight of Catrina hadn't done this. He knew he was never going to get an invitation to the house. He had to act. Put an end to this. Catrina wouldn't be home for some hours yet. He would go to the house, introduce himself. He needed to see the boy's face. For that matter he needed to see the woman's face. She reminded him of someone. He didn't know who. He could come up with some excuse for calling in on them. A courtesy call to all appearances when inside he was ferociously intent. Had he known it, his blue eyes were blazing. The boy had obviously inherited Catrina's glorious blonde hair. He wanted to believe the boy's eyes would be a crystalline green or even dark. The woman had dark hair. He had a clear sense her eyes would be dark as well.

He got out of the car, locked it with the button on his key. His expression was grim. He was intent on the task ahead. It could be a big mistake he was making. On the other hand it could prove to be a mind-blowing revelation.

He crossed the road, struggling for control.

The woman opened the door, a look of enquiry on her face. "Can I help you?" As she looked up at the tall, arrestingly handsome man at her door her expression splintered and her body began to shake slightly.

Stella's brain had turned to mush. She lost all track of time. Here before her in the flesh was a Carlisle. No doubting it. The Carlisle sapphire-blue, thickly lashed eyes. The height, the military-type bearing, the outstanding good looks. She remembered his late father, Geoffrey, had that thin aristocratic nose, the fine carriage, the set of the shoulders. An Englishman. Geoffrey had married that dreadful girl, Alicia Scott-Lennox, who had thought herself more royal than royalty itself. God knew why! She had hidden her worst side from Geoffrey. One had to wonder for how long?

"I think you can," the stranger who was never a stranger responded, unable to keep the shock and outrage out of his tone. Wyndham was stunned to see that the woman before him, the woman who had disappeared from all family life for more than a quarter century, was Stella Radclyffe. It was her sister, Annabel, who had remained. Annabel, the flighty one, the acknowledged beauty who had married a man old enough to be her father. Money, of course.

Well, the game was over now.

"You know who I am?" The tension in his tall, lean body revealed the extent of his shock. Indeed shock radiated off him.

Stella, too, was making a tremendous effort to pull herself together. "You're Lord Wyndham, of course," she said, with open hostility. "You became my father's heir." Here was the man who had not only broken Cate's heart, but had now returned to disrupt their happy lives.

"Which makes you a kinswoman of mine, Stella Radclyffe

that was." It was a statement, not a question, delivered with what she considered magnificent arrogance.

"I suppose there's no point in denying it." Stella threw back her head.

"No point at all," he agreed. "May I come in?" Behind her he could see into the spacious hallway, elegantly furnished with a curving staircase beyond it.

"I'm sorry." Stella stood firm, holding on to her not-inconsiderable nerve. "Cate should be here. She won't be home until well after six. Why do you want to see her anyway? You've done nothing but harm." Her breath rasped in her throat.

Harm? That gave him a jolt. He decided not to pursue it. "I'd like to see the boy," he replied. "Don't be afraid I will say anything to him. I just want to *see* him."

Stella's face had turned bone-white, but her tone was tightly controlled. "Not possible. My grandson has nothing whatever to do with you."

"Spare me," he groaned, having trouble processing what the hell was going on with this woman. "Why are you so frightened? What could you possibly have to hide? You and Catrina." His blue eyes slashed.

Stella's tongue, for once, was unguarded. "Aren't you the man who betrayed her?" she challenged. She was going out on the attack, feeling near hysterical under an avalanche of deep resentments.

"For goodness' sake!" He didn't deign to respond, the expression on his striking face openly contemptuous. "Allow me to see the boy and I'll go away. I give you my word."

He didn't need to add: *But I'll be back.*

Stella held up a hand. "I'm sorry."

"Are you?" he asked simply. "What did Catrina tell you about me—a pack of lies?"

"You're married, aren't you? You have children?"

Tell her.

He was about to when a child's voice called loudly and, it had to be said, belligerently from somewhere at the top of the stairs. "I'm here, Nan." The tone signalled the boy was ready to defend his nan and the house if need be.

"Do not upset him," Stella was reduced to begging.

"As if I would," he said shortly, maddened by her attitude. The next moment a boy who had to be around seven years old raced down the stairs, his expression growing more protective the closer he came to the front door. "Who are *you*?" He looked up at Wyndham, taking his grandmother's trembling hand. "Why are you standing there? What do you want?"

Wyndham's heart bounced, but remarkably his reply was both calm and quelling. "I was simply paying my respects to your grandmother. She happens to be a kinswoman of mine."

So why the strained faces? Jules pondered. "I don't believe you," he said flatly, though he was fairly certain the man was telling the truth.

"I could provide you with proof. I'm Julian Carlisle, by the way, and you're Jules, Catrina's son." Wyndham held out his hand.

It was such an authoritative hand, Jules was compelled to take it. This man *had* to be okay. He looked important.

"It's a great pleasure to meet you, Jules." Wyndham shook his son's hand, looking down into the Carlisles' vivid blue eyes. No mistaking them. Though the boy had Catrina's blond hair as he grew he would display more and more Carlisle physical characteristics. The height. The chiselled features. Right now he was just a beautiful, brave little boy coming swiftly to his grandmother's defence. Anyone would admire that. Wyndham did.

"How come my first name is the same as yours?" Jules asked, staring up at the man, his brain seeking answers.

Stella put a protective hand on his shoulder. "Jules," she hushed.

"Well, it's not such an uncommon name, is it?" Wyndham suggested and smiled.

That smile directed right at him made Jules' breath catch somewhere in his chest. He didn't know why except it was a *great* smile. People always told him he had a great smile. It struck him that despite the funny atmosphere he *liked* this man. He looked one hundred per cent trustworthy. Anyone would be proud to have him for a…for a…dad.

Jules turned his head to stare up at his grandmother, saw the worry on her face. "What's wrong, Nan?" he asked. Why wasn't Nan inviting their visitor in? She was normally softly spoken, but he had heard Nan speaking with frost bite in her tone. Was she really a relative of his? Then it hit Jules. The voices. Same kind of posh accent. Nan was English. His gaze flashed back to the man. The man was too. "You're Lord Wyndham, aren't you?" he asked as a door in his mind opened.

Wyndham could only nod. He felt like a man who had been robbed of what he would have held most precious.

His son.

His son denied him for long, empty years. He had thought of it as the abyss. What Catrina had done was diabolical. All right she had cut him out of her life. She had no right to cut out his child. He wanted to do something drastic. He wanted to rant and rage as he had never done. He had locked it all in. He wanted Catrina right there before him. Preferably on her knees, her slender neck bent, ready for the sword. He wanted the *truth*. He felt capable of forcing it out of her. But when he spoke it was with an air of apology. "My fault, Jules, I'm afraid. I gave your grandmother a shock. I should have rung ahead, but I wanted to surprise her."

Jules began to nod his understanding, then broke off as

further uncertainties set in. "There's something I don't understand," he said.

It was issued like a real challenge, Wyndham thought. The boy was displaying his intelligence and his finely tuned perceptions, exceptional for one so young.

"No matter, Jules." Wyndham began to turn away. "Your mother will explain it to you."

"Explain what? Wouldn't it be better if you did?" Jules started to follow the man as he walked down the short flight of stone steps.

Wyndham turned. "No, your mother will do it. Go back inside, Jules," he said with quiet but unmistakeable authority. He lifted a hand to Stella, who was standing like a pillar of salt. "I'll phone Catrina when I get back to the hotel," he said.

My God, I have to warn her, Stella thought.

"Goodbye now, Jules," he called.

"Goodbye, sir." The man's smile washed over Jules again. It was like sunlight. It restored Jules' sense of comfort and well-being.

"Will I see you again?" he called with a betraying eagerness in his voice. This was a real live lord. Wait until he told Noah! Not that either of them would want to be one. They were *Australian.*

Wyndham raised a hand. "Sure to, Jules," he said.

Try explaining this away, Catrina. Try it, just try it.

The words reeled away like a mantra in his head.

Once Stella shut the door, Jules wouldn't leave it alone. "You're his kinswoman. That's a relative, isn't it, Nan?"

Jules was into discovery. Next he'd be onto Ancestry.com. "Yes, darling," Stella said, desperate to get to the phone. "The funny thing is I never laid eyes on him until today."

"Why's that?" Jules grabbed at her hand. "Why have you

never gone back to England for a visit? Aunty Annabel used to visit you, didn't she? I think I remember her."

"You probably do, although you were only five."

"What happened to her?" Jules asked.

"Aunt Annabel died young, dear, because she never looked after herself. She mixed with the wrong people."

"That's sad. I hope her dying was peaceful?" Jules said from the depths of his tender heart.

"Very peaceful, darling," Stella assured him. "Now, what would you like for afternoon tea? Something light. I have roast chicken and all the trimmings for dinner."

Jules gave her the strangest look. "Don't you want to talk about it, Nan?"

She paused to look down at him. "What's *it*, darling?"

"I was listening from the top of the stairs. You sounded like you were a bit afraid of him. Were you?"

"Certainly not!" Stella pronounced firmly. "I suppose I was a bit overwhelmed. He is a lord, you know. The fifth Baron Wyndham."

"Aunt Annabel was a lady. Does that mean you were one too before you came to Australia? We don't have lords and ladies here, thank goodness. I think we should all be the same."

Stella's smile was grim. "You could be right. I was a very modest Miss Stella Radclyffe, as was Annabel." In fact both had had the title of The Honourable, but she didn't bother telling him that. "My sister, Annabel, married a hugely successful businessman, Sir Nigel Warren, who was knighted by the Queen. Therefore she had the title Lady Warren."

"I see. But it is better when everyone is the same," Jules pronounced, "yet part of me was impressed. I thought Lord Wyndham was really cool. He looks a bit like some painting I've seen in a book. Sort of haughty, but I think, kind. I can't wait for Mummy to get home. Should you ring her and tell her?"

Stella almost sighed aloud in relief. "What a good idea. You go upstairs and get changed and I'll ring your mother."

And that was what Stella did.

Catrina listened in silence, then said, "God help us all! He knows, doesn't he?"

"Of course he knows," Stella said with a severity that was palpable even over the phone. "I'd abandon any attempt to pull the wool over his eyes."

"Isn't it *eyes* what this is all about? Living proof," Cate said, halfway between gravity and black humour.

"Is it ever!" Stella rasped. "Jules liked him," she said, as though that were a betrayal.

"Of course he did!" Cate responded. "What's the big surprise? They're blood. I have to go, Stella. Thanks for warning me. Ashe won't let this lie. I kept the existence of his son from him for seven years. I suppose he had the right to know," she admitted unexpectedly.

"You remember what he did to you," Stella reminded her with some wrath. "Just don't panic. Be strong."

"You're the strong one, Stell."

"I'm not." Well, she *was*, but in all modesty it was her habit to dismiss it.

"You certainly are when it comes to pulling your weight. I want you to know I think you do a great job with Jules." Catrina put down the phone. The sky outside her floor-to-ceiling office window was a deep blue.

But a storm was coming.

Murphy Stiller, wearing another one of her power suits, barged into her office without knocking. "Finished the Mangan proposal yet?" Her ill humour was evident.

"Not only finished, I've run it all by Hugh," Cate said blithely. "Anything else I can help you with, Murphy?"

No reply. The usual glare.

"I mean, it's not as though we're buddies." A note of derision had entered her voice.

"Hardly." Murphy gave her a smile of sheer malevolence. "I don't care much for you."

"Not a lot of people care for you, Murphy," Cate pointed out. "Probably not even your mother." Cate once had been drawn into a long, informative chat with Murphy's large and formidable mother.

"Let's keep my mother out of this." Murphy bit down hard on her lip. "My mother is a tyrant. She's also a desperately unhappy woman."

"If so, I'm sorry to hear it." Mrs Stiller, like her daughter, Murphy, was a born bully with the devil in her. Blood would out.

"Well, I couldn't care less," Murphy cried, unrepentant. "She dotes on my brother, Alex, but she thinks I've never measured up."

Instantly Cate felt pity. Fancy growing up with Mrs Stiller for a mother. "I'm sure she doesn't. You're a highly successful woman."

Murphy didn't thank her for the comment. "So how did you and Lord Wyndham get along?" Her near-black eyes were full of innuendo. "Kept him happy, did you?"

"Get your head into gear," Cate said shortly. "How come you felt it necessary to tell him I had a son?"

Murphy had the grace to flush. "Tell you, did he?"

Cate kept her expression neutral. "It was of little interest to him, but I'm getting a bit tired of your interference in my private affairs, Murphy. You've done it many times. The next time I'll go to Hugh."

"And complain?" Murphy's loud challenge would have blown another woman to smithereens.

"You bet," Cate said. "I know you love your job, Murphy. Think about it."

Murphy Stiller's olive cheeks took on a hot flush. "Think you could get me fired? So poor old Hugh has the hots for you, does that make you think you're invincible?"

"Is anybody?" Cate asked. "I'm sick of these references to Hugh's attraction to me. Hugh is a hundred per cent loyal to his wife. So lay off, Murphy. Now I don't have time to talk, so you'll have to excuse me. Would you mind shutting the door when you go?"

Murphy did her stuff. She gave the door one almighty slam.

Thirty minutes later Cate was trying hard to focus on a mining lease, when the phone rang.

She knew who it was before she lifted the phone.

"Wyndham."

"What can I do for you, Wyndham?" She spoke with cool detachment. She could have been a great actress. No trouble at all. "Is something wrong?"

"Now I know the reason why you've been so worried." His tone was so much like a whiplash it brought the blood to her skin. "Make any excuse you like, but I expect to see you at my hotel in under a half hour."

"Impossible," she said. "I've work to do."

The steely tone was calculated to get anyone moving. "Thirty minutes," he said. "Don't show up, I'm coming after you. I can promise you it won't be pleasant. Far better we have our conversation here."

It reminded Cate of the many TV crime shows she had watched, where a suspect was offered the option of spilling the beans right where they stood, or going down to the police station.

She let the phone fall. She had to head off for his hotel.

CHAPTER SEVEN

He let her in. Fury was burning like a slow fuse. When it hit the target it would burst into a conflagration.

His target was her. Yet she threw her arms extravagantly into the air as if she didn't have a care in the world

It was the signal for him to turn on her, his body so taut Cate was made fully aware of the power in him. "I've never known anyone like you," he said, in a hard, unforgiving voice.

"So you used to say." Her comment was foolishly facetious, adding fuel to the fire.

"Don't make me angrier than I already am," he warned. "Your mother rang you, of course?"

"My adopted mother," Cate found herself saying, taking an armchair. "She's a jolly old Radclyffe, you know. You're related."

"That jolly old Radclyffe who just happened to have been born at Radclyffe Hall washed her hands of her own family. She's your *real* mother, your biological mother. She had to have a reason for running off to Australia. Pregnant no doubt, which doesn't make sense as she was a married woman."

"Stella had her reasons. She *did* adopt me. I have the papers."

He stared at her as though convinced she was a pathological liar. "I don't believe you."

Her own temper flared. "Harsh words aren't they? Especially coming from someone like you."

"Is that the best you can do?" he exclaimed, dropping into the chair opposite her. Even then his eyes were involuntarily drinking her in, he thought in disgust. "Your boy, Jules, is my son."

"What if I swear he isn't?'

"You could swear like the worst inmate in your worst jail. Jules is my son. You were pregnant when you left England."

"I wasn't."

He ignored that, his eyes ablaze.

"Okay, I was," she admitted. It would be too easy for him to prove paternity. That was if he wanted to. Her only hope was he would simply go away. "I wasn't really sure until a couple of months later. I should tell you it came as a huge shock. When the doctor told me I screamed so loud it's a wonder you didn't hear me deep in the Cotswolds."

He bent forward as though he couldn't bear to look at her. "This is it, is it?" he asked with contempt. "You're going to confront the gravest matter with your silly jokes."

"No joke, I assure you," she said so sharply he lifted his dark head. "Giving birth is no fun."

"God, Catrina," he breathed. "Have you even for a moment regretted not letting me know? I have rights. Have you forgotten about that, about common decency? I would have done everything in my power to help you."

She lit up with anger. "*How* exactly? Have money put into my bank account?"

His black brows knitted. "I would have come on the first plane."

She turned her head away. "That's as big a lie as it gets. You cut me out of your life, Ashe. You and your horrible mother."

That got to him. Horrible mother? He felt like shaking

her. "What does my mother have to answer for?" he rasped. "She was as shocked as I was by your defection. She stood by me. I couldn't have asked for stronger support."

Cate, too, was nearly jumping out of her skin. "Your mother was a *monster*," she cried.

He looked utterly shocked, so shocked she floundered. "She *was*." She registered she had lost it.

"My mother is dead," he said. His expression was fixed yet incredibly alert like a big cat about to pounce.

"What?" she gasped.

"Hard of hearing, are you? My mother is dead. She was very badly injured in a riding accident. She died a few days later in hospital."

Cate felt her skin blanch. "What can I say? I'm sorry? I *am* sorry, but your mother was hateful to me."

He gave an incredulous laugh. "Catrina, I'm finding this very hard to believe. If my mother was hateful to you I can only say she hid it extremely well."

"From *you*," Cate retorted. "I grant you she was pleasant enough right up until our last confrontation. Then she made it abundantly clear where she really stood. She told me it was time for me to get myself back off to Australia. Disappear from your life. I simply wasn't good enough. Marina only just made it. Perhaps she'd been aiming for one of the royal princesses?"

He felt as if his head were spinning. "What in the name of God are you talking about? You expect me to believe my own mother behaved in that way?"

"I don't care what you believe," she said flatly.

He lurched to his feet. "Catrina, try to see this my way, I beg you. Apart from anything else, my mother isn't around to refute these charges. All *I* know is, she was so upset she could barely show me your *pathetic* note."

An icy sensation enveloped Cate. "How could she show

you a note when I never *left* one?" she shouted. "Why would I, for God's sake? Like a coward—I never thought you were that—you scuttled off to London while your mother did your dirty work."

"Hey, hey, hey," he warned. "Go no further."

He looked furious, even disoriented, his eyes a stunning flame-blue. She decided it was time to beat a retreat, even though she knew he would never lay a hand on her.

"Don't you *dare* leave." His voice was a deep, dark purr low in his chest.

She took a panicky breath. "You can't touch me. I'll have you up on a charge." She made the empty threat.

"You'll have us *both* up," he said. "Come back and sit down, Catrina. I don't assault women, even women without a conscience, like you. What I'd really like to know is, how can such a lovely creature be so downright cruel?"

Her legs were so unsteady beneath her she had to resume her seat. "You were the one who screwed me up, Ashe. I loved you with all my heart."

He towered over her. "I won't listen to you."

"You listened to your mother. Don't you want to hear what *I* have to say?"

"Not right now," he said very tightly. "I don't think I could handle it. I just want you to admit one thing. Your child is my son."

"Hell with it!" she cried. "Yes, yes, *yes*!"

"That's all I need to know. My son, my precious, *precious* son!"

It was coming…it was coming…the Storm. Important she be ready. No one on earth would take Jules from her. "So what do you intend to do about it?" She threw out the challenge. "Have him over to England for the holidays? Let him mix with your kids?"

His eyes flashed lightning. "What makes you think I have kids?"

"Well, don't you?" She leapt to her feet again, unable to sit still. "Or is Marina barren? It can't be *you*. You got me pregnant in no time at all."

"You can never fix this, Cate," he said.

The first time he had ever used the shortened version of her name. It shook her badly. "That's irrelevant now. I want you to stay away from me, Ashe. Stay away from my son. I'll tell him about you in time. Not yet. Not until he's old enough to understand. I'd like to leave now."

"That's what you do, though, isn't it—*run*? What you can't deal with, you run from. Were you nervous about my taking up the peerage? What it might entail for you?"

She gave a laugh that was more than a little on the wild side. "Don't be so stupid."

"What was it, then?" he demanded. "Tell me. Tell me the truth and I'll let you go."

She was horrendously upset but she had to fight. Only how could she continue to attack his mother? Mothers were sacred. Sons always defended their mothers. That was the way of it. She knew how protective seven-year-old Jules was of her. "I did tell you, Ashe, but you wouldn't believe me," she said with more restraint. "I know your mother adored you. I know how much you loved her, your sisters, your family. You were the perfect son. She had lost her husband. She had to hold on to her son. To do that, she had to rule your life. Your mother didn't have a real problem with me until it became known you were heir to the baronetcy. She thought I was just a summer flirtation, a fling. Soon enough I would go back home. End of story. End of concern. You would marry Marina and live happily ever after."

"Except I didn't marry Marina," he exclaimed, trying to cope with what she was saying.

"What?" Her voice rose steeply despite her determination to keep calm. She stared at him with stunned eyes.

His tone was soft and deadly. "I didn't marry Marina. She married one of my closest friends. You met him. Simon Bolton."

Simon, of course. She shook her head, not able to conceal her amazement. "But she was deeply in love with you. I wasn't such a fool I didn't know that."

"Sadly I wasn't in love with her," he said with more than a trace of regret. "I was in love with some sort of a…" he hesitated, searching for the right word "…sociopath."

"To whom you were deeply attracted," she pointed out furiously. "Don't worry, there are a lot of sociopaths about," she said. "Mostly men. Women marry charming, generous, caring men only to find out a short time later their dark, abusive side. Only the other day, before the happy couple got to the wedding reception he bashed her up. You see, we're never really sure who we're dealing with. I learned that lesson fairly early in life. So who did you eventually marry? Hang on!" She held up a hand. "I think I know. It was Marina's friend, the dark-haired one with the lovely glowing skin and the unusual name…Talisa?"

He didn't answer, as though he didn't have to acknowledge it. Yet he had been prepared to be unfaithful to Talisa only nights ago, Cate thought.

"Think Talisa can handle your love child? It could come as a shock too difficult to bear."

His silence continued as though he were groping through a minefield to find answers. "I have your last note to me," he said finally. "Let me show it to you." His suit jacket was hanging over a chair. She saw his expensive crocodile-skin wallet lying on the table. He picked it up, extracting a folded, rather tattered-looking piece of paper.

"This is my note?" she asked in sharp derision. "I can't wait to read it."

Note, what note?

Much of life was a mystery.

"So how is my son doing at school?" he enquired as he passed the sheet of yellowing paper to her.

Cate frowned, gingerly beginning to open the sheet of paper up. "He's doing fine. He's clever. Like me."

"Or he's even cleverer. Like *me*."

Cate nodded impatiently, intent on absorbing the contents. They were handwritten in her rather distinctive script. To her horror, it looked like her handwriting only it *wasn't*. There was something terribly wrong here. She really needed a forensic tool to make a detailed inspection. Were there tiny breaks in the flowing script as if someone had rested a second before going on? She never did that. Her writing was continuous without break. Finally she made her decision, though she knew it would meet with extreme hostility. She looked directly at him. "Anybody, absolutely *anybody*, could have written this."

"*You're* the one," he returned trenchantly. "I compared it with all the little love notes you used to leave for me. 'How do I love thee? Let me count the ways.'"

"More like how do I *hate* thee."

"It's *your* handwriting, fine handwriting really with a few little eccentricities. The embellished C of Catrina, for instance. It's there."

"Of course it is. Essential to do it like that. Only you have to prove *I* was the one to do it. It might look like my handwriting but I didn't write this. Not in a million light years." Then it dawned on her. She spoke up knowing he would hate her. "Your mother wrote this," she said, not with a note of shock but comprehension. "I'm sure of it."

His mother? He suddenly felt a lack of oxygen, rallied fast. "Drop the tone and the accusation," he warned.

"Don't try intimidating me, Ashe," she said, angling her delicately determined chin. "Don't even think of it. I'm not the naïvely trusting girl I once was. You take a little moment to think about it. Your mother was a talented artist. I saw countless sketch books of her drawings over the years. Numerous sketches of you in particular, her darling only son. Your sisters were well back in the queue. They had to accept one of the realities of life. Mothers fixate on sons. Then there were Alicia's watercolours. She was gifted." Jules had followed in her footsteps; Cate had long since accepted that. Such was the permanence of *blood.* Jules had inherited Alicia's talent. His recent sketches of her and Stella were very good, even capturing their expressions. Jules had taken them to school and the art teacher had praised him, posting them up.

For a moment she felt real sadness, as though Alicia's presence was hovering over them. She covered up her angst by looking down again at the letter. It read:

Dearest Ashe,

Don't hate me but I can't bear to stay. You're lovely but I had no idea what I was getting myself into. I don't want your life. It scares me. The voice inside me is telling me to go home. You and I would never work. Not for long. You have Marina. She'll suit you far better than me. I'm not feeling good about it—I know we had started to make plans—but I realise now I'm not ready for any of it. I'm too young. The more I've thought it through, the surer I am I'm doing the right thing. By the time you read this I'll be back home where I belong. We had great times, but they're over.

Please don't try to contact me. That's the last thing I want. Have a good life.
Catrina.

Cate had to shut her eyes on the misery she had endured. The thoughts of betrayal she had battled so long might not have been so. Alicia had simply taken matters into her own autocratic hands.

"Not exactly an epic," she said, not letting her pain surface. "How many words—one hundred or so? Your mother, sadly, was a woman not to be trusted where you were concerned. She loved you. You loved her. It's terrible for me to have to speak about her with so much disrespect, but your mother wrote this. Not me." She fluttered the sheet of paper in the air. "Put it back in your wallet. Why have you carried it all these years anyway?"

"To remind me," he said with great abruptness.

"I would have thought you'd destroy it."

He was staring at her as though he was trying to look into her bruised and battered soul. Did he believe her? Mothers were sacrosanct.

Only Alicia had changed everything. She might be floating around somewhere but she no longer had her earthly force. "Get some forensic people onto it," Cate suggested. "It's not my writing, although at a cursory glance even I thought it was." His mother would have made a first-rate forger.

He was an expert in concealing his emotions, but there was something frightening in the intensity of his expression, the blaze in his eyes. "I cannot believe my own mother would have done anything to hurt me," he said with a twist to his mouth. "And so badly. I mean, she *saw* my pain, for God's sake. I loved and respected her even if I knew she was a mite possessive. But that was her nature." He continued to stare at Catrina, seeing a beautiful young woman with her golden hair and her crystal-clear green eyes with an unnatural clarity. How could such beauty hide so much darkness and deception? It didn't seem possible. He had to confront the possibility Catrina might well have been as much a victim as he was.

"Your mother built up a great case against me, Ashe," she said quietly, seeing his perceptions of his mother were badly shaken. "I'm equally sure she thought she was doing the right thing, protecting you from me. She thought I was the wrong person to become part of your life. You were to become the fifth Baron Wyndham. I didn't pass muster. You needed a *Somebody* at your side. That's the way you lot are. You needed an earl's daughter. You already had her—Marina. Marina was not part of this. Not part of your mother's manoeuvring. It was your mother who deliberately drove me away."

His handsome face bore such a torn expression. "Forget my poor mother for a moment. I can't handle it right now. You talk about deliberation? Then consider, if you will, you deliberately withheld from me the fact I had a son. You robbed me of my child for over seven years. You robbed me of so many great joys. I missed all of those early years, years that can never be retrieved. Justice must be served. I want my son back. Not only want, I *will* get him back, if I have to pursue you through the courts."

"It's not an easy task to separate a child from its mother, Ashe."

"I'll do it." He had to find a solution.

"You *can't*!"

A chink in the armour. "Watch me."

Her inner voice kicked in. *You can't offer him money to go away.* Some men would take it if the amount were big enough. But he wasn't one of them. For one thing he was rich. Far richer than she could ever be.

"Why would I expect you to show any loyalty to me?" Cate's voice was unnaturally calm. She looked up at him without anger, but a tremendous backwash of grief. "All your loyalty is and always has been to your mother. Believe her versions of events, Ashe. It suits you to do that. *I* know what happened. I remember all too clearly. The pain has never gone away. I never did have a chance. And don't try telling me you didn't know your mother was a fearful snob. Your sisters openly admitted that. They made a joke of it. And your Number One position in her life, her adored only son. Sons guaranteed the family name. Sons inherited. Ask them. They'll remember. If it's a question of a battle I know you're the one with the big guns, but I'll fight you to the death. Jules is mine. I raised him alone. My advice to you is to go home. No need to tell your family. They don't need to know. There's no reason whatever to bring scandal down on the illustrious family name." Now there was bitterness in her tone.

His eyes burned over her. "Much of public life is scandal, Catrina," he reminded her. "You'll be hearing from me."

"Go for it. But if you have samples of my handwriting, I'd advise you to take them to a handwriting expert. Let them check the capital C in particular. That's the flag. Your mother was clever, but not clever enough. She must have had a job carrying all that guilt around."

For a moment he couldn't speak. Singularly disturbing thoughts were whirring about in his head. "And what if this expert confirms it *is* your handwriting?"

"They won't," she said with utter conviction.

His expression had taken on a very determined cast. Indeed, everything about him was wound up so tight she went to the door.

"If they do confirm it's your handwriting, I'll destroy you," he warned, tremendously upset.

She laughed, totally without humour. "Except you destroyed me years ago."

That was her parting shot. Cate opened the door, allowing it to close after her.

She felt ill. What was it about mothers they could get away with just about anything? Alicia's efforts at forgery had been near perfect. She knew she wasn't the only woman whose romantic hopes had been dashed by the intervention of an overly possessive mother.

Only at long last Alicia was about to be found out.

That was if Ashe could bring himself to have her theory checked out. If he did, one problem would be solved. A far greater one remained. He had seen his beautiful son. He wanted him. He wanted to fit Jules into his family. Obviously he didn't think he would have a problem with Talisa. Why would he? She would adore him. Given a little time Talisa would settle.

Cate made the decision to see a solicitor right away.

No one would take her son from her. That wasn't about to happen. She wasn't frightened of a battle. She was up for it.

She faced the family solicitor of recent years, Gerald Enright, senior partner of the law firm Enright Matheson, across the expanse of his impressive partner's desk. Without an appointment Gerald had very kindly fitted her into his busy schedule, but she only had thirty minutes. Grateful, she had come prepared. She had it all in her head. A few pleasantries, enquiries after Stella, a great favourite, then Gerald listened in silence before summing up.

"I have to tell you I'm astonished by all this, Cate," he said. "Astonished matters have gone as far as they have. Either one of you could have got in touch with the other. So he's English and living there. That doesn't constitute a problem. Distance is no tyranny like in the old days."

She hadn't told him Ashe was the fifth Baron Wyndham and a recent client of Inter-Austral. She had referred to him only as Julian Carlisle.

"There is no doubt he is the father?" Gerald asked in his courtly voice. Gerald was a handsome man nearing sixty. He had a full head of silver hair, good unlined skin and piercing dark eyes. His grey suit and blue and silver silk tie were immaculate.

Cate shook her head. "None at all. To make matters worse, they share the same distinctive blue eyes. Electric-blue. Frankly it's incredible. My son has my blond colouring but he has Julian's eyes."

Gravely Gerald nodded. "Surely you don't expect him to go away, Cate? The fact you never told him he had a son casts a different light on matters. Clearly had he known he would have taken steps to gain custody of his child."

"I raised my son alone, Gerald. I'm not giving him up," Cate said, trying to control her emotions. Jules was her Achilles heel.

"You may *have* to share custody, my dear," Gerald pointed out. "So try to prepare yourself. You say he has the money to fight you?"

"He's a wealthy man," Cate said shortly. "Can I take out a restraining order against him?"

Gerald frowned. "He hasn't threatened you in any way?"

"Only to say he wants his son."

Gerald spread his manicured hands. "Fair enough, wouldn't you have said? We have fathers coming in here who've had a very tough time of it. I can't help thinking as a *man* the law as it stands is weighted heavily towards the mother. No wonder these dangerous protests are being staged by fathers. It's a desperate cry for attention."

"I agree." Cate's knees were beginning to shake. "So you're on his side?"

Gerald demurred. "As a lawyer, Cate, I must take a balanced view. Your Julian Carlisle has rights." He paused, the skin of his high forehead wrinkling. "Oddly enough the name rings a bell. Julian Carlisle…Julian Carlisle…" he mused. "I've heard the name, I'm sure, in the past week. No worries, it will come to me."

"I'll make it easy." Cate made the decision. "You'll find out anyway. Julian Carlisle is Lord Wyndham, the fifth Baron Wyndham. He's in Australia at the moment."

Gerald started to drum his fingernails on the desk top. "This whole business could get into the papers."

"I know that." She wanted to relax, but she couldn't.

"What about your job?" he asked. "Do you want to be in the papers? Hugh Saunders wouldn't like any member of his staff being caught up in legal proceedings, especially custody of a child."

"I'll lose everything before I lose my son." Cate's expression was closed.

"Perhaps you could bring Lord Wyndham here?" Gerald suggested, scrutinising her closely. "The three of us could talk. There has to be an amicable solution to this, Cate. No court will give you sole custody, given the circumstances and the calibre of the man you're up against. You must have cared for him once?"

Cate raised her beautiful light green eyes. "He was the love of my life," she said simply. "They say one person can ruin you for anyone else. They got it right."

"I'm not much of an expert." He gave a faint grimace. Gerald had been divorced ten or more years previously. His wife had remarried soon after the divorce, weirdly enough to a younger clone of Gerald.

"I don't know if I can persuade him to come in here," Cate

said. "We parted in anger. Anyway, he does his own thing. I haven't told you the full extent of his mother's interference."

"There's more?" Gerald expelled a breath.

Cate nodded, giving him the full picture.

"When he returned from London, his mother told him I had left a note, basically saying I wanted *out*, it was all too much for me, I was too young. She was a talented artist, very good at sketching. I didn't write any Dear John letter, Gerald. His mother wrote it."

Gerald's brows, black in contrast to his silver hair, lifted. "You're saying she forged it?"

"She made use of her talents," Cate said. "Though I didn't hang around long enough to sight it," she added with bitter regret. "God, I was eighteen. No age at all. I was so naïve I believed her. Ashe had taken himself off to London rather than tell me it was all over."

"And you believed her?" Gerald asked somewhat incredulously. Women in his experience were notorious liars.

Cate nodded. "In a way I was in awe of her. Alicia was a law unto herself."

"You should have stayed." Gerald rolled his Mont Blanc pen in his hands. "Given him a chance to explain."

"I know that *now*, Gerald. I didn't know it then," Cate said with deep regret.

"But surely if he loved you he should have come after you?" Gerald persisted. "Money no object and all that?"

"He believed his mother's version of events. That says it all. The terrible thing is liars regularly get to be believed. Why exactly is that?"

No reply from Gerald.

"They rely on being believed, that's why. The people they talk to *know* they're liars yet they're still believed. It's really weird, like people confessing to crimes they didn't commit.

People are seriously flawed. Me included. Alicia backed up her version of events with a forged letter. There are so many versions in life. Different versions. Different viewpoints. A half a dozen people can tell six entirely different stories." She took a deep breath, trying to steady herself. "I'm taking up your time, Gerald. It was very good of you to see me without an appointment. I can't keep your other clients waiting." She gathered up her handbag, then stood up.

"Why don't you put it to him, Cate? Surely Alicia has ceased to matter?'

"Oh, she matters," Cate said.

"She certainly left her mark on you. This is your opportunity to put things straight, Cate."

"Only if he brings in a handwriting expert."

"Okay, let's see what I can do." Gerald pulled out a drawer. "He couldn't do better than Georgie Warbuton. She's the best."

Cate brightened. "I've heard of her. She's a forensic document examiner, isn't she?"

Gerald handed over a business card. "Yes. Legal firms and the police have benefited from her amazing expertise. If there are flaws in the handwriting in your letter, Georgina will find it. Good luck."

"Thanks, Gerald," Cate said with real feeling. "I'll leave a message at his hotel."

"Strike while the iron's hot," Gerald urged. "You could cut out a lot of the angst, if you're prepared to be reasonable, Cate. No need to anger Lord Wyndham further. Give him a chance. At the very least the two of you should talk, with a mediator to hand. We're not just talking about the two of you. There's your boy. You don't want anything ugly around your boy. You said Jules took to him on sight?"

"Of course he did. He must have recognised his father at some subconscious level. I wasn't there."

* * *

Armed with Georgina's business card, she made the return journey to the hotel where Ashe was staying. She would leave a message for him at Reception. Outside the luxury hotel she paused a moment to ring Stella on her mobile.

"Hi, I'll be a little late. I've just come from Gerald's office. I need legal advice. Gerald sent you his very kindest regards."

"Dear Gerald," said Stella, very offhand.

"He really cares about you too, Stell," Cate said dryly. "Take my word for it. I'll tell you all about it when I get home."

"Take care, Catrina. Do not endanger yourself or your reputation in any way."

"But I've already done that," Cate said and cut the connection.

Over the years different people, mostly women, had tried their best to sling a little mud in her direction. Murphy Stiller for one. The problem boiled down to one thing. Envy. The belief Catrina Hamilton had unfair advantages over them. Little did they know!

Stepping briskly into the lobby, head down, she almost collided with someone. Surely it was impossible to know who you bumped into with your head down? Only all her senses went into overdrive. Her heart was pounding as hard as the first day she had met him. There had to be some primordial explanation for it. Even when her life was totally different, everything was the same.

"Back to see me?" he said, tempted to bundle her up and carry her off. The urge, however primitive, was irresistible. This was the love of his life. As simple and maybe as destructive as that.

She looked up into his handsome face. "Actually yes. Not to *see* you, but leave you a message."

"How good of you." He took her arm, leading her off to the plush seating area with its glass-topped tables. At this time of the afternoon the area was almost empty. Two smartly dressed matrons were sitting on the central banquet in animated conversation. A glorious arrangement of fig branches, cordyline leaves, lime-green liliums centred with gorgeous ruby-red peonies sat atop the cone-shaped pillar that rose above the banquet.

"Well, what is it?" he asked, courteously pulling out her chair.

Ashe had always had beautiful manners. She had loved him not simply because of his outstanding good looks, his privileged position in life, his confidence. He had other important qualities. He was kind, generous, courteous to everyone, as liberal-minded as his mother had been a class snob. "Thank you." She sat down, opening up her handbag to extract the card Gerald had given her. "If you're going to visit a handwriting expert, this woman is the best. She has a doctorate in Psychology but she's a forensic document examiner as well. She's made many appearances in court, big fraud cases, that kind of thing."

His raven head was bent as he stared down at the card.

"Her reputation is impeccable," Cate added for good measure.

"Unlike yours."

"Cheap shot."

Of a sudden his eyes met hers. "Okay, I apologise."

"I never thought I'd hear you say that, Ashe," she said, ultra-controlled, when all she could think was how much she had loved him. Lost him. Yet the magic remained alive. "Have you contacted home?" she asked, aware she was adopting more and more an upper-class English accent. It gave her some sort of bizarre satisfaction.

"I check in every day."

"Good for you. Does your wife know about me?"

He glanced away, then back at her. "That's funny," he said.

"Not too funny, I hope? Let me share the joke. I didn't rate a mention? Didn't some poet say after the great love there were minor ones? Which one was I?"

He didn't answer for a minute. Instead he raised a hand to a circling drinks waiter. "I'm not married, Catrina."

Her voice wouldn't work for her. She had never felt so shocked in her life. She wanted to say something, but couldn't. Her vocal cords weren't working.

"You look like you could use a drink," he said crisply. "Why don't I get us a glass of champagne?"

The suavity of his tone went a way to restoring her. "No—wait."

He ignored her. The waiter promptly arrived. He ordered. "I think you can have *one* glass without going over the limit."

"When were you going to tell me?"

"I *have* told you," he said, pretending to be taken aback. "Sometimes it's better not to do everything at once."

Her heart in her chest felt cramped. "I don't understand this. I'm twenty-six, that makes you—"

"Thirty-one," he supplied with a downward drag on his handsome mouth.

"You've never *thought* of getting married? I mean, you have to produce an heir, don't you? It's mandatory."

His eyes flashed. "I could tell you to go to hell, but since you ask, Catrina, I did *once* think of marriage. I already have an heir. Our son, Julian, is my heir."

Something in his tone turned her blood ice-cold. "I'll never deliver him up to you."

"Never say never," he warned.

The most shocking aspect was, some part of her was *rejoicing.* Ashe wasn't married. What did that make her? *Human, perhaps?* Ashe hadn't married Marina or what was her name—Talia, Tallis? She ought to say something.

He was the one to speak. "All these years wasted," he said. "But I guess it's a part of life."

"I'm not the only one to blame, Ashe." She put up a hand as though to tidy her already immaculately arranged blonde hair.

"That's just it," he said, like a stab. "You carry your own share of blame."

"Maybe, but I was too inexperienced and you weren't there. I believed your mother, Ashe. Just as you did. Your mother destroyed our relationship. Go see the handwriting expert. I can provide you with samples for comparison."

His hand suddenly shot out to grasp her narrow wrist. How warm her skin was. How satiny smooth. How sizzling the contact. He would never get over the craving to touch her. "You could doctor them."

Anger swept through her. Anger and a never-ending hunger. It was like living with a powerful addiction. "Careful, our drinks are coming," he warned.

The waiter duly arrived, delivering two glasses of champagne with a smile.

"Drink up, Catrina," Wyndham said, after the waiter had gone. "I can't stay long."

"Neither can I," she returned sharply. "I have to get home."

"To our boy? Tell me, what was really behind Stella's decision to emigrate to Australia? People have been talking about it for years. She could easily have adopted a child in England. Instead she left her home, her family, everyone she knew. It doesn't make sense. Not then. Not now."

"It doesn't have to, does it? They made their decision. Their lives. Let it lie."

The flame in his blue eyes flared up. "Only I'm not prepared to let anything lie."

"In that case you'll have the note examined by an expert who could study recent and old examples of my writing. I have journals I kept from years ago." Only she wouldn't want anyone sighting them. They were far too personal, too private. "Cheers," she said ironically, picking up her glass and taking a long drink, her mouth filling with bubbles.

"I ought to tell you I kept some old examples of your handwriting myself," he admitted.

She gave a sceptical laugh. "You're not going to tell me on your person?"

"I have copies," he replied, unperturbed by the taunt. "Olivia will send the originals."

"So you mean to have the letter tested?" She was lured into hope.

"I will if you come with me." The hardness was still in his voice. "If you allow me to see my son."

Cate experienced another moment of panic.

"Invite me for lunch at the weekend," he suggested.

"You don't belong in our world."

"I think otherwise. I'm sure our son will be happy to see me. My regards to Stella. I must tell the family I'm delighted to have found her after all these years."

It would all come out now. She was sure of it. But Annabel was dead. "Did any of them actually come to Australia to look her up?" she challenged.

"Well, of course her sister did, the notorious Annabel."

Cate bridled. "Notorious?"

"Keep calm. Annabel was somewhat on the wild side, I believe. At least that was the word. Her marriage to Warren was a farce. It suited him to have a beautiful young wife. Annabel apparently got in with a fast lot. Drink, drugs, the usual thing. I wouldn't really know. Before my time. I do know she came out to Australia, didn't she, that final time?"

"I don't want to talk about Annabel," Cate said, shaking her head. "The woman is dead."

"So is my mother. Actually no one wants to talk about

Annabel," he said. "A distant cousin of mine was madly in love with her at some phase of his young life."

The question flew out of her mouth. "And who was that?" This was her best chance of finding something out.

"Why do you want to know?" His glance sharpened.

"Excuse me for asking."

"It was a Ralph Stewart. Everyone called him Rafe. He was a friend of my father's."

"Was?" Cate noted the past tense. She had never heard of the man until very recently yet the news came as a heart-stopper.

"Why the interest?" he asked, leaning forward a little.

She had made a mistake with the intensity of tone. "I'm making conversation."

"Fine, except you sound like you really want to know." He sat back. "Rafe is very much alive. He's a prominent political figure. It's my father who is no longer with us."

"I regret I didn't know him," Cate offered quietly. Geoffrey Carlisle's tragic end was a subject never broached.

"Had he lived he would have inherited the title and all that went with it," he said.

"*Stella* should have," Cate, the feminist, shot back.

"I agree, but all the large estates were entailed. It was a protective measure. Only males could inherit, the original idea being to keep the land in the family. You do see the sense of it? Sisters marry into other families. Stella and her sister, Annabel, were handsomely provided for. The title and land passed to me."

"Are you sure Jules could be your heir?" she asked with some sarcasm. "He's that quaint term—illegitimate. That could disrupt your plans."

"Nothing will disrupt my plans," he said and meant it. "Julian will not lose out."

"And I'll never let him go, Ashe," she responded fiercely.

"I'll fight tooth and claw for him. You'll never take him off to England. He won't want to go. You'd better take that into account. Jules is an Australian, Ashe. He loves his own country. As do I. This issue will go to litigation. I've already consulted a solicitor."

She spoke with the inner toughness of a woman who had pride and confidence in herself. He couldn't help but admire her effrontery. "Won't do you a bit of good," he said. "You're heavily in my debt, Catrina. You knowingly and willingly deprived me of all knowledge of my son. Now you've come up with a last-ditch attempt at mitigation."

"If I give you my promise you can see my son you will see Georgina Warbuton?"

"*Our* son," he corrected. "He has your blond hair but as he gets older the Carlisle physical characteristics will emerge. He's tall for his age, well built. That cute nose will form into my *beak*, as you used to call it. He already has the Carlisle eyes. Stella would confirm that." He tapped the glass-topped table hard. "There's something all wrong here," he declared.

"Like what?" What she was feeling was alarm. Even her breathing was audible.

"My mother used to say you reminded her of someone." He stared across at her.

"Now that's just not believable. I was born here."

"You have your adoption papers?"

He held her eyes so she couldn't look down. "Of course I have," she scoffed. "They're nothing to do with you."

"You are the mother of my child." He was gravely intent on her.

"Well I wasn't good enough for you then—why go into my ancestry? There could well be a convict lurking in *my* biological family's tree."

He was still watching her. "Your biological mother could well be alive."

"She isn't." She'd had enough of this questioning.

"How do you know?" he shot back very fast.

"I checked. Don't know who my biological father was. Sorry. Can't help you there."

"And Stella applied for adoption here in Australia?"

She forced herself to stay calm. "Do I have to spell it out? Stella couldn't have children of her own. What else could she do? She wanted a new life. She wanted a child. That child was me. She's been a wonderful mother to me and grandmother to Jules."

His expression softened slightly. "I could see how devoted they are to each other." There was a deep tender sadness in his tone. "But there's a story here, Catrina." He looked directly at her. "And I'm going to find it out."

"Fine!" She threw up her head. "Pity you weren't like that years ago." Her voice bit so deep he almost flinched.

"One thing I am is *responsible*, Catrina," he replied. "I would have thought you knew that. I would have taken full responsibility for you and our child. I would have married you just as we planned. Correction—as *I* planned."

Catrina stood up, leaving the rest of the champagne in her glass untouched. "Well, it took your mother to sabotage your plans. I'll make the appointment to see Georgina Warbuton. I'll let you know when."

He too rose to his feet. "It had better be soon. I want to see Julian at the weekend." He glanced at his watch. "I have an appointment to keep."

"Don't let me hold you up."

"I'll walk you to your car."

"Don't bother." Strain was in her voice. "It's parked nearly a block away."

"No problem. I have time."

Out on the busy street he took her arm as they threaded their way through the crowd. She could feel the energy coming off his body. His subtle masculine cologne was in her nostrils. Ashe had some power, no other man in her life, and she had known quite a few very attractive men, had made her feel so female. So much the *Woman*. A woman to be greatly desired. He was Jules' father. The last thing she wanted was a viciously fought child-custody battle. It could destroy her and his well-ordered world. But the most important person in all this was Jules.

Their son.

CHAPTER EIGHT

WITH GERALD'S RECOMMENDATION Cate was able to make an after-hours appointment with Georgina Warbuton, who was on call as an expert witness in a current hot case involving massive fraud.

She picked up Ashe outside his hotel. He was waiting on the pavement, looking out for her car. He got in quickly, shut the door, effectively locking them in together. He looked very handsome in a mustard-coloured jacket, blue jeans, with a midnight-blue cotton shirt open at the throat. She felt her body go into insubordinate surges of desire. If this were a romance novel she'd be flinging herself at him with primitive abandon. Only this was real life.

"Seat belt," she prompted, not looking at him. Wiser to keep her eye on the traffic. Mother Nature had given Ashe far too many advantages.

"I do know how to do this," he pointed out. He slung the belt across him and locked it in. "Nice car."

"Thank you." He had made no comment the last time he was in it. "I have an excellent high-paying job."

"I know exactly how much you get," he said very dryly.

Cate was angered. "I beg your pardon." She flashed him an irate glance.

"It would be a good idea to watch the road," he said as a white Porsche pulled out right in front of them.

"I can't believe Hugh gave that away." Hugh was exceedingly discreet.

"It wasn't Hugh."

"Tell me. I want to know."

He glanced at her. She had a beautiful profile. He hadn't been celibate all these years, but just looking at Catrina was a bigger turn-on than full-blown sex with any other woman in all that time. Catrina was the real thing. A *femme fatale*. "You understand envy," he said. "I understand envy. People become envious. It's the way of the world."

"It was Murphy Stiller?"

He gave an exaggerated sigh. "I don't want to go into it. Settlement date for Isla Bella is ninety days hence. Thank you for your part in it."

"Lady McCready liked you. She's no snob, but Lord Wyndham did the trick. And then of course she knows about the trainloads of money. But surely you won't have the time for frequent visits?"

"I'll find time," he said. "Trustworthy caretakers are in place. They'll look after it for me. I'll allow my family and friends to use the island. You may even rate an invite. Julian certainly will."

"Jules won't go anywhere without me," she said sharply.

"Then you can come too."

All her resources, mind and body, were being put to work. "Oh, God, Ashe," she breathed. "Isn't ours a star-crossed story?"

He considered that for a long moment. "There's been far too much anguish, Catrina. I don't believe in love stories any more."

She felt tears come into her eyes. She blinked them away. "Do you have my notes with you?" she asked.

"Two samples. The ones we can actually use. The others

were a bit too personal. One would have thought you were desperately in love with me."

"I was. For a time." Occasionally one had to tell lies.

"It must have been difficult forgetting you ever cared?" he asked with a terrible calm.

"How was it for you?" She shot him a sparkling glance.

"I saw it as horrible treachery."

"On the basis of what your mother told you, then showed you. That's why we're going to consult Georgina Warbuton. I should warn you, you won't be able to go on exonerating your mother. I know how painful that will be. You can't claim total ignorance either. You knew your mother was dead set on Marina."

Knowledge of that was hitting him increasingly hard. He remained silent.

"Sorry, Ashe," said Cate. "Your mother had no conscience when it came to you and what she thought you should have. A different value system came into play."

Georgina Warbuton couldn't have been kinder, or nicer. A handsome woman in her late fifties, she welcomed them into her elegant terraced home. A tall, distinguished-looking man she introduced as her husband. After a few pleasantries, her husband left them.

They were offered tea, coffee, politely refused. Both of them were intent on getting answers. Georgina Warbuton shepherded them into her book-lined study, more like a library with floor-to-ceiling built-in bookcases on either side of a marble fireplace. A lovely flower painting of the Dutch school—it appeared to have been done with a palette knife—hung over it. The polished floor was covered with a beautiful vibrant Persian rug in deep reds and blues. There was room for a comfortable sofa and two matching armchairs covered in a beautiful blue silk-velvet picking up the colour in the rug and the blue of Ashe's shirt.

Dr Warbuton waited until they were seated before she took the sensitive documents into her long, expressive hands. Her keen gaze was very serious now. She was fully occupied with what was before her. "This shouldn't take long," she announced after a few moments, retreating behind her antique desk. There she switched on a table light with a strong beam, angling it towards her. Next she began to delve in a desk drawer.

To Cate, desperately hopeful, that sounded as though Dr Warbuton thought the outcome was a foregone conclusion.

Vindication.

For a moment her spirits soared, then crashed back to earth again.

Too late.

Cate looked over at the man she still loved. His hands were locked. He was looking down, his lean, athletic body perfectly still. For a split second she wanted to move across to him on the sofa, hold his hand. He had viewed Alicia with the eyes of a loving son. Blood was thicker than water.

Georgina Warbuton was examining the documents very closely now. Whatever she thought she was keeping quiet about it until she was absolutely sure.

There *couldn't* be a problem. There couldn't, Cate thought with a sinking feeling of dismay. Even the greatest art experts in the world had been tricked. Had Alicia been so clever she had even fooled an expert?

Finally Dr Warbuton looked up, her gaze intense. "It is my professional opinion, this letter—" she held up the contentious note "—is not the handwriting of Catrina here. It is in fact a clever forgery." Her voice was dispassionate, but her eyes were kind.

"You're absolutely sure?" Ashe asked gravely.

"I am." Dr Warbuton's answer was quiet. "If the matter is so very important to you, you could consult another handwriting expert, but they will tell you the same thing. If you care to come here, I can show you various markers."

Cate shook her head. She didn't want to see them. She didn't want to augment Ashe's pain. She looked to him as he sat mute.

Georgina Warbuton gave them both a moment. She could see how tremendously important verification of the document was. She had no doubt at all it had been carefully written by a hand other than the beautiful young woman in front of her. A clever hand. An artist's hand? The purpose? It was none of her business. She had to be entirely objective in her judgments.

Finally Ashe rose to his feet, his striking features taut. It was obvious he was feeling deep emotion. "That won't be necessary, Dr Warbuton," he said, respect in his voice. "You're a recognised expert in these matters. We won't proceed further."

Out in the street again she had to near run to keep pace with him, her face thrown up against the breeze, a strand of her hair coming loose, whipping across her cheek. Her body was humming with high-pitched nervous energy. Ashe's broad back, the set of his square shoulders, indicated he was battling a heavy load of tension.

He reached the car before she did.

"Are you getting in?" she asked, staring up into his taut face.

He touched an elegant hand to his temple. "I don't think so. I feel like walking."

"You don't know this part of the city," she said. "You could get lost. It's a long haul back to your hotel."

"I can always catch a cab," he said curtly.

"Please, Ashe." She tried to force balance, reason, into her voice. "I know you're upset."

He suddenly reached for her bare slender arms, clutching them hard. *"Upset?"* The expression on his handsome face was ravaged. "You were right!"

"Let me go, Ashe," she said quietly.

He released her with a sharp jerk. "God," he groaned. "Not one of us doubted her. Olivia, Leonie, me. We accepted her word, totally."

Cate, a mother herself, was now closer to understanding. "She was your mother, the strongest force in your life. The woman who had taken care of you from your very first breath. Your father wasn't there to make a judgment. I'm sure he would have handled things better."

"I can't answer that," he said, when he knew that would definitely have been the case. His father had been a highly intelligent man with wide-ranging briefs in very important work.

"You told me once your mother and father didn't agree on lots of things?" she suggested.

"My father saw things a whole lot clearer than my mother." His answer was brusque. "She tended to get very emotional."

"Not the best state to be in when you're trying to make an objective judgment. We all know that. Why don't you get in the car?" she urged. "I'll drive you back to the hotel."

They were well under way. But she hadn't composed herself sufficiently to take the next obstacle on board.

"Okay, my mother did a very wrong thing," he acknowledged tersely. "She had allowed herself to believe *my* life was hers. But *you*! I told you over and over I loved you deeply, Catrina. You were precious to me. You were part of my life; the whole twin souls bit. I told you I wanted to *share* my life with you. Yet you forgot all that the moment I turned my back."

"I was *young*, Ashe. Too young. Just a kid. You were five years older. Had I been five years older I may have handled it better. But your mother tied me up in knots. We both did the wrong thing. If your mother convinced *you*, think what an effect she had on me."

He shoved a hand through his wind-tousled hair. "You could have given yourself time to think it all through. I was home two days later. You could have stayed."

The sharp edges in his voice cut into her. "Ashe, I was told to back off in no uncertain terms. I really don't want this conversation. It's all too late."

"No, it isn't. I'm right *here*, Catrina, physically beside you. How many times did we make love?" he asked, in what seemed to her a totally disillusioned voice.

"One time too many," she said, then immediately shook her head. "I can't say that. I have my Jules."

"*Our* Jules," he said right on cue. "I just wish you'd told me. God knows you've had years."

The extraordinary thing was, in retrospect she had to ask herself why hadn't she? "The reason—or one of the reasons—was I believed you were married; probably had a couple of kids. I only had Jules. Please, Ashe. Just let it lie."

"I know my obligations," he said firmly.

They were nearing the hotel, one of the finest five-star hotels in the city. It was stunningly situated, overlooking the Harbour and the Opera House. "There's a parking spot. Grab it."

"I'm not coming in," she said briefly. Even with the air conditioning on, the interior of the car was steaming up.

"Grab it," he repeated in a crisp, authoritative tone. Ashe

had come a long way over the past years. He was no longer the young man she had known.

She felt far too agitated to argue. She had caught the flash in his eyes.

Inside the hotel he steered her seemingly solicitously towards the bank of lifts. "We have a custody agreement to work out."

"We have *no* custody agreement," she muttered, playing her part. "I want my son full time. I won't share him."

He only gave one of his elegant shrugs. "Neither of us wants to cause him grief. He's my son, too, Catrina. I would think your solicitor pointed this out to you. You've had Julian for the past seven years. It's your turn to make it up to me."

"So what do you want?" She was aware her emotions were getting out of hand. Always the see-saw. Up and down.

"Maybe we should talk about this in my suite," he said, lowering his voice as several hotel guests approached the lifts.

They were inside his spacious suite on the thirty-fourth floor. It was decorated in a sophisticated style with rich silks and exotic Honduran mahogany, but the emphasis was on comfort. There was a splendid view of the city's icons all aglitter through the series of triple-glazed soundproofed plate-glass windows.

"Sit down," he said, extending a hand towards one of the three-seater sofas, luxuriously upholstered.

"All I can give you is a half hour," she said, smoothing the skirt of her sleeveless silk cotton dress, printed in a medley of green and gold.

A black eyebrow shot up. "A half hour? That's it?"

"I have a lot of work lined up for tomorrow, Ashe. A good thing Hugh is handling your affairs himself."

"I suppose he would as he's the boss," he said dryly. "Want a drink?" He walked to the mini-bar.

"No," she answered. "Maybe a Perrier water."

He gave her a taut half smile. "Coming up. I'm not going to waive my right to see Julian at the weekend."

Cate felt herself stiffen. "You're not going to say anything to him?"

"As a matter of fact—" He made her wait until he had poured her a mineral water.

"As a matter of fact, *what*?" She was on tenterhooks.

"Of course I'm not going to say anything," he said, coming back towards her. "We both know the time isn't right."

"Is it *ever* going to be right, Ashe? I doubt it." She looked and felt unspeakably sad. Most of the previous night she had lain awake wondering what his plans would be. At such times her mind inevitably going back over the halcyon days they had spent together. The long walks, the conversations they'd had. They had talked about their hopes and their dreams, about art, literature, movies, religion, philosophy, politics, floated theories. They could talk about anything and find it immensely enjoyable. Both of them were born scholars always out to learn. Ashe had read Law and Economics at Oxford, graduating with a double first. If he had been thinking of following his father into British Intelligence, his father's death had made him rethink his plans.

He bent to put his glass down on the coffee table between the two sofas, then he shouldered out of his jacket, placing it over one of six chairs set around a glass-topped table in the dining area. Another lovely arrangement of flowers sat on the coffee table; a low celadon-coloured bowl of perfect velvety white gardenias that spread their ravishing perfume. No doubt they would be replaced the following day as they wilted but for now the blooms were astonishingly beautiful. Cate resisted the impulse to stroke a velvety petal. She didn't want to discolour it, though her own luminous skin looked just as stroke-able.

"You always did like white flowers," he said, taking a seat opposite her. "The rose gardens at the hall are quite famous now. People come from all over to view them on open days. I seem to remember your favourites. Snow Queen was one. It's one of the great roses, then there was the profusely flowering Iceberg—"

"And that wonderfully fragrant Bride," she broke in, fancying she could almost smell the perfume of the beautiful large, pure white rose with its exquisite form.

"There's a walled garden devoted entirely to white roses," he told her. "My idea. No need to ask what had prompted it," he said with some irony.

She looked up and their eyes locked. Always the quickening sensations in her body, the thrum of electricity. She *knew* the same electrical current was switched on in him. It was something neither of them seemed able to control. The very air was sexualised, exciting. "Cate," he murmured, "tell me this didn't happen. None of it happened."

The regret in his voice was echoed in her own. "I wish I could. I told you, we're star-crossed lovers."

"No one could take your place."

That cut to her heart, yet she said crisply, "And I bet there was no shortage of candidates. You'll find an eligible woman, Ashe, close to your rank."

His blue eyes burned. "Do stop talking rubbish. Prince William married his Kate. Prince Frederik married his Mary. Two great romances. My mother's mindset was from another time."

"God, Ashe, she was only in her mid-fifties then. Maybe she was channelling Queen Victoria?"

"Our present Queen had to marry a prince, or at the very least an earl. Ironic, isn't it? How times change. Princess

Margaret couldn't marry her divorced airman. Hard to believe now but it happened and she suffered."

"Your lot are still as stuffy," she said.

He frowned, although he knew in many cases it was true. "There's got to be a plausible explanation for Stella Radclyffe—your adopted mother, so you say—taking off for the other side of the world. She didn't attend her own father's funeral. Needless to say that was seized upon. Whereas Annabel, the supposed flighty one, was there. Decidedly odd. It wouldn't come as much of a surprise to me to find out *Annabel* was your biological mother." He looked surprised by his own observation.

Cate sprang to her feet. "That is so…so…"

"*Possible.* Sit down, Cate," he said with crisp authority. "I will get the answers, although I believe I've got one now. How's this for a hypothesis? Annabel fell pregnant. It would have created a great scandal at the time. She was unmarried, very young, pampered and adored. So what scheme did the sisters hatch?"

"I'm not following you at all." Of course she was. She resumed her seat, but pointedly glanced at her watch. Her heart was racing.

"No, you're not following me, you're way ahead. Always something to hide. That's you, isn't it, Catrina? When did you find out?" The blunt question was like a lash.

Of a sudden Cate gave up the deceit, torn by rage and shame. She was sick of it all, half frightened too. "Annabel came to visit Stella to be with someone who loved her and there to die. She had burned herself out."

"Sadly she did," he agreed in a sympathetic tone.

"But before she died she made a deathbed confession. She needed to get on the right side of the Big Guy up there. *She* was my biological mother. She had begged Stella to save her and her reputation. Big sister Stella came to the rescue, sacrificing herself. My mother didn't want me, you know," she said and tried to smile. "A baby would have sabotaged her plans."

Of course. That was it.

Ashe looked into her face, seeing a lifetime of tremendous hurt and pain of rejection. Pain of rejection gave credence to her story. Here was the mother of his child, living a large part of her life thinking herself an adopted child only to discover as a woman she had been deceived by someone who loved her, her own aunt, Stella. There would be long-reaching consequences of this.

"You must have been shocked, more at Stella than Annabel. Why didn't Stella tell you at some point much earlier?"

Cate rested her blonde head back on the sofa. "To be honest, I don't think she could get it out. I used to think I would never forgive her for not telling me."

"And have you? I'd say you still haven't forgiven her. Maybe you never will."

A sad smile was etched on Cate's face. "Bitterness taints, Ashe. I love Stella. She's my aunt, and Jules' great-aunt. She spent a lifetime looking out for her little sister and then looking after me."

"Did Annabel never reveal who your father is?" He could see tears behind the sparkle in her eyes, veiled by her long lashes.

"Maybe she didn't *know*." Her lovely mouth firmed into a disillusioned smile.

"Oh, she *knew*," Ashe retorted. "It's up to you now to find out."

It was such an effort to keep her voice steady. "I don't want to know either."

"I don't accept that. Your biological father may well have been in the same position as me." Ashe's tone hardened. "Have you ever considered Annabel mightn't have told him?"

She felt a sudden chill as though Annabel's shade were right behind her. "I have no idea. Both you and Stella have made the comment Rafe Stewart was madly in love with Annabel at the time. Do you recall anything your mother or father might have said?"

"Not in front of me or my sisters," he said. "We were kids. Rafe is, as I said, a prominent politician."

She stared at the area rug. "Is he married? I'm not saying there could be any connection, just asking the question."

"He's married, yes. To Helena Stewart, a lovely woman. She runs a very successful interior-decorating business."

"Children?"

He didn't answer. He appeared to be battling feelings of his own.

"Is that a no, then?" The room seemed very quiet now, as though the walls were listening.

"They had an only child, a son, Martin," he said finally. "Martin was a bit of a playboy. He was very handsome, very charming, very droll. But he was always in some kind of trouble with Rafe having to bail him out. He went into rehabilitation a number of times. Everyone hoped he'd beat his addiction, but in the end he died of an overdose. It took both Rafe and Helena years to pull out of it. Somehow they did."

Cate felt utter dismay. "How very, very tragic. What would have made a young man with everything in life become dependent on drugs?"

Ashe shrugged. "Once they start they can't stop. It's a tough world out there for young people these days. The availability, the peer pressure. Sometimes it must get so oppressive they feel driven to conform. Martin felt he lived very much in his father's shadow. He had the morbid fear he could never measure up, never meet the high expectations he thought were expected of him. His own harsh judgment, I have to tell you. His parents loved him. He was sent down from Oxford. He and another one of his druggie pals. Rich kids. It was all downhill from there. His sense of self-esteem gave out."

"It upset you, didn't it?"

"It greatly upset everyone who knew him. Death is no victory, no way out. What it was, was a tragic waste of a young life."

She could see he was still trying to grapple with Martin Stewart's death. "What did he look like?" she asked after a long moment, because somehow it seemed right.

Ashe exhaled heavily. "The girls used to call him Adonis. He was very handsome, as I said, but he settled for looking *louche*. That was the image he wanted to project." He was speaking now as though under a spell. "Martin had thick blond hair that he wore quite long." He touched his shoulders as an indicator. "He had lots of 'friends' but no close friends. The real friends were very worried about him. They tried to help him so he cut them out of his life. His so called 'friends' brought out the worst in him. But that was where he wanted to stay although it was a life sentence."

"I'm so sorry," Cate said. "I can only guess at the agony of his parents and his friends. Wasn't it Aristotle who said: The gods had no greater torment than for a mother to lose her child?"

"He might have said *father* too," Ashe answered for the fathers of the world.

"Maybe mothers have the edge in suffering? Not everyone has the strength to fight for life. To some, it must seem easier to throw it away."

He nodded grimly, looked away.

"Tell me something, Ashe." She felt compelled to forge ahead. "Do *I* resemble him at all?" Her question was calm enough but her heart was beating too fast for comfort.

"Sorry?" The sound of her voice brought him out of his reverie.

"Do *I* look like Martin? Straightforward question."

"God, Catrina!" He found himself staring back at her as though looking for enlightenment from above. Realisation began to press in on him. He had thought he was beyond surprise. Hadn't her colouring always struck him as familiar? She wasn't a copy of Martin, but she certainly could have been his sister!

"Hello, Ashe!" She wanted to jolt him into speech. "At least it's not a *hell no*!"

"Catrina, this is all too strange." The expression on his handsome face was both proud and moody. "If I said yes, I could be putting you on the wrong track entirely. Why don't you discuss it with Stella? That woman knows the story. Maybe the *whole* story. She would never have laid eyes on Martin, but she did know Rafe and as far as I recall she went to school with Rafe's sister, Penelope."

The veiled attack on Stella wasn't lost on her. "Stella has hardly said a blessed thing about either of them."

"She is without doubt a very secretive woman." Even a ruthless woman. Ashe's gaze was intense and highly speculative.

"This is an odd conversation we're having." Cate too was feeling decidedly uneasy.

"Well, it is *odd*, isn't it? Stella migrating to Australia to save her younger sister's reputation; refusing to acknowledge your true relationship, claiming she adopted you, presumably from an agency. Pretty hard to plead that down to a misdemeanour."

The misdemeanours were beginning to pile up. "She's very sorry for it now," Cate said.

"Maybe she could purge her sorrow telling you the truth?" he suggested crisply.

"Maybe it's too bad to tell—ever thought of that? I never questioned Stella, you know. I was always aware I looked *different*. Both Stella and Annabel had dark hair and dark eyes. Things might have been different had I been a carbon copy of my biological mother. As I'm not, I must take after my father. Whoever he may be," she said gravely. "You've experienced firsthand what deception can do, Ashe, your own mother forging a letter. People do it all the time. Letters, documents, anything where they have something to gain. Anyway—" she rose with determination to her feet "—I didn't come here to rehash the past."

"Then why *did* you come?" His blue eyes burned over her.

"You already know. *One*, you more or less compelled me. *Two*, so I could fix a time for you to see Jules. In my company, of course."

"Do you really think I'm going to jump on a plane with him?" he returned very dryly.

She made a mock face of apology.

"Actually I'd like to spend the whole day with him. Maybe this coming Sunday? We could go for a drive, have lunch somewhere. The Hunter Valley isn't all that far away, is it? The Blue Mountains, boat trip on the Harbour? One could never tire of seeing it from the water. Or as a seven-year-old Julian might like a trip to Taronga Park Zoo. I understand the location is fantastic with the best vantage points on Sydney Harbour. Maybe we can leave it to Julian to choose."

"We call him *Jules*," she said. Julian seemed to mark him as Ashe's son.

Ashe too was on his feet. He had moved too close to her, causing a swift reaction. Her heart was beating like a bird imprisoned in her chest.

"His *father* calls him Julian," he said in a voice that would have crushed another woman. But not Cate. "We can introduce the Jules later as we get to know each other." He had moved even nearer. The space between them was thrumming with heat. "So what time Sunday?"

"Ooh..." Something further was coming. "Nine suit you? I think Jules would like the zoo."

"Then the zoo it is," he said with just a touch of mockery.

She knew she mustn't touch him. Or he touch her. She knew she was only kidding herself. "Goodnight, Ashe."

"Goodnight, Catrina." He caught her wrist, twisted his fingers around it. "I'll come with you to your car." His eyes were full of strange lights.

"No need." Holding her hand, he had to register her whole body as drawn as taut as a wire. She felt as hot as if she were coming down with a fever.

"I've no intention of letting you go alone. A beautiful woman on her own is a target for unwanted attention."

"I've never had any trouble. *Really*, Ashe." She was in far more trouble where she was.

"Why sound so edgy? As much as part of me hates to admit it, I want to keep you beside me for ever."

"You sound like you're in crisis," she taunted. "You despise your own weakness."

"Don't you have the same problem?" he challenged, a note of cynicism creeping in.

"I've learned my lesson, Ashe. It wouldn't work. Then or now." She shifted away a fraction.

"Sure you didn't write that note?" He lifted an indolent hand to remove the pretty art-nouveau clasp that held back her hair. "There, doesn't that feel better?" he asked, unrepentant, as her beautiful hair, set free, slid forward in a smooth motion.

"You can't take that clip," she protested. "It's an antique piece." He had put it in his pocket.

"I'll give it back," he said. "Promise."

There was such an extraordinary aura about him, a whole

catalogue of advantages, the natural authority, the seeming calm and underneath a huge reserve of passion. It was shattering to know even if she wanted to, she couldn't break her bond with him.

"I don't know what we're doing here, Ashe, but if it's a ploy to soften me up, it won't work. You can't take Jules. My son is my life." The tremulous note in her voice gave her away.

"What if I take you as well?" he suggested, staring down at her in such a way it fired her blood. "Like it or not Julian is part of us both. What do you think he would say if you told him I was his father? Told him how circumstance ripped us apart. Told him how I lived to marry you, to make you my wife? What would he say if I told him when my back was turned, you vanished out of my life never to tell me *or* him we are father and son."

Of a sudden her nerve failed, ebbed away. "This is emotional blackmail, Ashe."

"I don't care what it is," he returned bluntly. "It's the *truth*."

"Jules is not ready for the truth, Ashe," she cried, knowing she was becoming overexcited. "I was wrong to come here."

A shadow crossed his handsome face. "But you've been wrong all along. I'm not going to give up my son, Catrina." There was a quiet but deadly firmness in his voice.

Colour rose beneath her skin as he confirmed her own thought. She turned on him, racked by conflicting emotions. "So where is it all going to end?"

He looked at her sharply weighing that up. "Don't you feel *some* guilt?" Anger spilled from eyes that were bluer than any Burmese sapphire.

"If we're going to make denunciations, what about *you*?" she hit back incautiously. "I'd say we're about even when it comes to making mistakes."

"Okay, okay." He partly agreed. "Only my plan is to put it right. You're not married. Neither am I. In a sense our lives were blown apart. Now I want you back in my life again. You're the mother of my son. I remind you that you were born of an English mother and almost certainly an English father. Don't you remember how you fitted in? You didn't think you would, but you did. The English side of you came to the fore. Julian's long vacation is coming up. May I make a suggestion? You could think about spending Christmas in England with me. You and Julian, Stella too if she wants to come. I would think she would like to return to her birthplace."

"What, as a visitor?" she retorted hotly when she felt a wave of near-happy anticipation. "Stella and my mother were born at Radclyffe Hall, Ashe. But *you* got it all. So does that mean you get to make all the decisions too?"

"Go file a complaint," he said caustically. "It was all legal, Catrina. *Your* grandfather, might I point out, made me his heir. Of course it would have been my father, but I was next in line. Julian one day may very well be the sixth Baron Wyndham. You can't change that."

"Try me!" She threw up her head. "Jules has already confided his ambition to anyone who will listen. He's aiming to become Prime Minister of Australia. He wants to put things right. He wants to be in a position to make life better for everyone. He won't change. He won't turn into an upper-class English boy packed off to boarding school as soon as he can toddle."

Ashe heard the conviction in her voice. He had to face the fact she could be right about their son and his long-term aims. He had fallen in love with Cate, reared in Australia where life was very open, confident and remarkably frank. Hadn't she been different from all the other girls in his circle?

"Understand me clearly," he said. "What Julian wants is important to me as well. I would never force a decision on him. But you've had our son for the past seven years. I am going to redress that. You can make it easy, or you can make it hard. It's up to you."

"So what roles do we play?" She swallowed with difficulty.

"I'll tell my sisters quietly all they need to know."

"I doubt they can keep it to themselves." She managed a derisory laugh.

"We *all* have experience of keeping things to ourselves, Catrina. You would know that better than most. Julian is their nephew, therefore they will do everything to protect him."

"In effect what I'm seeing is a Carlisle takeover."

His eyes flashed. "I'm not saying that at all, Catrina. I'm saying nothing concrete at the moment."

It was crisis point. The breath shook in her throat as she said, "But you will. When and if you do get to know more about Jules you might have to forfeit at least some of your plans. Since Jules was born I have been solely responsible for him."

"Because you omitted to inform me, his father," he shot back, rather bleakly.

That omission now hurt her. She strained away from him, but he held her fast.

"Cate!" he groaned.

She felt her heart constrict. "What happens if he doesn't like you and your family?"

"That's the worst possible scenario. Have you enough grace to accord me some understanding on this?"

"Not yet." He was moving much too fast. "Don't make me hate you, Ashe."

"I think I can handle it." His smile held a degree of self-mockery. "Besides you don't hate me at all. Life has caught up with us, Cate."

"But I'm not the Cate I used to be. Poor vulnerable little Cate. I'm *another* me. I have *another* life."

He had the sense he had a tigress by the tail. "Your *life* was supposed to be with me. Remember what you called it—*destiny.*"

He had touched a psychic nerve. "Destiny did a darn good job of mucking us up."

Within seconds their confrontation had moved from a kind of maddened frustration to a violent need to come together. To physically connect. There were layers upon layers of yearning beneath the conflict that was at best only skin deep.

"What I want to do now—what I *need* to do now is kiss you," he said in a voice seductive with want. His eyes devoured her face, came to rest on her mouth. "Your mouth is no different from what it used to be, do you know that? It's perfect. Perfect for me. Perfect for kissing. God, I couldn't count the kisses." His arms enfolded her, one hand very firm at her back.

Her whole body was pierced with awareness. "What is *this* going to solve, Ashe?" She knew where they were inexorably heading.

"That neither of us are going to fall in love with anyone else?"

"We've still got time." Only residual pride allowed her to say that.

"A lifetime won't be long enough for either of us to forget. I finally have you, Cate."

He looked down at her with intensity. He was mesmerising her and she was letting him. The effect was spine-tingling. "You think you do."

"I *know* I do," he said in his resonant voice. "The image of you has stayed with me. Cate, the eighteen-year-old girl, ravishingly pretty, now a true beauty. The fine bone structure of your face is more apparent. Your skin is as translucent as porcelain."

She knew she could have pulled away. Ashe would never handle her roughly. Only she stood there, held by his hypnotic gaze.

"Did you ever just once *mean* you loved me?" he asked as though he was trying to make sense of it all.

"I don't want to go back that far," she pleaded. Everything was totally different. Everything was the same.

"Let me remind you." He tipped up her chin, only to trail a line of kisses over her cheek to behind her ear. His mouth moved lower to nuzzle her neck, sending thrill after thrill shooting through her. How had she ever thought she could stop caring? His roving mouth came to rest in the warm hollow above her collarbone. "Remember this?" he asked dreamily.

She felt the coaxing caress of his hand. "Maybe..." Her voice shook. There was more to come. Nothing she could or would do to stop it. She was locked into a spell. She never had been able to withstand the spells Ashe wove. She was programmed to respond.

His mouth came down over hers, almost but not quite kissing her. "Seven long years," he muttered. "Misery for me. But a great thing happened to you, didn't it, Cate? You had our son." He pulled her in very tightly as though she would never be free to go.

A warm languor was sweeping through her, robbing her legs of strength. She had an idea she was leaning into him for support. She felt so light-headed it was as if she were weightless. His mouth was moving over her face and neck... He bent her backwards, kissing the shadowed cleft between her breasts.

Desire welled up as if from a gushing spring. "You hurt me badly."

"You hurt *me*."

"It still matters, Ashe," she gasped, hollow with yearning.

"Of course it does." The pads of his thumbs were working her erect nipples.

Reason was obliterated. She closed her eyes the better to lock in the ecstasy. No one had ever made love to her like Ashe. His hand was on the zipper of her dress. He pulled it down and the silken fold of fabric fell away from her, sliding to her feet. She stood in her undergarments. "I want you so badly," he said in such a quiet voice, it was barely a breath. "Don't fight me on this, Cate." His hands covered the slopes of her warm, smooth breasts.

I'm going to die of longing, she thought. Only just coping, she eased herself into him, her flesh melting like candle wax. "One last time?"

"And the one after, and the one after that…"

He lifted her slowly, easily, carrying her into the bedroom and laying her down on the king-sized bed. "You never know, you might like it. You certainly used to."

They were staring into one another's eyes, each seeking their own reflection. "It was different back then. I'm not the same. I was young."

His laugh was gently mocking. "You're the same." He passed a masterly hand over her body. It visibly quivered at his touch, awaiting further excitation. She was lying prone on the bed, her long legs extended, yet she felt as though he were drawing her up. "People change, but what we had lasts. I called it love. God knows what you called it, but you want me just as much as I want you." He lowered himself onto the side of the bed studying her, so beautiful, so womanly, so made for loving. "Go on, deny it. If you can." He began to caress her, his hand moving slowly over her, his palms against her flesh, her breasts, her stomach, his fingers sliding below the line of her briefs moving downwards, pressing, sending fiery sensations shooting through her. The sense of excitement, of utter intoxication, was extreme; the bursts of pleasure were such she thought she would come to a shuddering climax merely from the rotating movements of his long, caressing fingers.

That harsh breathing she suddenly realised was hers. She sounded very agitated. God, how she needed this! Her whole body was flowering, opening up to him. The needs of her body were in total control now. Her skin glittered with a faint dew as pressure built. She felt a crazed desperation to have him inside her.

"Ashe," she moaned like a woman only just holding it together. "Make love to me." Far, far into the night. At the same time what remained of cold reason told her:

He planned this. Planned it perfectly.

And you went along with it. Why?

She knew why. She was worn down by the years of intense loneliness, of the sense of deprivation, for that was what it had been without Ashe. Without love. Sex was a crucial part of it, but what they'd had had been more noble, engaging both mind and spirit. Still the lack of sex in the way she wanted it had weighed on her heavily. Now the drive towards fulfilment was gaining irresistible momentum.

She didn't realise it but tears were rolling down her cheeks. He bent his dark head, catching them up with his mouth as though each teardrop were as precious as a flawless diamond…

Naked, her skin gleamed like satin in the soft light. He had turned away swiftly to strip off his clothes, not bothering to hang them over anything, but discarding them where they fell. She called his name, begging him not to delay. She was desperate to merge her body with his.

It had been so long. So long. No one before or after her.

She was his woman, first and last. Rock-hard, Ashe moved towards the bed.

Their destinies were entwined.

He had found her. He had found his son.

They were his. He would never let them go. This was the most important mission of his life. His objective was to win. Nothing was as important to him as Catrina and Julian. They were his family.

He came to her, whispering into her open mouth, "Thy fate and mine are sealed."

CHAPTER NINE

CATE AND STELLA rarely had disagreements. They dealt calmly and considerately with one another and they had Jules in common. But when Cate arrived home much later than expected, Stella had the attitude of a woman on the warpath. Obviously there was some undisclosed crisis going on in her mind.

"Nearly twelve o'clock, right?"

"Hey, you gave me a fright." Cate actually jumped. Stella was standing right inside the front door. Her expression made Cate feel like a problematic teenager home much too late. "I didn't know I had to clock in and out." Cate tried a joke. "What's the problem?"

Stella's dark eyes were deeply shadowed. "We both know what the problem is," she said severely, as though Cate's past were being reactivated. "It's Julian Carlisle. He broke your heart once. Are you going to allow him to do it again?"

Cate groaned. "Stella, do you really want to get into this now?"

"Answer me." Stella spoke as if she had the right.

"With respect, I think that might be my business."

Stella wasn't about to apologise. "He wants Jules. You know that. He'll stop at nothing to get him. Jules, *my* Jules. *My* family."

Cate put her bag down, counting to ten. "Stella can we have this conversation at another time? I want to go to bed."

"But you've been to bed, haven't you?" Stella accused. Strong emotion was swirling at the backs of her eyes. "You have the look of a woman who's been very thoroughly bedded." Concrete evidence Cate had no moral strength. Like Annabel perhaps?

Cate shook her head. "I don't believe I'm hearing this, Stella. What I do is my business, not yours."

But Stella was on a roll, challenging as she had never been before. "It's clear to me you have no will of your own when he's around. You know how hard it's been getting over him. Now, you're back in the firing line."

Cate was dismayed and confused. Was this the Stella she had lived with all her life or a far more aggressive twin? "Stella, I'm not talking about this now," she said carefully. "You didn't have to wait up for me. I'm a grown woman. Not in *your* firing line. You're actually overstepping the mark."

"Am I now?" Stella gave a harsh laugh. "I certainly *did* have to wait up for you. I'm very worried about you, Catrina." She thrust her hair behind one ear.

"Well, you don't have to be." Cate backed away.

"I don't believe that," Stella hit back. "You should see yourself!'

To Cate's stunned ears it had a ring of *jealousy*. Was that possible? Stella was jealous of her? It seemed preposterous. Yet if it were so, she didn't know how to deal with it. She turned to look in the tall gilt-framed mirror over the hallway console. She did look different. She looked blazingly *alive*, an erotic creature still wearing the veils of ecstasy. "I look fine, though my hair is a bit on the messy side." Unlike its usual order, her hair tumbled in a thick golden mane. Even she knew she looked beautiful. What did Stella see?

Stella saw something she didn't like because her face was

a set mask. "I hope you took precautions?" she said severely, as though endlessly plagued by concerns in this regard. "We don't want a repeat of the last time."

"The last time?" This from kind-hearted Stella? Cate forced calm on herself.

"Like mother, like daughter," Stella affirmed, wringing her hands like a latter-day Lady Macbeth.

"Now that's uncalled for, Stella." Cate suddenly exploded. "It would be very unwise of us to continue this conversation."

But Stella, for the first time in living memory, was stripped of her calm façade. "No matter how clever you are, you're not ahead of the game," she said, just short of contempt. "You're still liable to make mistakes."

Cate's stomach was lurching sickly. "I thought we all were. *You're* making a mistake right now. This is *my* home, Stella, might I remind you. *I* pay the mortgage. You held on to your assets, which we both know are considerable. We've been very happy here. What's all this about anyway? You're saying I'm like Annabel, your *alleged* beloved little sister, maybe not so beloved after all?"

Stella's dark eyes glittered with intensity. This was a Stella from another world, another time. "Both of you brought a mess on yourselves and I had to deal with it. Beguiling little Annabel and her legions of lovers!" she exclaimed bitterly. "She didn't know about gentleness, tenderness, care. All she knew was running wild!"

"How dare you?" Cate found herself ready and willing to spring to her mother's defence. "Listen to the way you're talking. It's disgusting. You're talking about your dead sister and to *me*, her daughter. It's far more likely Annabel was a fascinating woman. That's why she had so many admirers. It's even possible you've totally misrepresented her. I see that now. You made confidences to people about your sister and people listened. You told me yourself you were much admired for your utter selflessness."

"I loved her," Stella continued as though she hadn't heard a word Cate said. "But I loved Ralph more. The tragedy was he didn't see me with Annabel around. It made no sense. Annabel wasn't anywhere near as stable as I. But men were like moths to the flame with her. Most people thought I was the nicer person and just as good-looking. Only I lacked the *look after me* image. It worked brilliantly for Annabel. I was the unselfish one who coped and endured."

"Here is a woman who has eaten the bread of righteousness," Cate quoted bleakly. "I hear what you say, Stella, now I'm making a belated assessment. You were *hugely* jealous of Annabel."

"Nonsense!"

Cate continued unimpressed. "You envied the excitement, the allure, that rippled around her. She couldn't help it. She was born that way. Please don't erode the love I have left for you, Stella. Say no more. Go to bed. Sleep on it."

"To be perfectly honest—"

"Have you ever been perfectly honest?" A hard core of grief and disillusionment was in Cate's voice.

"I've never felt better." Stella straightened her shoulders like a woman with a long list of good deeds behind her. "Seeing Julian Carlisle, now the two of you together, has brought it all back."

"What does it bring back, Stella?" Cate asked, moving into the living room. It was a precaution. Jules was a deep sleeper, but there was a possibility he could wake up at the sound of their voices. "You're saying you loved Rafe Stewart?" She had to press Stella into answering now. Stella might have the dubious gift of being able to wipe things from her mind, but *she* couldn't. She had to *know*.

"Stop being such a complete idiot! Of course I did. I was

mad about him. He was the most wonderful catch. He was attracted to me *first*, I was thrilled, but Annabel went after him. She felt no shame. She really needed to do penance."

Cate felt as if she had been pitched head first into hell. "What, *die*?" she exploded. "Annabel, my mother, deserved to die? And die relatively young? Are you saying all your years of self-sacrifice were no more than a cover-up orchestrated by you? I knew you didn't love Arnold. Poor old Arnold knew it too. He knew he was second best. You loved someone else. Did you marry Arnold on the rebound? To save face. You couldn't have Rafe, but eventually you learned you could have his child. *Me.* Is that it? Rafe Stewart is my father?" She drew closer to Stella, her voice soaring despite her efforts at restraint.

Jules woke with a fright. He sat up in bed, blinking his eyes. He could hear voices coming from downstairs. His mother and his grandmother were having an argument. It didn't seem possible. They all loved one another. Something was wrong. Immediately he resolved to get up. He had to go and check. He often thought of himself as a soldier, a brave soldier, a fighting man, going into battle. He would fight to the death for his mother. And Nan too, of course. But his mother was the most important person in the world to him.

He tripped over a rug, muttered a little swear word he wasn't supposed to say—all the kids did—then opened the door of his bedroom. He had left it ajar because he knew his mother always liked to kiss him goodnight. Most of the time he waited for it. But tonight he had fallen asleep. Out in the hallway the voices were louder. He moved very quietly to the top of the stairs, a lone little figure in pyjamas.

They *were* arguing. Just to know that was akin to what he thought an electric shock might be like. Nan was speaking in a voice he had never heard before. Or ever suspected she had. It was a voice that frightened him. Nan sounded as if she no longer loved his mother. She sounded as if she had been cheated in some way. Not by his mother, never!

Oh, please don't let this happen!

I must stop it.

For some reason not at all clear to him a vivid picture of Lord Wyndham sprang into his mind. Lord Wyndham was a man of authority. Moreover, he was a relative of Nan's, which meant there was an extended family connection to all of them. Lord Wyndham could help.

Nan's new-sounding voice hung in the air. "When are you going to tell the boy Carlisle is his father?" she asked tersely.

That came like a great clap of thunder. Stunned, Jules jerked to one side, in case he be obliterated by a bolt of lightning.

"I must tell him. I will tell him." His mother sounded tremendously upset. Her upset was transferring itself to him, forcing him to his knees. It was Nan who was going out on the attack. His mother was on the receiving end. He couldn't let that happen. The Jules he was, Jules Hamilton, had suddenly ceased to be. He was Jules Somebody Else. Why hadn't he put it all together? He was supposed to be smart. He wasn't smart at all. He was just a dumb kid who had lost all his powers.

Carlisle! That means Lord Wyndham is your father.

But his father had deserted his mother and him years ago. Jules felt as if he were drowning. Not that he *could* drown. He was a very good swimmer. But his legs suddenly felt so weak he sank onto the top step, his head in his hands. Now he was unashamedly listening. This was all about him, his mother and Lord Wyndham, who had never been there for them.

"He'd love that, wouldn't he?" Nan sounded close to snarling. Not like Nan at all. "He's always wanted a father."

"Why wouldn't he?" his mother broke in. "Everyone wants

a father, a loving father. You've always told me Annabel refused to name my father, even on her deathbed, but you've always known, haven't you, Stella? You've always known I'm Rafe Stewart's daughter. I was supposed to be the 'little cross' you took on. But you were actually *glad* to take me on, weren't you, Stella? You couldn't have him, but you had his child. You triumphed over Annabel there."

Jules found himself gasping for breath. What was happening here? He could almost wish he had stayed asleep.

"Do I detect a note of daughterly love?" Stella sounded scoffing. "You've always been so down on *Aunt* Annabel."

"How did you convince her to give me up?" It seemed to Jules there were tears in his mother's voice. His mother never cried. Not in front of him anyway. His mother was his life.

"It was easy," Nan said. "My influence over Annabel began when we were only small children. Our parents had one another. They didn't need us, especially after the Big Tragedy. You know, losing the heir. I convinced Annabel she was doing the right thing. She knew poor old Arnie and I would take the greatest care of you."

"Did Arnold know about Rafe?" his mother asked.

Rafe? Who was Rafe? Jules was struggling to understand but he couldn't take it all in.

"He may have guessed," Nan was saying. "He never knew. I certainly wasn't about to tell him."

His mother, who always sounded so bright and confident, now sounded deeply distressed. "Who the hell are you, Stella? How do I deal with the *two* of you? Stella One has been very good to me and to Jules. I thank her for that. But Stella Two, your alternate persona, is a formidable woman. I see how you built your life and my life on a pack of lies."

Nan's *new* voice burst out. "We could have gone on as before, *for ever*, if need be. The three of us, if only Carlisle hadn't come back into your life. And of course you still love him. How pathetic! So what does he want to do—take you both back to England? Don't think for a second he'll marry you. He didn't before."

Oh, Mummy, oh, Mummy. Jules wobbled to his feet. This wasn't fair. Nan didn't sound kind. She sounded cruel. It was important he be there for his mother.

"You're not the only designing woman in my life, Stella," his mother was saying. "You and Alicia Carlisle would have made a good match. I don't know which of you has done the greatest damage. I don't want to hear one more word from you. I'm going up to bed. We can't go on like this, Stella. You realise that. Not after all you've said."

There was the sound of high heels on the polished floor. His mother was coming upstairs.

"I love you, Catrina. I love Jules." Nan was calling to his mother in a hollow voice.

"What price love?" his mother answered.

Jules didn't know what to do. In a few moments his mother would reach the landing. He needed to talk to someone. He turned about, making a rush for the shelter of his bedroom. He knew he couldn't possibly sleep. Not after all he had heard. His head was still ringing with the sound of Nan's angry voice. Jules leapt into bed, pulling the light coverlet over him. He turned his face to the wall. He felt like crying, but dragged himself out of it. Soldiers didn't cry.

A few moments later he felt his mother's light kiss on his cheek.

"Goodnight, my darling," she said.

Goodnight, Mummy.

Your enemies are my enemies.

He spoke silently. He couldn't find a voice to answer her. He pretended to be sound asleep. It was what she would have wanted anyway. He knew perfectly well his mother would be tremendously upset to know he had overheard her argument with Nan.

Only she's not your nan, is she?

You have a father. You have a mother AND a father. Only your father denied you your birthright.

For a moment seven-year-old Jules was gripped by near-adult fury. *Why* had his father abandoned him and his mother? What his mother had told him wasn't good enough. He determined he would find out the real reason. He would have it out with this man, his father, Lord Wyndham. He didn't care if he was a lord or not. Titles had nothing to do with anything so far as he was concerned.

He would have it out with Mr Wyndham the very next day. The insult was so great.

You need to give me some answers. I'm nearly eight years old. I have a right to express my feelings.

Yet his beautiful mother—the most beautiful mother in the world—abandoned or not, had named him after his father. *Julian.* Why would she do that? Nothing made sense. Yet he knew what he had to do. He had to protect her.

Jules' heart was racing. He was in a bit of a panic. He waited until his mother drove away before he crossed to the other side of the road, pretending he was waiting for a school friend. The seconds seemed to be spinning into hours. As usual there were so many cars dropping off kids. He hoped Noah's mum would be late this morning. He didn't want to have to confront Noah. He was a man on a mission. It was a hot morning so he wasn't wearing Kingsley's distinctive school blazer. He should have had his hat on, but he didn't. His heart was now up in his throat. Sooner or later some conscientious mother was bound to ask him what he was doing. His mother always checked up on stray kids.

Like a miracle, a taxi double parked for a moment right

in front of him. One of the older boys got out, slamming the door. "What are you up to, Hamilton?" He fixed his eyes on the younger boy.

Jules saw a heaven-sent opportunity. "Hi, Daniel. I have to go back into town. I have a dentist appointment Mum forgot. My nan is going to take me." He appealed to the taxi driver. "Can you drive me back to the city, please? I have to meet my nan outside the Four Seasons Hotel. I have the money."

The taxi driver shouldn't have, but he said, "Right-o, hop in."

"I hope you're telling the truth, Hamilton?" the older boy asked, clearly dissatisfied with Jules' story.

"Please, don't hold us up, Daniel. I won't make it on time."

"All right, go, then," Daniel said. "But I'm going to check with your teacher," he warned.

"That's okay!" Jules waved a hand. "See you later."

"Playing the wag, are you?" the taxi driver, a jovial man, asked when they were under way.

"No, no! I need to get to the hotel. Please hurry."

"Better to keep to the speed limit," his driver chortled. The boy looked like an angel. Clearly he was not.

Safely inside the hotel, Jules marched straight up to Reception. For a minute or two the smart young woman behind the reception desk ignored him. "What are you doing here, little boy? Shouldn't you be at school?"

"I'm here to see Lord Wyndham," Jules answered, slightly intimidated despite himself.

The receptionist actually laughed. "Are you just! And who shall I say is calling?"

"Please tell him it's Jules," he said, squaring his shoulders. She needed to take him seriously.

"Jules who?" The receptionist placed the boy's age at around seven. He was a very handsome boy with thick blond hair and beautiful sapphire-blue eyes. His accent sounded English to her ears. He seemed excessively precocious for a kid his age. He really needed a set-down.

"Lord Wyndham knows me," Jules said without a blink. "I'm a relative of his." He formulated the words clearly.

"Of course you are!" the receptionist cried with splendid disbelief. Here was a kid of seven, going on seventy.

"May I speak to the manager?" Jules was eager to confront his father. He remembered his mother had asked to speak to the manager once when they were in Hong Kong. "If you could find him for me?" he suggested politely. "Or you could ring Lord Wyndham and check with him."

The receptionist's indignation became evident. She was seriously taken aback. Who did this kid think he was? "A great favourite of his, are you?"

"I did say I'm a relative," Jules reminded her.

The receptionist physically jerked back. "One minute," she said crisply. "You'll be in big trouble, sonny, if you're playing some sort of game. Sit down over there in the lobby." She pointed an officious hand.

"Thank you so much," said Jules, ever polite.

The receptionist's smile had a vague air of malevolence. *What a kid!* Anyone would think he was royalty! The receptionist, huffing to herself, put through the call to Lord Wyndham's suite. There was probably one chance in a million the drop-dead gorgeous Wyndham knew the boy. The kid was most likely up to some prank. But she had to hand it to him. He had *style.*

To her astonishment, when she told Lord Wyndham a boy called Jules was waiting for him in the lobby he told her he would be right down.

How about that? She could have short-circuited her career in hotel management. Come to think of it the boy had Lord

Wyndham's amazingly blue eyes and thick black lashes. He could very well be a relative.

She waited until Lord Wyndham walked into the lobby. She saw the tall, handsome British lord put his hand on the boy's shoulder, probably asking him what he was there for. The boy's face was upturned to him. He was speaking earnestly, with the look of someone who had a perfect right to be there. The next thing the two of them walked off towards the bank of lifts.

I ask you! Quite obviously the boy wasn't just any kid. He had identified himself as "Jules". Lord Wyndham had booked in as Julian Carlisle. She mulled over that nugget of information, wondering if it would be useful.

Cate was at her desk, when Stella rang. "What is it, Stella?" she asked, still not over her terrible upset at her aunt's behaviour. "I'm busy at the moment."

Stella lost no time relaying the news the school had rung. Jules had not turned up. He wasn't in class. An older boy Daniel Morris had spoken to him before school. Jules claimed he had to go into the city for a dentist appointment his mother had forgotten. He was to meet his grandmother. Jules got into the same cab the older boy had taken to school and told the cab driver he was meeting his grandmother at the Four Seasons Hotel.

The Four Seasons Hotel? Jules had gone to where Ashe was staying.

She was about to hang up on Stella, telling her she would handle it, only Stella chipped in, "He's gone to his father," she said. "His *father*, over *you*. Over *me*. He won't want us now."

Realisation dawned on Cate. Stella felt threatened, whereas she didn't feel threatened at all. She had come to see she had been given a chance in a million. The chance to put things right. Fate had brought her and Ashe together again despite the forces that had been at work against them. They would now have to work out the future. Right now, she had to ring the school, and then get herself to the Four Seasons Hotel. At that moment her job meant little to her. She had worked so hard, worked endless hours, all night sometimes. What did it add up to? She had known for years she was missing out on *real* life. She could no longer deny Ashe had a right to be part of his son's life. There were hard decisions to be made.

By the time Ashe made his phone call to Catrina—he had listened in silence to his son's impassioned stream of questions, before answering them as quietly and seriously as he knew how—he was told she had left work citing a family emergency. He swiftly put two and two together. She was coming to the hotel. Jules had told him all about the taxi ride into town. He walked away from the child into the other room to ring Stella. Jules had told him as well about "the fight" and the revelations that had emerged. For some reason Ashe realised he had queered his pitch with Stella, his kinswoman. This was instantly confirmed from the coldness of Stella's voice. Nevertheless he went on to assure her Jules was safe with him.

"Think you can show up when you like!" Her voice was startlingly loud in his ear.

"When and where I like, Stella," he said, dismayed by her reaction. "I'm paying you the courtesy of telling you my son and your great-nephew is safe."

"You want to know a secret?" Stella's icy voice came back at him in retaliation. "She's Rafe Stewart's daughter."

"Just as I thought." Ashe's reply was remarkably calm. "Does that set your conscience free, Stella? I should have recognised that wonderful colouring, the gold and the green. But you knew all along, didn't you? To think how you've deceived your own niece!"

"How could I not?" the gentle, unflappable Stella returned vehemently.

"That's not love," Ashe lamented. "You were driven by some form of *hate*."

"She was born looking so like him." Stella sounded as though she was talking more to herself than to him.

"The young man who was madly in love with Annabel, not you," Ashe said quietly. "I don't like to dwell on how you went about damaging Annabel's reputation. You were very cunning. You had to diminish her in people's eyes. Sadly you were often believed. Even I heard the stories of wicked little Annabel Radclyffe. Poor misjudged Annabel, I'd now say. Goodbye, Stella. I believe Catrina is on her way here. Her father, Rafe Stewart, will be thrilled out of his mind to finally meet her."

"Don't count on it!" Stella made a harsh grunting noise.

"I am counting on it. Rafe will know who she is before ever a word is spoken. You force-fed Catrina a pack of lies." His tone told her plainly she had acted very badly.

"I have a special gift for them," Stella retorted, unfazed. Then, to his dismay, laughed. "We got on well without you. And Rafe," she said. "Now you've got the lot!"

"What goes around, comes around, Stella," was his reply.

When a knock came, Jules rushed to the door. "That will be Mummy," he cried excitedly.

"Well, let her in, Julian," Ashe advised calmly. He was still recovering from being taken to task with a vengeance by a small boy who just happened to be his son. He couldn't think of a single soul who had confronted him thus unless it was Jules' mother. It was made very clear to him protecting his mother was central to Jules' existence. He, the father, was perceived as the man who had disavowed them. That was his son's world as it was and as he saw it. He had used all his powers of persuasion to get the boy to sit down so they could talk it out, even to the extent of getting into human relationships and moral issues. He had pointed out Jules would find as an adult there were always harsh realities in life to confront. He had set out his case. He had left it to Jules to determine the outcome. It was tremendously important for his son to understand the circumstances that had driven him and Catrina apart. He thought he might have been pushing a seven-year-old boy to his extreme limits but his son's high intelligence was well on display. Catrina had reared their son well. She had given him a childhood of stability and love. Jules was a confident child. For one so young he had achieved an impressive state of equilibrium. The silent rages that he had quite naturally harboured against his missing father had been at long last addressed. Hopefully the scars would fade.

His son's question gave him the answer. "Is everything going to be all right?" It was clear he had become an authority figure.

"Of course it is, Julian. Open the door," Ashe bid him calmly.

Mother and son fell into one another's arms. "Don't you ever do that again!" Cate cried, bending over her precious child. "Not *ever*!" she repeated fiercely, her eyes moving over Jules' blond head to find Ashe. Ashe nodded to her, knowing she was reading his mind. Their son's issues had been addressed. "Why didn't you speak to me, Jules?" Cate turned back to her son. "You should have spoken to me."

He had already been told that by his father. Still, he spoke his mind. "I had to handle this myself." His blue eyes were very bright. "But I'm very sorry, Mum, if you were worried."

"Worried!" Cate echoed, casting her eyes up to heaven.

"All's well that ends well." Ashe spoke gently from behind them. "Come in, Catrina. Shut the door. You've rung the school?"

"Of course." She looked into his face, all her old love for him surging back. One could live a lifetime and still not know the evils that existed inside other people's souls. Jealousy was a deadly sin. The people that were closest to them—for Ashe, his mother; for her, her aunt Stella—had caused so much damage it was a miracle they had finally won through. It was their job now to refocus on the future and what was best for their son. Ashe wanted him. He wanted her. Past history would not be allowed to tarnish the future.

"You'll be in a spot of bother at school, Julian," Ashe was telling his son.

"What can they do to me?" Jules kept his arm around his mother, feeling a great upsurge of happiness, of *family.* "They wouldn't expel me, would they?"

"No, but you won't get off scot-free." Ashe made it perfectly clear. "You may have thought you were doing the right thing, but you weren't. There was your mother to be considered, and others. The school has a duty of care. It's a very serious matter when a child takes it into their head to go AWOL."

"I know what that means," said Jules. "Away without leave?"

"It does." Ashe nodded. His son had confided he liked to think of himself as a soldier. No bad thing at all.

"It was a blessing Daniel told your teacher." Cate sighed in relief.

Jules pulled a wry face. "I knew he would. He suspected I wasn't telling the truth, anyway."

"Your taxi driver has a problem." Cate was reminded. "He shouldn't have taken you on as a passenger."

"I think he thought it was a joke." Jules tried to get the jovial taxi driver off the hook. "So did the receptionist downstairs. She thought I was having her on."

"Regardless, there are rules to be obeyed, Julian," Ashe said firmly. "Rules of good behaviour have to pertain."

"Yes, sir." Jules dipped his head respectfully. "Do I have to go back to school today?" he asked, looking from one to the other, hoping they would say no.

"Yes, you do," Ashe said, putting an end to his son's speculation. "We'll go with you. But you have to make your own apologies. No excuses."

"I can do that," Jules said, cheering up enormously. They were going together. He, his mother and now his *father*! It was wonderful, *wonderful*, knowing his father wanted him. His father had confided the whole story to him, man to man. His father had told him his mother, Catrina, was the great love of his life.

That made two of them.

He watched while his mother walked into his father's outstretched arms. He watched his father bend his dark head to kiss her, a really super-duper kiss, just like the movies. He didn't mind in the least. Mothers and fathers were supposed to kiss one another.

"I expect I'll enjoy Christmas in England," he suddenly announced to his startled parents. "I know so many carols. And there could be *snow*! Wouldn't that be wonderful, Mum?"

His mother's beautiful smile quivered. "Wonderful, Jules!" she seconded.

"Right!" His father stretched out an imperious hand. "Time to go back to school, Julian, and face the music."

"Okay. I know I've done wrong." Jules held out both his hands. "Can I tell the kids my dad has come for me? Can I?"

"I don't see why not," Cate said, lacing her fingers through his, while his father took his other hand.

"I know 'Stille Nacht, Heilige Nacht' in German," Jules told his father proudly. "I really would love to be able to speak several languages. You told me my grandfather, my *real* grandfather, could."

"Then you've got a head start," said Lord Julian Wyndham. "I can help you. I speak a couple myself."

"Maybe we can take Nan too," Jules said. "Back to England, I mean, for the trip. I'm sure she'll apologise for getting so angry. I expect she was worried."

It was obvious to them both Jules was waiting for their answer.

"We'll see," said his mother. "Now, best get going."

"Face the music," said Jules, a bounce in his step. He had fantasised about having a great dad. A great dad would have made his world complete.

Now he had one.

CHAPTER TEN

Christmas.
Radclyffe Hall.
England.

JULES CROSSED THE great hall of this wonderful old house where Nan had been born. Why hadn't anyone told him? Adults seemed to keep so much to themselves. He didn't know why and he wouldn't know for a long time. But when he'd first caught sight of the beautiful old manor house set high on the hill he had burst out, "Things like this only happen in fairy tales, don't they, Mum?" The sight had enchanted him.

She had ruffled his hair and given him the loveliest smile. "Actually they happen more often than we think, my darling." He had never seen his mother look more beautiful or more happy. She even called him Julian now and then and he pretended not to notice. Anyway, he didn't mind. Julian seemed to suit him better here in England.

He loved England. He thought London was a splendid city with so many monuments and so much history. He had stood in awe outside Buckingham Palace where the Queen lived. The Queen was still Queen of Australia. He was loving everything, but he missed home and he missed his friends, particularly Noah. Radclyffe Hall and the beautiful countryside were special but it did rain a lot and it was very *cold.*

He had never been so cold in his life, even with lots of warm clothes on, a beanie pulled down over his forehead and over his ears. Woollen mittens. Now that wasn't *cool.* The cold wrapped around him but he was starting to get a bit used to it. Acclimatisation they called it. He didn't know if it would ever happen though. He loved the *sun.*

He missed Nan too, but she had decided to stay at home. Before they'd left she had told his mother she was giving a good deal of thought to marrying their family solicitor, Gerald Enright. He didn't have a clue why she would want to marry Mr Enright—he was a nice man but quite old—but his mother said they would suit very well.

He pushed open the heavy door of what his father called the Yellow Drawing Room, with a feeling of glorious anticipation, shutting it quietly behind him. It was early morning. No one had spotted him as he had come down the stairs, though he had heard brisk footsteps from somewhere at the rear of the grand house. A row of luxury cars stood at the front of the house in the huge circular drive with all the pudding-shaped bushes his father told him were yews. He had studied with interest the Bentleys, the Rolls and two Mercedes. It was cold enough for snow to fall, he thought, but the longed-for snow hadn't fallen as yet. He knew it would. He was so looking forward to it.

Passing under the great chandeliers, Jules crossed the beautiful, big room to where the great Christmas tree glittered and shone. His mother and his aunt Olivia had decorated it with a delirium of fantastically beautiful and plentiful baubles—gorgeous jewelled butterflies Aunty Olivia had taken out of storage for this year's festivities. Many of the ornaments were very old, handed down through the generations. So the tree looked absolutely splendid, even more so at night when all the dazzling fairy lights were turned on.

His mother and Aunt Olivia had had to stand on ladders to decorate the higher branches.

Around the base of the tree were swags and swags of presents wrapped up in sumptuous papers and embellished with ribbons. Silver-sprayed bare branches in tall blue and white Chinese pots stood over at the long windows. Bronze deers had been placed beside them. Garlands of silver and scarlet flowers, with lots of greenery in between and lovely little ornaments that included white doves, were strung along the chimney piece of the white marble fireplace. They had all worked hard to make it happen. Even the banisters of the great staircase had been decorated with hanging bunches of green foliage and big red baubles tied with silver, gold and scarlet ribbon. He thought he would carry a vivid memory of that Christmas tree, the first he would see at Radclyffe Hall, for the rest of his life.

Aunt Olivia had a son, Peter, a bit younger than he. They were cousins. Fancy that! Already they got on well. In fact, they had accepted one another right off. He and Peter had been allowed to help. Afterwards, his father had taken him upon his shoulders to place the Christmas angel at the top of the tree. Everyone had clapped, making his heart swell with happiness. He started to think of all the generations of his family, the Radclyffes, who had looked on the Christmas tree with awe. Years after he would be told the whole story. But this was *now*.

Aunt Leonie and her family would be arriving this morning. Other relatives had already arrived. They were house guests in a home that had so many bedrooms it could have been a small hotel. It was going to be one "splendid do!" said one of his father's guests, a lovely man, called Mr Stewart, who was a famous politician. He was so looking forward to the two of them having a talk. Mr Stewart had promised. Of course he had already confided to Mr Stewart he wanted to be a politician too. In fact, Prime Minister of Australia was his long-term goal.

"So you've made up your mind?" Mr Stewart had asked with such kindness and keen interest in his face.

"Yes, sir."

"Then you have a goal, Julian?"

"Yes, I do, sir. I want to live a life that has meaning."

For a moment Mr Stewart looked startled, then he stared right into the small boy's eyes, blue like a gas flame. Carlisle eyes. "There's wisdom deep inside you, Julian. We need men and women of wisdom. Stick with your goal."

"I will, sir." Jules was thrilled by Mr Stewart's words of encouragement. Mr Stewart was a great man.

"And I'll be following your progress closely." Mr Stewart had clasped his shoulder as if he meant to be a part of his life. When they had first met, Mrs Stewart had bent to kiss his face. She was a lovely lady with soft, gentle, haunted eyes that made him want to comfort her. He knew now just being an adult there could be sad, scary times. He had already seen most people's lives weren't without sadness. His mother had been sad for a long time. Yet she had always said, "We have to find a quiet place to nurture the spirit, Jules. Try our hardest to be positive."

He thought so too. What he didn't realise was it was quite an insight for a boy of seven going on eight. Jules had in fact made a profound impact on everybody. Aunt Olivia had hugged him and hugged him, crooning, *"Julian, Julian,"* over and over, cradling his head. When she had kissed him there were tears in her eyes. Everyone seemed to really like him. And he liked them. It gave him a wonderful feeling, like opening a window on the magical power of belonging. It was going to be the best Christmas of his life. He hoped everyone would sing in church. He had been practising his carols. He knew they were all going to the village church later on in the morning. He believed people should pray. There was no need to bottle up all one's troubles. Tell God and He would listen. Hadn't He listened to him?

Christmas Day went off splendidly. Cate and Olivia had consulted with Cook to come up with a mouth-watering menu. There were entrées and main courses. Roast turkey and roast goose. Jules had never tried that one before, but he liked it. Plenty of yummy desserts, including little meringue snowmen, jolly little fellows, their hats made out of black decorating icing, black button eyes, an upturned red mouth and down the front of the snowman's chest, a red scarf. Cook had made them especially for the children. They were a big hit. There was Christmas pudding, of course, that was brought flaming to the table. It was all so different from Christmas at home where the sun blazed and everyone ate lots of seafood, prawns, crabs with lovely, fresh white meat, lobster and large platters of different salads. Afterwards, when the meal settled they all headed off for the beach and a cooling swim.

There was a lovely warmth around the gleaming dining-room table with its decorative swag running its full length of the centre. The table was so long there was plenty of room for everyone to spread out. The joy of it all had caught Jules a bit by surprise. His father's family and his father's extended family had welcomed him and his mother, tucking them neatly and lovingly into the fold. It seemed to him that was what Christmas was all about.

It was Mr Stewart who put word to it. "'Remembrance, like a candle, burns brightest at Christmastime.'"

Everyone had clapped and Mr Stewart had said with a laugh, "I can't take the credit. That lies with a Mr Charles Dickens."

* * *

Much later that night, when the entire household had long since retired, Catrina and Ashe lay together in his great warm bed, their bodies spooned into one another. Ashe had his arms around the woman he loved, the woman he had lost, the woman he had regained, the mother of his son. He could feel every bone in her slender body; his hand cupped her small, perfect breast like a creamy-white rosebud unfurled. He adored her.

"What are you thinking?" he murmured into her ear.

"How happy I am." She gave a voluptuous sigh, turning on her back to face him, looking up into his bluer than blue eyes. "Safe, secure, loved. As a family we're united. What more could I want?"

He bent and languidly, but very sensually, kissed her mouth. "I can't make Jules into a little Pom."

They both laughed. Recognition of that fact had set him back, but he was admiring of his son's firm mindset even at age seven. Julian was having a wonderful time but it was clear after the long vacation was over in early February he wanted to go home.

Home was Australia. Ashe had the definite notion his son thought he, as his father, would take charge of the whole situation and find a solution.

"He wants to go home, Ashe," Cate said, as if he needed any reminder. "He's loving it here, but he calls Australia home. So do I." She placed her hands against his chest, her tapering fingers tangling in his light chest hair.

"So it's up to me." It wasn't a question.

"Darling, I'm not saying that. I'm—"

"You *are*." He kissed her again. "You're so beautiful. Naked you look like a mermaid with your green eyes and long, golden hair. Rafe is thrilled out of his mind. He told me over and over he thinks Jules is an amazing little fellow. So does dear

Helena. What makes Rafe happy makes Helena happy. They're in your life now, my love."

"I know and I feel blessed." Cate meant it. "Everyone has been so beautiful to me."

"That's because *you're* beautiful." He smoothed her tumbled hair from her forehead, pressing her back into the pillows. "Julian told me he loves to draw you because you're so beautiful."

Tears swam into Cate's eyes. Jules had told her that too.

"And you're going to make an exquisite bride," said Jules' father. The two of them had agreed on an April wedding at Radclyffe Hall. Beyond that, they were still trying to work out what was best for them as a family. Wherever Ashe was, Cate would go. Ashe was her world. Only he wasn't her *entire* world. There was their son. Many of her hopes could well be sunk, but she realised neither of them was prepared to destabilise Jules. After all, he was a young man with big plans.

"How mysterious is the way destiny works." Ashe kissed her open mouth, breathing in her sweet breath. "I intend to have a word with Liv and Bram in the morning," he said, as though he had finally reached a mulled-over decision.

"What about?" Cate's green eyes, which had been shut in rapture, snapped open.

"We're looking for a solution, aren't we? We could have one if Liv and Bram agree."

Cate sat up in bed, not bothering to pull the sheet over her naked body. Ashe knew every inch of her. "You have a plan?"

"Do I?" He lay back, pulling her down over the top of him. One arm locked around her back. "Well, it's a practical solution until Jules is much older and better able perhaps to make up his mind. I'm going to offer the house and the running of the estate to Liv and Bram. They absolutely love it here—always have—and Peter can go to the excellent village school until he's ready to be sent to whatever school they choose.

They will act as custodians. I want nothing from them. They will live rent free. Bram will get paid as the manager of the estate. It's a suggestion I'm going to put to them."

Cate was too close to tears to speak. "You mean you're prepared to come and live in Australia?" she asked, as if a great blessing had descended on her. "But what about all you have *here*, to say nothing of your business interests?"

"My darling Cate, don't worry. Clever businesswoman that you are, you know business can be conducted from virtually anywhere. Besides, I like Australia. I like the people. You and Julian especially. Sydney is a beautiful and liveable city. I can't say I won't have to make a lot of trips around the globe. I will. I need to oversee my interests, which I remind you will become yours. I want you on board, not only as my wife, but as my business partner. Your input would be much appreciated."

She felt such a degree of relief she nearly shouted aloud with joy. "I don't know what to say, Ashe."

"Say, what a wonderful solution." He afforded her his beautiful smile.

"It's a *marvellous* solution, providing you're absolutely sure?"

"I'm absolutely sure I want you and our son in my life. Since Julian is dead set on being Prime Minister of Australia, that is where we must reside."

It made wonderful sense. "I'm fine with that. But aren't you taking Olivia's and Bram's falling in with the plan a little bit for granted?"

"Not really. This is the kind of life they both want. I think they'll grab the opportunity with both hands. This house is big enough to shelter us all. It may turn out that Julian will renounce the baronetcy after I'm gone. Who knows? That's a decision he will have to make in the future. Peter may well become the sixth Baron Wyndham. Meanwhile I intend to stick around for a very long time."

"And we may well have more children," Cate pointed out, a brilliant light in her eyes.

"You're planning on more children, then?" Ashe asked in a low, provocative voice.

"Well, we can *try*!" Cate laughed, her hand moving with great sensuous delight down over his superb body. "I love you. Love you. Love you," she cried. "My darling, my dearest, Ashe. I plan on telling you every day of our lives."

"And I'll be holding you to that!" Ashe promised. "Do you know I realise now, no matter past desolations, I've lived with the possibility of one day seeing you again," he admitted with wonderment.

"I did too." Cate sighed blissfully, thinking the great joys of the present were folding away all the unhappiness of the past. "What if we had missed one another?"

A hush fell over them at the thought. "We haven't. Fate has smiled on us." Ashe leaned down to kiss her, his love flowing like a benediction. "It's given us back our one true soul mate."

"And our son." Cate felt doubly blessed.

"I see a tiny bit of me in there?" He stared into her eyes, capturing his own image.

"A lot!'

"My father too," Ashe mused. "The way Julian talks it's as though my father has come alive."

"My father has come alive for me." Tears caught in Cate's eyes and throat. "He is such a fine man. He didn't know about me. Isn't that terrible?"

"Terrible indeed," Ashe confirmed with only the mildest irony.

"My mother and my aunt made sure of that. I wonder if Stella ever feels shame for the things she's done?"

"I'd be a tad astonished if she did," Ashe said dryly. "Stella obviously has the capacity for blotting away guilt and shame. Some people are like that. They can never admit to wrongdoing. It's always somebody else's fault if things turn out badly."

"The textbook narcissist?" Cate suggested quietly. "She was happy when there were only the three of us. She does love Jules."

"Until he rebelled," Ashe pointed out firmly. "No rebelling allowed. *You* were okay as long as you remained with no permanent partner in your life. Stella might have had to go then. She must have feared that."

"Well, now she's making a life of her own." Cate sighed. "I think Gerald deserves more. Or at least a warning. But the great thing is *I* have all of my men in my life. It's the way it was supposed to have happened. I suppose even destiny can sometimes get things wrong."

"Be grateful this time it's got it *right*!" Ashe said emphatically. "Are we, or are we not, the perfect match?"

Cate touched her fingers gently to his mouth. "You get your answer when you've made love to me again."

Love was a revelation. It was also a miracle when all the forces of the universe conspired to bring two people together.

These forces had various names. Fate, Destiny, Chance. Call it what you will.

* * * * *

CONVENIENTLY HIS PRINCESS

OLIVIA GATES

To my family and friends, who give me all I need…
love, understanding, encouragement and space, to
keep on writing…and enjoying it. Love you all.

One

"You want me to marry Kanza the Monster?"

Aram Nazaryan winced at the loudness of his own voice.

Not that anyone could blame him for going off like that. Shaheen Aal Shalaan had made some unacceptable requests in his time, but *this* one warranted a description not yet coined by any language he knew. And he knew four.

But the transformation of his best and only friend into a meddling mother hen had been steadily progressing from ignorable to untenable for the past three years. It seemed that the happier Shaheen became with Aram's kid sister Johara after they had miraculously reunited and gotten married, the more sorry for Aram he became and the more he intensified his efforts to get his brother-in-law to change what he called his "unlife."

And to think he'd still been gullible enough to believe that Shaheen had dropped by his office for a simple visit. Ten minutes into the chitchat, he'd carpet bombed him with emotional blackmail.

He'd started by abandoning all subtlety about enticing him to go back to Zohayd, asking him point-blank to come *home*.

Annoyed into equal bluntness, he'd finally retorted that Zohayd was Shaheen's home, not his, and he wouldn't go back there to be the family's seventh wheel, when Shaheen and Johara's second baby arrived.

Shaheen had only upped the ante of his persistence. To prove that he'd have a vital role and a full life in Zohayd, he'd offered him his job. He'd actually asked him to become Zohayd's freaking minister of economy!

Thinking that Shaheen was pulling his leg, he'd at first laughed. What else could it be but a joke when only a royal Zohaydan could assume that role, and the last time Aram checked, he was a French-Armenian American?

Shaheen, regretfully, hadn't sprouted a sense of humor. What he had was a harebrained plan of how Aram could *become* a royal Zohaydan. By marrying a Zohaydan princess.

Before he could bite Shaheen's head off for that suggestion, his brother-in-law had hit him with the identity of the candidate he thought *perfect* for him. And *that* had been the last straw.

Aram shot his friend an incredulous look when Shaheen rose to face him. "Has conjugal bliss finally fried your brain, Shaheen? There's no way I'm marrying that monster."

In response, Shaheen reeled back his flabbergasted expression, adjusting it to a neutral one. "I don't know where you got that name. The Kanza I know is certainly no monster."

"Then there are two different Kanzas. The one I know, Kanza Aal Ajmaan, the princess from a maternal branch of your royal family, has earned that name and then some."

Shaheen's gaze became cautious, as if he were dealing with a madman. "There's only one Kanza…and she is delightful."

"Delightful?" A spectacular snort accompanied that exclamation. "But let's say I go along with your delusion and agree that she is Miss Congeniality herself. Are you out of your mind even suggesting her to me? She's a kid!"

It was Shaheen's turn to snort. "She's almost thirty."

"Wha…? No way. The last time I saw her she was somewhere around eighteen."

"Yes. And that was over ten years ago."

Had it really been that long? A quick calculation said it had been, since he'd last seen her at that fateful ball, days before he'd left Zohayd.

He waved the realization away. "Whatever. The eleven or twelve years between us sure hasn't shrunk by time."

"I'm eight years older than Johara. Three or four years' more age difference might have been a big deal back then, but it's no longer a concern at your respective ages now."

"That may be your opinion, but I…" He stopped, huffed a laugh, shaking his finger at Shaheen. "Oh, no, you don't. You're not dragging me into discussing her as if she's actually a possibility. She's a monster, I'm telling you."

"And I'm telling you she's no such thing."

"Okay, let's go into details, shall we? The Kanza I knew was a dour, sullen creature who sent people scurrying in the opposite direction just by glaring at them. In fact, every time she looked my way, I thought I'd find two holes drilled into me wherever her gaze landed, fuming black, billowing smoke."

Shaheen whistled. "Quite the image. I see she made quite an impression on you, if after over ten years you still recall her with such vividness and her very memory still incites such intense reactions."

"Intense *unfavorable* reactions." He grunted in disgust. "It's appalling enough that you're suggesting this marriage of convenience at all but to recommend the one…creature who ever creeped the hell out of me?"

"Creeped?" Shaheen tutted. "Don't you think you're going overboard here?"

He scowled, his pesky sense of fairness rearing its head. "Okay, so perhaps *creeped* is not the right word. She just… disturbed me. *She* is disturbed. Do you know that horror once went around with purple hair, green full-body paint and pink contact lenses? Another time she went total albino rabbit with white hair and red eyes. The last time I saw her she had blue hair and zombie makeup. *That* was downright creepy."

Shaheen's smile became that of an adult coddling an unreasonable child. "What, apart from weird hair and eye color and makeup experimentation, do you have against her?"

"The way she used to mutter my name, as if she was casting a curse. I always had the impression she had some… goblin living inside her wisp of a body."

Shaheen shoved his hands inside his pockets, the image of complacency. "Sounds like she's exactly what you need. You could certainly use someone that potent to thaw you out of the deep freeze you've been stuck in for around two decades now."

"Why don't I just go stick myself in an incinerator? It would handle that deep freeze much more effectively and far less painfully."

Shaheen only gave him the forbearing, compassionate look of a man who knew such deep contentment and fulfillment and was willing to take anything from his poor, unfortunate friend with the barren life.

"Quit it with the pitying look, Shaheen. My temperature is fine. It's how I am now.… It's called growing up."

"If only. Johara feels your coldness. I feel it. Your parents are frantic, believing they'd done that to you when you were forced to remain with your father in Zohayd at the expense of your own life."

"Nobody forced me to do anything. I chose to stay with Father because he wouldn't have survived alone after his breakup with Mother."

"And when they eventually found their way back to each other, you'd already sacrificed your own desires and ambitions and swerved from your own planned path to support your family, and you've never been able to correct your course. Now you're still trapped on the outside, watching the rest of us live our lives from that solitude of yours."

Aram glowered at Shaheen. He was happy, incredibly so, for his mother and father. For his sister and best friend. But when they kept shoving his so-called solitude in his face, he felt nothing endearing toward any of them. Their solicitude only chafed when he knew he couldn't do anything about it.

"I made my own choices, so there's nothing for anyone to feel guilty about. The solitude you lament suits me just fine. So put your minds the hell at ease and leave me be."

"I'll be happy to, right after you give my proposition serious consideration and not dismiss it out of hand."

"Said proposition deserves nothing else."

"Give me one good reason it does. Citing things about Kanza that are ten years outdated doesn't count."

"How about an updated one? If she's twenty-eight—"

"She'll be twenty-nine in a few months."

"And she hasn't married yet—I assume no poor man has taken her off the shelf only to drop her back there like a burning coal and run into the horizon screaming?"

Shaheen's pursed lips were the essence of disapproval. "No, she hasn't been married or even engaged."

He smirked in self-satisfaction at the accuracy of his projections. "At her age, by Zohaydan standards, she's already long fossilized."

"How gallant of you, Aram. I thought you were a progressive man who's against all backward ideas, including ageism. I never dreamed you'd hold a woman's age against her in anything, let alone in her suitability for marriage."

"You know I don't subscribe to any of that crap. What I'm saying is if she is a Zohaydan woman, and a princess, who didn't get approached by a man for that long, it is proof that she is generally viewed as incompatible with human life."

"The exact same thing could be said about you."

Throwing his hands up in exasperation, he landed them on his friend's shoulders. "Listen carefully, Shaheen, because I'll say this once, and we will not speak of this again. I will not get married. Not to become Zohaydan and become your minister of economy, not for any other reason. If you really need my help, I'll gladly offer you and Zohayd my services."

Shaheen, who had clearly anticipated this as one of Aram's answers, was ready with his rebuttal. "The level of involvement needed has to be full-time, with you taking the top job and living in Zohayd."

"I have my own business..."

"Which you've set up so ingeniously and have trained your deputies so thoroughly you only need to supervise operations from afar for it to continue on its current trajectory of phenomenal success. This level of efficiency, this uncanny ability to employ the right people and to get the best out of them is exactly what I need you to do for Zohayd."

"*You* haven't been working the job full-time," he pointed out.

"Only because my father has been helping me since he abdicated. But now he's retreating from public life completely. Even with his help, I've been torn between my family, my business and the ministry. Now we have another baby on the way and family time will only increase. And Johara is becoming more involved in humanitarian projects that require my attention, as well. I simply can't find a way to juggle it all if I remain minister."

He narrowed his eyes at Shaheen. "So I should sacrifice my own life to smooth out yours?"

"You'd be sacrificing nothing. Your business will continue as always, you'd be the best minister of economy humanly possible, a position you'd revel in, and you'll get a family...something I know you have always longed for."

Yeah. He was the only male he knew who'd planned at

sixteen that he'd get married by eighteen, have half a dozen kids, pick one place and one job and grow deep, deep roots.

And here he was, forty, alone and rootless.

How had that happened?

Which was the rhetorical question to end all rhetorical questions. He knew just how.

"What I longed for and what I am equipped for are poles apart, Shaheen. I've long come to terms with the fact that I'm never getting married, never having a family. This might be unimaginable to you in your state of familial nirvana, but not everyone is made for wedded bliss. Given the number of broken homes worldwide, I'd say those who are equipped for it are a minority. I happen to be one of the majority, but I happen to be at peace with it."

It was Shaheen who took him by the shoulders now. "I believed the exact same thing about myself before Johara found me again. Now look at me…ecstatically united with the one right person."

Aram bit back a comment that would take this argument into an unending loop. That it was Shaheen and Johara's marriage that had shattered any delusions he'd entertained that he could ever get married himself.

What they had together—this total commitment, trust, friendship and passion—was what he'd always dreamed of. Their example had made him certain that if he couldn't have that—and he didn't entertain the least hope he'd ever have it—then he couldn't settle for anything less.

Evidently worried that Aram had stopped arguing, Shaheen rushed to add, "I'm not asking you to get married tomorrow, Aram. I'm just asking you to consider the possibility."

"I don't need to. I have been and will always remain perfectly fine on my own."

Eager to put an abrupt end to this latest bout of emotional wrestling—the worst he'd had so far with Shaheen—he started to turn around, but his friend held him back.

He leveled fed-up eyes on Shaheen. *"Now what?"*

"You look like hell."

He felt like it, too. As for how he looked, during necessary self-maintenance he'd indeed been seeing a frayed edition of the self he remembered.

Seemed hitting forty did hit a man hard.

A huff of deprecation escaped him. "Why, thanks, Shaheen. You were always such a sweet talker."

"I'm telling it as it is, Aram. You're working yourself into the ground…and if you think I'm blunt, it's nothing compared to what Amjad said when he last saw you."

Amjad, the king of Zohayd, Shaheen's oldest brother. The Mad Prince turned the Crazy King. And one of the biggest jerks in human history.

Aram exhaled in disgust. "I was right there when he relished the fact that I looked 'like something the cat dragged in, chewed up and barfed.' But thanks for bringing up that royal pain. I didn't even factor him in my refusal. But even if I considered the job offer/marriage package the opportunity of a lifetime, I'd still turn it down flat because it would bring me in contact with *him.* I can't believe you're actually asking me to become a minister in that inhuman affliction's cabinet."

Shaheen grinned at his diatribe. "You'll work with me, not him."

"No, I won't. Give it up, already."

Shaheen looked unsatisfied and tried again. "About Kanza…"

A memory burst in his head. He couldn't believe it hadn't come to him before. "Yes, about her and about abominations for older siblings. You didn't only pick Kanza the Monster for my best match but the half sister of the Fury herself, Maysoon."

"I hoped you'd forgotten about her. But I guess that was asking too much." Wryness twisted Shaheen's lips. "Maysoon was a tad…temperamental."

"A tad?" he scoffed. "She was a raging basket case. I barely escaped her in one piece."

And she'd been the reason that he'd had to leave Zohayd and his father behind. The reason he'd had to abandon his dream of ever making a home there.

"Kanza is her extreme opposite, anyway."

"You got that right. While Maysoon was a stunning if unstable harpy, Kanza was an off-putting miscreant."

"I diametrically differ with your evaluation of Kanza. While I know she may not be…sophisticated like her womenfolk, Kanza's very unpretentiousness makes me like her far more. Even if you don't consider those virtues exciting, they would actually make her a more suitable wife for you."

Aram lifted a sarcastic brow. "You figure?"

"I do. It would make her safe and steady, not like the fickle, demanding women you're used to."

"You're only making your argument even more inadmissible, Shaheen. Even if I wanted this, and I consider almost anything admissible in achieving my objectives, I would draw the line at exploiting the mousy, unworldly spinster you're painting her to be."

"Who says there'd be any exploitation? You might be a pain in the neck that rivals even Amjad sometimes but you're one of the most coveted eligible bachelors in the world. Kanza would probably jump at the opportunity to be your wife."

Maybe. Probably. Still…

"No, Shaheen. And that's final."

The forcefulness he'd injected into his voice seemed to finally get to Shaheen, who looked at him with that drop-it-now-to-attack-another-day expression that he knew all too well.

Aram clamped his friend's arm, dragging him to the door. "Now go home, Shaheen. Kiss Johara and Gharam for me."

Shaheen still resisted being shoved out. "Just assess the

situation like you do any other business proposition before you make a decision either way."

Aram groaned. Shaheen was one dogged son of a king. "I've already made a decision, Shaheen, so give it a rest."

Before he finally walked away, Shaheen gave him that unfazed smile of his that eloquently said he wouldn't.

Resigned that he hadn't heard the last of this, Aram closed the door after him with a decisive click.

The moment he did, his shoulders slumped as his feet dragged to the couch. Throwing himself down on it, he decided to spend yet another night there. No need for him to go "home." Since he didn't have one anyway.

But as he stretched out and closed his eyes, his meeting with Shaheen revolved in his mind in a nonstop loop.

He might have sent Shaheen on his way with an adamant refusal, but it wasn't that easy to suppress his own temptation.

Shaheen's previous persuasions hadn't even given him pause. After all, there had been nothing for him to do in Zohayd except be with his family, who had their priorities—of which he wasn't one. But now that Shaheen was dangling that job offer in front of him, he could actually visualize a real future there.

He'd given Zohayd's economy constant thought when he'd lived there, had studied it and planned to make it his life's work. Now, as if Shaheen had been privy to all that, he was offering him the very position where he could utilize all his talents and expertise and put his plans into action.

Then came that one snag in what could have been a once-in-a-lifetime opportunity.

The get-married-to-become-Zohaydan one.

But…should it be a snag? Maybe convenience was the one way he *could* get married. And since he didn't want to get married for real, perhaps Shaheen's candidate *was* exactly what he needed.

Her family was royal but not too high up on the tree of

royalty as to be too lofty, and their fortune was nowhere near his billionaire status. Maybe as Shaheen had suggested, she'd give him the status he needed, luxuriate in the boost in wealth he'd provide and stay out of his hair.

He found himself standing before the wall-to-wall mirror in the bathroom. He didn't know how he'd gotten there. Meeting his own eyes jogged him out of the preposterous trajectory of his thoughts.

He winced at himself. Shaheen had played him but good. He'd actually made him consider the impossible.

And it was impossible. Being in Zohayd, the only place that had been home to him, being with his family, being Zohayd's minister of economy were nice fantasies.

And they would remain just that.

Miraculously, Shaheen hadn't pursued the subject further.

Wonders would never cease, it seemed.

The only thing he'd brought up in the past two weeks had been an invitation to a party he and Johara were holding in their New York penthouse tonight. An invitation he'd declined.

He was driving to the hotel where he "lived," musing over Shaheen dropping the subject, wrestling with this ridiculously perverse sense of disappointment, when his phone rang. Johara.

He pressed the Bluetooth button and her voice poured its warmth over the crystal-clear connection.

"Aram, please tell me you're not working or sleeping."

He barely caught back a groan. This must be about the party, and he'd hate refusing her to her ears. It was an actual physical pain being unable to give Johara whatever she wanted. Since the moment she'd been born, he'd been a *khaatem f'esba'ha,* or "a ring on her finger," as they said in Zohayd. He was lucky that she was part angel or she would have used him as her rattle toy through life.

He prayed she wouldn't exercise her power over him, make it impossible for him to turn down the invitation again. He was at an all-time low, wasn't in any condition to be exposed to her and Shaheen's happiness.

He imbued his voice with the smile that only Johara could generate inside him no matter what. "I'm driving back to the hotel, sweetheart. Are you almost ready for your party?"

"Oh, I am, but…are you already there? If you are, don't bother. I'll think of something else."

He frowned. "What is this all about, Johara?"

Sounding apologetic, she sighed. "There's a very important file that one of my guests gave me to read, and we'd planned to discuss it at the party. Unfortunately, I forgot it back in my office at Shaheen's building, and I can't leave now. So I was wondering if you could go get the file and bring it here to me?" She hesitated. "I'm sorry to take you out of your way and I promise not to try to persuade you to stay at the party, but I can't trust anyone else with the pass codes to my filing cabinets."

"You know you can ask me anything at all, anytime."

"Anything but come to the party, huh?" He started to recite the rehearsed excuse he'd given Shaheen, and she interjected, "But Shaheen told me you did look like you needed an early night, so I totally understand. And it's not as if I could have enjoyed your company anyway, since we've invited a few dozen people and I'll be flitting all over playing hostess."

He let out a sigh of relief for her letting him off the hook, looking forward to seeing them yet having the excuse to keep the visit to the brevity he could withstand tonight. "Tell me what to look for."

Twenty minutes later, Aram was striding across the top floor of Shaheen's skyscraper.

As he entered Johara's company headquarters, he

frowned. The door to her assistants' office, which led to hers, was open. Weird.

Deciding that it must have been a rare oversight in their haste to attend Johara and Shaheen's soiree, he walked in and found the door to his sister's private office also ajar. Before he could process this new information, a slam reverberated through him.

He froze, his senses on high alert. Not that it took any effort to pinpoint the source of the noise. The racket that followed was unmistakable in direction and nature. Someone was inside Johara's office and was turning it upside down.

Thief was the first thing that jumped into his mind.

But no. There was no way anyone could have bypassed security. Except someone the guards knew. Maybe one of Johara's assistants was in there looking for the file she'd asked him for? But she had been clear she hadn't trusted anyone else with her personal pass codes. So could one of her employees be trying to break into her files?

No, again. He trusted his gut feelings, and he knew Johara had chosen her people well.

Then perhaps someone who worked for Shaheen was trying to steal classified info only she as his wife would be privy to?

Maybe. Calling the guards was the logical next step, anyway. But if he'd jumped to conclusions it could cause unnecessary fright and embarrassment to whomever was inside. He should take a look before he made up his mind how to proceed.

He neared the door in soundless steps, not that the person inside would have heard a marching band. A bulldozer wouldn't have caused more commotion than that intruder. That alone was just cause to give whomever it was a bit of a scare.

Peeping inside, he primed himself for a confrontation if need be. The next moment, everything in his mind emptied.

It was a woman. Young, slight, wiry. With the thickest

mane of hair he'd ever seen flying after her like dark flames as she crashed about Johara's office. And she didn't look in the least worried she'd be caught in the act.

Without making a conscious decision, he found himself striding right in.

Then he heard himself saying, "Why don't you fill me in on what you're looking for?"

The woman jumped in the air. She was so light, her movement so vertical, so high, it triggered an exaggerated image in his mind of a cartoon character jumping out of her skin in fright. It almost forced a laugh from his lips at its absurdity yet its appropriateness for this brownie.

The laugh dissolved into a smile that hadn't touched his lips in far too long as she turned to him.

He watched her, feeling as if time was decelerating, like one of those slow-motion movie sequences that signified a momentous event.

He heard himself again, amusement soaking his drawl. "I hear that while searching for something that evidently elusive, two sets of hands and eyes, not to mention two brains, are better than one."

With his last word, she was facing him. And though her face was a canvas of shock, and he could tell from her shapeless black shirt and pants that the tiny sprite was unarmed, it felt as if he'd gotten a kick in his gut.

And that was before her startled expression faded, before those fierce, dark eyes flayed a layer off his skin and her husky voice burned down his nerve endings.

"I should have known the unfortunate event of tripping into your presence was a territorial hazard around this place. So what brings you to your poor sister's office while she's not around? Is no one safe from the raids of The Pirate?"

Two

Aram stared at the slight creature who faced him across the elegant office, radiating the impact of a miniature force of nature, and one thing reverberating through his mind.

She'd recognized him on the spot.

No. More than that. She *knew* him. At least knew *of* him.

She'd called him "The Pirate." The persona, or rather the caricature of him that distasteful tabloids, scorned women and disgruntled business rivals had popularized.

She seemed to be waiting for him to make a comeback to her opening salvo.

A charge of electricity forked up his spine, then all the way up to his lips, spreading them wider. "So I'm The Pirate. And what do you answer to? The Tornado? The Hurricane? You did tear through Johara's office with the comparative havoc of one. Or do you simply go with The Burglar? A very messy, noisy, reckless one at that?"

She tilted her head, sending her masses of glossy curls tumbling over one slim shoulder. He could swear he heard them tutting in sarcastic vexation that echoed the expression on her elfin face.

It also poured into her voice, its timbre causing something inside his rib cage to rev. "So are you going to stand there like the behemoth that you are blocking my escape route and sucking all oxygen from the room into that ridiculously massive chest of yours, or are you going to give a fellow thief a hand?"

His lips twitched, every word out of hers another zap lashing through his nerves. "Now, how is it fair that I assist you in your heist without even having the privilege of knowing who I'm going to be indicted with when we're caught? Or are formal introductions not even necessary? Perhaps your spritely self plans on disappearing into the night, leaving me behind to take the fall?"

Her stare froze on him for several long seconds before she suddenly tossed her hair back with a careless hand. "Oh, right…I remember now. Sorry for that. I guess having you materialize behind me like some genie surprised me so much it took me a while to reboot and access my memory banks."

He blinked, then frowned. Was she the one who'd stopped making sense, or had his mind finally stopped functioning? It *had* been increasingly glitch riddled of late. He had been teetering on the brink of some breakdown for a long time now, and he'd thought it was only a matter of time before the chasm running through his being became complete.

So had his psyche picked now of all times to hit rock bottom? But why *now,* when he'd finally found someone to jog him out of his apathy, even if temporarily; someone he actually couldn't predict?

Maybe he'd blacked out or something, missed something she'd said that would make her last words make sense.

He cleared his throat. "Uh…come again?"

Her fed-up expression deepened. "I momentarily forgot how you got your nickname, and that you continue to live down to it, and then some."

Though the jump in continuity still baffled him, he went along. "Oh? I'm very much interested in hearing your dissection of my character. Knowing how another criminal mastermind perceives me would no doubt help me perfect my M.O."

One of those dense, slanting eyebrows rose. "Invoking the code of dishonor among thieves? Sure, why not? I'm charitable like that with fellow crooks." That obsidian gaze poured mockery over him. "Let's see. You earned your moniker after building a reputation of treating other sentient beings like commodities to be pillaged then tossed aside once their benefit is depleted. But you reserve an added insult and injury to those who suffer the terrible misfortune of being exposed to you on a personal level, as you reward those hapless people by deleting them from you mind. So, if you're seeking my counsel about enhancing your performance, my opinion is that you can't improve on your M.O. of perfectly efficient cruelty."

Her scathing portrayal *was* the image that had been painted of him in the business world and by the women he'd kept away by whatever measures necessary.

When his actions had been exaggerated or misinterpreted and that ruthless reputation had begun to be established, he'd never tried to adjust it. On the contrary, he'd let it become entrenched, since that perceived cold-bloodedness did endow him with a power nothing else could. Not to mention that it supplied him with peace of mind he couldn't have bought if he'd projected a more approachable persona. This one did keep the world at bay.

But the only actual accuracy in her summation was the personal interactions bit. He didn't crowd his recollections with the mundane details of anyone who hadn't proved worth his while. Only major incidents remained in his memory—if stripped from any emotional impact they might have had.

But…wait a minute. Inquiring about her identity had triggered this caustic commentary in the first place. Was she obliquely saying that he didn't remember *her,* when he should?

That was just not possible. How would he have ever forgotten those eyes that could reduce a man to ashes at thirty paces, or that tongue that could shred him to ribbons, or that wit that could weave those ribbons into the hand basket to send him to hell in?

No way. If he'd ever as much as exchanged a few words with her, not only would he have remembered, he would probably have borne the marks of every one. After mere minutes of being exposed to her, he felt her eyes and tongue had left no part of him unscathed.

And he was loving it.

God, to be reveling in this, he must be sicker than he'd thought of all the fawning he got from everyone else—especially women. Though he knew *that* had never been for *him.* During his stint in Zohayd, it had been his exotic looks but mainly his closeness to the royal family that had incited the relentless pursuit of women there. After he'd become a millionaire, then a billionaire… Well, status and wealth were irresistible magnets to almost everyone.

That made being slammed with such downright derision unprecedented. He doubted if he would have accepted it from anyone else, though. But from this enigma, he was outright relishing it.

Wanting to incite even more of her verbal insults, he gave her a bow of mock gratitude. "Your testimony of dishonor honors me, and your maligning warms my stone-cold heart."

Both her eyebrows shot up this time. "You have one? I thought your species didn't come equipped with those superfluous organs."

His grin widened. "I do have a rudimentary thing somewhere."

"Like an appendix?" A short, derogatory sound purred in the back of her throat. "Something that could be excised and you'd probably function better without? Wonder why you didn't have it electively removed. It must be festering in there."

As if compelled, he moved away from the door, needing a closer look at this being he'd never seen the likes of before. He kept drawing nearer as she stood her ground, her glare one that could have stopped an attacking horde.

It only made getting even closer imperative. He stopped only when he was three feet away, peering down at this diminutive woman who was a good foot or more shorter than he was yet feeling as if he was standing nose to nose with an equal.

"Don't worry," he finally said, answering her last dig. "There is no reason for surgical intervention. It has long since shriveled and calcified. But thank you from the bottom of my vestigial heart for the concern. And for the counsel. It's indeed reassuring to have such a merciless authority confirm that I'm doing the wrong thing so right."

He waited for her ricocheting blitz, anticipation rising. Instead, she seared him with an incinerating glance before seeming to delete *him* from her mind as she resumed her search.

By now he knew for certain that she wasn't here to do anything behind Johara's back. Even when she'd readily engaged him in the "thieves in the night" scenario he'd initiated, and rifling through the very cabinets he himself was here to search…

It suddenly hit him, right in the solar plexus, who this tempest in human form was.

It was *her*.

Kanza. Kanza Aal Ajmaan.

Unable to blink, to breathe, he stood staring at her as she kept transferring files from the cabinets, plopping them down on Johara's desk before attacking them with a speed and focus that once again flooded his mind's eye with images of hilarious cartoon characters. He had no clue how he'd even recognized her. Just as she'd accused him, his memories of the Kanza he'd known over ten years ago had been stripped of any specifics.

All he could recall of the fierce and fearsome teenager she'd been, apart from the caricature he'd painted for Shaheen of her atrocious fashion style and the weird, bordering-on-repulsive things she'd done with her hair and eyes, was that it had felt as if something ancient had been inhabiting that younger-than-her-age body.

A decade later, she still seemed more youthful than her chronological age, yet packed the wallop of this same primal force. But that was where the resemblance ended.

The Mad Hatter and Wicked Witch clothes and makeup and extraterrestrial hair, contact lenses and body paint were gone now. From the nondescript black clothes and the white sneakers that clashed with them, to the face scrubbed clean of any enhancements, to the thick, untamed mahogany tresses that didn't seem to have met a stylist since he'd last seen her, she had gone all the way in the other direction.

Though in an opposite way to her former self, she was still the antithesis of all the svelte, stylish women who'd ever entered his orbit, starting with her half sisters. Where they'd been overtly feminine and flaunting their assets, she made no effort whatsoever to maximize any attributes she might have. Not that she had much to work with. She was small, almost boyish. The only big thing about her was her hair. And eyes. Those were enormous. Everything else was tiny.

But that was when he analyzed her looks clinically. But when he experienced them with the influence of the being they housed, the spirit that animated them…that was when his entire perception changed. The pattern of her features, the shape of her lips, the sweep of her lashes, the energy of her movements… Everything about her evolved into something totally different, making her something far more interesting than pretty.

Singular. Compelling.

And the most singular and compelling thing about her was those night eyes that had burned to ashes any preformed ideas of what made a woman worthy of a second glance, let alone constant staring.

Though he was still staring after she'd deprived him of their contact, he *was* glad to be relieved of their all-seeing scrutiny. He needed respite to process finding her here.

How could Shaheen bring her up a couple of weeks ago only for him to stumble on her here of all places when he hadn't crossed paths with her in ten years? This was too much of a coincidence. Which meant…

It wasn't one. Johara had set him up.

Another realization hit simultaneously.

Kanza seemed to be here running his same errand. Evidently Johara had set her up, too.

God. He was growing duller by the day. How could he have even thought Shaheen wouldn't share this with Johara, the woman where half his soul resided? How hadn't he picked up on Johara's knowledge or intentions?

Not that those two coconspirators were important now. The only relevant thing here was Kanza.

Had she realized the setup once he'd walked through that door? Was that why she'd reacted so cuttingly to his appearance? Did she take exception to Johara's matchmaking, and that was her way of telling her, and him, "Hell, no!"?

If this was the truth, then that made her even more interesting than he'd originally thought. It wasn't conceit, but as Shaheen had said, in the marriage market, he was about as big a catch as an eligible bachelor got. He couldn't imagine any woman would be averse to the idea of being his wife—if only for his status and wealth. Even his reputation was an irresistible lure in that arena. If women thought they had access, it only made him more of a challenge, a dangerous bad boy each dreamed she'd be the one to tame.

But if Kanza was so immune to his assets, so opposed

to exploring his possibility as a groom, that alone made her worthy of in-depth investigation.

Not that *he* was even considering Shaheen and Johara's neat little plan. But he *was* more intrigued by the moment by this…entity they'd gotten it into their minds was perfect for him.

Suddenly, said entity looked up from the files, transfixed him in the crosshairs of her fiercest glare yet. "Don't just stand there and pose. Come do something more useful than look pretty." When she saw his eyebrows shoot up, her lips twisted. "What? You take exception to being called pretty?"

He opened his mouth to answer, and her impatient gesture closed it for him, had him hurrying next to her where she foisted a pile of files on him and instructed him to look for the very file Johara had sent him here to retrieve.

Without looking at him, she resumed her search. "I guess pretty is too mild. You have a right to expect more powerful descriptions."

He gave her engrossed profile a sideways glance. "If I expect anything, it certainly isn't that."

She slammed another file shut. "Why not? You have the market of *halawah* cornered after all."

Halawah, literally sweetness, was used in Zohayd to describe beauty. That had him turning fully toward her. "Where *do* you come up with these things that you say?"

She flicked him a fleeting glance, closed another file on a sigh of frustration. "That's what women in Zohayd used to say about you. Wonder what they'd say now that your *halawah* is so exacerbated by age it could induce diabetes."

That had a laugh barking from his depths. "Why, thanks. Being called a diabetes risk is certainly a new spin on my supposed good looks."

She tsked. "You know damn well how beautiful you are."

He shook his bemused head at what kept spilling from those dainty lips, compliments with the razor-sharp edges of insults. "No one has accused me of being beautiful before."

"Probably because everyone is programmed to call men handsome or hunks or at most gorgeous. Well, sorry, buddy. You leave all those adjectives in the dust. You're all-out beautiful. It's really quite disgusting."

"Disgusting!"

"Sickeningly so. The resources you must devote to maximizing your assets and maintaining them at this…level…" She tossed him a gesture that eloquently encompassed him from head to toe. "When your looks aren't your livelihood, this is an excess that should be punishable by law."

An incredulous huff escaped him. "It's surreal to hear you say that when my closest people keep telling me the very opposite—that I'm totally neglecting myself."

She slanted him a caustic look. "You have people who can bear being close to you? My deepest condolences to them."

He smiled as if she'd just lavished the most extravagant praise on him. "I'll make sure to relay your sympathies."

Another withering glance came his way before she resumed her work. "I'll give mine directly to Johara. No wonder she's seemed burdened of late. It must be quite a hardship having you for an only brother in general, not to mention having to see you frequently when she's here."

His gaze lengthened on her averted face. Then suddenly everything jolted into place.

Who Kanza *really* was.

She was the new partner that Johara had been waxing poetic about. Now he replayed the times his sister had raved about the woman who'd taken Johara's design house from moderate success to household-name status, this financial marketing guru who had never actually been mentioned by name. But he had no doubt now it was Kanza.

Had Johara never brought up her name because she didn't want to alert him to her intentions, making him resistant to meeting Kanza and predisposed to finding fault with her if he did? If so, then Johara understood him better than Shaheen did, who'd hit him over the head with his intentions and Kanza's name. That *had* backfired. Evidently Johara had reeled Shaheen in, telling her husband not to bring up the subject again and that she'd handle everything from that point on, discreetly. And she had.

Another certainty slotted into place. Johara had kept her business partner in the dark about all this for the same reason.

Which meant that Kanza had no clue this meeting wasn't a coincidence.

The urge to divulge everything about their situation surged from zero to one hundred. He couldn't wait to see the look on her face as the truth of Johara and Shaheen's machinations sank in and to just stand back and enjoy the fireworks.

He turned to her, the words almost on his lips, when another thought hit him.

What if, once he told her, she became stilted, self-conscious? Or worse, *nice?* He couldn't bear the idea that after their invigorating duel of wits, her revitalizing lambasting, she'd suddenly start to sugarcoat her true nature in an attempt to endear herself to him as a potential bride. But worst of all, what if she shut him out completely?

From what he'd found out about her character so far, he'd go with scenario number three as the far more plausible one.

Whichever way this played out, he couldn't risk spoiling her spontaneity or ending this stimulating interlude.

Deciding to keep this juicy tidbit to himself, he said, "Apart from burdening Johara with my existence, I was actually serious for a change. Everyone I meet tells me I've never looked worse. The mirror confirms their opinion."

"I've smacked people upside the head for less, buddy." She narrowed her eyes at him, as if charting the trajectory of the smack he'd earn if he weren't careful. "Nothing annoys me more than false modesty, so if you don't want me to muss that perfectly styled mane of yours, watch it."

Suddenly it was important for him to settle this with her. "There is no trace of anything false in what I'm saying—modesty or otherwise. I really have been in bad shape and have been getting progressively worse for over a year now."

This gave her pause for a moment, something like contrition or sympathy coming into her eyes.

Before he could be sure, it was gone, her fathomless eyes glittering with annoyance again. "You mean you've looked better than this? Any better and you should be…arrested or something."

Something warm seeped through his bones, brought that unfamiliar smile to his lips again. "Though I barely give the way I look any thought, you managed what I thought impossible. You flattered me in a way I never was before."

She grimaced as if at some terrible taste. "Hello? Wasn't I speaking English just now? Flattering you isn't among the things I would ever do, even at gunpoint."

"Sorry if this causes you an allergic reaction, but that is exactly what you did, when I've been looking at myself lately and finding only a depleted wretch looking back at me."

She opened her mouth to deliver another disparaging blow, before she closed it, her eyes narrowing contemplatively over his face.

"Now I'm looking for it. I guess, yeah, I see it. But it sort of…roughens your slickness and gives you a simulation of humanity that makes you look better than your former overly polished perfection. Figures, huh? Instead of looking like crap, you manage to make wretched and depleted work for you."

He abandoned any pretense of looking through the files and turned to her, arms folded over his chest. "Okay. I get it. You despise the hell out of me. Are you going to tell me what I ever did to deserve your wrath, Kanza?"

When she heard her name on his lips, something blipped in her eyes. It was gone again before he could latch on to it, and she reverted back to full-blast disdain mode. "Give the poor, depleted Pirate an energy bar. He's exerted himself digging through his hard drive's trash and recognized me. And even after he did, he still asks. What? You think your transgressions should have been dropped from the record by time?"

"Which transgressions are we talking about here?"

"Yeah, with multitudes to pick from, you can't even figure out which ones I'm referring to."

"Though I'm finding your bashing delightful, even therapeutic, my curiosity levels are edging into the danger zone. How about you put me out of my misery and enlighten me as to what exactly I'm paying the price for now?"

Her lips twisted disbelievingly. "You've really forgotten, haven't you?" At his unrepentant yet impatient nod, she rolled her eyes and turned back to the files, muttering under her breath. "You can go rack your brains with a rake for the answer for all I care. I'm not helping you scratch that itch."

"Since there's no way I've forgotten anything I did to you that could cause such an everlasting grudge..." He paused, frowned then exclaimed, "Don't tell me this is about Maysoon!"

"*And* he remembers. In a way that adds more insult to injury. You're a species of one, aren't you, Aram Nazaryan?"

Before he could say anything, she strode away, clearly not intending to let him pursue the subject. He could push his luck but doubted she'd oblige him.

But at least he now knew where this animosity was coming from. While he hadn't factored in that this would be her stance regarding the fiasco between him and Maysoon, it seemed she had accumulated an unhealthy dose of prejudice against him from the time he'd been briefly engaged to her half sister. And she'd added an impressive amount of further bias ever since.

She slammed another filing cabinet shut. "This damn

file isn't here." She suddenly turned on him. "But you are. What the hell are you doing here, anyway?"

So it had finally sunk in, the improbability of his stumbling in on her here in his sister's office.

Having already decided to throw her off, he said, "I was hoping Johara would be working late."

She frowned. "So you don't know that she and Shaheen are throwing a party tonight?"

"They are?" This had to be his best acting moment ever.

She bought it, as evidenced by her return to mockery. "You forgot that, too? Is anything of any importance to you?"

He approached her again with the same caution he would approach a hostile feline. "Why do you assume it's me who forgot and not them who neglected to invite me?"

"Because I'd never believe either Johara or Shaheen would neglect anyone, even you."

When he was a few feet away, he looked down at her, amusement again rising unbidden. "But it's fully believable that I got their invitation and tossed it in the bin unread?"

She shrugged. "Sure. Why not? I'd believe you got a dozen phone calls, too, or even face-to-face invitations and just disregarded them."

"Then I come here to visit my sister because I'm disregarding her?"

"Maybe you need something from her and came to ask for it, even though you won't consider going to her party."

He let out a short, delighted laugh. "You'll go the extra light-year to think the worst of me, won't you?"

"Don't give me any credit. It's you who makes it exceptionally easy to malign you."

Hardly believing how much he was enjoying her onslaught, he shook his head. "One would think Maysoon is your favorite sister and bosom buddy from the way you're hacking at me."

The intensity of her contempt grew hotter. "I would have

hacked at you if you'd done the same to a stranger or even an enemy."

"So your moral code is unaffected by personal considerations. Commendable. But what *have* I done exactly, in your opinion?"

Her snort was so cute, so incongruous, that it had his unfettered laugh ringing out again.

"Oh, you're good. With three words you've turned this from a matter of fact to a matter of opinion. Play another one."

"I'm trying hard to."

"Then *el'ab be'eed.*"

This meant *play far away.* From her, of course.

Something he had no intention of doing. "Won't you at least recite my charges and read me my rights?"

She produced her cell phone. "Nope. I bypassed all that and long pronounced your sentence."

"Shouldn't I be getting parole after ten years?"

"Not when I gave you life in the first place, no."

His whole face was aching. He hadn't smiled this much in…ever. "You're a mean little thing, aren't you?"

"And you're a sleazy huge thing, aren't you?"

He guffawed this time.

Wondering how the hell this pixie was doing this, triggering his humor with every acerbic remark, he headed back to Johara's desk. "So are we done with your search mission? Or going by the aftermath of your efforts, search-and-destroy operation?"

"Just for that," she said as she placed a call, "you put everything back where it belongs."

"I don't think even Johara herself can accomplish that impossibility after the chaos you've wrought."

She flicked him one last annihilating look, then dismissed him as she started speaking into the phone without preamble. "Okay, Jo, I can't find anything that might be the file you described, and I've gone through every shred of paper you got here."

"You mean *we* did." Aram raised his voice to make sure Johara heard him.

An obsidian bolt hit him right between the eyes, had his heart skipping a beat.

He grinned even more widely at her. He had no doubt Johara *had* heard him, but it was clear she'd pretended she hadn't, since Kanza's wrath would have only increased if Johara had made any comment or asked who was with her.

And he'd thought he'd known everything there was to know about his kid sister. Turned out she wasn't only capable of the subterfuge of setting him and her partner up, but of acting seamlessly on the fly, too.

Kanza was frowning now. "What do you mean it's okay? It's not okay. You need the file, and if it's here, I'll find it. Just give me a better description. I might have looked at it a dozen times and didn't recognize it for what it was."

Kanza fell silent for a few moments as Johara answered. He had a feeling she was telling Kanza a load of ultra-convincing bull. By now, he was 100 percent certain that file didn't even exist.

Kanza ended the conversation and confirmed his deductions. "I can't believe it! Johara is now not even sure the file is here at all. Blames it on pregnancy hormones."

Hoping his placating act was half as good as Johara's misleading one, he said, "We only lost an hour of turning her office upside down. Apart from the mess, no harm done."

"First, there's no *we* in the matter. Second, I was here an hour before you breezed in. Third, you *did* breeze in. Can't think of more harm than that. But the good news is I now get to breeze out of here and put an end to this unwelcome and torturous exchange with you."

"Aren't you even going to try to ameliorate the destruction you've left in your wake?"

"Johara insisted I leave everything and just rush over to the party."

So she was invited. Of course. Though from the way she was dressed, no one would think she had anything more glamorous planned than going to the grocery store.

But it was evident she intended to go. That must have been Johara and Shaheen's plan A. They'd invited him to set him and Kanza up at the soirée. And when he'd refused, Johara had improvised find-the-nonexistent-file plan B.

Kanza grabbed a red jacket from one of the couches, which he hadn't noticed before, and shrugged it on before hooking what looked like a small laptop bag across her body.

Then, without even a backward glance at him, she was striding toward the door.

He didn't know how he'd managed to move that fast, but he found himself blocking her path.

This surprised her so much that she bumped into him. He caught an unguarded expression in those bottomless black eyes as she stumbled back. A look of pure vulnerability. As though the steely persona she'd been projecting wasn't the real her, or not the only side to her. As though his nearness unsettled her so much it left her floundering.

A moment later he wondered if he'd imagined what he'd seen, since the look was now gone and annoyance was the only thing left in its place.

He tried what he hoped was the smooth charm he'd seen others practice but had never attempted himself. "How about we breeze out of here together and I drive you to the party?"

"You assume I came here…how? On foot?"

"A pixie like you might have just blinked in here."

"Then I can blink out the same way."

"I'm still offering to conserve your mystic energies."

"Acting the gentleman doesn't become you, and any attempt at simulating one is wasted on me since I'm hardly a damsel in distress. And if you're offering in order to score points with Johara, forget it."

"There you go again—assigning such convoluted motives to my actions when I'm far simpler than you think. I've decided to go to the party, and since you're going, too, you can save your pixie magic, as I have a perfectly mundane car parked in the garage."

"What a coincidence. So do I. Though mine is mundane for real. While yours verges on the supernatural. I hear it talks, thinks, takes your orders, parks itself and knows when to brake and where to go. All it has left to do is make you a sandwich and a cappuccino to become truly sentient."

"I'll see about developing those sandwich- and cappuccino-making capabilities. Thanks for the suggestion. But wouldn't you like to take a spin in my near-sentient car?"

"No. Just like I wouldn't want to be in your near-sentient presence. Now *ann eznak*...or better still, *men ghair eznak*." Then she turned and strode away.

He waited until she exited the room before moving. In moments, his far-longer strides overtook her at the elevators.

Kanza didn't give any indication that she noticed him, going through messages on her phone. She still made no reaction when he boarded the elevator with her and then when he followed her to the garage.

It was only when he tailed her to her car that she finally turned on him. *"What?"*

He gave her his best pseudoinnocent smile and lobbed back her parting shot. "By your leave, or better still without it, I'm escorting you to your car."

She looked him up and down in silence, then turned and took the last strides to a Ford Escape that was the exact color of her jacket. Seemed she was fond of red.

In moments, she drove away with a screech right out of a car chase, which had him jumping out of the way.

He stood watching her taillights flashing as she hit the

brakes at the garage's exit. Grinning to himself, he felt a rush of pure adrenaline flood his system.

She'd really done it. Something no other woman—no other person—had ever done.

She'd turned him down.

No…it was more that that. She'd *rebuffed* him.

Well. There was only one thing he could do now.

Give chase.

Three

Kanza resisted the urge to floor the gas pedal.

That…rat was following her.

That colossal, cruelly magnificent rat.

Though the way he made her feel was that *she* was the rat, running for her life, growing more frantic by the breath, chased by a majestic, terminally bored cat who'd gotten it in his mind to chase her…just for the hell of it.

She snatched another look in the rearview mirror.

Yep. There he still was. Driving safely, damn him, keeping the length of three cars between them, almost to the inch. He'd probably told his pet car how far away it should stick to her car's butt. The constant distance was more nerve-racking than if he'd kept approaching and receding, if he'd made any indication that he was expending any effort in keeping up with her.

She knew he didn't really want to catch her. He was just exercising the prerogative of his havoc-inducing powers. He was doing this to rattle her. To show her that no one refused him, that he'd do whatever he pleased, even if it infringed on others. Preferably if it did.

It made her want to slam the brakes in the middle of the

road, force him to stop right behind her. Then she'd get down, walk over there and haul him out of his car and… and… What?

Bite mouthfuls out of his gorgeous bod? Swipe his keys and cell phone and leave him stranded on the side of the road?

Evidently, from the maddening time she'd just spent in his company, he'd probably enjoy the hell out of whatever she did. She *had* tried her level worst back in Johara's office, and that insensitive lout had seemed to be having a ball, thinking every insult out of her mouth was a hoot. Seemed his jaded blood levels had long been toxic and now any form of abuse was a stimulant.

Gritting her teeth all the way to Johara and Shaheen's place, she kept taking compulsive glances back at this incorrigible predator who tailed her in such unhurried pursuit.

Twenty minutes later, she parked the car in the garage, filled her lungs with air. Then, holding it as if she was bracing for a blow, she got out.

Out of the corner of her eye she could estimate he'd parked, too. Three empty car places away. He was really going the distance to maintain the joke, wasn't he?

Fine. Let him have his fun. Which would only be exacerbated if she made any response. She wouldn't.

When she was at the elevator, she stopped, a groan escaping her. Aram had frazzled her so much that she'd left Johara and Shaheen's housewarming present, along with the Arabian horse miniature set she'd promised Gharam, in the trunk.

Cursing him to grow a billion blue blistering barnacles, she turned on her heel and stalked back to the car. She passed him on her way back, as he'd been following in her wake, maintaining the equivalent of three paces behind her.

Feeling his gaze on her like the heaviest embarrassment she'd ever suffered, she retrieved the boxes. Just as the tailgate clicked closed, she almost knocked her head against it in chagrin. She'd forgotten to change her sneakers.

Great. This guy was frying her synapses even at fifty paces, where he was standing serenely by the elevator, awaiting her return. Maybe she should just forget about changing the sneakers. Or better still, hurl them at him.

But it was one thing to skip around in those sneakers, another to attend Johara and Shaheen's chic party in them. It was bad enough she'd be the most underdressed one around, as usual.

Forcing herself to breathe calmly, she reopened the tailgate and hopped on the edge of the trunk. He'd just have to bear the excitement of watching her change into slightly less nondescript two-inch heels. At least those were black and didn't clash like a chalk aberration on a black background.

In two minutes she was back at the elevators, hoisting the boxes—each under an arm. Contrary to her expectations, he didn't offer to help her carry them. Then he didn't even board the elevator with her. Instead, he just stood there in that disconcerting calm while the doors closed. Though she was again pretending to be busy with her phone, she knew he didn't pry his gaze from her face. And that he had that infuriating smile on his all the time.

Sensing she'd gotten only a short-lived respite since he was certain to follow her up at his own pace, she knew her smile was on the verge of shattering as Johara received her at the door. It must have been her own tension that made her imagine that Johara looked disappointed. For why would she be, when she'd already known she hadn't found her file and had been the one to insist Kanza stop searching for it?

Speculation evaporated as Johara exclaimed over Kanza's gifts and ushered her toward Shaheen and Gharam. But barely three minutes later, Johara excused herself and hurried to the door again.

Though Kanza was certain it was *him,* her breath still

caught in her throat, and her heart sputtered like a malfunctioning throttle.

Ya Ullah... Why was she letting this virtuoso manipulator pull her strings like this?

The surge of fury manifested in exaggerated gaiety with Shaheen and Gharam. But a minute later Shaheen excused himself, too, and rushed away with Gharam to join his wife in welcoming his so-called best friend. She almost blurted out that Aram was here only to annoy her, not to see him or his sister, and that Shaheen should do himself a favor and find himself a new best friend, since *that* one cared about no one but himself.

Biting her tongue and striding deeper into the penthouse, she forced herself to mingle, which usually rated right with anesthesia-free tooth extractions on her list of favorite pastimes. However, right now, it felt like the most desirable thing ever, compared to being exposed to Aram Nazaryan again.

But to her surprise, she wasn't.

After an hour passed, throughout which she'd felt his eyes constantly on her, he'd made no attempt to approach her, and her tension started to dissipate.

It seemed her novelty to him had worn off. He must be wondering why the hell he'd taken his challenge this far—at the price of suffering the company of actual human beings. Ones who clearly loved him, though why, she'd never understand.

She still welcomed the distraction when Johara asked her to put the horse set in their family living room away from Gharam's determined-to-take-them-apart hands. The two-and-a-half-year-old tyke was one unstoppable girl who everyone said took after her maternal uncle. Clearly, in nature as well as looks.

She'd finished her chore and was debating what was more moronic—that she was this affected by Aram's presence or that her relief at the end of this perplexing interlude was mixed with what infuriatingly resembled letdown—when it felt as if a thousand volts of electricity zapped her. His dark, velvety baritone that drenched her every receptor in paralysis.

It was long, heart-thudding moments before what he'd said made sense.

"I'm petitioning for a reopening of my case."

She didn't turn to him. She couldn't.

For the second time tonight, he'd snuck up on her, startling the reins of volition out of her reach.

But this time, courtesy of the building tension that had been defused in false security, the surprise incapacitated her.

When she didn't turn, it was Aram who circled her in a wide arc, coming to face her at that distance he'd been maintaining, as if he was a hunter who knew he had his quarry cornered yet still wasn't taking any chances he'd get a set of claws across the face.

And as usual with him around, she felt the spacious, ingeniously decorated room shrink and fade away, her senses converging like a spotlight on him.

It was always a shock to the system beholding him. He was without any doubt the most beautiful creature she'd ever seen. Damn him.

She'd bet it was beyond anyone alive not to be awed by his sheer grandeur and presence, to not gape as they drank in the details of what made him what he was. She remembered with acute vividness the first time she'd seen him. She *had* gaped then and every time she'd seen him afterward, trying to wrap her mind around how anyone could be endowed with so much magnificence.

He lived up to his pseudonym—a pirate from a fairy tale, imposing, imperious, mysterious with a dark, ruthless edge to his beauty, making him…utterly compelling.

It still seemed unbelievable that he was Johara's brother. Apart from both of them possessing a level of beauty that was spellbinding, verging on painful to behold, they looked nothing alike. While Johara had the most amazing golden hair, molten chocolate eyes and thick cream complexion, Aram was her total opposite. But after she'd seen both their parents, she'd realized he'd manifested the absolute best in both, too.

His eyes were a more dazzling shade of azure than that of his French mother's—the most vivid, hypnotic color she'd ever seen. From his mother, too, and her family, he'd also inherited his prodigious height and amplified it. He'd added a generous brush of burnished copper to his Armenian-American father's swarthy complexion, a deepened gloss and luxury to his raven mane and an enhanced bulk and breadth to his physique.

Then came the details. And the devil was very much in those. A dancing, laughing, knowing one, aware of the exact measure of their unstoppable influence. Of every slash and hollow and plane of a face stamped with splendor and uniqueness, every bulge and sweep and slope of a body emanating maleness and strength, every move and glance and intonation demonstrating grace and manliness, power and perfection. All in all, he was glory personified.

Now, exuding enough charisma and confidence to power a small city, he towered across from her, calmly sweeping his silk black jacket out of the way, shoving his hands into his pockets. The movement had the cream shirt stretching over the expanse of virility it clung to. Her lips tingled as his chiseled mouth quirked up into that lethal smile.

"I submit a motion that I have been unjustly tried."

Aram's obvious enjoyment, not to mention his biding his time before springing his presence on her again, made retaliation a necessity.

Her voice, when she managed to operate her vocal cords, thankfully sounded cool and dismissive. "And I submit you've not only gotten away with your crimes but you've been phenomenally rewarded for them."

"If you're referring to my current business success, how are you managing to correlate it to my alleged crimes?"

She fought not to lick the dryness from her lips, to bite into the numbness that was spreading through them. "I'm managing because you've built said success using the same principles with which you perpetrated those crimes."

His eyes literally glittered with mischief, becoming bluer before her dazzled ones. "Then I am submitting that those principles you ascribe to me and your proof of them were built around pure circumstantial evidence."

Her eyebrows shot up. "So you're not after a retrial. What you really want is your whole criminal record expunged."

He raised those large, perfectly formed hands like someone blocking blows. "I wouldn't dream of universally dismissing my convictions." His painstakingly sculpted lips curled into a delicious grin. "That would be pushing my luck. But I do demand an actual primary hearing of my testimony, since I distinctly remember one was never taken."

Although she felt her heart sputtering out of control, she tried to match his composure outwardly. "Who says you get a hearing at all? You certainly didn't grant others such mercy or consideration."

The scorching amusement in those gemlike eyes remained unperturbed. "By others you mean Maysoon, I assume?"

"Hers was the case I observed firsthand. As I am a stickler for justice, I will not pass judgment on those I know of only through secondhand testimonies and hearsay."

His eyes widened on what looked like genuine surprise. Yeah, right. As if he could feel anything for real.

"That's very…progressive of you. Elevated, even." At her baleful glance, something that simulated seriousness took over his expression. "No, I mean it. In my experience, when people don't like someone, they demonize them wholesale, stop granting them even the possibility of fairness."

She pursed her lips, refusing to consider the possibility of his sincerity. "Lauding my merits won't work, you know."

"In granting me a hearing?"

"In granting you leniency you haven't earned and certainly don't deserve." He opened his mouth, and she raised her hand. "Don't you think you've taken your joke far enough?"

For a moment he looked actually confused before a careful expression replaced uncertainty. "What joke, exactly?"

She rolled her eyes. "Spare me."

"Or you'll spear me?" At her exasperated rumble, he raised his hands again, the coaxing in his eyes rising another notch. "That *was* lame. But I really don't know what you're talking about. I am barely keeping up with you."

"Yeah, right. Since you materialized behind me like some capricious spirit, you've been ready with something right off the smart-ass chart before I've even finished speaking."

He shook his head, causing his collar-length mane to undulate. "If you think that was easy, think again. You're making me struggle for every inch before you snatch it away with your next lob. For the first time in my life I have no idea what will spill out of someone's lips next, so give me a break."

"I would ask where you want it, but I have to be realistic. Considering our respective physiques, I probably can't give you one without the help of heavy, blunt objects."

The next moment, all her nerves fired up as he proceeded to subject her to the sight and sound of his all-out amusement, a demonstration so…virile, so debilitating, each peal was a new bolt forking through her nervous system.

When he at last brought his mirth under control, his lips remained stretched the widest she'd seen them, showing off that set of extraordinary white teeth in the most devastating smile she'd had the misfortune of witnessing. He even wiped away a couple of tears of hilarity. "You can give me compound fractures with your tongue alone. As for your glares, we're talking incineration."

Hating that even when he was out of breath and wheezing, he sounded more hard-hitting for it, she gritted out, "If I could do that, it would be the least I owe you."

"What have I done *now?*" Even his pseudolament was scrumptious. This guy needed some kind of quarantine. He shouldn't be left free to roam the realm of flimsy mortals. "Is this about the joke you've accused me of perpetrating?"

"There's no accusation here—just statement of fact. You've been enjoying one big fat joke at my expense since you stumbled on me in Johara's office."

His eyes sobered at once, filling with something even more distressing than mischief and humor. Indulgence? "I've been relishing the experience immensely, but not as a joke and certainly not at your expense."

Her heart gave her ribs another vicious kick. She had to stop this before her heart literally bruised.

She raised her hands. "Okay, this is going nowhere. Let's say I believe you. Give me another reason you're doing this. And don't tell me that you care one way or the other what I think in general or what I think of you specifically. You don't care about what anyone thinks."

The earnestness in his eyes deepened. "You're right. I care nothing for what others think of me."

"And you're absolutely right not to."

That seemed to stun him yet again. "I am?" At her nod, he prodded, "That includes *everyone?*"

She nodded again. "Of course. What other people think of you, no matter who they are, is irrelevant. Unsolicited opinions are usually a hindrance and a source of discontentment, if not outright unhappiness. So carry on not caring, go take your leave from Johara and Shaheen and return to your universe where no one's opinion matters…as it shouldn't."

"At least grant me the right to care or not care." Those unbelievable eyes seemed to penetrate right through her as his gaze narrowed in on her. “And whether it comes under caring or not, I do happen to be extremely interested in your opinion of me. Now, let me escort you back to the party. Let me get us a drink over which we’ll reopen my case and explore the possibility of adjusting your opinion of me—at least to a degree.”

She arched a brow. “You mean you’d settle for adjusting my opinion of you from horrific to just plain horrid?”

“Who knows, maybe while retrying my case, your unwavering sense of justice will lead you to adjusting it to plain misjudged.”

“Or maybe just downright wretched.”

He hit her with another of his pouts. Then he raised the level of chaos and laughed again, his merriment as potent as everything else about him. “I’d take that.”

Trying to convince her heart to slot back into its usual place after its latest somersault, she again tried her best glower. It had no effect on him, as usual. Worse. It had the opposite effect to what she’d perfected it for. He looked at her as if her glare was the cutest thing he’d seen.

She voiced her frustration. “You talk about my incinerating glares, but I could be throwing cotton balls or rose petals at you for all the effect they have on you.”

“It’s not your glares that are ineffective. It’s me who’s discovering a penchant for incineration.”

Instead of appeasing her, it annoyed her more. “I’ll have you know I’ve reduced other men to dust with those scowls. No one has withstood a minute in my presence once I engaged annihilate mode.” She lifted her chin. “But you seem to need specifically designed weapons. If I go along with you in this game you got it in your mind to play, it’ll be so I can find out if you have an Achilles’ heel.”

“I have no idea if I have that.” His gaze grew thoughtful. “Would you use it to…annihilate me if you discovered it?”

She gave him one of her patented sizing-up glances and regretted it midway. She must quit trying her usual strategies with him. Not only because they always backfired, but it wasn't advisable to expose herself to another distressing dose of his wonders.

She returned to his eyes, those turquoise depths that exuded the ferocity of his intellect and the power of his wit, and found gazing into them just as taxing to her circulatory system.

She sighed, more vexed with her own inability to moderate her reactions than with him. "Nah. I'll just be satisfied knowing your Achilles' heel exists and you're not invulnerable. And maybe, if you get too obnoxious, I'll use my knowledge as leverage to make you back off."

That current of mischief and challenge in his eyes spiked. "It goes against my nature to back off."

"Not even under threat of…annihilation?"

"Especially then. I'd probably beg you to use whatever fatal weakness you discover just to find out how it feels."

"Wow. You're jaded to the point of numbness, aren't you?"

"You've got me figured out, don't you? Or do you? Shall we find out?"

It was clear this monolith would stand there and spar with her until she agreed to this "retrial" of his. If she was in her own domain or on neutral ground, or at least somewhere without a hundred witnesses blocking her only escape route, she would have slammed him with something cutting and walked out as she'd done in Johara's office.

But she couldn't inflict on her friends the scene this gorgeous jerk would instigate if he didn't have his way. She bet he knew she suffered from those scruples, was using the knowledge to corner her into participating in his game.

"You're counting on my inability to risk spoiling Johara and Shaheen's party, aren't you?"

His blink was all innocence, and downright evil for it. "I thought you didn't care what other people thought."

"I don't, not when it comes to how I choose to live my

life. But I do care about what others think of my actions that directly impact them. And if I walk out now, you'll tail me in the most obvious, disruptive way you can, generating curiosity and speculation, which would end up putting a damper on Johara and Shaheen's party." Her eyes narrowed as another thought hit her. "Now I am wondering if maybe they *didn't* extend an invitation to you after all because they've been burned by your sabotage before."

He pounced on that, took it where she couldn't have anticipated. "So you're considering changing your mind about whether I was invited? See? Maybe you'll change your mind about everything else if you give me a chance."

She blew out a breath in exasperation. "I only change my mind for the worse…or worst."

"You're one tiny bundle of nastiness, aren't you?" His smile said he thought that the best thing to aspire to be.

She tossed her head, infusing her disadvantaged stature with all the belittling she could muster. "Again with the size references."

"It was you who started using mine in derogatory terms. Then you moved on to my looks, then my character, then my history, and if there were more components to me, I bet you'd have pummeled through them, too."

Refusing to rise to the bait, she turned around and stomped away.

He followed her. Keeping those famous three steps behind. With his footfalls being soundless, she could pinpoint his location only by the chuckles rumbling in the depths of his massive chest. When those ended, his overpowering presence took over, cocooning her all the way to the expansive reception area.

Absorbed in warding off his influence, she could barely register the ultraelegant surroundings or the dozens of chic people milling around. No one noticed her, as usual, but everyone's gaze was drawn to the nonchalant predator behind her. Abhorring the thought of having everyone's eyes on her by association once they realized he was following her, she continued walking where she hoped the least amount of spectators were around.

She stepped out onto the wraparound terrace that overlooked the now-shrouded-in-darkness Central Park, with Manhattan glittering like fiery jewels beyond its extensive domain. Stopping at the three-foot-high brushed stainless steel and Plexiglas railings, gazing out into the moonlit night, she shivered as September's high-altitude wind hit her overheating body. But she preferred hypothermia to the burning speculation that being in Aram Nazaryan's company would have provoked. Not that she'd managed to escape that totally. The few people who'd had the same idea of seeking privacy out here did their part in singeing her with their curiosity.

She hugged herself to ward off the discomfort of their interest more than the sting of the wind. He made it worse, drenching her in the dark spell of his voice.

"Can I offer you my jacket, or would I have my head bitten off again?"

Barely controlling a shudder, she pretended she was flipping her hair away. "Your head is still on your shoulders. Don't push your luck if you want to keep it there."

His lips pursed in contemplation as he watched her suppress another shudder. "You're one of those independent pains who'd freeze to death before letting people pay them courtesies, aren't you?"

"You're one of those imposing pains who force people into the cold, then inflict their jackets on them and call their imposition courtesy, aren't you?"

"I would have settled for remaining inside where it's toasty. You're the one who led me out here to freeze."

"If you're freezing, don't go playing Superman and volunteering your jacket."

That ever-hovering smile caught fire again. "How about we both mosey on round the corner? Since you're the one who decided to hold my retrial thirty floors up and in the open, I at least motion to do it away from the draft."

"You're also one of those gigantic pains who love to marvel at the sound of their own cleverness, aren't you?" She tossed the words back as she walked ahead to do as he'd suggested.

His answer felt like a wave of heat carrying on the whistling wind. "Just observing a meteorological fact."

As he'd projected, the moment they turned the corner, the wind died down, leaving only comfortable coolness to contend with.

She turned to him at the railings. "Stop right there." He halted at once, perplexity entering his gaze. "You're in the perfect position to shield me from any draft. A good use at last for this superfluous breadth and bulk of yours."

Amusement flooded back into his eyes, radiated hypnotic azure in the moonlight. "So you're only averse to voluntary courtesy on my part, but using me as an unintentional barrier is okay with you."

"Perfectly so. I don't intend to suffer from hypothermia because of the situation you imposed on me."

"I made you come out here?"

"Yes, you did."

"And how did I do that?"

"You made escaping the curiosity, not to mention the jealousy, of all present a necessity."

"Jealousy!" His eyebrows disappeared into the layers of satin hair the wind had flopped over his forehead.

"Every person in there, man or woman, would give anything to be in my place, having your private audience." She gave an exaggerated sigh. "If only they knew I'd donate the *privilege* if I could with a sizable check on top as bonus."

His chuckle revved inside his chest again and in her bones. "That *privilege* is nontransferable. You're stuck with it. So before we convene, what shall I get you?"

"Why shouldn't I be the one to get you something?"

His nod was all concession. "Why shouldn't you, indeed?"

She nodded, too, slowly, totally unable to predict him and feeling more out of her depth by the second for it. "Be specific about what you prefer. I hate guessing."

"I'm flabbergasted you're actually considering my preferences. But I'll go with anything nonalcoholic. I'm driving." Considering he'd placed his order, she started to turn around and he stopped her. "And, Kanza…can you possibly also make it something nonpoisoned and curse free?"

Muttering "smart-ass" and zapping him with her harshest parting glance, which only dissipated against his force field and was received by another chuckle, she strode away.

On reentering the reception, she groaned out loud as she immediately felt the weight of Johara's gaze zooming in on her. She'd no doubt noticed Aram marching behind her across the penthouse and must be bursting with curiosity about how they'd met and why that older brother of hers had gotten it into his mind to follow her around.

Johara just had to bear not knowing. She couldn't worry about her now. One Nazaryan at a time.

She grabbed a glass of cranberry-apple juice from a passing waiter and strode back to the terrace, this time exiting from where she'd left Aram. As soon as she did, she nearly tripped, as her heartbeat did.

Aram was at the railing, two dozen paces away with his back to her. He was silhouetted against the rising moon, hands gripping the bar, looking like a modern statue of a Titan. The only animate things about him were the satin stirring around his majestic head in the tranquil breeze and the silk rustling around his steel-fleshed frame.

But apart from his physical glory, there was something about his pose as he stared out into the night—in the slight slump of his Herculean shoulders, dimming that indomitable vibe—that disturbed her. Whatever it was, it forced her to reconsider her disbelief of his assertion that he'd never felt worse. Made her feel guilty about how she'd been bashing him, believing him invincible.

Then he turned around, as if he'd felt her presence, and his eyes lit up again with that potent merriment and mischief, and all empathy evaporated in a wave of instinctive challenge and chagrined response.

How was it even possible? That after all these years he remained the one man who managed to wring an explosive mixture of fascination and detestation from her?

From the first time she'd laid eyes on him when she'd been seventeen, she'd thought him the most magnificent male in existence, one who compounded his overwhelming physical assets with an array of even more impressive superiorities. He'd been the only one who could breach her composure and tongue-tie her just by walking into a room. That had only earned him a harder crash from the pedestal she'd placed him on, when he'd proved to be just another predictable male, one who considered only a woman's looks and status no matter her character. Why else would he have gotten involved with her spoiled and vapid half sister? Her opinion of him would have been salvaged when he'd walked away from Maysoon, if—and it was an insurmountable if—he hadn't been needlessly, shockingly cruel in doing so.

Remembered outrage rose as she stopped before him and foisted the drink into his hand. It rose higher when she couldn't help watching how his fingers closed around the glass, the grace, power and economy of the movement. It made her want to whack herself and him upside the head.

She had to get this ridiculous interlude over with.

"Without further ado, let's get on with your preposterous retrial."

That gargantuan swine gave a superb pretense of wiping levity from his face, replacing it with earnestness.

"It's going to be the fastest one in history. Your indictment was unequivocal and the evidence against you overwhelming. Whatever her faults, Maysoon loved you, and you kicked her out of your life. Then when she was down, you kicked her again—almost literally and very publicly. You left her in a heap on the ground and walked away unscathed, and then went on to prosper beyond any expectations. While she went on to waste her life, almost self-destruct in one failed relationship after another. If I'd judged your case then, I would have passed the harshest sentence. In any retrial, I'd still pronounce you guilty and judge that you be subjected to character execution."

Four

Aram stared at the diminutive firebrand who was the first woman who'd ever fetched him a drink, then followed up by sentencing his character to death.

Both action and indictment should have elated the hell out of him, as everything from her tonight had. But the expected exhilaration didn't come; something unsettling spread inside him instead. For what if her opinion of him was too entrenched and he couldn't adjust it?

He transferred his gaze to the burgundy depths in the glass she'd just handed him, collecting his thoughts.

Although he'd been keeping it light and teasing, he knew this had suddenly become serious. He had to be careful what to say from now on. If he messed this up, she'd never let him close enough again to have another round. That would be it.

And he couldn't let that be it. He wasn't even going to entertain that possibility. He might have lost many things in his life, but he wasn't going to lose this.

He raised his eyes to meet hers. It was as if they held pieces of the velvet night in their darkest depths. She was waiting, playing by the rules he'd improvised, giving him a chance to defend himself. He had no doubt it would be his one and only chance. He had to make it work.

He inhaled. "I submit that your so-called overwhelming evidence was all circumstantial and unreliable. I did none of the things you've just accused me of. Cite every shred of evidence you think you have, and I'll debunk each one for you."

Her face tilted up at him, sending that amazing wealth of hair cascading with an audible sigh to one side. "You didn't kick Maysoon out of your life?"

"Not in the way you're painting."

"How would you paint it? In black-and-white? In full color? Or because the memory must have faded—in sepia?"

"Who's being a smart-ass now?" At her nonchalant shrug, he pressed on. "What do you know about what happened between Maysoon and me? Apart from her demonizing accounts and your own no less prejudiced observations?"

"Since my observations were so off base, why don't you tell me your own version?"

Having gotten so used to her contention, he was worried by her acquiescence.

He exhaled to release the rising tension. "I assume you knew what your half sister was like? Maybe the impossible has happened and she's evolved by age, but back then, she was…intolerable."

"But of course you found that out after you became engaged to her."

"No. Before."

As he waited for her censure to surpass its previous levels, her gaze only grew thoughtful.

There was no predicting her, was there?

"And you still went through with it. Why?"

"Because I was stupid." Her eyes widened at his harsh admission. She must have thought he'd come up with some excuse to make his actions seem less pathetic and more defensible. He would have done that with anyone else. But with her, he just wanted to have the whole truth out. "I wanted to get married and have a family, but I had no idea how to go about doing that. I thought I'd never leave Zohayd at the time and I'd have to choose a woman from those available. But there was no one I looked at twice, let alone considered for anything lasting. So when Maysoon started pursuing me…"

"Watch it." Her interjection was almost soft. It stopped him in his tracks harder than if she'd bitten it off. "You'll veer off into the land of fabrication if you use this rationale for choosing Maysoon. Using the pursuit criterion, you should have ended up with a harem, since women of all ages in Zohayd chased after you."

"Now who's taking a stroll in the land of exaggeration? Not all women were after me. Aliyah and Laylah, for instance, considered me only one of the family. And you didn't consider me human at all, I believe, let alone male."

Her eyes glittered with the moon's reflected silver as she ignored his statement concerning her. "And that's what? Two females out of two million?"

"Whatever the number of women who pursued me, they were after me as an adventure, and each soon gave up when I made it clear I wasn't into the kind of…entertainment they were after. I wanted a committed relationship at the time."

"And you're saying that none wanted that? Or that none seemed a better choice than Maysoon for said relationship?"

"Compared to Maysoon's pursuit, they were all slouches. And your sister did look like the best deal. Suitable age, easy on the eyes and very, very determined. Sure, she was volatile and superficial, but when her pursuit didn't wane for a whole year, I thought it meant she *really* liked what she saw."

"Her along with everyone with eyes or a brain wave."

Again she managed to make the compliment the most

abrasive form of condemnation, arousing that stinging pleasure he was getting too used to.

"I'm not talking about my alleged 'beauty' here. I thought she liked *me,* and that meant a lot then. I knew how I was viewed in the royal circles in Zohayd, what my attraction was to the women you cite as my hordes of pursuers. I was this exotic foreigner of mixed descent from a much lower social class that they could have a safe and forbidden fling with. Many thought they could keep me as their boy toy."

Something came into her eyes. Sympathy? Empathy?

It was probably ridicule, and he was imagining things.

"You were hardly a boy," she murmured.

"Their gigolo, then. In any event, I thought Maysoon viewed me differently. Her pursuit in spite of our class differences and the fact that I was hardly an ideal groom for a princess made me think she was one of those rare women who appreciated a man for himself. I thought this alone made up for all her personal shortcomings. And who was I to consider those when I was riddled with my own?" He emptied his lungs on a harsh exhalation. "Turned out she was just attracted to me as a spoiled brat would be to a toy she fancied and couldn't have. Most likely because some of the women in her inner circle must have made me a topic of giggling lust, maybe even challenge, and being pathologically competitive herself, she wanted to be the one to triumph over them."

Kanza's eyes filled with skepticism, but she let it go unvoiced and allowed him to continue.

"And the moment she did she started trying to strip me bare to dress me up into the kind of toy she had in mind all along. She started telling me how I must behave, in private and public, how I must distance myself from my father, whom she made clear she considered the hired help." He drew in a sharp inhalation laden with his still-reverberating chagrin on his father's account. "And it didn't end there. She dictated who I should get close to, how I must kiss up to Shaheen's brothers now that he was gone, play on my former relationship with him to gain a 'respectable' position within the kingdom and wheedle financial help in setting up a business like theirs so I would become as rich as possible."

The cynicism in Kanza's eyes had frozen. There was nothing in them now. A very careful nothing. As if she didn't know how to react to the influx of new information.

He went on. "And she was in a rabid hurry for me to do all that. She couldn't wait to have me pick up the tab of her extravagant existence—which she'd thought so disadvantaged—and informed me that as her husband it would be my duty to raise her up to a whole new level of excess." He scrubbed a hand across his jaw. "In the four months' duration of the engagement, I was so stunned by the depths of her shallowness, so taken aback by the audacity of her demands and the intensity of her tantrums, that I didn't react. Then came the night of that ball."

She'd been there that night. In one of those horrific getups and alien makeup. He now remembered vividly that she'd been the last thing he'd seen as he'd walked out, standing there over Maysoon, glaring at him with loathing in her eyes.

There was nothing but absorption in her eyes now. She was evidently waiting to see if his version of that ill-fated night's events would change the opinion she'd long held of him, built on her interpretation of its events.

He felt that his next words would decide if she'd ever let him near again. He had to make them count. The only way he could do that was to be as brutally honest as possible.

"Maysoon dragged me to talk to King Atef and Amjad. But when I didn't take her heavy-handed hints to broach the subject of the high-ranking job she'd heard was open, or the loan she'd been pushing me to ask for, she decided to take control. She extolled my economic theories for Zohayd and made a mess of outlining them. Then she proceeded to massacre my personal business plans, which I'd once made the mistake of trying to explain to her. She became terminally obvious as she bragged how anyone getting on with me on the ground level with a sizable investment would reap *millions*." He huffed a bitter laugh. "For a mercenary soul, she knew nothing about the real value of money, since she'd never made a cent and had never even glanced at her own bills."

There was only corroboration in Kanza's eyes now. Knowing her half sister, she must have known the accuracy of this assessment.

He continued. "Needless to say, King Atef and Amjad were not impressed, and they must have believed I'd put her up to it. I was tempted to tell them the truth right then and there, that I'd finally faced it that I was just a means to an end to subsidize her wasteful life. Instead, I attempted to curtail the damage she'd done as best I could before excusing myself and making my escape. Not that she'd let me walk away."

Wariness invaded her gaze. She must have realized he'd come to the point where he'd finally explain the fireworks that had ended his life in Zohayd and formed her lasting-till-now opinion of him.

He shoved his hands into his pockets. "She stormed after me, shrieking that I was a moron, a failure, that I didn't know a thing about grabbing opportunities and maximizing my connections. She said my potential for 'infiltrating' the higher echelons of the royal family was why she'd considered me in the first place and that if I wanted to be her husband I'd do anything to ingratiate myself to them and provide her with the lifestyle she deserved."

Her wince was unmistakable. As if, even if she knew full well Maysoon was capable of saying those things and harboring those motivations, she was still embarrassed for her, ashamed on her account.

Suddenly he wanted to go no further, didn't want to

cause her any discomfort. But she was waiting for him to go on. Her eyes were now prodding him to go on.

He did. "It was almost comical, but I wasn't laughing. I wasn't even angry or disappointed or anything else. I was just…done. So I told her that I would have done anything for the woman I married if she had married me for me and not as a potential meal ticket. Then I walked away. Maysoon wasn't the first major error in judgment I made in Zohayd, but she was the one I rectified."

He paused for a moment, then made his concluding statement, the one refuting her major accusation. "If your half sister has been wasting her life and self-destructing, it's because that's what she does with her capriciousness and excesses and superfluous approach to life—not because of anything *I* did to her. And she's certainly not spinning out of control on my account, because I never counted to her."

Kanza stared up at Aram for what felt like a solid hour after he'd finished his *testimony.*

She could still feel his every word all over her like the stings of a thousand wasps.

She'd never even imagined or could have guessed about his situation back in Zohayd, how he'd been targeted and propositioned, how he'd felt unvalued and objectified.

And she'd been just as guilty of wronging him. In her own mind, in her own way, she had discriminated against him, too, if in the totally opposite direction to those women he'd described. While they'd reduced him to a sexual plaything in their minds, or a stepping-stone to a material goal, she'd exalted him to the point where she'd been unable to see beyond his limitless potential. She hadn't suspected that his untouchable self-possession could have been a facade, a defense; had believed him confident to the point of arrogance; equated his powerful influence with ruthlessness; and had assumed that he could have no insecurities, needs or vulnerabilities.

But…wait. *Wait.* This story was incomplete. He'd left out a huge part. A vital one.

She heard her voice, low, strained, wavering on a gust of wind that circumvented the shield of his body. "But you ended up doing what she advised you to do. She just didn't reap the benefit of her efforts, since you kicked her out of your life on her ear and soared so high on your own."

"Now what the hell are you talking about?"

She pulled herself to her full five-foot-two-plus-heels height, attempting to shove herself up into his face. "Did you or didn't you seek the Aal Shalaan Brotherhood in providing you with their far-reaching connections and fat financial support on your launch into billionairedom?"

"Is this what she said I did?" His scoff sounded furious for the first time. So this was his inapproachable line, what would rouse the indolent predator—any insinuations maligning the integrity and autonomy of his success. "And why not? I did know that there was no limit to her vindictiveness, that she'd do and say anything to punish me for escaping her talons. What else did she accuse me of? Maybe that I abused her, too?"

Her own outrage receded at the advance of his, which was so palpable she had no doubt it was real. Her answer stuck in her throat.

She no longer wanted to continue this. She hadn't wanted to start it in the first place. But his eyes were blazing into hers, demanding that she let him know the full details of Maysoon's accusations. And she had to tell him.

"She said you…exploited her, then threw her aside when you had enough of her."

His eyes narrowed to azure lasers. "By exploited, she meant…sexually?" She nodded, and he gave a spectacular snort, a drench of cold sarcasm underscoring his affront. "Would you believe that I never slept with her?"

"Last I heard, 'sleeping' with someone wasn't a prerequisite of being intimate."

"All right, I did try to be a gentleman and spare you the R-rated language. But since being euphemistic doesn't work in criminal cases, let me be explicit. I never had sex with her. In *any* form. *She* did instigate a few instances of heavy petting—which I didn't reciprocate and put an end to when she tried to offer me…sexual favors. Bottom line…beyond a few unenthusiastic-on-my-part kisses, I never breached her 'purity.' And I wasn't even holding back. I just never felt the least temptation. And when I started seeing her true colors and realized what she really wanted from me, I even became repulsed."

Every word had spiked her temperature higher. To her ears, her every instinct, each had possessed the unmistakable texture of truth. But sanctioning them as the new basis for her belief, her view of the past and his character was still difficult. Mainly because it went against everything she'd believed for so long, about him, about men in general.

Feeling her head would burst on fire, she mumbled, "You're telling me you could be so totally immune to a woman as beautiful as Maysoon when she was so very willing, too? I never heard that mental aversion ever interfered with a man's…drive. Maybe you are not human after all."

"Then get this news flash. There are men who don't find a beautiful, willing woman irresistible."

"Yes. Those men are called gay. Are you? Did you maybe discover that you were when you failed to respond to Maysoon?"

She knew she was being childish and that there was no way he was gay. But she was floundering.

"I 'failed to respond' to Maysoon because I'm one of those men who recognizes black widows and instinctively recoils from said intimacies out of self-preservation. Feeling you're being set up for long-term use and abuse is far more effective than an ice-cold shower. Of course, in hindsight, the fact that I was not attracted to her from the start should have been the danger bell that sent me running. But as I said, I was stupid, thinking that marriage didn't have to include sexual compatibility as a necessary ingredient, that beggars shouldn't be choosers."

He shook his head on a huff of deep disgust. "Lord, now I know why everyone treated me as if I was a sexual predator. Even knowing what she's capable of, I never dreamed she'd go as far as slandering herself in a conservative kingdom where a woman's 'honor' is her sexual purity, in order to paint me a darker shade of black."

That was the main reason Kanza had been forced to believe her half sister. She hadn't been able to imagine even Maysoon would harm herself this way if it hadn't been true. And once she'd believed her in this regard, everything else had been swallowed and digested without any thought of scrutiny. But now she couldn't even consider *not* believing him. This was the truth.

This meant that everything she'd assumed about him was a lie. Which left her…where?

Nowhere. Nowhere but in the wrong and not too happy about being forced to readjust her view of him.

Which didn't actually amount to anything. Her opinion had never mattered to anyone—especially not to Aram. All this new information would do now was torment her with guilt over the way she'd treated him. She'd always prided herself on her sense of justice, yet she'd somehow allowed prejudice to override her common sense where he'd been concerned.

The other damage would be to have her rekindled fascination with him unopposed by that buffering detestation. Although it wouldn't make any difference to him how she changed her opinion of him, she couldn't even chart the ramifications to herself. There was no way this wouldn't be a bad thing to her. Very bad.

Snapping out of her reverie, she realized he wasn't even done "testifying" yet. "Now I come to my deposition about your other accusation—of enlisting the Aal Shalaan Brotherhood's help in 'soaring so high.'"

She waved him off, not up to hearing more. "Don't bother."

"Oh, I bother. Am bothered. Very much so."

"Well, that's your problem. I've heard enough."

"But I haven't said enough." He frowned as a shudder shook her. "For a hurricane, it seems you're not impervious to fellow weather conditions. Let's get inside, and I'll field all the curiosity and jealousy you dragged us out here to avoid."

She shuddered again—and not with cold. She was on the verge of combusting with mortification. "It's not the cold that's bothering me."

He gave her one of those patient looks that said he'd withstand any amount of resistance and debate…until he got his way. Then he suddenly advanced on her.

Trapped with the terrace railings at her back, she couldn't have moved if she'd wanted to. She was unable to do anything but stand there helplessly watching him as he neared her in that tranquil prowl, shrugging off his jacket. Then, without touching her, he draped her in it. In what it held of his heat, his scent, his…essence.

For paralyzed moments, feeling as if she was completely enveloped in him, she gazed way up into those preternatural eyes, that slight, spellbinding smile, a quake that originated from a fault line at her very core threatening to break out and engulf her whole.

Before it did, he stepped away, resumed the position she'd told him to maintain as her windshield.

"Now that you're warm, I don't have to feel guilty about rambling on. To explain what happened, I have to outline what happened after that showdown at the ball. I basically found myself a pariah in Zohayd, and I very soon was forced to take the decision to leave. I was preparing to when the Aal Shalaan Brotherhood came to me—all but Amjad, of course. They attempted to dissuade me from leaving, assured me they knew me too well to believe Maysoon's accusations, that they'd resolve everything with their family and Zohaydan society at large if I stayed. They did offer to help me set up my business, to be my partners or to finance me until it took off. But I declined their offer."

She again tried to interject with her insistence that she didn't need him to explain. She believed that had been another of Maysoon's lies. "Aram, I—"

He held up a hand. "Don't take my word for it. Go ask them. I wanted no handouts, but even more, I wanted nothing to maintain any ties to Zohayd after I decided to sever them all forever. I'd remained in Zohayd in the first place for my father, but I felt I hadn't done him any good staying, and after Maysoon's stunt, I knew my presence would cause him nothing but grief." He paused before letting out his breath on a deep sigh. "I had also given up on Shaheen coming back. It was clear that the reconciliation I'd thought being in Zohayd would facilitate wouldn't come to pass."

She heard her voice croaking a question that had long burned in the back of her mind. "Are you going to tell me that Shaheen was to blame for this breakup and alienation, too?"

She hadn't been able to believe the honorable Shaheen could have been responsible for such a rift. Learning of that estrangement after Maysoon's public humiliation *had* entrenched her prejudice against Aram, solidifying her view of him as a callous monster who cast the people who cared for him aside.

Though said view had undergone a marked recalibration, she hoped he'd blame Shaheen as he'd blamed Maysoon. This would put him back in the comfortable dark gray zone.

His next words doused that hope.

"No, that was all my doing. But don't expect me to tell you what I did that was so bad that he fled his own kingdom to get away from me."

"Why not?" she muttered. "Aren't you having a disclosure spree this fine night?"

"You expect me to spill all my secrets all at once?" His feigned horror would have been funny if she was capable of humor now. "Then have nothing more to reveal in future encounters?"

"Did I ask you to tell me *any* secrets? You're the one who's imposing them on me."

His grin was unrepentant. "Let me impose some more on you, then. Just a summation, so grit your teeth and bear it. So…rather than following Maysoon's advice and latching onto Shaheen's brothers for financing, connections and clout, I turned down their generous offers. I had the solid plan, the theoretical knowledge and some practical experience, and I was ready to take the world by storm."

Her sense of fairness reared its head again. "And you certainly did. I am well aware of the global scope of your business management and consultation firm. Many of the major conglomerates I worked with, even whole countries, rely on you to set up, manage and monitor their financial and executive departments. And if you did it all on your own, then you're not as good as they say—you're way better."

Again her testimony seemed to take him by surprise.

His eyes had taken that thoughtful cast again as he said, "Though I'm even more intrigued than ever that you know all that, and I would have liked to take all the credit for the success I've achieved, it didn't happen quite that way. The beginning of my career suffered from some…catastrophic setbacks, to say the least."

"How so?"

Those brilliant eyes darkened with something…vast and too painful. But when he went on, he gave no specifics. "Well, what I thought I knew—my academic degrees, the experience I had in Zohayd—hadn't prepared me for jumping off the deep end with the sharks. But I managed to climb out of the abyss with only a few parts chomped off and launched into my plans with all I had. But I wouldn't have attained my level of success if I hadn't had the phenomenal luck of finding the exact right people to employ. It was together that we 'soared so high.'"

Not taking all the credit for his achievements cast him in an even better light. But there was still one major crime nothing he'd said could exonerate.

"So Maysoon might have been wrong—*was* wrong—about how you made your fortune. But can you blame her for thinking the worst of you? My opening statement in this retrial stands. You didn't have to be so unbelievably cruel in your public humiliation of her."

His stare fixed her for interminable moments, something intense roiling in its depths, something like reluctance, even aversion, as if he hated the response he had to make.

Seeming to reach a difficult decision, he beckoned her nearer.

He thought she'd come closer than that to him? Of her own volition? And why did he even want her to?

When she remained frozen to the spot, he sighed, inched nearer himself. She felt his approach like that of an oncoming train, her every nerve jangling at his increasing proximity.

He stopped a foot away, tilted his head back, exposing his neck to her. She stared at its thick, corded power, her mind stalling. It was as if he was asking her to…to…

"See this?" His purr jolted her out of the waywardness of her thoughts. She blinked at what he was pointing at. Three parallel scars, running from below his right ear halfway down his neck. They'd been hidden beneath his thick, luxurious hair. A current rattled through her at the sight of them. They were clearly very old, and although they weren't hideous, she could tell the injury *had* been. It was because his skin was that perfect, resilient type that healed with minimum scarring that they'd faded to that extent.

He exhaled heavily. "I ended my deposition at the moment I walked away, thought it enough, that any more was overkill. But seems nothing less than full disclosure will do here." He exhaled again, his eyes leveled on hers, totally serious for the first time. "Maysoon gave me this souvenir. She wouldn't let me go just like that. I barely dodged before she slashed across my face and took one eye out."

Kanza shuddered as the scene played in her mind. She did know how hysterical Maysoon could become. She could see her doing that. And she was left-handed…

"I pushed her off me, rushed to the men's room to stem the bleeding and had to lock the door so she wouldn't barge in and continue her frenzy. I got things under control and cleaned myself up, but she pounced on me as soon as I left the sanctuary of the men's room. I couldn't get the hell out of the palace without crossing the ballroom, and I kept pushing her off me all the way there, but once we got back inside, she started screeching.

"As people gathered, she was crying rivers and saying I cheated on her. I just wanted out—at any cost. So I said, 'Yes, I'm the bad guy, and isn't she lucky she's found out before it was too late?' When I tried to extricate myself, she flung herself on the ground, sobbing hysterically that I'd hit her. I couldn't stand around for the rest of her show, so I turned away and left."

He stopped, drew in a huge breath, let it out on a sigh. "But my deposition wouldn't be complete without saying that I've long realized that I owe her a debt of gratitude for everything she did."

Now, *that* stunned her. "You do?"

He nodded. "If her campaign against me hadn't forced me to leave Zohayd, I would have never pursued my own destiny. My experience with her was the perfect example of *assa an takraho sha'an wa howa khairon lakkom.*"

You may hate something and it is for your best.

He'd said that in perfect Arabic. Hearing his majestic voice rumbling the ancient verse was a shock. Maysoon had spoken only English to him, making her think he hadn't learned the language. But it was clear he had—and perfectly. There wasn't the least trace of accent in his pronunciation. He'd said it like a connoisseur of old poetry would.

He cocked that awesome head at her. "So now that you've heard my full testimony, any adjustment in your opinion of me?"

Floundering, wanting for the floor to split and snatch her below, she choked out, "It—it *is* your word against hers."

"Then I am at a disadvantage, since she is your half sister. Though that should be to her disadvantage, since you're probably intimate with all her faults and are used to taking her testimony about anything with a pound of salt. But if for some reason you're still inclined to believe her, then there is only one way for me to have a fair retrial. I demand that you get to know me as thoroughly as you know her."

"What do you mean, get to know you?" She heard the panic that leaped into her voice.

He was patient indulgence itself. "How do people get to know each other?"

"I don't know. How?"

The same forbearance met her retort. "How did you get to know anyone in your orbit?"

"I was thrown with them by accidents of birth or geography or necessity."

That had his heart-stopping smile dawning again. "I'm tempted to think you've been a confirmed misanthrope since you exited the womb."

"According to my mother, they barely extracted me surgically before I clawed my way out of her. She informed me I spoiled the having-babies gig for her forever."

His eyes told her what he thought of her mother. Yeah, him and everyone in the civilized world.

Then his eyes smiled again. "It's a calamity we don't have video documentation of your entry into the world. That would have been footage for the ages. So—" he rubbed his hands together "—when will our next reconnaissance session be?"

Her heart lodged in her throat again. "There will be no next anything."

"Why? Have you passed your judgment again, and it's still execution?"

"No, I've given you a not-guilty verdict, so you can go gallop in the fields free. Now, *ann eznak...*"

"Or better still, *men ghair ezni,* right?"

"See? You can predict me now. I was only diverting when you couldn't guess what I'd say next, but now that you've progressed to completing my sentences, my entertainment value is clearly depleted. Better to quit while we're ahead."

"I beg to differ. Not that I am or was after 'entertainment.' Will you suggest a time and venue, or will you leave it up to me?"

She could swear flames erupted inside her skull.

"You've had your retrial, and I want to salvage what I can of this party," she growled. "Now get out of my way."

As if she hadn't said anything, his eyes laughed at her as he all but crooned, "So you want me to surprise you?"

"Argh!"

Foisting his jacket at him, she pushed past him, barely resisting the urge to break out into a sprint to escape his nerve-fraying chuckles.

She felt those following her even after she'd rejoined the party, when there was no way she could still hear him.

And he thought she'd expose herself to him again?

Hah.

One cataclysmic brush with Aram Nazaryan might have been survivable. But enduring another exposure?

No way.

After all, she didn't have a death wish.

Five

"I see you've found Kanza."

Aram stopped midstride across the penthouse, groaning out loud.

Shaheen. Not the person he wanted to see right now.

But then, he wanted to see no one but that keg of unpredictability who'd skittered away from him again. Though he was betting she wouldn't let him find her again tonight.

While Shaheen wasn't going anywhere before he rubbed his nose in some choice I-told-you-sos.

Deciding on the best defense, he engaged offensive maneuvers. "*Found* her? Don't you mean you and your coconspirator wife threw us together?"

"*I* did nothing but put my foot in it. It's *your* kid sister who pushed things along. But she only 'threw' you two together. You could have extracted yourself in five minutes if she'd miscalculated. But obviously she didn't. From our estimations, you've spent over five hours in Kanza's company. To say you found her...compatible is putting it mildly."

"*Hold* it right there, buddy." He shook his finger at Shaheen. "You're not even going down that road, you hear? I just *talked* to the...to the... God, I can't even find a name for her. I can't call her girl or woman or anything that… run-of-the-mill. I don't know what the hell she is."

"As long as it's not monster or goblin anymore, that's a huge development."

"No, she's certainly neither of those things." And Kanza the Monster hadn't even been his name for her. It had been Maysoon's and her friends'. That alone should have made him disregard it. He'd adopted it only because he couldn't find an alternative. And Kanza *had* unsettled the hell out of him back then. She still did—if in a totally different way. One he still couldn't figure out. "All night I've been thinking sprite, brownie, pixie…but none of that really describes her either."

"The word you're looking for is…treasure."

Aram stared at his friend. *"Treasure?"*

Then he blinked. *Kanz* meant treasure. Kanza was the feminine form. How had he never focused on her name's meaning?

Though… "Treasure isn't how I'd describe her, either."

"No?" Shaheen quirked an eyebrow. "Maybe not…yet. She can't be categorized, anyway."

"You got *that* right. But that's as right as you get. I'm not about to ask for her hand in marriage, so put a lid on it."

"Your…caution is understandable. You met her—the grown-up her, anyway—only hours ago. You wouldn't be thinking of anything beyond the moment yet."

"Not yet, not ever. Can't a man enjoy the company of an unidentifiable being without any further agenda?"

Knowing amusement rose in Shaheen's eyes. "You tell me. Can he?"

"*Yes,* he can. And he fully intends to. And he wants you and your much better half to butt out and stay out of this. Let *him* have *fun* for a change, and don't try to make this into anything more than it is. Got it?"

Shaheen nodded. "Got it."

He threw his hands in the air. "Why didn't you argue? Now I know I'm in for some nasty surprise down the road."

Abandoning his pretense of seriousness, Shaheen grinned teasingly. "From where I'm standing, you consider the surprise you got a rather delightful one."

"Too many surprises and one is bound to wipe out all good ones before it. It's basic Surprise Law." Folding his arms across his chest, he shot his friend a warning look. "Keep your royal noses out of this, Shaheen. I'm your senior, and even if you don't think so, I do know what's best for me, so permit me the luxury of running my own personal life."

Shaheen's grin only widened. "I already said I…*we* will. Now chill."

"Chill?" Aram grimaced. "You just managed to give me an anxiety attack. God, but you two are hazards."

Shaheen took him around the shoulder. "We've done our parts as catalysts. Now we'll let the experiment progress without further intervention."

He narrowed his eyes at him. "Even if you think I'm messing it up? You won't be tempted to intervene then?"

Shaheen wiggled one eyebrow. "That worry would motivate you not to mess it up, wouldn't it?"

He tore himself away. "Shaheen!"

Shaheen laughed. "I'm just messing with you. You're on your own. Just don't come crying one day that you are."

"I won't." He tsked. "And quit making this what it isn't. I only want to put my finger on what makes her so… unquantifiable."

Sighing dramatically, Shaheen played along. "I guess it's because she's nothing anyone expects a princess, let alone a professional woman, to be. Before she became Johara's partner, I only heard her being described as mousy, awkward, even gauche."

"*What?* Who the hell were those people talking about?"

"*You* had that Kanza the Monster conviction going, too."

"At least 'monster' recognized the sheer force of her character."

Shaheen shrugged. "I think she's simply nice."

An impressive snort escaped him. "Who're you calling nice? That's the last adjective in the English language to describe her. She's no such vague, lukewarm, *benign* thing."

Shaheen's lips twitched. "After an evening in her company, you seem to have become *the* authority on her. So how would *you* describe her?"

"Didn't you hear me when I said that I don't *know* what she is? All I know is that she's an inapproachable bundle of thorns. An unstoppable force of nature, like a…a… hurricane."

"That's more of a natural disaster."

He almost muttered "smart-ass" in the exact way Kanza had to him. He *was* exasperated with having his enthusiasm interpreted into what Shaheen and Johara wanted it to be. When it was like nothing he'd ever felt. It was as unpredictable as that hurricane in question.

One thing he knew for certain, though. He wasn't trying to define it or to direct it. Or expect anything from it. And he sure as hell wasn't attempting to temper it. Not to curb Shaheen's expectations, not for anything.

"Whatever. It's the one description that suits her."

"That would make her Hurricane Kanza."

With that, Shaheen took him back to Johara, where he endured her teasing, too. And he again made her and her incorrigibly romantic spouse promise that they wouldn't interfere.

Then as he left the party, he thought of the name Shaheen had suggested.

Hurricane Kanza. It described her to a tee.

After he'd compared her effect on Johara's office to one a lifetime ago, she had proceeded to tear through him with the uprooting force of one. All he wanted to do now was hurtle into her path again and let her toss him wherever she would.

But she wouldn't do it of her own accord. She must still be processing the revelations that, given her sense of justice, *must* have changed her opinion of him. But it no doubt remained an awkward situation for her, since her prejudice had been long held, and Maysoon was still her half sister.

Not that he would allow any of that to stand in his way. He fully intended to get exposed to her delightful destruction again and again, no matter what it took.

Now he just had to plan his next exposure to her devastation.

Aram eyed Johara's office door, impatience rising.

Kanza was in a morning meeting with his sister. Once that was over, he planned to…intercept her.

He'd done so every day for the past two weeks. But the sprite had given him the slip each time. He never got in more than a few words with her before she blinked out on him like her fellow pixies did. But what words those had been. Like tastings from gourmet masterpieces that only left him starving for a full meal again.

He'd let her wriggle away as part of his investigation into her components and patterns of behavior. It had pleased the hell out of him that he still found the first inscrutable and the second unforeseeable. But today he wasn't letting that steel butterfly flutter away. She was having a whole day in his company. She just didn't know it yet.

Johara's assistants eyed him curiously, no doubt wondering why he was here, *again.* And why he didn't just walk right into his sister's office. That had been his first inclination, to corner that elusive elf in there.

He'd reconsidered. Raiding Kanza's leisure time was one thing. Marauding her at work was another. He'd let her get business out of the way before swooping in and sweeping her away on that day off Johara said she hadn't taken in over a year. He'd arranged a day off himself. The first whole one he'd had in…ever.

The office door was suddenly flung open, and Johara's head popped out, golden hair spilling forward. "Aram—come in, please."

He was on his feet at once, buoyed by the unexpected thrill of seeing Kanza now, not an hour or more later. "I thought you were having a meeting."

"When did that ever stop you?" Johara's grin widened as he ruffled her hair. "But as luck would have it, the day you chose to go against your M.O., I found myself in need of that incomparable business mind of yours, big brother."

He hugged her to his side, kissing the top of her head lovingly. "At your service always, sweetheart."

His gaze zeroed in on Kanza like a heat-seeking missile the moment he entered the office. Déjà vu spread its warmth inside his chest when he found her standing by the filing cabinets, like that first night. The only difference was the office was in pristine order. It had looked much better to him after she'd exercised her hurricane-like powers.

He noticed the other two people in the room only when they rose to salute him. All his faculties converged on that power source at the end of the office, even when he wasn't looking at her.

Then he did, and almost laughed out loud at the impact of her disapproving gaze and terse acknowledgment.

"Aram."

While it no longer sounded like a curse, it was…eloquent. No, more than that. Potent. Her unique, patented method of cutting him down to size.

Johara dragged back his attention, explaining their problem. Forcing himself to shift from Kanza to business mode, Aram turned to his sister's concerns.

After he'd gotten a handle on the situation, he offered solutions, only for Kanza to point out the lacking in some and the error in others. But she did so without the least contention or malice, as most would have when they considered someone to be infringing on their domain. In fact, there was nothing in her analysis except an earnest endeavor to reach the best possible solution.

Aram ascribed his lapse to close exposure to her, but he was lucid enough to know he was in the presence of a mind that rivaled his in his field. Having met only a handful of those in his lifetime, who'd been much older and wielding far more experience, he was beyond impressed.

As the session progressed, what impressed him even more was that she didn't compete with him, challenge him or harp on his early misjudgment. She deferred to his superior knowledge where he possessed it and put all her faculties at his disposal during what became five intensive hours of discussion, troubleshooting and restructuring.

Once they reached the most comprehensive plan of action, Johara leaped to her feet in excitement. "Fantastic! I couldn't have dreamed of such a genius solution! I should have teamed you and Kanza up a long time ago, Aram."

He couldn't believe it.

How had he not seen this as another of Johara's blatant efforts to show him how *compatible* they were? Would he *never* learn?

He twisted his lips at Johara for breaching their *noninterference* pact again as he rose to his feet. "And now that you did, how about we celebrate this breakthrough? It's on me."

Johara's eyes were innocence incarnate. "Oh, I wish. I have tons of boring, artistic stuff to take care of with Dana and Steve. You and Kanza go celebrate for us."

If anyone had told him before that business with Kanza that his kid sister was an ingenious actress, he wouldn't have believed it. But though he didn't approve of her underhanded methods, he was thankful for the opportunity she provided to get Kanza alone.

He turned to the little spitfire in question, gearing up for another battle, but Kanza simply said, "Let's go, then. I'm starving. And, Aram, it's on me. I owe you for those shortcuts you taught me today."

His head went light as the tension he'd gathered for the anticipated struggle drained out of him. Then it began to spin, at her admission that she'd learned from him, at her willingness to reward the favor.

Exchanging a last glance that no doubt betrayed his bewilderment with Johara, who was doing less than her usual seamless job of hiding her smug glee, he followed Kanza the Inscrutable out of the office.

Kanza walked out of Johara's office with the most disruptive force she'd ever encountered following her and a sense of déjà vu overwhelming her.

In the past two weeks he'd been taking this "get to know him" to the limit, had turned up everywhere to trail her as he was doing now. Instead of getting used to being inundated in his vibe and pervaded by his presence, each time the experience got more intense, had her reeling even harder.

And she still couldn't find one plausible reason why he was doing this.

The possibility that he was attracted to her had been the first one she'd dismissed. The idea of Aram Nazaryan, the epitome of male perfection, being romantically interested in her was so ludicrous it hadn't lasted more than two seconds of perplexed speculation before it had evaporated. Other reasons hadn't held water any better or longer.

So, by exclusion, one theory remained.

That he was nuts.

The hypothesis was loosely based on Johara's testimony.

With his repeated appearances of late, which Johara hadn't tied to Kanza, Johara had started talking about him. Among the tales from the past, mostly of their time in Zohayd, she'd let slip she believed he'd been sliding into depression. Kanza had barely held back from correcting Johara's tentative diagnosis to *manic*-depression, according to that inexplicable eagerness and elation that exuded from him and gleamed in his eyes.

Johara believed it was because he'd long been abusing his health and neglecting his personal life by working so much. Again, Kanza had barely caught back a scoff. In the past two weeks he hadn't seemed to work at all. How else could he turn up everywhere she went, no matter the time of day? Her only explanation was that he'd set up his business with such efficiency that its success was self-perpetuating and he could take time off whenever the fancy struck him.

But according to Johara, he had been working himself to death for years, resulting in being cut off from humanity and lately even becoming physically sick. It had been why she and Shaheen came so often to New York of late, staying for extended periods of time, to try to alleviate his isolation and stop his deterioration.

Not that Johara thought they were succeeding. She felt that their intimacy as husband and wife left Aram unable to connect with either of them as he used to, left him feeling like an outsider, even a trespasser. But she truly believed he needed the level of attachment he'd once shared with them to maintain his psychological health. Bottom line, she was worried that his inability to find anyone who fulfilled that need, along with his atrocious lifestyle, was dragging him to the verge of some breakdown.

But this man, stalking her like a panther who'd just discovered play and couldn't contain his eagerness to start a game of all-out tackle and chase, seemed nothing like the morose, self-destructive loner Johara had described. Which made *her* theory the only credible explanation. That his inexplicable pursuit of her was the first overt symptom of said breakdown.

Not that she was happy with this diagnosis.

While it had provided an explanation for his behavior, it had also influenced hers.

She'd dodged him so far, because she'd thought he'd

latched on to her in order to combat his ennui, and she hadn't fancied being used as an antidote to his boredom. But the idea that his behavior wasn't premeditated—or even worse, was a cry for help—had made it progressively harder to be unresponsive.

"So where do you want to take me?"

Doing her best not to swoon at the caress of his fathomless baritone, she turned to him as they entered the garage. "I'm open. What do you want to eat?"

"You pick." He grinned as he strode ahead, leading the way to his car. Seemed it was time for that spin in his near-sentient behemoth, a black-and-silver Rolls-Royce Phantom that reportedly came with a ghastly half-million-dollar price tag.

She stopped. "Okay, this goes no further."

That dazzling smile suddenly dimmed. "You're taking back your invitation?"

"I *mean* we're not going in circles, each insisting the other chooses. I already said I'm open to whatever you want, and it wasn't a ploy for you to throw the ball back in my court, proving you're more of a gentleman. I always say exactly what I mean."

His smile flashed back to its debilitating wattage. "You have no idea what a relief that is. But I'm definitely more of a gentleman. It's an incontestable anatomical fact."

She made no response as he seated her in his car's passenger seat. She wasn't going to take this exchange that lumped him and anatomy together any further. It would only lead to trouble.

Focusing instead on being in his car, she sank into the supple seashell leather while her feet luxuriated in the rich, thick lamb's wool, feeling cosseted in the literal lap of luxury.

After veering that impressive monster into downtown traffic, he turned to her. "So why did you suddenly stop evading me?"

Yeah. Good question. Why did she?

She told him the reason she'd admitted to herself so far. "I took pity on you."

"Yes." He pumped his fist. At her raised eyebrow, he chuckled. "Just celebrating the success of my pitiful puppy-dog-eyed efforts."

"If that's what you were shooting for, you missed the mark by a mile. You came across as a hyper, blazing-eyed panther."

Those eyes flared with enjoyment. "Back to the drawing board, then. Or rather the mirror, to practice. But if that didn't work…what did?"

And she found herself admitting more, to herself as well as to him. "It got grueling calculating the lengths you must have gone to, popping up wherever I went. It had me wondering if you're one of those anal-retentive people who must finish whatever they start, and I was needlessly prolonging both of our discomfort. I also had to see what would happen if I let go of the tug-of-war."

"You'll enjoy my company." At her sardonic sideways glance, he laughed. "Admit it. You find me entertaining."

She found him…just about everything.

"*Not* the adjective I'd use for you," Kanza said with a sigh.

"Don't leave me hanging. Lay it on me."

Her gaze lengthened over his dominant profile. She'd been candid in her description of his outward assets. Was it advisable to be her painfully outspoken self in expounding on what she thought of his more essential endowments?

Oh, what the hell. He must be used to fawning. Her truthfulness, though only her objective opinion, wouldn't be more than what he'd heard a thousand times before.

She opened her mouth to say she'd use adjectives like *enervating,* like a bolt of lightning, and *engulfing,* like a rising flood—and as if to say the words for her, thunder rolled and celestial floodgates burst.

He didn't press her to elucidate, because even with the efficiency of the automatic wipers, he could barely see through the solid sheets of rain. Thankfully, they seemed to have arrived at the destination he'd chosen. The Plaza Hotel, where Johara had mentioned Aram stayed.

As he stopped the car, she thought they should stay inside until the rain let up. They'd get soaked in the few dozen feet to the hotel entrance. Then he opened her door, and lo and behold…an umbrella was ingeniously embedded there. In moments, he was shielding her from the downpour and leading her through the splendor of the iconic hotel. But it wasn't until they stepped into the timeless Palm Court restaurant that she felt as if she'd walked into a scene out of *The Great Gatsby.*

She took in the details as she walked a step ahead among tables filled with immaculate people. Overhanging gilded chandeliers, paneled walls, a soaring twenty-foot green-painted and floral-patterned ceiling and 24-karat gold-leafed Louis XVI furniture, all beneath a stunning stained-glass skylight. Everything exuded the glamour that had made the hotel world famous while retaining the feel of a French country house.

After they were seated and she opted for ordering the legendary Plaza tea, she leveled her gaze back on him and sighed. "Is that your usual spending pattern? This hotel, that car?"

"I am moderate, aren't I?" At her grimace, he upped his teasing. "I was eyeing a Bugatti Veyron, but since there are no roads around to put it through its two-hundred-and-fifty-miles-per-hour paces, I thought paying three times as much as my current car would be unjustified." He chuckled at her growl of distaste. "Down, girl. I can afford it."

"And that makes it okay? Don't you have something better to do with your money?"

"I do a *lot* of better things with my money. And then, it's my only material indulgence. It's in lieu of a home."

"Meaning?"

"Meaning I've never bought a place, so I consider my cars my only home."

This was news. Somewhat…disturbing news. She'd thought he'd been staying in this hotel for convenience, not that he'd never had a place to call home.

"But…if you're saying you don't splurge on your accommodations, it would be *far* more economical—and an investment—to buy a place. A day here is an obscene amount of money down the drain, and you've been here almost a *year*."

His nod was serene. "My suite goes for about twenty grand a night." At her gasp, his lips spread wide. "Of which I'm not paying a cent. I am a major shareholder in this hotel, so I get to stay free."

Okay. She should have known a financial mastermind like him wouldn't throw money around, that he'd invest every cent to make a hundred. It was a good thing their orders had arrived so she'd have it instead of crow after she'd gone all self-righteous on him.

She felt him watching her and pretended to have eyes only on the proceedings as waiters heaped varieties of tea, finely cut sandwiches, scones, jam, clotted cream and a range of pastries on the table.

They had devoured two irresistible scones each, and mellow live piano music had risen above the buzz of conversation, when he broke the silence.

"This place reminds me of the royal palace in Zohayd. Not the architecture, but something in the level of splendor. The distant resemblance is…comforting."

The longing, the melancholy in his reminiscing about the place where he'd lived a good portion of his youth, tugged at her heart…a little too hard.

Suddenly his smile dawned again. "So ask me anything."

Struggling with the painful tautness in her throat, she eyed him skeptically. "Anything at all?"

His nod was instantaneous. "You bet."

It seemed Johara had been correct. He did need someone to share things with that he felt he could no longer share with his sister or brother-in-law. And as improbable as it was, he seemed to have elected her as the one he could unburden himself to. His selection had probably been based on her ability to say no to him, to be blunt with him. That must be a total novelty for him.

But she also suspected there was another major reason she was a perfect candidate for what he had in mind. Because he didn't seem to consider her a woman. Just a sexless buddy he could have fun with and confide in without worrying about the usual hassles a woman would cause him.

She had no illusions about what she was, how a man like him would view her. But that still had mortification warring with compassion in her already tight chest. Compassion won.

Feeling the ridiculous urge to reach across the table for his hand, to reassure him she was there for him, even if he thought her a sprite, she cleared her throat. "Tell me about the rift between you and Shaheen."

He nodded. "Did Johara tell you how we came to Zohayd?"

"Oh, no! You're planning to tell me your whole life story to get to one incident in its middle?"

"Yep. So you'll understand the factors leading up to the incident and the nature of the players in it."

"Can I retract my request?" She pretended glibness.

"Nope. *Dokhool el hammam mesh zay toloo'oh.*"

Entering a bathroom isn't like exiting it. What was said in Zohayd to signify that what was done couldn't be undone.

And she was beginning to realize what that really meant.

Living life knowing a man like him existed had been fine with her as long as he'd been just a general concept—not a reality that could cross hers, let alone invade it.

But now that she was experiencing him up close, she feared it would irrevocably change things inside her.

And the peace she'd once known would be no more.

Six

Pretending to eat what seemed to have turned to ashes, Kanza watched Aram as he poured her tea and began sharing his life story with her.

"Before I came to Zohayd at sixteen, my father used to whisk me, Johara and Mother away every year or so to yet another exotic locale as he built his reputation as an internationally rising jeweler. When I told my peers that I'd trade what they thought an enchanted existence in the glittering milieus of the rich and famous for a steady, boring life in a small town, dweeb and weirdo were only two of the names they called me. I learned to keep my mouth shut, but I couldn't learn to stop hating that feeling of homelessness. My defense was to go to any new place as if I was leaving the next day, and I remained in self-imposed isolation until we left."

She gulped scalding tea to swallow the lump in her throat. So his isolation had deeper roots than Johara even realized. And she'd bet she was the first one he'd told this to.

He went on. "I had a plan, though. That the moment I hit eighteen, I'd stay put in one place, work in one job forever, marry the first girl who wanted me and have a brood of kids. That blueprint for my future was what kept me going as the flitting around the world continued."

She gulped another mouthful, the heaviness in her chest increasing. His plans for stability had never come to pass. He was forty and as far as she knew, apart from the fiasco with Maysoon, he'd never had any kind of relationship.

So how had the one guy who'd planned a family life so early on, who'd craved roots when all others his age dreamed of freedom, ended up so adrift and alone?

He served them sandwiches and continued. "Then my father's mentor, the royal jeweler of Zohayd, retired and his job became open. He recommended Father to King Atef…."

Feeling as if a commercial had burst in during a critical moment, she raised a hand. "Hey, I'm from Zohayd and I know all the stories. How your father became the one entrusted with the Pride of Zohayd treasure is a folktale by now. Fast forward. Tell me something I don't know. I hate recaps."

His eyes crinkled at her impatience—he was clearly delighted she was so riveted by his story. "So there I was, jetting off to what Father said was one of the most magnificent desert kingdoms on earth, feeling resigned we'd stay for the prerequisite year before Father uprooted us again. Then we landed there. I can still remember, in brutal vividness, how I felt as soon as my feet touched the ground in Zohayd. That feeling of…belonging."

God. The emotions that suddenly blazed from him… Any moment now she was going to reach for that box of tissues.

"That feeling became one of elation, of certainty, that I'd found a home—that I *was* home—when I met Shaheen." His massive chest heaved as he released an unsteady breath. "Did Johara tell you how he saved her from certain death that day?"

She shook her head, her eyes beginning to burn.

"She was a hyperactive six-year-old who made me age

running after her. Then I take my eyes off her for a minute and she's dangling from the palace's balcony. I was too far away, and Father failed to reach her, and she was slipping. But then at the last second, Shaheen swooped in to snatch her out of the air like the hawk he's named after.

"I was there the next second, beside myself with fright and gratitude, and that kindred feeling struck me. And from that day forward, he became my first and only friend. As he became Johara's first and only love."

She let out a ragged breath. "Wow."

"Yeah." He leaned back in his chair. "It was indescribable, having the friendship of someone of Shaheen's caliber—a caliber that had nothing to do with his status. But though he felt just as closely bonded to me, considered me an equal, I knew the huge gap between us would always be unbridgeable. I grew more uncomfortable by the day when Johara started to blossom, and I became certain that her emotions for Shaheen weren't those of a friend but those of a budding woman in love.

"By the time she was fourteen, worry poisoned every minute I spent with Shaheen, which by then almost always included Johara. Though the three of us were magnificent together, I thought Shaheen's all-out indulgence of Johara would lead to catastrophe, for Johara, for my whole family. Then my anxiety reached critical mass…"

"Go on," she rasped when he paused, unable to wait to hear the rest.

He raked a hand through his dark, satin hair. "We were having a squash match, and I started to trounce a bewildered Shaheen. The more Johara cheered him to fight back, the more vicious I became. Afterward in the changing room, I tore into Shaheen with all my pent-up resentment. I called him a spoiled prince who made a game of manipulating people's emotions. I accused him of encouraging her crush on him—which he knew was beyond hopeless—just for fun. I demanded he stop leading her on or I'd tell his father King Atef…so he'd *order* him never to come near Johara again.

"Shaheen was flabbergasted. He said Johara was the little sister he'd never had. I only sneered that his affections went far beyond an older brother's, as I should know as her *real* one. He countered that while he didn't know what having a sister was like, Johara was his 'girl'—the one who 'got' him like no one else, even me, and he did love her… in every way but *that* way.

"But I was way beyond reason, said that his proclamations meant nothing to me—I cared only about Johara—and that he was emotionally exploiting her, and I wouldn't stand idly by waiting for him to damage her irrevocably."

She couldn't imagine how he'd felt at the time. Sensing the powerful bond between his best friend and sister, having every reason to believe it would end in devastation and being forced to risk his one friendship to protect his one sister. It must have been terrible, knowing that either way he'd lose something irreplaceable.

Grimacing with remembered pain, Aram placed his forearms on the table, his gaze fixed on the past. "Outrage finally overpowered Shaheen's mortification that I could think such dishonorable things of him. His bitterness escalated as my conviction faltered, then vanished in the face of his intense affront and hurt. But there was no taking back what I'd said or threatened. Then it was too late, anyway.

"Shaheen told me he'd save me the trouble of running to his father with my demands for him to cease and desist. He'd never come near Johara again. Or me. He carried out his pledge, cutting Johara and me off, effective immediately."

It was clear the injury of those lost years had never fully healed. And though Shaheen and Johara were now happily married and Aram's friendship with Shaheen had been restored, it seemed the gaping wound where his friend had been torn out had been only partially patched. Because there was no going back to the same closeness now that Shaheen's life was so full of Johara and their daughter while Aram had found nothing to fill the void in his own life. Except work. And according to Johara, it was nowhere near enough.

"Just when I thought Shaheen's alienation was the worst thing that could happen to me, Mother suddenly took Johara and left Zohayd. I watched our family being torn apart and was unable to stop it. Then I found myself left alone with a devastated father who kept withdrawing into himself in spite of all my efforts. I tried to grope for my best friend's support, hoping he'd let me close again, but he only left Zohayd, too, dashing any hope for a reconciliation."

So she had been totally wrong about him in this instance, too. It hadn't been not caring that had caused that breach; it had been caring too much. And it had cost him way more than she'd ever imagined.

He went on. "With all my dreams of making a home for myself in Zohayd over, I wanted to leave and tried to persuade Father to leave with me, too, but I backed off when I realized his service to the king and kingdom was what kept him going. Knowing I couldn't leave him, I resigned myself that I'd stay in Zohayd as long as he lived."

It must have been agonizingly ironic to get what he wanted, that permanent stay in Zohayd, but for it to be more of an exile than a home.

As if he'd heard her thoughts, he released a slow, deep breath. "It was the ultimate irony. I was getting what I'd hoped for all my life—stability in one place, just without the roots or the family, to live there in an isolation that promised to become permanent." *Isolation.* There was that word again. "Then, six years after everyone left Zohayd, I took a shot at forging that family I'd once dreamed of…and you now know what happened next."

She nodded, her throat tight. "And you ended up being forced to leave."

He sighed deeply again. "Yeah. So much happened after

that. Too much. And I've never stayed in one place longer than a few months since. I hadn't wanted to. Couldn't bear to, even. Then three years ago, Shaheen and Johara ended up getting married. I was right about the nature of their involvement." He smiled whimsically. "I just jumped the gun by twelve years." Another deep sigh. "Then suddenly I had my friend back, Mother reconciled with Father and my whole family was put back together—just in Zohayd, where I could no longer be."

Swallowing what felt like a rock, she wondered if he'd elaborate on the intervening years, the "too much" he'd said with such aversion. He didn't.

He'd done what he'd set out to do, told her the story that explained his rift with Shaheen. Anything else would be for another day. If there would be one.

From the way her heart kept twisting, it wasn't advisable to have one. Exposure to him when she'd despised him, thought him a monster, had been bad enough. Now that she saw him as not only human but even empathetic, further exposure could have catastrophic consequences. For her.

His eyes seemed to see her again, seeming to intensify in vividness as he smiled like never before. A heartfelt smile. "Thank you."

Her heart fired so hard it had her sitting forward in her chair. "Wh-what for?"

The gentleness turning his beauty from breathtaking to heartbreaking deepened. "You listened. And made no judgments. I think you even…sympathized."

She struggled to stop the pins at the back of her eyes from dissolving in an admission of how moved she was. "I did. It was such a tragic and needless waste, all those years apart. For all of you."

His inhalation was sharp. The exhalation that followed was slow, measured. "Yes. But they're back together now."

They. Not we.

He didn't seem to consider he had his family and friend

back. Worse, it seemed he didn't consider himself part of the family anymore. And though his expression was now carefully neutral, she sensed he was…desolate over the belief. What he seemed to consider an unchangeable fact of his life now.

After that, as if by unspoken agreement, they spent the rest of their time in the Palm Court talking about a dozen things that weren't about lost years or ruined life plans.

After the rain stopped, he took her out walking, and they must have covered all of Central Park before it was dark.

She didn't even feel the distance, the exertion or the passage of time. She saw nothing, heard and smelled and felt nothing but him. His company was that engrossing, that gratifying. The one awful thing about spending time with him was that it would come to an end.

But it didn't. When she'd thought their impromptu outing was over, he insisted she wasn't going home until she was a full, exhausted mass unable to do anything but fall into bed. She hadn't even thought of resisting his unilateral plans for the rest of the evening. This time out of time would end soon enough, and she wasn't going to terminate it prematurely. She'd have plenty of time later to regret her decision not to.

Over dinner, their conversation took a turn for the funny, then the hilarious. On several occasions, his peals of goose-bump-raising laughter incited many openmouthed and swooning stares from besotted female patrons, while *she* was leveled with what's-*she*-doing-with-that-god glares, not to mention the times the whole restaurant seemed to be turning around to see if there was a hyena dining with them.

When he drove her back to her apartment building, he parked two blocks away—just an excuse to have another walk.

As they walked in companionable silence, she felt the impulsive urge to hook her arm in his, lean on him through the wind. It wasn't discretion that stopped her but the fact that he hadn't attempted even a courteous touch so far.

At her building's entrance, he turned to her with expectation blazing in those azure eyes. "So same time tomorrow?"

Her heart pirouetted in her chest at the prospect of another day with him.

But… "We went out at *one* today!"

He shrugged. "And?"

"And I have work."

He waved dismissively. "Take the day off."

"I can't. Johara…"

"Will shove you out of the office if she can to make you take some time off. She says you're a workaholic."

"Gee. She says the same about you."

"See? We both need a mental-health day."

"We already had one today."

"We worked our asses off for five hours in the morning. Tomorrow is a *real* day off. With all the trimmings. Sleeping in, then going crazy being lazy and doing nothing but eating and chatting and doing whatever pops into our minds till way past midnight."

And he'd just described her newfound vision of heaven.

Then she remembered something, and heaven seemed to blink out of sight. She groaned, "I really can't tomorrow."

Disappointment flooded his gaze, but only for a second. Then eagerness was back full steam ahead. "The day after tomorrow, then. And at noon. No…make it eleven. *Ten.*"

Her heart tap-danced. She did her best not to grin like a loon, to sound nonchalant as she said, "Oh, all right."

He stuck his hands at his hips. "Got something more enthusiastic than that?"

"Nope." She mock scowled. "That's the only brand available. Take it or…take it."

"I'll take it, and take it!" He took a step back as if to dodge a blow, whistled. "Jeez. How did something so tiny become so terrifying?"

She gave a sage nod. "It's an evolutionary compensatory mechanism to counteract the disadvantaged size."

"Vive la évolution." And he said it in perfect French, reminding her he spoke that fluently, too.

She burst out laughing.

Minutes later, she was still chuckling to herself as she entered her apartment. God, but that man was the most unprecedented, unpredictable, unparalleled fun she'd ever had.

She met her eyes in her foyer's mirror, wincing at what she'd never seen reflected back…until now. Unmistakable fever in her cheeks and soppy dreaminess in her eyes. Aram had put it all there without even meaning to.

Yeah. He was boatloads of fun. Too bad he was also a mine of danger.

And she'd just agreed to another daylong dose of deadly exposure.

Seven

"So how's my Tiny Terror doing this fine day?"

Kanza leaned against the wall to support legs that always went elastic on hearing Aram's voice. Not to mention the heart that forgot its rhythm.

You'd think after over a month of daily and intensive exposure, she'd have developed some immunity. But she only seemed to be getting progressively more susceptible.

She forced out a steady, "Why, thank you, I'm doing splendidly. And you, Hulking Horror?"

Right on cue, his expected laugh came, boisterous and unfettered. He kept telling her that she had the specific code that operated his humor, and almost everything she said tickled him mercilessly. She'd been liberally exercising that power over him, to both their delight.

In return, the gift of his laughter, and knowing that she could incite it, caused her various physical and emotional malfunctions.

She was dealing with the latest bout when he said, laughter still permeating his magnificent voice, "I'm doing spectacularly now that my Mighty Miniature has taken me well in hand. You ready? I'm downstairs." Yeah, he never even asked to come up. "And hurry! I have something to show you."

"Uh-uh. Don't play that game with me." She took a look in the mirror and groaned. Not a good idea to inspect herself right before she beheld him. The comparison was just too disheartening. She slammed out of her apartment in frustration and ran into the elevator that a neighbor had just exited. "Tell me what it is. I have severe allergies to surprises."

"Just so we won't end up in the E.R., I'll give you a hint." His voice had that vibrant edge of excitement she'd been hearing more of late as they planned trips they'd take and projects they'd do together. "It's things people live in."

Her heart sputtered in answering excitement. "You bought an apartment! Oh, congrats."

"Hey, you think me capable of making a decision without consulting my Mini Me?"

The elevator opened to reveal him. And it hit her all over again with even more force than last time. How…shattering his beauty was.

But with the evidence of his current glory, she knew he'd been right. When she'd met him again six weeks ago, he *had* been at his lowest ebb. Ever since then, he'd been steadily shedding any sign of haggardness. He was now at a level that should be prohibited by law, like any other health hazard.

And there she was, the self-destructive fool who willingly exposed herself to his emanations on a daily basis. And without any protection.

Not that there was any, or that she'd want it if there was. She'd decided to open herself up to the full exposure and to hell with the certain and devastating side effects.

As usual, without even taking her arm or touching her in any way whatsoever, he rushed ahead, gesturing eagerly for her to follow. She did. As she knew by now, she always would.

Once in his car and on their way, he turned to her. "I'm

taking you to see the candidates. I'm signing the contract of the one you'll determine I'll feel most comfortable in."

Her jaw dropped. "And I'm supposed to know that… how?"

His sideways glance was serenity itself. "Because you know everything."

"Hey." She turned in her seat. "Thanks for electing me your personal oracle or goddess or whatever, but no thanks. You can't saddle me with this kind of responsibility."

"It's your right and prerogative, O Diminutive Deity."

She rolled her eyes. "What ever happened to free will?"

"Who needs that when I have you?"

"If it was anyone else, I'd be laughing. But I know you're crazy enough to sign a contract if I as much as say a word in preference of one place." His nod reinforced her projection. "What if you end up hating my choice?"

"I won't." His smile was confidence incarnate. "And that's not crazy, but the logical conclusion to the evidence of experience. Everything you choose for me or advise me to do turns out to be the perfect solution for me. Case in point, look at me."

And she'd been trying her best not to. Not to stare, anyway. He gestured at his clothes. "You pointed this out in a shop yesterday, said I'd look good in it."

Yeah, because you'd look good in anything. You'd make a tattered sac look like haute couture.

"Even though I thought I'd look like a cyanotic parrot in this color…" A deep, intense purple that struck incredible hues off his hair and eyes. "I bought it on the way here based solely on your opinion. Now I think I've never worn anything more complimenting."

Her lips twisted in mockery, and with a twinge at how right he was. He looked the most vital and incandescent he'd ever been. "Pink frills would compliment you, Aram."

"Then I'll try those next."

A chuckle overpowered her as imaginings flooded her mind. "God, this I have to see."

His grin flashed, dazzling her. "Then you will." Suddenly his face settled into a seriousness that was even more hard-hitting. "All joking aside, I'm not being impulsive here. I'm a businessman, and I make my decisions built on what works best. And *you* work best."

"Uh, thanks. But in exactly what way do I do that?"

"Your perception is free from the distortions of inclinations. You cut to the essence of things, see people and situations for what they are, not what you'd prefer them to be, and don't let the background noise of others' opinions distract you." He slid her that proud, appreciative glance that he bestowed on her so frequently these days. "You proved that to me when you accepted my word and adjusted your opinion of me, guided only by your reading of me against overwhelming circumstantial evidence and long-standing misconceptions. It's because you're so welcoming of adjustments and so goal oriented that you achieve the best results in everything. I mean, look at me..."

Oh, God, not again. Didn't he have any idea what it did to her just being near him, let alone looking more closely at him than absolutely necessary?

No, he didn't.

He had no idea whatsoever how he made her feel.

She sighed. "I'm looking. And purple does become you. Anything else I should be looking at?"

"Yes, the miracle you worked. You took a fed-up man who was feeling a hundred years old and turned him into that eager kid who skips around doing all the things he'd long given up on. And you did it by just being your no-nonsense self, by just reading me right and telling me everything you thought and exactly what I have to hear."

She almost winced. She wasn't telling *everything* she thought. Not by a long shot. But her thoughts and feelings where he was concerned were her responsibility. She had no right to burden him with what didn't concern him.

But he was making it harder by the minute to contain those feelings within her being's meager boundaries.

He wasn't finished with his latest bout of unwitting torment. "You yanked me out of the downward spiral I was resigned to plunge into until I hit rock bottom. So, yes, I'm sure your choice of abodes will be the best one for me. Because you've been the best thing that has ever happened to me."

The heart that had been squeezing harder with every incredible word almost burst.

To have him so eloquently reinforcing her suspicion that he'd come to consider her the replacement best friend/sister he needed was both ecstasy and agony.

Feeling the now-familiar heat simmering behind her eyes, she attempted to take this back to lightness. "What's with the seriousness? And here I was secure in the fact that you're incapable of being that way around me."

His smile was so indulgent that she felt something coming undone right in her very essence. "I'm always serious around you. Just in a way that's the most fun I've ever had. But if you feel I'm burdening you with making this choice…"

And she had to laugh. "Oh, shut up, you gigantic weasel. After all the sucking up you did, and all the puppy-dog-eyed persuasion that you *have* perfected in front of that mirror, you have the audacity to pretend that I have a choice here?"

His guffaw belted out, almost made her collapse onto herself. "Ah, Kanza, *you* are the most fun I've ever had."

Yeah. What every girl wanted to hear from the most divine man on earth. That she made him laugh.

But she'd already settled for that. For anything with him. For as long as she could have it. Come what may.

He brought the car to a stop in front of a building that felt vaguely familiar. As he opened his door, she jumped out so he wouldn't come around to open hers, since opening doors and pulling back seats for her seemed to be the only acts that indicated that he considered her female.

When he fell into step beside her, she did a double take.

They were on Fifth Avenue. Specifically in front of one of the top Italian-renaissance palazzo-style apartment buildings in Manhattan.

Forgetting everything but the excitement of apartment hunting, she turned to him with a whoop. "I used to live a block from here." And she'd found the area only "vaguely familiar." He short-circuited her brain even more than she'd thought. "God, I loved that apartment. It was the only place that ever felt like home."

His eyebrows shot up. "Zohayd didn't feel like that?"

"Not really. You know what it was like."

He frowned and, if possible, became more edible than ever. "Actually, I have no idea how it was like for you there. Because you never told me." As soon as they entered the elevator, he turned to her with a probing glance. "How did we never get to talk about your life in Zohayd?"

She shrugged. "Guess we had more important things to discuss. Like how to pick the best avocado."

His lips pursed in displeasure. "That alone makes me realize how remiss I've been and that there is a big story here. One I won't rest until I hear."

She waved him off. "It's boring, really."

His pout was adamant. "I live to be bored by you."

The last thing she wanted to do was tell him about her disappointment-riddled life in Zohayd. But knowing him, he'd persist until she told him. The best she could hope for was to distract him for now.

She took the key from his hand as they got off the elevator. "Which apartment?"

He pointed out the one at the far end of the floor.

As they sauntered in that direction, he looked down at her. "So about this old place of yours—if it felt like home, and I'm assuming your new place doesn't, why did you move?"

"A friend from Zohayd begged me to room with her, as she couldn't live alone, and the new place was right by her work. Then she up and got married on me and went back to Zohayd, and I never got around to going back to my place. But now that you might be buying a place this close, it would save us a lot of commuting if I got it back. Hope it's still on the market."

"Choose this apartment, and I'll *make* it on the market."

"Oh. Watch out, world, for the big, bad tycoon. He snaps his fingers and the market yelps and rolls over."

He gave her a deep bow. "At your service."

They laughed and exchanged wit missiles as they entered the opulent duplex through a marble-framed doorway. Then she fell silent as she beheld what looked straight out of the pages of *Architectural Digest.* Sweeping, superbly organized layouts with long galleries, an elegant staircase, lush finishes, oversize windows, high ceilings and a spacious terrace that wrapped around two sides of the apartment. It was even furnished to the highest standards she'd ever seen and very, very much to her taste.

In only minutes of looking around, she turned to Aram. "Okay, no need to see anything more. Or any other place. I hereby proclaim that you will find utmost comfort here."

He again bowed deeply, azure flames of merriment leaping in his eyes. "My Minuscule Mistress, thy will be done."

And in the next hour, it was. He immediately called the Realtor, who zoomed over with the contracts. Aram passed them to her to read before he signed, and she made some amendments before giving him the green light. From then on, it took only minutes for the check to be handed over and the Realtor to leave the apartment almost bouncing in delight.

Aram came back from walking the lady to the front door, his smile flooding his magnificent new place in its radiance.

"Now to inaugurate the apartment with our first meal." He threw himself down beside her on the elegant couch. "So what are we eating?"

She cocked an eyebrow at him and tsked. "This inability to make decisions without my say-so is becoming worrisome."

He slid down farther on the couch, reclining his big, powerful body more comfortably. "I've been making business decisions for countless employees, clients and shareholders for the past eight years. I'm due for a perpetual vacation from making minor- to moderate-sized decisions for the rest of my personal life."

She gave him her best stern scowl, which she resignedly knew he thought was the most adorable thing ever. "And I'm the one who's supposed to pick up the slack and suddenly be responsible for your decisions as well as mine?"

He nodded in utmost complacency. "You do it so well, so naturally. And it's your fault. You're the one who got me used to this." His gaze became that cross between cajoling and imploring that he'd perfected. "You're not leaving me in the lurch now, are you?"

"Stop with the eyes!" she admonished. "Or I swear I'll blindfold you."

"What a brilliant idea. Then besides making decisions for me, you'll have to lead me around by the hand. Even more unaccountability for me to revel in."

She threw her hands up. "Sushi, okay. Here's your decision before I find myself taking over your business, too, while you go indulge in the teenage irresponsibility you evidently never had."

Chuckling, he got out his phone. Then he proceeded to ask her exactly what kind of sushi they were eating, piece by piece, until she had to slam him with a cushion.

After they'd wiped off the delicious feast, he was pouring her jasmine tea when she noticed him looking at her in an even more unsettling, contemplative way.

"What?" she croaked.

"I was wondering if you were always this interesting."

"And I'm wondering if you were always this condescending. Oh, wait, you were even worse. You used to look at me like I was a strange life-form."

"You *were* a strange life-form. I mean, green body makeup? And pink contacts? Pink? Did you have those custom-made?" He rejoined her on the couch with his own cup. "What statement were you making?"

She was loath to remember those times when she'd felt alone even while deluged by people. When she used to look at him and know that *nogoom el sama a'arablaha*—that the stars in the sky were closer than he was. Now, though he was a breath away, he remained as distant, as impossible to reach.

She sighed, shaking free from the wave of melancholy. "One of my stepmothers, Maysoon's mother, popularized Kanza the Monster's name until everyone was using it. So I decided to go the whole hog and look the part."

His eyes went grim, as if imagining having his hands on those who'd been so inconsiderate with her. Knowing him, she didn't put it past him that he would act on his outrage on behalf of her former self.

"What made you give it up?" His voice was dark with barely suppressed anger. "Then go all the way in the other direction, doing without any sort of enhancement?"

She shrugged. "I developed an allergy to makeup."

His lips twitched as his anger dissolved into wry humor. "Another allergy?"

"Not a real one. I just realized that regardless of whether makeup makes me look worse or better, I was focusing too much on what others thought of me. So I decided to focus on myself. Be myself."

That pride he showered on her flooded his gaze. "Good for you. You're perfect just the way you are."

Kanza stared at him. In any romantic movie, as the hero

professed those words, he would have suddenly seen his dorky best friend in a new light, would have realized she was beautiful in his eyes and that he wanted her for more than just a friend.

Before her heart imploded with futility, she slid down on the couch, pretending she thought it a good moment for one of those silent rituals they exercised together.

Inside her, there was only cacophony.

Aram considered her perfect.

Just not for him.

Eight

Aram sank further into tranquility and relaxation beside Kanza, savoring the companionable silence they excelled at together, just as they did at exhilarating repartee.

Just by being here, she'd turned this place, which he'd felt ambivalent toward until she'd entered it and decided she liked it, into a home. He'd decided to have one at last only because she'd said she would always stay in New York and make it hers.

He sighed, cherishing the knowledge that expanded inside him with each passing hour.

She was really her name. A treasure.

And to think that no one, even Shaheen and Johara, realized how much of one she really was.

He guessed she was too different, too unexpected, too unbelievable for others to be able to fathom, let alone to handle.

She was perfect to him.

It was hard to believe that only six weeks ago he hadn't had her in his life. It felt as if his existence had *become* a life only once she'd entered it.

And it seemed like a lifetime ago when Shaheen had

suggested her as a convenient bride, convinced she'd consider his assets and agree to the arrangement. If Shaheen only knew her, he would have known that she'd sign a contract of enslavement before she would a marriage of convenience. If he'd known how unique, how exceptional she was, he wouldn't have even thought of such an unworthy fate for her.

She'd achieved her success in pursuit of self-realization and accomplishment, not status and wealth—things she cared nothing about and would certainly never wish to attain through a man. She'd even made it clear she didn't consider marriage a viable option for herself. But among the many misconceptions about her had been his own worry that his initial fascination would fade, and she'd turn out to be just another opportunistic woman who'd use any means necessary to reel in a husband.

But the opposite had happened. His fascination, his admiration, his pleasure at being with her intensified by the minute. For the first time, he found himself attracted to the *whole* woman, his attraction not rooted in sexuality or sustained by it. He had to use Shaheen's word to describe what they were. Compatible. They were matched on every level—personally, professionally, mentally and emotionally. Her every quality and skill meshed with and complemented his own. She was his equal, and his superior in many areas.

She was *just* perfect.

Just yesterday, Shaheen had asked him for an update on whether he'd changed his mind about Kanza now that he'd gotten to know her.

He'd said only that he had, leaving it at that.

What he'd really meant was that he had changed his mind about *everything.*

The more he was with Kanza, the more everything he'd believed of himself—of his limits, inclinations, priorities and everything he'd felt before her—changed beyond all recognition.

She made him work hard for her respect and esteem, for the pleasure and privilege of his presence in her life, for her gracing his with hers. She gave him what no one had ever given him before, not even Shaheen or Johara. She *reveled* in being with him as much as he did with her. She *got* him on every level. She accepted him, challenged him, and when she felt there were things about him that needed fixing—and there were *many*—she just reached inside him with the magic wand of her candor and caring and put it right.

She'd turned his barren existence into a life of fulfillment, every day bringing with it deeper meanings, invigorating discoveries and uplifting experiences.

The only reason he'd fleetingly considered Shaheen's offer had been for the possibility of filling his emptiness with a new purpose in life and the proximity of his family. Now he found little reason to change his status quo. For what could possibly be better than this?

It was just perfection between them.

So when Shaheen had asked for an update, really asking about projected developments, he couldn't bear thinking of any. How could he when any might tamper with this blissful state? He was *terrified* anything would happen to change it.

They were both unconcerned about the world and its conventions, and things were flourishing between them. He only hoped they would continue to deepen in the exact same way. So even if he wanted to, he certainly wasn't introducing any new variable that might fracture the flawlessness.

For now, the only change he wanted to introduce was removing the last barrier inside him. He wanted to let her into his being, fully and totally.

So he did. "There's something I haven't told you yet. Something nobody knows."

She turned to him, her glorious mass of hair rustling as if it was alive, those unique obsidian eyes delving deep inside his recesses, letting him know she was there for him always.

Just gazing into them he felt invincible. And secure that he could share everything with her, even his shame.

"It happened a few months after I left Zohayd…." He paused, the long-repressed confession searing out of his depths. He braced himself against the pain, spit it out. "I got involved in something…that turned out to be illegal, with very dangerous people. I ended up in prison."

That had her sitting up. And what he saw on her face rocked through him. Instantaneous reassurance that, whatever had happened, whatever he told her, it wouldn't change her opinion of him. She was on his side. Unequivocally.

And as he'd needed to more frequently of late, he took a moment to suppress the desire to haul her to him and crush her in the depths of his embrace with all his strength.

The need to physically express his feelings for her had been intensifying every day. But she'd made no indication that she'd accept that. Worse. She didn't seem to want it.

It kept him from initiating anything, even as much as a touch. For what if even a caress on her cheek or hair changed the dynamic between them? What if it made her uneasy and put her on her guard around him? What if he then couldn't take it back and convince her that he'd settle for their previous hands-off status quo, forever if need be?

He brought the urge under control with even more difficulty than he had the last time it had assailed him, his voice sounding as harsh as broken glass as he went on, "I was sentenced to three years. I was paroled after only one."

Her solemn eyes were now meshed with his. He felt he was sinking into the depths of their unconditional support, felt understood, cosseted, protected. It was as if she was reaching to him through time, to offer him her strength to tide him through the incarceration, to soothe the wounds and erase his scars.

"For good behavior?" Her voice was the gentlest he'd ever heard it.

He barked a mirthless laugh. "Actually, they probably

wanted me out to get rid of me. I was too much trouble, gave them too many inmates to patch up. I almost killed a couple. I spent over nine months of that year in solitary. The moment they let me out, I put more inmates in the infirmary and I was shoved back there."

"You ended up being…solitary too many times throughout your life."

She'd mused that as if to herself. But he felt her soft, pondering words reaching down inside him to tear out the talons he'd long felt sunk into his heart. Making him realize that it hadn't been the solitude itself that had eaten at him but the notion that he'd never stop being alone.

But now she was here, and he'd never be alone again.

Her smile suddenly dawned, and it lit up his entire world. "But you still managed to make the best of a disastrous situation in your own inimitable way."

"It wasn't only my danger to criminal life-forms that got me out. I was a first-time offender, and I was lucky to find people who believed that I had made a mistake, not committed a crime. Those allies helped me get out, and afterward, they supported my efforts to…expunge my record."

The radiance of her smile intensified, scorching away any remnants of the ordeal's despondency and indignity. "So you're an old hand at expunging your record. And I wasn't the first one who believed in you."

He didn't know how he stopped himself from grabbing her hands, burying his lips and face in them, grabbing *her* and burying his whole being in her magnanimity and faith.

He expended the urge on a ragged breath. "You're the first and only one who did with only the evidence of my word."

She waved that away. "As you so astutely pointed out the first night, I do know Maysoon. That was a load of evidence in your favor, once I'd heard both sides of the story."

He wasn't about to accept her qualification. "No. You

employed this unerring truth-and-justice detector of yours without any backing evidence. You read *me.* You believed *me.*"

Her eyes gleamed with that indulgence that melted him to his core. "Okay, okay, I did. Boy, you're pushy."

"And you believed me again now," he insisted, needing to hear her say it. "When I said I didn't knowingly commit a crime, even when I gave you no details, let alone evidence."

Teasing ebbed, as if she felt he needed the assurance of her seriousness. "Yes, I did, because I know you'd always tell me the truth, the bad before the good. If you'd been guilty, you would have told me. Because you know I can't accept anything but the truth and because you know that whatever it was, it wouldn't make a difference to me."

Hot thorns sprouted behind his eyes, inside his heart. Everything inside him surged, needing to mingle with her.

He had to end these sublime moments before he…expressed how moved he was by them, shattering them instead.

He first had to try to tell her what her belief meant to him. "Your trust in me is a privilege and a responsibility that I will always nurture with pride and pleasure."

Her gaze suddenly escaped his, flowed down his body.

By the time they rose back, he was hard all over. Thankfully, her eyes were intent on his, full of contemplation.

"Though you're so big, with no doubt proportionate strength, it never occurred to me you'd be that capable of physical violence."

The vice that had released his heart suddenly clamped around it again. "Does this…disturb you?"

Her laugh rang out. "Hello? Have you met me? It *thrills* me. I would have loved to see you decimate a few thugs and neuter some bullies."

His hands, his whole being itched, ached. He just wanted to squeeze the hell out of her. He wanted to contain her, assimilate her and never let her go again.

He again held back with all he had, then drawled, "And to think something so minuscule could be so bloodthirsty."

She grinned impishly. "You've got a lot to learn about just what this deceptive exterior hides, big man."

Though her words tickled him and her smile was unfettered, he was still unsettled. "Is it really no problem for you to change your perception of me from someone who's too civilized to use his brute strength to someone who relishes physical violence?"

She shook her head, her long, thick hair falling over her slight shoulders down to her waist. "I don't believe you 'relish' it, but you'll always do 'what works best.' At the time, violence was the one thing that would keep the sharks away. So you used it, and to maximum efficiency, as is your way with everything. I'm only lamenting that there's no video documentation of those events for *me* to cheer over."

The delight she always struck in his heart overflowed in an unbridled guffaw. "I can just see you, grabbing the popcorn and hollering at the screen for more gore. But I might be able to do something about your desire to see me on a rampage. I can pull some strings at the prison and get some surveillance-camera footage."

She jumped up to her knees on the couch, nimble and keen as a cat. "Yes, yes, please!"

"Uh…I'm already regretting making the offer. You might think you can withstand what you'd see, but it was no staged fight like those you see on TV. There was no showmanship involved, just brutality with only the intent to survive at whatever cost."

She tucked her legs as if she was starting a meditation session, her gaze ultraserious. "That only makes it even more imperative to see it, Aram. It was the ugliest, harshest, most humiliating test you've ever endured and your deepest scar. I need to experience it in more than imagination, even if in the cold distance of past images, so I'd be able to share it with you in the most profound way I need to."

Stirred through to his soul, he swallowed a jagged lump of gratitude. "You just have to want it and it's done."

"Oh, I so want it. Thank you." Before he pounced with a thank-*you,* she probed, "You've really been needing to confide this all this time. Why didn't you?"

She was killing him with her ability to see right into his depths. She was reviving him with it, reanimating him.

"I was…ashamed. Of my weakness and stupidity. I wanted to prove to Shaheen and his brothers that I didn't need their help after all, that I'd make it on my own. And I got myself involved in something that looked too good to be true because I was in such a hurry to do it. And I paid the price."

She tilted her head to the side, as if to look at him from another perspective. "I can't even imagine what it was like. When you were arrested, when you were sentenced, when you realized you might have destroyed your future, maybe even tainted that of your family. That year in prison…"

He wanted to tell her that she was imagining it just fine, that her compassion was dissipating the lingering darkness of that period, erasing the scars it had left behind. But his throat was closed, his voice gone.

The empathy in her gaze rose until it razed him. "But I can understand the ordeal was a link in the chain that led to your eventual decline. Not the experience itself as much as the reinforcement of your segregation. You couldn't share such a life-changing experience with your loved ones, mainly because you wanted to protect them from the agony they would have felt on your behalf. But that very inability to bare your soul to them made you pull further away emotionally, and actually exacerbated your solitude."

When he finally found his voice, it was a hoarse, ragged whisper. "See? You do know everything."

Her eyes gentled even more. "Not everything. I'm still unable to fill some spaces. You were going strong for years after your imprisonment. Was that only *halawet el roh?*"

Literally sweetness of the soul. What was said in Zohayd to describe a state of deceptive vigor, a clinging to life when warding off inevitable deterioration or death.

"Now that you mention it, that's the best explanation. I came out of prison with a rabid drive to wipe out what happened, to right my path, to make up for lost time. I guess I was trying to run hard and fast enough to escape the memories, to accumulate enough success and security to fix the chasm the experience had ripped inside me and that threatened to tear me open at any moment."

Her eyes now soothed him, had him almost begging her to let her hand join in their caress. "Johara told me you were at the peak of fitness, at least physically, three years ago when you attended their wedding in Zohayd. From her observations, you started deteriorating about two years ago. Was there a triggering event? Like when it sank in that they were a family now? Did their togetherness—especially with your parents' reconciliation—leave you feeling more alone than ever?"

He squeezed his eyes on a spasm of poignancy. "You get me so completely. You get me better than I get myself."

Wryness touched her lips. "It was Johara who gave me the code to decipher your hieroglyphics when she said she felt as if her and Shaheen's intimacy left you unable to connect with either of them on the same level as you used to."

"She's probably right. But it's not only my own hang-ups. Neither of them has enough left to devote to anyone else. A love like that fills up your being. And then there's the massive emotional investment in Gharam and their coming baby."

Something inscrutable came into her eyes, intensifying their already absolute darkness.

Seeming to shake herself out of it, whatever it was, she continued searching his recesses. "So *was* there a triggering physical event? That made your health start to deteriorate?"

"Nothing specific. I just started being unable to sleep

well, to eat as I should. Everything became harder, took longer and I did it worse. Then each time I got even a headache or caught a cold, it took me ages to bounce back. My focus, my stamina, my immunity were just shot. I guess my whole being was disintegrating."

"But you're back in tip-top shape now."

It was a question, not a statement, worry tingeing it.

He let his gaze cup her elfin face in lieu of his hands. "I've never been better. And it's thanks to you."

Her smile faltered as she again waved his assertion away. "There you go again, crediting me with miracles."

"You *are* a miracle. My Minute Miracle. Not that size has anything to do with your effect. *That's* supreme."

He jumped to his feet, feeling younger and more alive than he'd ever felt, needing to dive headfirst into the world, doing everything under the sun with her. He rushed to fetch their jackets, then dashed back to her. "Let's go run in the rain. Then let's hop on my jet and go have breakfast anywhere you want. Europe. South America. Australia. Anywhere."

She donned her jacket and ran after him out of the apartment with just as much zeal. "How about the moon?"

Delighted at her willingness to oblige him in whatever he got it in his mind to say or do, he said, "If it's what you want, then I'll make it happen."

She pulled one of those funny faces that he adored. "And I wouldn't put it past you, too. Nah…I'll settle for something on terra firma. And close by. I have to work in the morning, even if you're so big and important now you no longer have to."

He consulted his watch. "If we leave for Barbados in an hour, I'll have you at work by ten."

Her disbelief lasted only moments before mischief and excitement replaced it. "You're on."

Nine

"It's…good to hear your voice, Father."

Kanza hated that hesitation in her voice. Whatever her father's faults, she did love him. Did miss him.

Yeah. She did. But, and it was a huge but, after ten minutes of basking in the nostalgia of early and oblivious childhood when her father had been her hero, she always thudded back to reality and was ready not to see him again for months.

"It's great to hear yours, *ya bnayti.*"

His calling her *my daughter,* instead of bestowing a personalized greeting with her name included, annoyed her. He called his other eight daughters that, with the same indiscrimination. She thought he used it most times because he forgot the name of the one he was talking to.

Curbing her irritation, and knowing her father never called unless he had something to ask of her, she said, "Anything I can do for you, Father?"

"*Ya Ullah,* yes. Only you can help me now, *ya bnayti.* I need you to come back to Zohayd at once."

Ten minutes later, she sat staring numbly into space.

She'd tried to wriggle out of saying yes. She'd failed.

She was really going back to Zohayd. Tonight.

Her father had begged her to board the first flight to Zohayd. Beyond confirming that no one was dead or severely injured, he'd said no more about why he needed her back so urgently.

She reserved a ticket online, then packed a few essentials. She wouldn't stay a minute longer than necessary.

Not that there was a reason to hurry back.

Not from the evidence of the past two weeks anyway.

It had been then, six weeks after that magical time in Aram's new apartment and the breakfast in Barbados, that Aram had suddenly become insanely busy. He'd neglected his work so much that the accumulation had become critical.

She understood. Of *course,* she did. She knew exactly how many people depended on him, what kind of money rode on his presence and expertise. She'd been neglecting her work, too, but Johara had picked up the slack, and she was not so indispensable that her absence would cause the same widespread ripples his had. She appreciated this fully. Mentally. But otherwise…

The fact was, he'd spoiled her. She'd gotten reliant on seeing him each and every day, on being able to pick up the phone, day or night, and he'd be eager and willing to grant her every wish, to be there with her at no notice. When that had suddenly come to an abrupt end, she'd gone into withdrawal.

God. She'd turned into one of those clingy, needy females. At least in her own mind and psyche. Outwardly, she was her devil-may-care self. At least, she hoped she was.

But she was something else, too. Moronic. The man had a life outside her, even if for three months straight it had seemed as if he didn't. She'd known real life would reassert itself at one point. So she should stop whining *now.*

And now that she thought of it without self-pity, going to Zohayd was a good thing. She'd been twiddling her thumbs until she and Johara started the next project. And by the time she was back, he would have sorted himself enough to be able to see her again—at least more than he had the past two weeks.

She speed-dialed his number. The voice she now lived to hear poured into her brain after the second ring.

"Kanza—a moment please..." His voice was muffled as he talked to someone.

Feeling guilty for interrupting him when he'd told her he wouldn't have a free moment before seven, she rushed on. "I just wanted to tell you I'm going home in a couple of hours."

More muffled words, then he came back to her. "That's fantastic. About time."

That she hadn't expected. "It—it is?"

"Sure, it is. Listen, Kanza, I'm sorry, but I *have* to finish this before the Saudi Stock Exchange opens. 'Bye now."

Then he hung up.

She stared at the phone.

Last night, he'd said he'd see her later tonight. But she'd just told him she wouldn't be able to see him because she was traveling and he'd sounded...glad?

Had she unwittingly let her disappointment show when he'd been unable to see her for the past two weeks, and he now thought it was a good idea if she did something other than wait for him until his preoccupation lightened and he could see her again?

But he hadn't even asked why she was going or how long she'd stay. Sure, he'd been in a hurry, but he could have said something other than *fantastic* or *about time*. He could have said he'd call later to get details.

So was it possible he was just glad to get her off his back? Could it be that what she'd thought were unfounded feelings of impending loss had just been premonition? Was the magical interlude with him really over?

She'd known from the start he'd just needed someone to help him through the worst slump in his life. Now that he was over it, was he over his need for her?

That made sense. Terrible sense. And it was only expected. She'd dreaded that day, but she'd known it would come. She'd just kept hoping it would not come so soon. She wasn't ready to give him up yet.

But when would she ever be? How could she ever be… when she loved him?

Suddenly a sob tore out of her. Then another, and another until she was bent over, tears raining on the ground, unable to contain the torrent of anguish anymore.

She loved him.

She would forever love him.

And she would have remained his friend forever, asking nothing more but to have the pleasure and privilege of his nearness, of his appreciation, of his completion. Of his need.

But it seemed he no longer needed her.

Now he'd recede, but never really end it as he would have with a lover. She would see him again and again whenever life threw them together. And each time, he'd expect her to be his buddy, would chat and tease and reminisce and not realize that she missed him like an amputee would a limb.

Maybe going to Zohayd now *was* a blessing in disguise. Maybe she should stay until he totally forgot about her.

The moment Aram finished his last memo for the night, he pounced on his phone to call Kanza. Before he did, Shaheen walked into his office.

A groan escaped him that he had to postpone the call—and seeing her—for the length of Shaheen's visit.

His brother-in-law whistled. "*Ya Ullah,* you missed me *that* much?"

Aram winced. His impatience must be emblazoned across his whole body. And he'd been totally neglecting his friend as of late. But he'd been reserving every hour, every moment, every spare breath for Kanza.

"Actually I do miss you, but—" he groaned again, ran his fingers through his hair "—you know how it is."

Shaheen laughed. *"Menn la'ah ahbaboh nessi ashaboh." He who finds his loved ones forgets his friends.*

He refused to comment on Shaheen's backhanded reference to Kanza as his loved one. "As much as I'd love to indulge your curiosity, Shaheen, I have to go to Kanza now. Let's get together some other time. Maybe I'll bring Kanza over to your home, hmm?"

Shaheen blinked in surprise. "You're going to Zohayd?"

Aram scowled. "Now, where did that come from? Why should I go to Zohayd?"

"Because you said that you're going to Kanza, who's on her way to Zohayd right now."

Aram glanced at his watch, then out of the jet's window, then back at his watch.

Had it always taken that long to get to Zohayd?

It felt as if it had been a day since he'd boarded his jet—barely an hour after Shaheen had said Kanza was heading there.

He was still reverberating with disbelief. With...panic.

His condition had been worsening since it had sunk in that the "home" Kanza had meant was Zohayd. According to Johara, Kanza was returning there at her father's urgent demand. Kanza herself didn't know why. Shaheen hadn't been able to understand why he'd be so agitated that she was visiting her family and would probably be back in a few days.

But he'd been unable to listen, to Shaheen or the voice of reason. Nothing had mattered but one thing.

The need to go after her.

A tornado was tearing through him. His gut told him something was wrong. Terribly wrong.

For how could she go like that without saying goodbye?

Even if she had to rush, even if he'd been swamped, the Kanza he knew would have let him see her before separation was imposed on them.

So why hadn't she? Why hadn't she made it clear where she was going? If he'd known, he would have rushed to her, would have paid the millions that would have been lost for a chance to see her even for a few minutes before she left. She had to know he would have. So why hadn't she given him the chance to? Hadn't it been as necessary for her to see him this last time as it was for him?

Was he not as necessary to her as she was to him?

He'd long been forced to believe his necessity to her differed from hers to him. He'd thought that as long as the intimacy remained the same, he'd just have to live with the fact that its…texture wasn't what he now yearned for.

But what if he was losing even that? What if not saying goodbye now meant that she *could* eventually say goodbye for real? What if that day was even closer than his worst nightmares?

What if that day was here?

He couldn't even face that possibility. He'd lost his solitariness from the first time he'd seen her. She'd proceeded to strip him of his self-containment, his autonomy. He'd known isolation. But he hadn't realized what loneliness was until he'd heard from Shaheen that she'd left.

She'd become more than vital to him. She'd become… home.

What if he could never be anything like that to her?

What if he caught up with her in Zohayd and she only thought he was out of his mind hurtling after her like that?

Maybe he was out of his mind. Maybe everything he'd just churned himself over had no basis in fact. Maybe…

His cell phone rang. He fumbled with it, his fingers going numb with brutal anticipation. *Kanza.* She'd tell him why she hadn't said goodbye. And he'd tell her he'd be with her in a couple of hours and she could say it to his face.

The next moment disappointment crashed through him. Johara.

He couldn't hold back his growl. "What is it, Johara?"

A silent beat. "Uh…don't kill the messenger, okay?"

"What the hell does that mean? Jo, I'm really not in any condition to have a nice, civil conversation right now. For both our sakes, just leave me alone."

"I'm sorry, Aram, but I really think you need to know, so you'd be prepared."

"Know what? Be prepared for what?" A thousand dreads swooped down on him, each one shrieking Kanza, Kanza, *Kanza...* "Just spit it out!"

"I just got off the phone with Kanza's father. He said he needed me to know as Kanza's best friend that Prince Kareem Aal Kahlawi has asked for her hand in marriage."

Kanza thought it was inevitable.

She would end up killing someone.

For now, storming through her father's house, slamming her old bedroom door behind her was all the venting she could do.

She leaned against it, letting out a furious shriek.

Of all the self-involved, self-serving, unfeeling… Argh!

To think that was why her father had dragged her back here!

Couldn't she kill him? And her sisters? Just a little bit…?

Her whole body lurched forward, every nerve firing at once.

She stopped. Moving. Breathing. Even her heart slowed down. Each boom so hard her ears rang.

That must be it. Why she thought she'd heard…

"Kanza."

Aram.

God. She was starting to hear things. Hear him. When he was seven thousand miles away. This was beyond pathetic….

"Kanza. I know you're there."

Okay. She wasn't *that* pathetic.

"I saw you tearing out of the living room, saw you going

up. I know this is your room. I know you're in there now. Come to the window. *Now,* Kanza."

That last "now" catapulted her to the French doors. She barely stopped before she shot over the balcony's balustrade.

And standing down there, among the shrubs below, in all his mind-blowing glory, was Aram.

Azure bolts arced from his eyes and a wounded lion's growl came from his lips. "What are you *doing* here?"

Her head spun at the brunt of his beauty under Zohayd's declining sun and the absurdity of his question.

She blinked, as if it would reboot her brain. "What are *you* doing here? In Zohayd? And standing beneath my window?"

He stuck his fists at his hips. He looked…angry? And agitated. Why? "What does it look like? I'm here to see you."

She shook her head, confusion deepening. He must have left New York just a few hours after she had. Had he come all the way here to find out why she had? After he'd basically told her to scram? Why not just call? What did it all mean?

Okay. With the upheaval of this past day, her brain was on the fritz. She could no longer attempt to make any sense of it.

She pinched the bridge of her nose. "Well, you saw me. Now go away before all my family comes out and finds you here. With the way you've been shouting, they must be on their way."

He widened his stance, face adamant planes and ruthless slashes. "If you don't want them to see me, come down."

"I can't. If I go down and try to walk through the front door, I'll have twenty females on my case…and I don't want the ulcer I've acquired in the last hours to rupture."

"Then *climb* down."

That last whisper could have sandpapered the manor's facade. "Okay, Aram, I know you're crazy, but even in your insanity you can see that the last foothold is twenty feet above splat level."

He shrugged. "Fifteen max. I'll catch you."

Closing her mouth before it caught one of the birds zooming back to their nests at the approach of sunset, she echoed his pose, fists on hips. "If you want to reenact Shaheen's stunt with Johara, I have to remind you that she was six at the time."

That shrug again. "You're not that much bigger now."

She coughed a chagrined laugh. "Why, thanks. Just what every grown woman wants to hear."

He sighed. "I meant the ratio of your size to mine, compared to that of fourteen-year-old Shaheen to six-year-old Johara." He suddenly snarled again, his eyes blazing. "Stop arguing. I can catch you, easy. You know I've been exercising."

Yeah, she knew. She'd attended many a mind-scrambling session, seen what he looked like with minimal clothing, flexing, bulging, sweating, flooding a mile's radius with premium, lethal testosterone.

"But even in my worst days, I would have been able to catch you. I always knew I was that big for a reason, but I just never knew what it was. Now I know. It's so I could catch you."

Her mouth dropped open again.

What that man kept *saying.*

What would he say when he was actually in love...?

That thought made her feel like jumping off the balcony—and not so he could catch her.

She inhaled a steadying, sanity-laced breath. "Oh, all right. Just because I know you'll stand there until I do. Or worse, barge into the house to come up here and have a houseful of your old fans pick your bones. I hope you know I'm doing this to save your gorgeous hide."

His smile was terse. "Yes, of course. I'm, as always, eternally indebted to you. Now hurry."

Mumbling under her breath about him being a hulk-sized brat who expected to get his way in everything, she took one last bracing breath and climbed over the balustrade.

As she inched down over the steplike ledges, he kept a running encouragement. "You're doing fine. Don't look down. I'm right here."

Slipping, she clung to the building, wailed, "Shut *up,* Aram. God, I can't believe what you can talk me into."

He just kept going. "Keep your body firm, not tense, okay? Now let go." When she hesitated, his voice suddenly dropped into the darkest reaches of hypnosis. "Don't worry, I'll catch you, *ya kanzi.*"

My treasure.

All her nerves unraveled. She plummeted.

Her plunge came to a jarring, if firm and secure, end.

He'd caught her. Easy, as he'd said. As if he'd snatched her from a three-foot drop. And she was staring up into those vivid, luminescent eyes that now filled her existence.

Without one more word, he swept her along through the manicured grounds and out of her father's estate.

She reeled. Not from the drop, but from her first contact with him. His flesh pressed to hers, his warmth enveloping her, his strength cocooning her. Being in his arms, even if in this context, was like…like…going home.

Even if the feeling was imaginary, she'd savor it. He was here, for whatever reason, and their…closeness wasn't over.

Not yet.

She let go, let him take her wherever he would.

Aram brooded at Kanza as she walked one step ahead.

He could barely let her be this far away. He'd clutched her all the way out of her father's estate, almost unable to let her go to put her into the car. As if by agreement, they hadn't said anything during the drive. But it hadn't been the companionable silence they'd perfected. By the time they'd arrived, he'd expended his decimated willpower so he wouldn't roar, demanding she tell him what was wrong.

She turned every few steps, as if to check if he was maintaining the same distance. Her glances felt like the sustenance that would save him from starvation. But they didn't soothe him as they'd always done. There was something in them that sent his senses haywire. Something…wary.

He couldn't bear to interpret this. Any interpretation was just too mutilating. And could be dead wrong anyway. So he wouldn't even try.

She stopped at the railings of the upper-floor terrace, turning to him. "Don't tell me you bought this villa in your half hour in Zohayd before popping up beneath my window."

He barely caught back a groan of relief. Her voice. Her teasing. God, he *needed* them.

"Why? Do you think I'm not crazy enough to do it?"

Her smile resembled her usual ones. But not quite. "Excellent point. Since you're crazier, you might have also bought the sea and desert in a ten-mile radius."

A laugh caught in his throat, broke against the spastic barrier of tension. "It's Shaheen's. Now tell me what the hell you're doing here. And why you left without telling me."

Her eyes got even more enormous. "I did tell you."

He threw his arms wide in frustration. "How was I supposed to know you meant Zohayd when you said home?"

"Uh…is this a new crisis? What else could I have meant?"

"Your old New York apartment, of course. The one you said felt like home, the one I got you back the lease for. I thought you were finally ready to move there again."

"That's why you thought it fantastic when I said I was going home," she said, as if to herself. "You thought it was about time I was down the street from you."

He gaped at her. "Are you *nuts?* You thought I would *actually* think it fantastic for you to come out here and leave me alone in New York? Contrary to popular belief, I'm not that evolved. I might support your doing something that doesn't involve me if it makes you happy, even accept that it could take you away from me—for a little while—but be okay, let alone ecstatic about it? No way."

Her eyes kept widening with his every word. At his last bark, her smile flashed back to its unbridled vivacity.

"Thanks for letting me know the extent of your evolution. Now quit snarling at me. I have a big enough headache being saddled with making decisions for more than you now, in not only one but *two* weddings."

It felt as if a missile had hit him.

No. She couldn't be talking about a wedding already. He couldn't allow it. He wouldn't. He'd…

Two weddings?

His rumble was that of a beast bewildered with too many blows. "What the hell are you talking about?"

"My last two unmarried sisters' weddings. With each from a different mother and with how things are in Zohayd where weddings are battlefields, they've reached a standoff with each other and with their bridegrooms' families. It seems there's more hope of ending a war than reaching an agreement on the details of the weddings. Enter me—what Father thinks is his only hope of defusing the situation."

He frowned. "Why you?"

Her lips twisted whimsically. "Because I'm what Father calls the 'neutral zone.' With me as the one daughter of the woman who gave birth to me then ran off with a big chunk of my father's wealth, I am the one who has always given him no trouble, having no mother to harass him on my behalf. And being stuck as the middle sister between eight half sisters, four each from a stepmother, it made me the one in his brood of nine female offspring that no one is jealous of, therefore not unreasonably contentious with." She sighed dramatically. "I was always dragged to referee, because both sides don't consider me a player in the family power games at all. Now Father has recruited me to get all these hysterical females off his back and hopefully get those weddings under way and over with."

What about the groom who proposed to you? That... prince? *Why aren't you telling me about him?*

The questions backlashed in his chest. He couldn't give this preposterous subject credence by even mentioning it.

There was only one thing to ask now.

"Is it me?"

She stared up at him, standing against the winter sunset's backdrop, its fire reflecting gold on her skin and striking flames from the depths of her onyx eyes and the thick mahogany satin tresses that undulated around her in the breeze. She was the embodiment of his every taste and desire and aspiration. And the picture of incomprehension.

But he could no longer afford the luxury of caution. Not when he had the grenade of that...*prince's*...proposal lying there between them. Not when letting the status quo continue could give it a chance to explode and cost him everything.

He halved the step he'd been keeping between them. "You're the only one who's ever told me the whole truth, Kanza. I need you to give it to me now."

Her gaze flickered, but she only nodded. She would give him that truth. Always.

And that truth might end his world.

But he had to have it. "I believe in pure friendship between a man and a woman. But when they share... everything, I can't see how there'd be no physical attraction at all. So, again, is it me? Or are you generally not interested?"

No total truth came from her. Just total astonishment.

He groaned. "It's clear this has never even crossed your mind. And I've been content with what we share, delighted our friendship is rooted in intellectual and spiritual harmony—and I was willing to wait forever for anything else. But I feel I don't have forever anymore. And I can't live with the idea that maybe you just aren't aware of the possibilities, that if I can persuade you to give it a try, you might…not hate it."

Still nothing. Nothing but gaping.

And he put his worst fear into words. "Were you stating your personal preferences that first night? When you said I was disgustingly pretty? Do your tastes run toward something, I don't know, rougher or softer or just not…this?" He made a tense gesture at his face, his body. "Do you have an ideal of masculinity and I'm just not it?"

Her cheeks and lips were now hectic rose. Her voice wavered. "Uh… I'm really not sure…"

Neither was he. If it would be even adequate between them. If he could even please her.

But he felt everything for her, wanted everything with her, so he had to try.

He reached for her, cupped her precious head and gazed down into her shocked eyes. "There's one way to make sure."

Then he swooped down and took her lips.

At the first contact with her flesh, the first flay of her breath, a thousand volts crackled between them, unleashing everything inside him in a tidal wave.

Lashed by the ferocity of his response and immediacy of her surrender, he captured her dainty lower lip in a growling bite, stilling its tremors, attempting to moderate his greed. She only cried out, arched against him and opened her lips wider. And her taste inundated him.

God…her *taste.* He'd imagined but couldn't have possibly anticipated her unimaginable sweetness. Or the perfume of her breath or the sensory overload of her feel. Or what it would all do to him. Everything about her mixed in an aphrodisiac, a hallucinogen that eddied in his arteries and pounded through his system, snapping the tethers of his sanity.

He could have held back from acting on his insanity, could have moderated his onslaught if not for the way she melted against him, blasting away all doubts about her capacity for passion in the inferno of her response. Her moans and whimpers urged him on to take his possession from tasting to clinging to wrenching.

His hands shook with urgency as he gathered her thighs, opened her around his bulk, pinned her against the railings with the force of his hunger. Plundering her with his tongue, he drove inside her mouth, thrust against her heat, losing rhythm in the wildness, losing his mind.

But even without a mind or will, his love for this irreplaceable being was far more potent than even his will to live. She did mean more than life to him.

Tearing out of their merging, rumbling at the sting of separation, he looked down at the overpowering sight of the woman trembling in his arms. "Do you want this, Kanza? Do you want *me?*"

Her dark eyes scorched him with what he'd never dreamed of seeing in them: drugged sensuality and surrender. Then they squeezed in languorous acquiescence.

He needed more. A full disclosure, a knowing consent.

"I will take everything you have, devour everything you are, give you all of me. Do you understand? Is this what you want? What you need? *Everything* with me, now?"

His heart faltered, afraid to beat, waiting for her verdict. Then its valves almost burst as her parted, passion-swollen lips quivered on a ragged, drawn-out sigh.

A simple, devastating, "Yes."

Ten

Kanza heard herself moaning "yes" to Aram as if from the depths of a dream. What *had* to be a dream.

For how could this be reality? How could she be in Aram's arms? How could it be that he'd been devouring her and was now asking for more, for everything?

The only reason she believed it was real was that no dream could be this intense, this incredible. And because no dream of hers about him had been anything like this.

In her wildest fantasies, Aram, her indulgent friend, had been gentle in his approach, tender in his passion.

But the Aram she'd known was gone. In his place was a marauder: wild, almost rough and barely holding back to make certain she wanted his invasion and sanctioned his ferocity.

And she did. Oh, how she did. She'd said yes. Couldn't have said more. She could barely hold on to consciousness as she found herself swept up in the throes of his unexpected, shocking passion. The thrill of his dominance, the starkness of his lust tampered with everything that powered her, body and being. Her brain waves blipped, her heartbeat plunged into arrhythmia, her every cell swelled, throbbed, screamed for his possession and assuagement.

She'd thought she'd been aroused around him. Now she knew what arousal was. This mindlessness, this avalanche of sensations, this need to be conquered, dominated, ravished. By him, only him.

Almost swooning with the force of need, she delighted in openly devouring him, indulging her greed for his splendor. He loomed above her, the fiery palette of the horizon framing his bulk, accentuating his size, setting his beauty ablaze. The tempest in his eyes was precariously checked. He was giving her one last chance to recant her surrender. Before he devastated her.

She would die if he didn't.

The only confirmation she was capable of was to melt back into his embrace, arching against him in fuller surrender.

Growling something under his breath, he bent toward her. Thinking he'd scoop her up into his arms, carry her inside and take full possession of her, she felt shock reverberate when he started undoing her shirt. He planned to make love to her out here!

There was no one around in what looked like a hundred-mile radius, but she still squirmed. One arm firmed around her only enough to still her as his other hand drifted up her body and behind her to unclasp her bra. The relief of pressure on her swollen flesh buckled her legs.

He held her up, his eyes roving her body in fierce greed as he rid her of her jacket, shirt and bra. The moment her breasts spilled out, he bared his teeth, his lips emitting a soft snarl of hunger. Before she could beg for those lips and teeth on her, his hand undid her pants. She gaped as he dropped to his knees, spanning her hips in his hands' girdle of fire; his fingers hooked into both pants and panties and swept both off her, along with her shoes.

Suddenly his hands reversed their path, inflaming her flesh, rendering her breathless, and he stilled an inch from her core.

She shook—and not with cold. If it wasn't for the cooling air, she might have spontaneously combusted.

Then he lit her fuse, raising eyes like incendiary precious stones. *"Ma koll hada'l jamaal? Kaif konti tekhfeeh?"*

Hearing him raggedly speaking Arabic, asking how she had hidden all this beauty, made her writhe. "Aram… please…"

"*Aih*...I'll please you, *ya kanzi.*" His face pressed to her thighs, her abdomen, his lips opening over her quivering flesh, sucking, nibbling everywhere like a starving man who didn't know where to start his feast. Her fingers convulsed in his silky hair, pressed his face to her flesh in an ecstasy of torment, unable to bear the stimulation, unable to get enough. He took her breasts in hands that trembled, pressed them, cradled them, kneaded and nuzzled them as if they were the most amazing things he'd ever felt. Tears broke through her fugue of arousal. "Please, Aram…"

He closed his eyes as if in pain and buried his face in her breasts, inhaling her, opening his mouth over her taut flesh, testing and tasting, lavishing her with his teeth and tongue. *"Sehr, jonoon, ehsasek, reehtek, taamek..."*

Magic, madness, your feel, your scent, your taste...

Her mind unraveled with every squeeze, each rub and nip and probe, each with the exact force, the exact roughness to extract maximum pleasure from her every nerve ending. He layered sensation with each press and bite until she felt devoured, set aflame. Something inside her was charring.

Her undulations against him became feverish, her clamoring flesh seeking any part of him in mindless pursuit of relief. Her begging became a litany until he dragged an electric hand between her thighs, tormenting his way to her core. The heel of his thumb delved between her outer lips at the same moment the damp furnace of his mouth finally clamped over one of the nipples that screamed for his possession. Sensations slashed her nerves.

Supporting her collapsing weight with an arm around

her hips, he slid two fingers between her molten inner lips, stilling at her entrance. "I didn't think that I'd ever see you like this, open for me, on fire, hunger shaking you apart, that I would be able to pleasure you like this…."

He spread her legs, placed one after the other over his shoulders, opening her core for his pleasure and possession. Her moans now merged into an incessant sound of suffering.

He inhaled her again, rumbling like a lion maddened at the scent of his female in heat, as she was. Then he blew a gust of acute sensation over the knot where her nerves converged. She bucked, her plea choking. It became a shriek when he pumped a finger inside her in a slow, slow glide. Sunset turned to darkest night as she convulsed, pleasure slamming through her in desperate surges.

Her sight burst back to an image from a fantasy. Aram, fully clothed, kneeling between her legs…her, naked, splayed open over his shoulders, amidst an empty planet all their own.

And he'd made her climax with one touch.

Among the mass of aftershocks, she felt his finger, still inside her, pumping…beckoning. Her gasp tore through her lungs as his tongue joined in, licked from where his finger was buried inside her upward, circling her bud. Each glide and graze and pull and thrust sent hotter lances skewering through her as if she hadn't just had the most intense orgasm of her life. It was only when she sobbed, bucked, pressed her burning flesh to his mouth, opening herself fully to his double assault, that his lips locked on her core and really gave it to her, had her quaking and screaming with an even more violent release.

She tumbled from the explosive peak, drained, sated. Stupefied. What had just happened?

Her drugged eyes sought his, as if for answers.

Even in the receding sunset they glowed azure, heavy with hunger and satisfaction. "You better have really enjoyed this, because I'm now addicted to your taste and pleasure."

Something tightened inside her until it became almost painful. She was flabbergasted to recognize it as an even fiercer arousal. Her satisfaction had lasted only a minute, and now she was even hungrier. No. Something else she'd never felt before. Empty. As if there was a gnawing void inside her that demanded to be filled. By him. Only ever him.

She confessed it all to him. "The pleasure you gave me is nothing like I ever imagined. But I hope you're not thinking of indulging your addiction again. I want pleasure *with* you."

All lightness drained from his eyes as he reached for her again. He cupped her, then squeezed her mound possessively, desensitizing her, the ferocious conqueror flaring back to life. "And you will have it. I'll ride you to ecstasy until you can't beg for more."

Her senses swam with the force of anticipation, with the searing delight of his sensual threat. Her heart went haywire as he swept her up in his arms and headed inside.

In minutes, he entered a huge, tastefully furnished suite with marble floors, Persian carpets and soaring ceilings. At the thought that it must be Johara and Shaheen's master suite, a flush engulfed her body.

A gigantic circular bed draped in chocolate satin spread beneath a domed skylight that glowed with the last tendrils of sunset. Oil lamps blazed everywhere, swathing everything in a golden cast of mystery and intimacy.

Sinking deeper into sensory overload, she tried to drag him down on top of her as he set her on the bed. He sowed kisses over her face and clinging arms as he withdrew, then stood back looking down at her.

His breath shuddered out. "Do you realize how incredible you are?" Elation, embarrassment, but mainly disbelief gurgled in her throat. "Do you want to *see* how incredible I find you?"

That got her voice working. "Yes, *please*."

She struggled up to her elbows as he started to strip, exposing each sculpted inch, showing her how incredible *he* was. Her eyes and mouth watered, her hands stung with the intensity of need to explore him, revel in him. He did have the body of a higher being. It was a miracle he wore clothes at all, didn't go through life flaunting his perfection and driving poor inferior mortals crazy with lust and envy.

Then he stepped out of his boxers, released the…proof of how incredible he found her, and a spike of craving and intimidation had her collapsing onto her back.

She'd felt he was big when he'd pressed against her what felt like a lifetime ago back on the terrace. But this… What if she couldn't accommodate him, couldn't please him?

But she had to give him everything, had to take all he had. Her heart would stop beating if he didn't make her his now. *Now.*

His muscles bunched with barely suppressed desire as he came down onto the bed, his hunger crashing over her in drowning waves. "No more waiting, *ya kanzi*. Now I take you. And you take me."

"Yes." She held out shaking arms as he surged over her, impacted her. She cried out, reveling in how her softness cushioned his hardness. Perfect. No, sublime.

He dragged her legs apart even as she opened them for him. He guided them around his waist, his eyes seeking hers, solicitous and tempestuous, his erection seeking her entrance. Finding it both hot and molten, he bathed himself in her flowing readiness in one teasing stroke from her bud to her opening.

On the next stroke, he growled his surrender, sank inside her, fierce and full.

The world detonated in a crimson flash and then disappeared.

In the darkness, she heard keening as if from the end of

a tunnel, and everything was shuddering. Then she went nerveless, collapsed beneath him in profound sensual shock.

She didn't know how long existence was condensed into the exquisite agony. Then the world surged back on her with a flood of sensations, none she'd ever felt before.

She found him turned to stone on top of her, face and body, eyes wild with worry. "It's your first time."

As she quivered inside and out, a laugh burst out, startling them both. "As if this is a surprise. Have you met me?"

The consternation gripping his face vanished and was replaced by sensuality and tenderness. "Oh, yes, I have. And oh, yes, it is—*you* are a surprise a second."

He started withdrawing from her depths.

The emptiness he left behind made her feel as if she'd implode. "No, don't go…don't stop…."

Throwing his head back, he squeezed his eyes. "I'm going nowhere. In consideration of your mint condition, I'm just trying to adjust from the fast and furious first time I had in mind to something that's slower and more leisurely…." He opened his eyes and gazed down at her. "I would only stop if you wanted me to."

Feeling the emptiness inside her threatening to engulf her, she thrust her hips upward, uncaring about the burning, even needing it. "I'd die if you stop."

His groan was as pained, as if she'd hurt him, too. "Stopping would probably finish me, as well. For real."

She thrust up again, crying out at the razing sensations as he stretched her beyond her limits. "You'd still stop… if I asked?"

A hand stabbed through her hair, dragged her down by its tether to the mattress, pinning her there for his ferocious proclamation. "I'd die if you asked."

Her heart gave a thunderclap inside her chest, shaking her like an earthquake. Tears she'd long repressed rose and poured from her very depths.

She surged up, clung to him, crushed herself against his

steel-fleshed body. "*Ya Ullah, ya* Aram, I'd die for you, too. Take me, leave no part of me, finish me. Don't hold back, hurt me until you make it better…."

"*Aih, ya kanzi,* I'll make it better. I'll make it so much better…." He cupped her hips in both hands, tilted them into a fully surrendering cradle for his then ever so slowly thrust himself to the hilt inside her.

It was beyond overwhelming, being occupied by him, being full of him. The reality of it, the sheer meaning and carnality of it, rocked her to the core. She collapsed, buried under the sensations.

He withdrew again, and she cried out at the unbearable loss, urged him to sink back into her. He resisted her writhing pleas, his shaft resting at her entrance before he plunged inside her again. She cried out a hot gust of passion, opening wider for him.

He kept her gaze prisoner as he watched her, gauging her reactions, adjusting his movements to her every gasp and moan and grimace, waiting for pleasure to submerge the pain. He kept her at a fever pitch, caressing her all over, suckling her breasts, draining her lips, raining wonder over her.

Then her body poured new readiness and pleasure over him, and he bent to drive his tongue inside her to his plunging rhythm, quickening both, until she felt a storm gathering inside her, felt she'd shatter if it broke.

His groan reverberated inside her mouth. "Perfection, *ya kanzi,* inside and out. Everything about you, with you."

Everything inside her tightened unbearably, her depths rippling around him, reaching for that elusive something that she felt she'd perish if she didn't have it, now, now.

She cried out, "Please, Aram, please, give it to me now, everything, *everything….*"

And he obliged her. Tilting her toward him, angling his thrusts, he drove into her with the exact force and speed she needed until he did it, shattered the coil of tension.

She heaved up beneath him so hard she raised them both in the air before crashing back to the bed. Convulsion after convulsion tore through her, clamped her around him. Her insides splintered on pleasure too sharp to register at first, then to bear, then to bear having it end.

Then she felt it, the moment his body caught the current of her desperation, a moment she'd replay in her memory forever. The sight and feel of him as he surrendered inside her to the ecstasy the searing sweetness of their union had brought him.

She peaked again as he threw his head back to roar his pleasure, feeding her convulsions with his own, pouring his release on her conflagration, jetting it inside her in hot surges until she felt completely and utterly filled.

Nothingness consumed her. For a moment, or an hour. Then she was surging back into her body, shaking, weeping, aftershocks demolishing what was left of her.

He *had* finished her, as she'd begged him to.

Then he was moving, and panic surged. She clung to him, unable to be apart from him now. He pressed soothing kisses to her swollen eyes, murmuring reassurance in that voice that strummed everything in her as he swept her around, took her over him, careful not to jar her, ensuring he remained inside her.

Then she was lying on top of him, the biggest part of her soul, satiated in ways she couldn't have imagined, at once reverberating with the enormity of the experience, and in perfect peace for the first time in her life.

She lay there merged with him, fused to him, awe overtaking her at everything that had happened.

Then her heart stopped thundering enough to let her breathe properly, to raise her head, to access her voice.

She heard herself asking, "What—what was…that?"

He stared up at her, his eyes just as dazed, his lips twitching into a smile. "I…have absolutely no idea. So *that* was sex, huh?"

"Hey…that's my line."

"Then you'll have to share it with me."

He withdrew from her depths carefully, making her realize that his erection hadn't subsided. His groan echoed her moan at the burn of separation. He soothed her, suckling her nipples until she wrapped herself around him again.

Unclasping her thighs from around him, he gave a distressed laugh. "You might think you're ready for another round of devastation, but trust me, you're not." He propped himself on his elbow, gathered her along his length, looking down at her with such sensual indulgence, her core flowed again. "It's merciful I had no idea it would be like this between us or I would have pounced on you long ago."

Feeling free and incredibly wanton, she rubbed her hands down his chest and twined her legs through his. "You should have."

He pressed into her, daunting arousal undiminished, body buzzing with vitality and dominance and lust. "I should make you pay for all these times you looked at me as if I was the brother you never had."

She arched, opening for his erection, needing him back inside her. "You should."

He chuckled, a dozen devils dancing in his incredible eyes. "Behave. You're too sore now. Give it an hour or two, then I'll…make you pay."

"Make me pay now. I loved the way you made me sore so much I almost died of pleasure. Make me sore again, Aram."

"And all this time I was afraid you were this sexless tomboy. Then after one kiss, that disguise you wear comes off and there's the most perfectly formed and uninhibited sex goddess beneath it all. You almost did kill me with pleasure, too."

"How about we flirt with mortal danger some more?"

"Sahrah."

Calling her *enchantress,* he crushed her in his arms and

thrust against her, sliding his erection up and down between the lips of her core, nudging her nub over and over.

The pleasure was unimaginable, built so quickly, a sweet, sharp burn in her blood, a tightening in her depths that now knew exactly how to unfurl and undo her. She opened herself wide for him, let him pleasure her this way.

Feeling the advance tremors of a magnificent orgasm strengthening, she undulated faster against him. Her pleas became shrieks as pleasure tore through her.

He pinned her beneath him as she thrashed, bucked, gliding over his hardness to the exact pressure and rhythm to drain her of the last spark of pleasure her body needed to discharge.

Then, kneeling between her splayed legs, he pumped his erection a few last times and roared as he climaxed over her.

She'd never seen anything as incredible, as fulfilling as watching him take his pleasure, rain it over the body he'd just owned and pleasured. The sight of his face in the grip of orgasm…

Then he was coming down half over her, mingling the beats of their booming hearts.

"Now I might have a heart attack thinking of all the times I was hard as steel around you and didn't realize this—" he made an explicit gesture at all of her spread beneath him, no doubt the very sight of abandon "—was in store for me if I just grabbed you and plunged inside you."

"Sorry for wasting your time being so oblivious."

His eyes were suddenly anxious, fervent. "You wasted nothing. I was just joking. I can never describe how grateful I am that we became friends first. I wouldn't change a second we had together, *ya kanzi.* Say you believe that."

She brought him down to her. "I believe *you.* Always. And I feel exactly the same. I wouldn't change a thing."

She didn't know anything more but that she was surrounded by passion and protection and sinking into a realm of absolute safety and contentment…

* * *

She woke up to the best sight on the planet.

A naked Aram standing at the window, gazing outside through a crack in the shutters. From the spear of light, she judged it must be almost sunset again. He'd woken her up twice through the night and day, showed her again and again that there was no limit to the pleasure they could share.

As if feeling her eyes on him, he turned at once, his smile the best dawn she'd ever witnessed.

She struggled to sit up in bed as he brought her a tray. Then he sat beside her, feeding her, cossetting her. The blatant intimacy in his eyes suddenly made her blush as everything they'd done together washed over her. She buried her flaming face in his chest.

He laughed out loud. "You're just unbearably cute being shy now after you blew my mind and every cell in my body with how responsive and uninhibited you are."

"It's a side effect of being transfigured, being a first timer," she mumbled against the velvet overlying steel of his skin and flesh.

"I was a first timer, too." She frowned up at him. "I *was* as untried as you in what passion—towering, consuming, earth-shattering passion—was like. So the experience was just as transformative for me as it was for you."

Joy overwhelmed her, had her burrowing deeper in his chest. "I'll take your word for it."

He chuckled, raised her face. "Now I want to take *your* word. That you won't do what your sisters did."

"What do you mean?"

"That you won't ask for a million contradictory details. That you won't do a thing to postpone our wedding."

Eleven

"What do you mean *wedding?*"

Aram's smile widened as Kanza sprang up, sitting like the cat she reminded him of, switching from bone-deep relaxation to full-on alertness in a heartbeat. Everything inside him knotted and hardened again as his gaze roved down that body that had taught him the meaning of "almost died of pleasure."

He reached an aching hand to cup that breast that filled it as if it was made to its measurement. "I mean our wedding."

"Our…" Her face scrunched as if with pain. "Stop it right this second, okay? Just…don't. *Don't,* Aram."

His heart contracted so hard it hurt. "Don't what?"

"Don't start with 'doing the right thing.'"

He frowned. "What the hell do you mean by that?"

She rose to her knees to scowl down at him. "I mean you think you've seduced a 'virgin,' had unprotected sex with her a handful of times and probably put a kid inside her by now. Having long been infected with Zohaydan conservatism, you think it's unquestionable that you have to marry me."

He rose to his knees, too, towering over her, needing to

overwhelm her and her faulty assumptions before this got any further. "If there is a kid in there, I'd want with every fiber of my being to be its father...."

"And that's no reason to get married."

He pressed on. "And to be the best friend, lover and husband of its mother for as long as I live...and if there's really a beyond, I'd do anything to have dibs on that, too."

The chagrined look in her eyes faltered. "Well, that only applies if there was actually a...kid. I assure you there is no possibility of one. It's the wrong time completely. So don't worry about that."

He reached for her, pressing her slim but luscious form to his length. "Does this look like a worried man to you?"

She leaned back over his arm, her eyes wary. "This looks like a...high man to me."

"I am. High on you, on the explosively passionate chain reaction we shared." He ground his erection harder into her belly, sensed her ready surrender. "And it's really bad news there isn't a possibility of a kid in there right now. I really, really want to put one in there. Or two. Or more."

Her eyes grew hooded. "What's the rush all of a sudden, about all that life-changing stuff?"

"I don't know." He bent to suckle her earlobe, nip it, before traveling down her neck and lower. "Maybe it's my biological clock. Turning forty does things to a man, y'know?"

She squirmed out of his arms, put a few inches' distance between them. "Since you'll live to a gorgeous, vital hundred, you're not even at the midpoint yet, so chill."

He slammed her back against him. "I don't *want* to chill. I've been chilling in a deep freeze all my life. Now that I've found out what burning in searing passion is like, I'll never want anything else but the scorching of your being. I love you, *ya kanzi,* I more than love you. I adore and worship you. *Ana aashagek.*"

She lurched so hard, she almost broke his hold.

"You—you do?"

He stared into her eyes, a skewer twisting in his gut at what filled them. God, that vulnerability!

Unable to bear that she'd feel that way, he caught her back, holding her in the persuasion of his hands and eyes. "How can you even doubt that I do?"

That precious blush that he'd seen only since last night blazed all over her body. "It's not you I doubt, I guess."

He squeezed her tighter, getting mad at her. "How can you doubt yourself? Are you nuts? Don't you know—"

"How incredible I am? No, not really. Not when it comes to you, anyway. I couldn't even dream that you could have emotions for me. That's why I kept it so strictly chummy. I didn't see how you'd look at me as a woman, thought that I must appear a 'sexless tomboy' to you."

"I was afraid *you* thought you were that. This wasn't how *I* saw you." He filled his hand with her round, firm buttock, pushed the evidence of how he saw her against her hot flesh.

As she undulated against him, her voice thickened. "I was never sexless where you were concerned."

"Don't go overboard now. You were totally so at the beginning. Probably till last night."

Her undulations became languorous, as if he was already inside her, thrusting her to a leisurely rhythm. "If you only knew the thoughts I had where you were concerned."

"And what kind of thoughts were those?"

She rubbed her breasts against him, her nipples grazing against his hair-roughened chest. "Feverishly licentious ones. At least I thought they were. You proved me very uncreative."

He crushed her against him to stop her movements. He had to or he'd be inside her again, and they wouldn't get this out of the way. "If you'd had thoughts of even wanting to hold my hand, you hid them well. Too well, damn it."

Her hands cupped his face, her eyes filling with such tenderness, such remembered pain. "I couldn't risk putting you on edge or having you pull back if you realized

I was just another woman who couldn't resist you. I was afraid it would mar our friendship, that I wouldn't be able to give you the companionship you needed if you started being careful around me. I couldn't bear it if you lost your spontaneity with me."

The fact that she'd held back for him, as he'd done for her, was just more proof of how right they were for one another. "When did you start feeling this way about me?"

"When I was around seventeen."

That flabbergasted him. "But you hated the sight of me!"

"I hated that in spite of all your magnificent qualities you seemed to be just another predictable male who'd go for the prettiest female, no matter that she had nothing more to recommend her. Then I hated that you also seemed so callous—you could be cruel to someone who was so out of your league. But mostly, I hated how you of all men made me feel, when I knew I couldn't even dream of you."

"I beg you, dream of me now," he groaned, burrowing his face into her neck. "Dream of a lifetime with me. Let yourself love me, *ya kanzi*."

"I far more than love you, Aram. *Ana aashagak kaman*."

To hear her say she felt the same, *eshg,* stronger than adoration, more selfless than love, hotter than passion, was everything. What he had been born for. For her.

Lowering her onto the bed, he gazed deep into her eyes as she wound herself around him. "I've been waiting for you since I was eighteen. And you had to go get born so much later, make me wait that much longer."

Tears streamed among unbridled smiles. "You can take all the waiting out on me."

Taking her lips, her breath, he pledged, "Oh, I will. How I will."

Floating back to her father's house, Kanza felt like a totally different woman from the one who'd left it over twenty-four hours ago.

She was so high on bliss that she let her family subject her to their drama with a smile. She might have spent three years living autonomously in New York, but once on Zohaydan soil, she must act the unmarried "girl," who could do whatever she wanted during "respectable hours" provided she spent the nights under her father's roof.

To shut them up, she told them of Aram's proposal.

Her news boggled everyone's mind. It seemed beyond their comprehension that she, the one undesirable family member they'd thought would die a spinster, hadn't gotten only one, but two incredible proposals in the space of two days. One from a prince, which she'd dared turn down on the spot, and the other from Aram, someone far bigger and better than any prince. It seemed totally unacceptable to her sisters and stepmothers that she'd marry the incomparable Aram of all men, when *they* had all settled for *far* lesser men.

At least Maysoon was absent, as usual, pursuing her latest escapades outside Zohayd and unconcerned with the rest of her family or their events. Kanza would at least be spared what would have been personal venom, with her history with Aram.

Feeling decidedly Cinderella-like, she thought it was poetic when her prince strolled in. Reading the situation accurately, Aram proceeded to give her family strokes. Showing them he couldn't keep his eyes or hands or even lips off her, he declared he wouldn't wait more than three days for their wedding. A wedding he'd finance from A to Z—unlike her sisters' grooms who divided costs—and that the nuptials would be held at the royal palace of Zohayd.

As her family reeled that Kanza would get a wedding that topped that of a member of the ruling family and in the royal palace, too—where most of them had rarely set foot—Aram took her father aside to discuss her *mahr*. As the dowry or "bride's price" was paid to the father, Aram let everyone hear that her father could name *any* number.

As his *shabkah* to Kanza, the bride's gift, he was writing his main business in her name.

Kanza let him deluge her in extravagant gestures and tumbled deeper in love with him. He was defending her against her family's insensitivity and honoring her in front of them and all of Zohayd by showing them there were no lengths he wouldn't go to for the privilege of her hand.

She'd later tell him that her *mahr* was his heart and her *shabkah* was his body.

But then, he already knew that.

Now that she was as rock-stable certain of his love as he was of hers, she was ready to marry him right there on the spot. Three days felt like such an eternity. Couldn't they just elope?

Kanza really wished they *had* eloped.

Preparing for the wedding, even though Aram had taken care of most of the arrangements, was nerve-racking.

At least now it would be over in a few hours.

If only it would start *already.* The hour until it did felt like forever. Not that anyone else seemed to think so. Everyone kept lamenting that they didn't have more time.

"It's a curse."

Maram, the queen of Zohayd, and Johara's sister-in-law, threw her hands in the air as she turned from sending two of her ladies-in-waiting for last-minute adjustments in Kanza's bridal procession's bouquets. The florist had sent white and yellow roses instead of the cream and pale gold Aram had ordered, which would go with all the gowns.

"No matter what—" Johara explained Maram's exclamation "—we end up preparing royal weddings in less and less time."

Kanza grinned at all the ladies present, still shell-shocked that all the women of the royal houses of Zohayd, Azmahar and even Judar were here to help prepare her wedding. "Take heart, everyone. This is only a *quasi*-royal wedding."

"It is a bona fide royal one around here, Kanza." That was Talia Aal Shalaan, Johara's other sister-in-law. "It's par for the course when you're a friend or relative to any of the royal family members. And you and Aram are both to so many of us. But this is an all-time crunch, and there is no earthshaking cause for the haste as there was in the other royal weddings we've rushed through preparing here."

"Aram can't wait." Johara giggled, winking to her mother, then to Kanza. "That *is* earthshaking."

Talia chuckled. "Another imperious man, huh? He'll fit right in with our men's Brotherhood of Bigheadedness."

Maram pretended severity. "Since this haste is only at his whim, this Aram of yours deserves to be punished."

"Oh, I'll punish him." Kanza chuckled, then blushed as Jacqueline Nazaryan, her future mother-in-law, blinked.

Man, she liked her a lot, but it would be a while until the poised swan of a French lady got used to Kanza's brashness.

Maram rolled her eyes. "And if he's anything like my Amjad, he'll love it. I applaud you for taming that one. I never saw Amjad bristle around another man as he does around Aram. A sign he's in a class of his own in being intractable."

"Oh, Aram is nothing of the sort…." Kanza caught herself and laughed. "*Now.* He told me how he locked horns with Amjad when he lived here, and I think it's because they *are* too alike."

Maram laughed. "Really? Someone who's actually similar to my Amjad? *That* I'd like to see. We might need to put him in a museum."

As the ladies joined in laughter, Carmen Aal Masood came in. Carmen was the event planner extraordinaire whose services Aram had enlisted in return for contributing an unnamed fortune to a few of her favorite charities, and the wife of the eldest Aal Masood brother, Farooq, who gave up the throne of Judar to marry her. The Aal Masoods were also Kanza's relatives from their Aal Ajmaan mother's side.

Yeah, it was all tangled up around here.

"So you ready to hop into your dress, Kanza?" Carmen said, carrying said dress in its wrapping.

Kanza sprang to her feet. "Am I! I can't wait to get this show on the road."

Lujayn, yet another of Johara's sisters-in-law, the wife of Shaheen's half brother Jalal, sighed. "At least you're eager for your wedding to start. Almost every lady here had a rocky start, and our weddings felt like the end of the world."

Farah, the wife of the second-eldest Judarian prince, Shehab Aal Masood, raised her hand. "I had my end of the world *before* the wedding. So I was among the minority who were deliriously happy during it."

"Kanza doesn't seem deliriously happy." Aliyah, King Kamal Aal Masood of Judar's wife—the queen who wore black at her own wedding then rocked the whole region when she challenged her groom to a sword duel on global live feed—gave Kanza a contemplative look. "You're treating it all with the nonchalance of one of the guests. Worse, with the impatience of one of the caterers who just wants it over with so she can get the hell home."

Kanza belted a laugh as she ran behind the screen. "I just want to marry the man. Don't care one bit how I do it."

Feeling the groans of her half sisters flaying her, she undressed and jumped into her gown. They were almost *haybeedo*—going to lay eggs—to have anything like her wedding. And for her to not only have it but to not care about having it must be the ultimate insult to injury to them.

Sighing, she came out from behind the screen.

Her sisters and stepmothers all gaped at her. Yeah, she'd gaped, too, when she'd seen herself in that dress yesterday at the one and only fitting. If you could call it a dress. It was on par with a miracle. Another Aram had made come true.

Before she could get another look at herself in the mirror, the ladies flocked around her, adjusting her hair and veil and embellishing her with pieces of the Pride of Zohayd treasure that King Amjad and Maram were lending her.

Then they pulled back, and it was her turn to gasp.

Who was that woman looking back at her?

The dress's sumptuous gradations of cream and gold made everything about her coloring more vivid, and the incredible amalgam of chiffon, lace and tulle wrapped around her as if it was sculpted on her. The sleeveless, corsetlike, deep décolleté top made her breasts look full and nipped her waist to tiny proportions. Below that, the flare of her hips looked lush in a skirt that hugged them in crisscrossing pleats before falling to the floor in relaxed sweeps. And all over it was embroidered with about every ornament known to humankind, from pearls to sequins to cutwork to gemstones. Instead of looking busy, the amazing subtleness of colors and the denseness and ingeniousness of designs made it a unique work of art. Even more than that. A masterpiece.

Aram had promised he'd tell her how he'd had it made in only two days, if she was very, very, *very* good to him.

She intended to be superlative.

Looking at herself now—with subtle makeup and her thick hair swept up in a chignon that emphasized its shine and volume, with the veil held in place by a crown from the legendary royal treasure, along with the rest of the priceless, one-of-a-kind jewels adorning her throat, ears, arms and fingers—she had to admit she looked stunning.

She wanted to look like that more from now on.

For Aram.

The new bouquets had just arrived when the music that had accompanied bridal processions in the region since time immemorial rocked the palace.

Kanza ran out of the suite with her royalty-studded procession rushing after her, until Johara had to call out for her to slow down or they'd all break their ankles running in their high heels.

Kanza looked back, giggling, and was again dumbfounded by the magnitude of beauty those women packed. They themselves looked like a bouquet of the most perfect flowers in their luscious pale gold dresses. Those royal men of theirs sure knew how to pick women. They had been blessed by brides who were gorgeous inside and out.

As soon as they were out in the gallery leading to the central hall, Kanza was again awed by the sheer opulence of this wonderland of artistry they called the royal palace of Zohayd. A majestic blend of Persian, Ottoman and Mughal influences, it had taken thousands of artisans and craftsmen over three decades to finish it in the mid-seventeenth century. It felt as if the accumulation of history resonated in its halls, and the ancient bloodlines that had resided and ruled in it coursed through its walls.

Then they arrived at the hall's soaring double doors, heavily worked in embossed bronze, gold and silver Zohaydan motifs. Four footmen in beige-and-gold outfits pulled the massive doors open by their ringlike knobs. Even over the music blaring at the back, she heard the buzz of conversation pouring out, that of the thousand guests who'd come to pay Aram respects as one of the world's premier movers and shakers.

Inside was the octagonal hall that served as the palace's hub, ensconced below a hundred-foot high and wide marble dome. She'd never seen anything like it. Its walls were covered with breathtaking geometric designs and calligraphy, its eight soaring arches defining the space at ground level, each crowned by a second arch midway up, with the upper arches forming balconies.

At least, that had been what it was when she'd seen it yesterday. Now it had turned into a scene right out of *Arabian Nights.*

Among the swirling sweetness of *oud,* musk and amber

fumes, from every arch hung rows of incense burners and flaming torches, against every wall breathtaking arrangements of cream and gold roses. Each pillar was wrapped in gold satin worked heavily in silver patterns, while gold dust covered the glossy earth-tone marble floor.

Then came the dozens of tables that were lavishly decorated and set up in echoes of the hall's embellishment and surrounded by hundreds of guests who looked like ornaments themselves, polished and glittering. Everyone came from the exclusive realm of the world's most rich and famous. They sparkled under the ambient light like fairy-tale dwellers in Midas's vault.

Then the place was plunged into darkness. And silence.

Her heart boomed more loudly than the boisterous percussive music that had suddenly ended. After moments of stunned silence, a wildfire of curious murmuring spread.

Yeah. Them and her both. This wasn't part of the planned proceedings. Come to think of it, not much had been. Aram had been supposed to wait at the door to escort her in. She hadn't given it another thought when she hadn't found him there because she'd thought he'd just gotten restless as her procession took forever to get there, and that he'd simply gone to wait for her at the *kooshah,* where the bride and groom presided over the celebrations, keeping the *ma'zoon*—the cleric who'd perform the marriage ritual—company.

So what was going on? What was he up to?

Knowing Aram and his crazy stunts, she expected anything.

Her breathing followed her heartbeat in disarray as she waited, unmoving, certain that there was no one behind her anymore. Her procession had rustled away. This meant they were in on this. So this surprise was for her.

God, she hated surprises.

Okay, not Aram's. She downright adored those, and had,

in fact, gotten addicted to them, living in constant anticipation of the next delightful surprise that invariably came.

But really, now wasn't the time to spring something on her. She just wanted to get this over with. And get her hands back on him. Three days without him after that intensive… initiation had her in a constant state of arousal and frustration. By the end of this torture session, she'd probably attack and devour him the moment she had him alone….

"Elli shoftoh, gabl ma tshoofak ainayah.
Omr daye'e. Yehsebooh ezzai alaiah?"

Her heart stopped. Stumbled. Then stopped again.

Aram. His voice. Coming from…everywhere. And he'd just said…said…

All that I've seen, before my eyes saw you.
A lifetime wasted. How can it even be counted life?

Her heart began ricocheting inside her chest. Aram. Saying exactly what she felt. Every moment before she was with him, she no longer counted as life.

But those verses… They sounded familiar….

Suddenly a spotlight burst in the darkness. It took moments until her vision adjusted and she saw…saw…

Aram, rising as if from the ground at the far end of the gigantic ballroom, among swirling mist. In cream and gold all over, looking like a shining knight from a fantasy.

As he really was.

Music suddenly rose, played by an orchestra that rose on a huge platform behind him, wearing complementary colors.

She recognized the overture. *Enta Omri,* or *You Are My Lifetime.* One of the most passionate and profound love songs in the region. That was why the verses had struck a chord.

Not that their meaning had held any before. Before Aram, they'd just been another exercise in romantic hyperbole. Now that he was in her heart, every word took on a new meaning, each striking right to her foundations.

He now repeated the verses but not by speaking them.

Aram was *singing.* Singing to *her.*

Everything inside her expanded to absorb every nuance of this exquisite moment as it unfolded, to assimilate it into her being.

She already knew he sang well, though it was his voice itself that was unparalleled, not his singing ability. They'd sung together while cooking, driving, playing. He always sang snippets of songs that suited a situation. But nothing local.

While his choice and intention overwhelmed her with gratitude and happiness, the fact that he knew enough about local music to pick this song for those momentous moments stunned her all over again with yet another proof that Aram knew more about her homeland than she did. Not to mention loved it way more.

He was descending the steps from the platform where the orchestra remained. Then he was walking toward her across the huge dance floor on an endless gold carpet flanked by banks of cream rose petals. All the time he sang, his magnificent, soul-scorching voice filling the air, overflowing inside her.

"Ad aih men omri ablak rah, w'adda ya habibi.
Wala da'a el galb ablak farhah wahda.
Wala da'a fel donia ghair ta'am el gerah."
How much of my lifetime before you passed and was lost.
With a heart tasting not a single joy but only wounds.

She shook, tears welling inside her.

Yes, yes. Yes. Exactly. *Oh, Aram...*

He kept coming nearer, his approach a hurricane that uprooted any lingering despondencies and disappointments, blowing them away, never to be seen again.

And he told her, only her, everything in his heart.

"Ebtadait delwa'ti bas, ahheb omri.
Ebtadait delwa'ti akhaf, lal omr yegri."
Only now I started to love my lifetime.

Only now I started to fear its hasty passage.

Every word, everything about him, overwhelmed her. It was impossible, but he was even more beautiful now, from the raven hair that now brushed his shoulders, to the face that had never looked more noble, more potent, every slash carved deeper, every emotion blazing brighter, to the body that she knew from extensive hands-on…investigation was awe incarnate. To make things worse and infinitely better, his outfit showcased his splendor to a level that would have left her speechless, breathless, even without the overkill of his choice of song and his spellbinding performance.

The costume echoed her dress in colors, from the cream-and-gold embroidered cape that accentuated his shoulders and made him look as if he'd fly up, up and away at any moment to the billowing-sleeved gold shirt that was gathered by a cream satin sash into formfitting coordinating pants, which gathered into light beige matte-leather boots.

She was looking at those when he stopped before her, unable to meet his eyes anymore. Her heart had been racing itself to a standstill, needed respite before she gazed up at him and into the full force of his love up close.

His hands reached for her, burned on her bare arms. Quivers became shudders. She raised her eyes, focused on the mike in front of lips that were still invoking the spell.

His hands caressed her face, cupped it in their warmth and tenderness, imbuing her with the purity of his emotions, the power of their union. And he asked her:

"Ya hayat galbi, ya aghla men hayati.
Laih ma abelneesh hawaak ya habibi badri?"
Life of my heart, more precious than my life.
Why didn't your love find me earlier, my love?

Shudders became quakes that dismantled her and dislodged tears from her depths. She waited, heart flailing uncontrollably, for the last verse to complete the perfection.

"Enti omri, elli ebtada b'noorek sabaho."
You are my lifetime, which only dawned with your light.

Music continued in the closing chords, but she no longer heard anything as she hurled herself into his arms.

She rained feverish kisses all over his face, shaking and quaking and sobbing. "Aram…Aram…too much…too much…everything you are, everything with you, from you…" She burrowed into his containment and wept until she felt she'd disintegrate.

He hugged her as if he'd assimilate her, bending to kiss her all over her face, her lips, raggedly reciting the verses, again and again.

She thought a storm raged in the background. It wasn't until she expended her tears and sobs that she realized what it was. The thunder of applause and whistles and hoots among the lightning of camera flashes *and the video flood-lights.*

Drained, recharged, she looked up at her indescribable soul mate, her smile blazing through the upheaval. "This should get record hits on YouTube."

It was amazing, watching his face switch from poignancy to elation to devilry.

Only she could do this to him. As he was the one who could make her truly live.

"Maybe this won't." He winked. "But *this* surely will."

Before she could ask what "this" was, he turned and gestured, and for the second time tonight he managed to stun her out of her wits.

Openmouthed, she watched as hundreds of dancers in ethnic Zohaydan costumes, men in flowing black-and-white robes and women with waist-length hair and in vibrant, intricately embroidered floor-length dresses, poured onto the huge dance floor from all sides, *including* descending by invisible harnesses from the balconies. Drummers with all Zohaydan percussive instruments joined in as they formed facing queues and launched into infectiously energetic local dances.

He caught her around the waist, took her from gravity's

dominion into his. “Remember the dance we learned at that bar in Barbados?” She nodded hard enough to give herself a concussion. He swung her once in the air before tugging her behind him to the dance floor. “Then let’s dance, *ya kanzi.*”

Though the dance was designed to a totally different rhythm, somehow dancing to this melody worked and, spectacularly, turned out to be even more exhilarating.

Soon all the royal couples were dancing behind them as they led the way, and before long, the whole guest roster had left the tables and were circled around the dance floor clapping or joining the collective dances.

As she danced with him and hugged him and kissed him and laughed until she cried, she wondered how only he could do this—change the way she felt about anything to its opposite. This night she’d wished would be over soon, she suddenly wished would never end.

But even when it did, life with Aram would only begin.

Twelve

Aram clasped Kanza from behind, unable to let her go for even a moment as she handed back the Pride of Zohayd jewelry to the royal guards at the door.

He had to keep touching her to make himself believe this was all real. That she was his wife now. That they were in their home.

Their home.

The fact that it was in Zohayd made it even more unbelievable.

He'd thought he'd lost Zohayd forever. But she'd given it back to him, as she'd given him everything else. Though she'd never loved Zohayd as he loved it, she'd consented to make it her home again.

After seeing her among her family, he now realized why Zohayd had never held fond memories for her. But he was determined to set things right and would put those people in their place. They'd never impact her in any way again.

Now he hoped he could make her see Zohayd as he saw it.

But at any sign of discomfort, they'd leave. He just wanted

her happy, wanted her to have everything. Starting with him and his whole life.

She closed the door then turned and wrapped herself around him. “I just can never predict you.”

He tasted her lips, her appreciation. “I hope this keeps me interesting.”

Her lips clung to his as she kneaded his buttocks playfully, sensuously. He still couldn’t believe, couldn’t get enough of how uninhibited she was with him sexually. It was as if the moment he’d touched her she’d let him in all the way, no barriers.

“Don’t you dare get more interesting or I’ll expire.”

“You let me know the level of ‘interesting’ I can keep that’s optimum for your health.”

“You’re perfect now. You’ll always be perfect.” She squeezed him tighter. “Thank you, *ya habibi*. For the gift of your song. And every other incredible thing you did and are.”

His lips explored her face, loving her so much it was an exquisite pain. “I had to give you a wedding to remember.”

“As long as it had you, it would have been the best memory, as everything you are a part of is. *And* it would have been the best possible earthly event. But that…that was divine.” Her eyes adored him, devoured him. “Have I told you lately just how out of my mind in love with you I am?”

His heart thundered, unable to wait anymore. He needed union with her. Now.

His hands shook as he undid her dress, slid it off her shoulders. “Last time was ten minutes ago. Too long. Tell me again. *Show* me. You haven’t shown me in *three* damn days.”

She tore back at his clothes. “Thought you’d never ask.”

He shoved off the dress that he’d had ten dressmakers work on day and night, telling himself he couldn’t savor her beauty now. He had to lose himself in her, claim her heart, body and soul.

The beast inside him was writhing. This. This flesh. This spirit. This tempest of a woman. Her. It demanded her. And it wouldn't have her slow or gentle. Their lifelong pact had to be sealed in flesh, forged in the fires of urgency and ferociousness. And she wanted that, too. Her eyes were engulfing him whole, her breathing as erratic as his, her hands as rabid as she rid him of his shackles.

He pressed her to the door, crashed his lips down on hers. Her cry tore through him when their mouths collided. He could only grind his lips, his all, against hers, no finesse, no restraint. The need to ram into her, ride her, spill himself inside her, drove him. Incessant groans of profound suffering filled his head, his and hers. He was in agony. Her flesh buzzed its equal torment beneath his burning hands.

He raised her thighs around his hips, growled as her moist heat singed his erection. His fingers dug into her buttocks as he freed himself, pushed her panties out of the way, and her breasts heaved, her hardened nipples branding his raw flesh where she'd torn his shirt off.

Her swollen lips quivered in her taut-with-need face. "Aram…fill me…"

The next moment, he did. He drove up into her, incoherent, roaring, invading her, overstretching her scorching honey. Her scream pierced his soul as she consumed him back, wrung him, razed him.

He rested his forehead against hers, completely immersed in her depths, loved and taken and accepted whole, overwhelmed, transported. He listened to her delirium, watching her through hooded eyes as she arched her graceful back, giving him her all, taking his. Blind, out of his mind and in her power—in her love—he lifted her, filled his starving mouth and hands with her flesh, with the music of her hunger. He withdrew all the way then thrust back, fierce and full, riding her wild cry. It took no more than that. One thrust finished her. And him. Her satin screams echoed his roars as he jetted his essence inside her. Her convulsions spiked with the first splash of his seed against her womb. Her heart hammered under his, both spiraling out of control as the devastating pleasure went on and on and on and the paroxysm of release destroyed the world around them.

Then it was another life. Their new life together, and they were merged as one, rocking together, riding the aftershocks, sharing the descent.

Then, as she always did, she both surprised and delighted him. "That was one hell of an inauguration at the very entrance of our new home. Who needs breaking a bottle across the threshold when you can shatter your bride with pleasure?"

Squeezing her tighter, he looked down at her, his heart soaring at the total satisfaction in her eyes. "I am one for better alternatives."

"That was the *best*. You redefine mind-blowing with every performance. I'm not even sure my head is still in place."

Chuckling, proud and grateful that he could satisfy her that fully, he gathered his sated bride into his arms and strode through the still-foreign terrain of their new home.

Reaching their bedroom suite, he laid her down on the twelve-foot four-poster bed draped in bedcovers the color of her flesh and sheets the color of her hair. She nestled into him and went still, soaking in the fusion of their souls and flesh.

Thankfulness seeped out in a long sigh. "One of the incredible things about your size is that I can bundle you all up and contain you."

She burrowed her face into his chest. "Not fair. I want to contain you, too."

Tightening his arms around her, he pledged, "You have. You do."

* * *

"It is such a relief to be back home in Zohayd."

Kanza looked up from her laptop as Johara waddled toward her, just about to pop.

Johara and her family had returned to Zohayd since her wedding to Aram two months ago. Their stay in New York *had* only been on Aram's account. The moment he'd come to Zohayd, they'd run home.

She smiled at her friend and now new sister-in-law. "I would have never agreed before, but with Aram, Zohayd has become the home it never was to me."

Johara, looking exhausted just crossing their new base of operations, plopped down beside her on the couch. "We knew you'd end up together."

Kanza's smile widened. "Then you knew something I didn't. I had no idea, or even hope, for the longest time."

"Yeah." Johara nodded absently, leafing through the latest status report. "When the situation revolves around you, it's hard to have a clear enough head to see the potential. But Shaheen and I knew you'd be perfect for each other and gave you a little shove."

Her smile faltered. "You did? When was that?"

Johara raised her head, unfocused. Then she blinked. "Oh, the night I sent you to look for that file."

A suspicion mushroomed then solidified into conviction within the same heartbeat. "There was no file, was there?"

Johara gave her a sheepish look. "Nope. I just had to get you both in one place."

Unease stirred as the incident that had changed her life was rewritten. "You sent him to look for the nonexistent file, too, so he'd stumble on me. You set us up."

Johara waved dismissively. "Oh, I just had you meet."

The unease tightened. "Did Aram realize what you did?"

"I'm sure he did when he found you there on his same mission."

So why had he given her different reasons when she'd asked him point-blank what he'd been doing there?

But… "He could have just thought you asked me to do the same thing. He had no reason to think you were setting us up."

"Of course he did. Shaheen had suggested you to him only a couple of weeks before."

"*Suggested* me…how?"

"How do you think? As the most suitable bride for him, of course." Johara's grin became triumphant. "Acting on my suggestion, I might add. And it turns out I was even more right than I knew. You and Aram are beyond perfect."

So their meeting hadn't been a coincidence.

But… "Why should Aram have considered your suggestion? It isn't as if he was looking for a bride."

Johara looked at her as if she asked the strangest things. "Because we showed him what a perfect all-around package you are for him—being you…*and* being Zohaydan. We told him if you married, you'd have each other, he'd have Zohayd back, I'd have my brother back, my parents their son and Shaheen his best friend."

Kanza didn't know how she'd functioned after Johara's blithe revelations.

She didn't remember how she'd walked out of the office or how she'd arrived home. Home. Hers and Aram's. Up until two hours ago, she'd been secure, certain it was. Now…now…

"Kanzi."

He was here. Usually she'd either run to greet him or she'd already be at the door waiting for him.

This time she remained frozen where she'd fallen on the bed, dreading his approach. For what if when he did, when she asked the inevitable questions, nothing would be the same again?

She felt him enter their bedroom, heard the rustle of his

clothes as he took them off. He always came home starving for her, made love to her before anything else, both always gasping for assuagement that first time. Then they settled to a leisurely evening of being best friends and patient, inventive and very, very demanding lovers.

At least, that was what she'd believed.

If everything hadn't started as she'd thought, if his motivations hadn't been as pure as she'd believed them to be, how accurate was her perception of what they shared now?

The bed dipped under his weight, rolling her over to him. He completed the motion, coming half over her as soon as her eyes met his. He'd taken off his jacket and shirt, and he now loomed over her, sculpted by virility gods and unbending discipline and stamina, so hungry and impatient. And her heart almost splintered with doubt and insecurity.

Was it even possible this god among men could truly want her to that extent?

His lips devoured her sob of despair as he rid her of her clothes, sought her flesh and pleasure triggers, cupped the breasts and core that were swollen and aching with the need for him that not even impending heartbreak could diminish.

"Kanza...*habibati...wahashteeni...kam wahashteeni.*"

Her heart convulsed at hearing the ragged emotion in his voice as he called her his love, told her how much he'd missed her. When it had only been hours since he'd left her side.

He slid her pants off her legs, and they fell apart for him. He rose to free his erection, and as she felt it slap against her belly, hot and thick and heavy, everything inside her fell apart, needing his invasion, his affirmation.

Holding her head down to the mattress by a trembling grip in her hair, feeding her his tongue, rumbling his torment inside her, he bathed himself in her body's begging for his, then plunged into her.

That familiar expansion of her tissues at his potency's advance was as always at first unbearable. Then he withdrew and thrust back, giving her more of him, and it got better, then again and again until it was unbearable to have him withdraw, to have him stop. He didn't stop, breaching her to her womb, over and over, until he was slamming inside her with the exact force and speed and depth that would…would…

Then she was shrieking, bucking beneath him with a sledgehammer of an orgasm, the force of it wrenching her around him for every spark of pleasure her body was capable of, wringing him of every drop of his seed and satisfaction.

Before he collapsed on top of her in the enervation of satiation, he as usual twisted around to his back, taking her sprawling on top of him.

Instead of slowing down, her heart hurtled faster until it was rattling her whole frame. It seemed it transmitted to Aram as he slid out of their merging, turned her carefully to her back and rose above her, his face gripped with worry.

"God, what is it, Kanza? Your heart is beating so hard."

And it would stop if she didn't ask. It might shrivel up if she did and got the answers she dreaded.

She had no choice. She had to know.

"Why didn't you tell me that Johara and Shaheen nominated me as a bride for you?"

Thirteen

Kanza's question fell on Aram like an ax.

His first instinct was to deny that he knew what she was talking about. The next second, he almost groaned.

Why had he panicked like that? How could he even consider lying? It was clear Johara or Shaheen or both had told her, but why, he'd never know. But though it wasn't his favorite topic or memory, his reluctance to mention it had resulted in this awkward moment. But that was all it was. He'd pay for his omission with some tongue-lashings, and then she'd laugh off his failure to provide full disclosure about this subject as he did everything else, and that would be that.

He caressed her between the perfect orbs of her breasts, worry still squeezing his own heart at the hammering that wasn't subsiding beneath his palm. "I should have told you."

He waited with bated breath, anticipating the dawning of devilry, the launch of a session of stripping sarcasm.

Nothing came but a vacant, "Yes. You should have."

When that remained all she said and that heart beneath his palm slowed down to a sluggish rhythm, he rushed to qualify his moronically deficient answer. "There was nothing to tell, really. Shaheen made the suggestion a couple of weeks before I met you. I told him to forget it, and that was that."

Another intractable moment of blankness passed before she said, "But Johara set us up that first night. And you must have realized she had. Why didn't you say something then? Or later? When you started telling me everything?"

All through the past months, unease about this omission had niggled at him. He'd started to tell her many times, only for some vague…dread to hold him back.

"I just feared it might upset you."

"Why should it have, if it was nothing? It's not that I think I'm entitled to know everything that ever happened in your life, but this concerned me. I had a right to know."

He felt his skull starting to tighten around his brain. "With the exception of this one thing, I *did* tell you everything in my life. And it was because this concerned you that I chose not to mention it. Their nomination, as well-meaning as it was, was just…unworthy of you."

"But you did act on that nomination. It was why you considered me."

His skull tightened another notch. "No. *No.* I didn't even consider Shaheen's proposition. Okay, I did, for about two minutes. But that was before I saw you that night. If I thought about it again afterward, it was to marvel at how wrong Shaheen was when he thought you'd agree to marry me based on my potential benefits. There's no reason to be upset over this, *ya kanzi.* Johara and Shaheen's matchmaking had nothing to do with us or the soul-deep friendship and love that grew between us."

"Would you have considered me to start with if not for *my* potential benefits?"

"You had none!"

"Ah, but I do. Johara listed them. Stemming from being me and being Zohaydan, as she put it."

"Why the hell would she tell you something like that?

Those pregnancy hormones have been scrambling her brain of late."

"She was celebrating the fact that it all came together so well for all of us, especially you."

"I don't care what she or anyone else thinks. I care about nothing but you. You *know* that, Kanza."

She suddenly let go of his gaze, slipped out of his hold. He watched her with a burgeoning sense of helplessness as she got off the bed, then put on her clothes slowly and unsteadily.

He rose, too, as if from ten rounds with a heavyweight champion, stuffing himself back into his pants, feeling as if he'd been hurled from the sublime heights of their explosively passionate interlude to the bottom of an abyss.

Suddenly she spoke, in that voice that was hers but no longer hers. Expressionless, empty. Dead. "I was unable to rationalize the way you sought me out in the beginning. It was why I was so terrified of letting you close. I needed a logical explanation, and logic said I was nowhere in your league—nothing that could suit or appeal to you."

"You're *everything* that—"

Her subdued voice drowned the desperation of his interjection. "But I was dying to let you get close, so I pounced on Johara's claims that you needed a best friend, then did everything to explain to myself how I qualified as that to you. But her new revelations make much more sense why you were with me, why you married me."

"I was with you because you're everything I could want. I married you because I love you and can't live without you."

"You do appear to love me now."

"*Appear?* Damn it, Kanza, how can you even say this?"

"I can because no matter how much you showed me you loved me, I always wondered *how* you do. *What* I have that the thousands of women who pursued you don't." He again tried to protest the total insanity of her words when lashing pain gripped her face, silencing him more effectively than a skewer in his gut. "When I couldn't find a reason why, I thought you were responding to the intensity of my emotions for you. I thought it was my desire that ignited yours. I did know you needed a home and I thought you found it in me. But your home has always been Zohayd. You just needed someone to help you go home and to have the family and set down the roots you yearned for your entire life."

Unable to bear one more word, he swooped down on her, crushed her to him, stormed her face with kisses, scolding her all the while. "Every word you just said is total madness, do you hear me? You are everything I never dreamed to find, everything I *despaired* I'd never find. I've loved you from that first moment you turned and smacked me upside the head with your sarcasm, then proceeded to reignite my will to exist, then taught me the meaning of being alive."

He cradled her face in his hands, made her look at him. "*B'Ellahi, ya hayati,* if I ever needed your unconditional belief, it's now. My life depends on it, *ya habibati.* I beg you. Tell me you believe me."

Her reddened eyes wavered, then squeezed in consent.

Relief was so brutal his vision dimmed. He tightened his grip on her, reiterating his love.

Then she was pushing away, and alarm crashed back.

Her lips quivered on a smile as she squirmed out of his arms. "I'm just going to the bathroom."

He clung to her. "I'm coming with you."

"It's not that kind of bathroom visit."

"Then call me as soon as it is. There's these new incense and bath salts that I want to try, and a new massage oil."

Her eyes gentled, though they didn't heat as always, as she took another step away. "I'll just take a quick shower."

"Then I'll join you in that. I'll…"

Suddenly the bell rang. And rang.

Since they'd sent the servants away for the night as usual, so they'd have the house and grounds all to themselves, there was no one to answer the door. A door no one ever came to, anyway. So who could this be?

Cursing under his breath as Kanza slipped away, he ran to the door, prepared to blast whoever it was off the face of the earth.

He wrenched the door open, and frustration evaporated in a blast of anxiety when he found Shaheen on his doorstep half carrying an ashen-faced Johara.

He rushed them inside. "God, come in."

Shaheen lowered Johara onto the couch, remained bent over her as Aram came down beside her, each massaging a hand.

"What's wrong? Is she going into labor?"

"No, she's just worried sick," Shaheen said, looking almost sick himself.

Johara clung feebly to the shirt he hadn't buttoned up. "I talked with Kanza earlier, and I think I put my foot in it when I told her how we proposed her to you."

"You *think?*"

At his exclamation, Shaheen glared at him, an urgent head toss saying he wanted a word away from Johara.

Gritting his teeth, he kissed Johara's hot cheek. "Don't worry, sweetheart. It was nothing serious," he lied. "She just skewered me for never mentioning it, and that was it. Now rest, please. Do you need me to get you anything?"

She shook her head, clung to him as he started to rise. "Is it really okay? She's okay?"

He nodded, caressed her head then moved away when she closed her eyes on a sigh of relief.

He joined Shaheen out of her earshot. "God, Shaheen, you shouldn't be letting her around people nowadays. She unwittingly had Kanza on the verge of a breakdown."

Shaheen squeezed his eyes. "*Ya Ullah*... I'm sorry, Aram. Her pregnancy is taking a harder toll on her this time, and I'm scared witless. Her pressure is all over the place and she loses focus so easily. She said she was celebrating how well everything has turned out for you two and only remembered when she came home that Kanza didn't know how things started." He winced. "Then she kept working herself up, recalling how subdued Kanza became during the conversation, the amount of questions she'd asked her, and she became convinced she'd made a terrible mistake."

"She did. God, Shaheen, Kanza kept putting two and two together and getting fives and tens and hundreds. But right before you came she'd calmed down at last."

Hope surged in his friend's eyes. "Then everything is going to be fine?"

He thought her spiraling doubts had been arrested, but he was still rattled.

He just nodded to end this conversation. He needed to get back to Kanza, close that door where he'd gotten a glimpse of hell once and for all.

Shaheen's face relaxed. "Phew. What a close call, eh? Now that that's settled, please tell me when are you going to take my job off my hands? In the past five months since I offered you the minister of economy job, juggling it with everything else—" he tossed a worried gesture in Johara's direction "—has become untenable. I really need you on it right away."

"So this is why you *have* to become Zohaydan."

Kanza's muffled voice startled Aram so much he staggered around. He found her a dozen feet away at the entrance to their private quarters. Her look of pained realization felt like a bullet through his heart.

Her gaze left his, darting around restlessly as if chasing chilling deductions. "Not just to make Zohayd your home, but you need to be Zohaydan to take on such a vital position. But as only members of the ruling house have ever held it, you have to become royalty, through a royal wife."

"Kanza…"

"Kanza…"

Both he and Shaheen started to talk at once.

Her subdued voice droned on, silencing them both more effectively than if she'd shouted. "Since there are no high-ranking princesses available, you had to choose from lower-ranking ones. And in those, I was your only viable possibility. The spinster who never got a proposal, who'd have no expectations, make no demands and pose no challenge or danger. I was your only safe, convenient choice."

He pounced on her, trembling with anxiety and dismay, squeezed her shoulders, trying to jog her out of her surrender to macabre projections. "No, Kanza, hell, *no.* You were the most challenging, *in*convenient person I've ever had the incredible fortune to find."

She raised that blank gaze to his. "But you didn't find me, Aram. You were pushed in my direction. And as a businessman, you gauged me as your best option. Now I know what you meant when you said I 'work best.' For I do. I'm the best possible piece that worked to make everything fall into place without resistance or potential for trouble."

He could swear he could see his sanity deserting him in thick, black fumes. "How can you think, let alone say, *any* of this? After all we've shared?"

Ignoring him, she looked over at Shaheen. "Didn't you rationalize proposing me to him with everything I just said?"

He swung around to order Shaheen to shut up. Every time he or Johara opened their mouths they made things worse.

But Shaheen was already answering her. "What I said was along those lines, but not at all—"

"Why didn't you all just tell me?" Kanza's butchered cry not only silenced Shaheen but stopped Aram's heart. And that was before her agonized gaze turned on him. "I would have given you the marriage of convenience you needed if just for Johara and Shaheen's sake, for Zohayd's. I would have recognized that you'd make the best minister of economy possible, would have done what I could to make it happen without asking for anything more. But now…now that you made me hope for more, made me believe I had more—all of you—I can't go back…and I can't go on."

"Kanza."

His roar did nothing to slow her dash back to the bedroom. It only woke Johara up with a cry of alarm.

Reading the situation at a glance, Johara struggled up off the couch, gasping, "I'll talk to her."

Unable to hold back anymore, dread racking him, he shouted, "*No.* You've talked enough for a lifetime, Johara. I was getting through to her, and you came here to *help* me some more and spoiled everything."

Shaheen's hand gripped his arm tight, admonishing him for talking to his sister this way for any reason, and in her condition. "Aram, get hold of yourself—"

He turned on him. "I *begged* you never to interfere between me and Kanza. Now she might never listen to me, never believe me again. So *please,* just leave. Leave me to try to salvage what I can of my wife's heart and her faith in me. Let me try to save what I can of our marriage, and our very lives."

Forgetting them as he turned away, he rushed into the bedroom. He came to a jarring halt when he found Kanza standing by the bed where they'd lost themselves in each other's arms so recently, looking smaller than he'd ever seen her, sobs racking her, tears pouring in sheets down her suffering face.

He flew to her side, tried to snatch her into his arms. Her feeble resistance, the tears that fell on his hands, corroded through to his soul.

Shaking as hard as she was, he tried to hold the hands that warded him off, moist agony filling his own eyes. "Oh, God, don't, Kanza…don't push me away, I beg you."

She shook like a leaf in his arms, sobs fracturing her words. "With everything in me…I do…I *do* want you to have everything you deserve. I was the happiest person on earth when I thought that I was a big part of what you need…to thrive, to be happy…."

"You are *everything* I need."

She shook her head, pushed against him again. "But I'll always wonder…always doubt. Every second from now on, I'll look at you and remember every moment we had together and…see it all differently with what I know now. It will…abort my spontaneity, my fantasies…twist my every thought…poison my every breath. *And I can't live like this.*"

Even in prison, during those endless, hopeless nights when he'd thought he'd be maimed or murdered, he'd never known terror.

But now…seeing and hearing Kanza's faith, in him—in herself—bleed out, he knew it.

Dark, drowning, devastating.

And he groveled. "No, I beg you, Kanza. I beg you, please…don't say it. Don't say it…."

She went still in his arms as if she'd been shot.

That ultimate display of defeat sundered his heart.

Her next words sentenced him to death.

"The moment you get your Zohaydan citizenship and become minister, let me go, Aram."

Fourteen

It was as harsh a test of character and stamina as Kanza had always heard it was.

But being in the presence of Amjad Aal Shalaan in Kanza's current condition was an even greater ordeal than she'd imagined.

She'd come to ask him as her distant cousin, but mainly as the king of Zohayd, to expedite proclaiming Aram a Zohaydan subject and appointing him to the position of minister.

After the storm of misery had racked her this past week, inescapable questions had forced their way from the depths of despair.

Could she leave Aram knowing that no matter what he stood to gain from their marriage, he did love her? Could she punish him and herself with a life apart because his love wasn't identical to hers, because of the difference in their circumstances?

Almost everyone thought she had far more to gain from their marriage than he did, especially with news spreading of the minister's position. Her family had explicitly expressed their belief that marrying him would raise her to undreamed-of status and wealth.

But she expected him to believe she cared nothing about those enormous material gains, to know for certain that they were only circumstantial. She would have married him had he been destitute. She would continue to love him, come what may. So how could she not believe him when he said the same about his own projected gains? Could she impose a separation on both of them because her ego had been injured and her confidence shaken?

No. She couldn't.

Even if she'd never be as certain as she'd been before the revelations, she would heal and relegate her doubts to the background, where they meant nothing compared to truly paramount matters.

Once she had reached that conclusion, she'd approached a devastated Aram and tried everything to persuade him that he must go ahead with his plans, to persuade him that she'd overreacted and was taking everything she'd said back.

He'd insisted he'd *never* had plans, didn't want anything but her and would never lift a finger to even save his life if it meant losing her faith and security in the purity of his love.

So here she was, taking matters into her own hands.

She was getting him what he needed, what he was now forgoing to prove himself to her.

Not that she seemed to be doing a good job of championing his cause.

That cunning, convoluted Amjad had been keeping her talking for the past half hour. It seemed he didn't buy the story that she wished Aram to be Zohaydan as soon as possible for the job's sake…that Shaheen needed Aram to take over before Johara gave birth.

He probed her with those legendary eyes of his, confirmed her suspicion. "So, Kanza, what's your *real* rush? Why do you want your husband to become Zohaydan so immediately? He can assume Shaheen's responsibilities without any official move. I'd prefer it, to see if my younger brother wants to hand his closest friend the kingdom's fate as a consolation prize for the 'lost years,' or if he is really the best man for the job."

"He is that, without any doubt."

Those eyes that were as vividly emerald as Aram's were azure flashed their mockery. "And of course, that's not the biased opinion of a woman whose head-over-heels display during her wedding caused my eyes to roll so far back in my skull it took weeks to get them back into their original position?"

"No, *ya maolai.*" It was a struggle to call him "my lord," when all she wanted to do was chew him out and make him stop tormenting her. "It's the very objective opinion of a professional in Aram's field. While there's no denying that you, Shaheen and your father have been able to achieve great things running the ministry, I believe with the unique combination of his passion for the job and for Zohayd, and with the magnitude of his specific abilities and experience, Aram would surpass your combined efforts tenfold."

Amjad's eyebrows shot up into the hair that rained across his forehead. "Now, *that's* a testimony. I might be needing your ability to sell unsellable goods quite soon."

"As reputedly the most effective king Zohayd has ever known, I hear you've achieved that by employing only the best people where they'd do the most good. I trust you wouldn't let your feelings for Aram, whatever they are, interfere with the decision to make use of him where he is best suited."

He spread his palm over his chest in mock suffering. "Ah, my feelings for Aram. Did he tell you how he broke my heart?"

You, too? she almost scoffed.

Not that Aram had broken hers. It was she who'd churned herself out with her insecurities.

But that big, bored regal feline would keep swatting her until she coughed up an answer he liked.

She tried a new one. "I'm pregnant."

And she was.

She'd found out two days after Johara's revelations. She hadn't told Aram.

"I want Aram to be Zohaydan before our baby comes."

Amjad raised one eyebrow. "Okay. Good reason. But again, what's the rush? Looking at you, I'd say you have around seven months to go. And you seem to want this done last week."

"I need Aram settled into his new job and his schedule sorted out with big chunks of time for me and the baby."

"Okay. Another good reason. Want to add a better one?"

"I haven't told Aram he's going to be a father yet. I wish him to be Zohaydan before I do to make the announcement even more memorable."

His bedeviling inched to the next level. "You have this all figured out, haven't you?"

"Nothing to figure out when you're telling the truth."

Those eyes said "liar." Out loud he said, "You're tenacious and wily, and you're probably making Aram walk a tightrope to keep in your favor…."

"Like Queen Maram does with you, you mean?"

He threw his head back on a guffaw. "I like you. But even more than that, you must be keeping that pretty, pretty full-of-himself Aram in line. I like *that.*"

"Are we still talking about Aram, *ya maolai?*"

His cruelly handsome face blazed with challenge and enjoyment. "And she can keep calling me *ya maolai* with a straight face, right after she as much as said, 'I'd put you over my knee, you entitled brat, if I possibly could.'"

Even though he didn't seem offended in the least by the subtext of her ill-advised retort, the worry that she might end up spoiling Aram's chances was brakes enough.

"I thought no such thing, *ya maolai.*"

He hooted. "Such a fantastic liar. And that gets you extra

points. Now let's see if you can get a gold star. Tell me the real reason you're here, Kanza."

Nothing less would suffice for this mercilessly shrewd man who had taken one of the most internally unstable kingdoms in the region, brought it to heel and was now leading it to unprecedented prosperity.

So she gave him the truth. "Because I love Aram. So much it's a constant pain if I can't give him everything he needs. And he *needs* a home. He needs *Zohayd*. It's part of his soul. It *is* his home. But until it is that for real, he'll continue to feel homeless, as he's felt for far too long. I don't want him to feel like that one second longer."

Amjad narrowed his eyes. He was still waiting. He knew there was just a bit more to the truth, damn him.

And she threw it in. "I didn't want to expose his vulnerability to you of all people, to disadvantage him in this rivalry you seem to have going."

His lips twisted. "You don't consider this rivalry would be moot and he'd be in a subordinate position once he becomes a minister in my cabinet, in a kingdom where I'm king?"

"No. On a public, professional level, Aram would always hold his own. No one's superior office, which has nothing to do with skill or worth, would disadvantage him. But I was reluctant to hand you such intimately personal power over him. I do now only because I trust you won't abuse it."

It seemed as if he gave her a soul and psyche scan, making sure he'd mined them for every last secret he'd been after.

Seemingly satisfied that he had, Amjad flashed her a grin. "Good girl. That took real guts. Putting the man you love at my mercy. And helluva insight, too. Because I am now bound by that honor pact you just forced on me to never abuse my power over your beloved, I'm definitely going to be making use of this acumen and power of persuasion of yours soon. And as your gold star, you get your wish."

Her heart boomed with relief.

He went on. "Just promise you will not be too good to Aram. You'd be doing him a favor exercising some…*severe* love. Otherwise his head will keep mushrooming, when it's already so big it's in danger of breaking off his neck."

She rose, gave him a tiny bow. "I will consult with Queen Maram about the best methods of limiting the cranial expansion of pretty, pretty full-of-themselves paragons, *ya maolai.*"

His laugh boomed.

She could hear him still laughing until she got out of hearing range. The moment she was, all fight went out of her.

This had been harder than she'd thought it would be.

But she'd done it. She'd gotten Aram the last things he needed. Now to convince him that it wouldn't mean losing her.

For though she was no longer secure in the absoluteness of his need for her, and only her, she'd already decided that anything with him would always remain everything she needed.

Amjad did far better than she'd expected.

The morning after her audience with him, he sent her a royal decree. It proclaimed that in only six hours, a ceremony would be held at the royal palace to pronounce her husband Zohaydan. And to appoint him as the new minister of economy.

She flew to Aram's home office and found him just sitting on the couch, vision turned inward.

The sharp, ragged intake of breath as she came down on his lap told her he'd been so lost in his dark reverie he hadn't noticed her entrance. Then as she straddled him, the flare of vulnerability, of entreaty in his eyes, made ever-simmering tears almost burst free again.

Ya Ullah, how she loved him. And she'd starved for him.

She hadn't touched him since that night, unable to add passion to the volatile mix. He hadn't tried to persuade her again. Not because he didn't want to. She knew he did. He'd gone instantly hard between her legs now, his arousal buffeting her in waves. He'd been letting her guide him into what she'd allow, what she'd withstand.

She'd show him that for as long as he wanted her, she was his forever. That he was her everything.

She held his beloved head in her hands, moans of anguish spilling from her lips as they pressed hot, desperate kisses to his eyes, needing to take away the hurt in them and transfer it into herself. He groaned with every press, long and suffering, and remorse for the pain she'd caused him during her surrender to insecurity came pouring out.

"I'm sorry, Aram. Believe me, please. I *didn't* mean what I said. It was my insecurities talking."

He threw his head back on the couch, his glorious hair fanning to frame his haggard face. "*I'm* sorry. And you had every right to react as you did."

She pressed her lips to his, stopping him from taking responsibility. She wanted this behind them. "No, I didn't. And you have nothing to be sorry about."

His whole face twisted. "I just am. So cripplingly sorry that you felt pain on my account, no matter how it happened."

She kissed him again and again. "Don't be. It's okay."

"No, it's not. I can't bear your uncertainty, *ya habibati.* I can't breathe, I can't *be*...if I don't have your belief and serenity. I'd die if I lost you."

"I'm never going anywhere. I was being stupid, okay? Now quit worrying. You have more important things to worry about than my insecurities."

"I worry about nothing but what you think and feel, *ya kanzi.* Nothing else is important. Nothing else even matters."

"Then you have nothing to worry about. Since only

you…only us, like *this*...matters to me, too." Her hands feverishly roved over him, undoing his shirt, his pants. She rained bites and suckles over his formidable shoulders and torso, releasing his daunting erection. A week of desolation without him, knowing that his seed had taken root inside her, made the ache for him uncontrollable, the hunger unstoppable.

But it was clear he wouldn't take, wouldn't urge. He'd sit there and let her do what she wanted to him, show him what she needed…take all she wanted. And she couldn't wait.

She shrugged off her jacket, swept her blouse over her head, snapped off her bra and bunched up her skirt. She rose to her knees to offer him her breasts, to scale his length. He devoured her like a starving man, reiterating her name, his love.

Her core flowed as she pushed aside her panties then sank down on him in one stroke. Her back arched at the shock of his invasion. Sensations shredded her. *Aram.* Claiming her back, taking her home. Her only home.

She rose and fell over him, their mouths mating to the same rhythm of their bodies. He forged deeper and deeper with every plunge, each a more intense bolt of stimulation. She'd wanted it to last, but her body was already hurtling toward completion, every inch of him igniting the chain reaction that would consume her.

As always, he felt her distress and instinctively took over, taking her in his large palms, lifting her, thrusting her on that homestretch to oblivion until the coil of need broke, lashing through her in desperate surges of excruciating pleasure.

"Aram, *habibi,* come with me…."

He let go at her command, splashing her walls with his essence. And she cried out her love, her adoration, again and again. *"Ahebbak, ya hayati, aashagak."*

Aram looked up at Kanza as she cried out and writhed the last of her pleasure all over him, wrung every drop of his from depths he'd never known existed before collapsing over him, shuddering and keening her satisfaction.

She'd taken her sentence back, had again expunged his record, giving him the blessing of continuing as if nothing had happened. She'd called him her love and life again. She'd made soul-scorching love to him.

So why wasn't he feeling secure that this storm was over?

She was stirring, her smile dawning as she let him know she wanted to lie down.

Maneuvering so she was lying comfortably on her side on the couch, he got her the jacket she reached for. She fished an envelope from its pocket. At its sight, his heart fisted.

He recognized the seal. The king of Zohayd's. He was certain what this was.

With a radiant smile, she foisted it on him. And sure enough, it was what he'd expected. She'd gone and gotten him everything that just a week ago she'd thought he'd married her to get.

And she'd made love to him before presenting it to him to reassure him that accepting this wouldn't jeopardize their relationship. She was giving him everything she believed he needed. Zohayd as his home. The job that would be the culmination of his life's work, putting him on par with the ruling family.

He again tried to correct her assumptions about his needs. "I need only you, *ya kanzi*…."

"How many times will I tell you I'm okay now? I just showed you how okay I was."

"But we still need to talk."

She kissed him one last time before sitting up. "And we will. As much as you'd like. After the ceremony, okay? Just forget about everything else now."

Could *she* forget it, or would she just live with it? When she'd said before that she couldn't?

He feared *that* might be the truth. That she was just giving in to her love, her need for him, but even more, his love and need for her. But in her heart, she'd never regain her total faith in him, her absolute security in his love.

"Let's get you ready," she said as she pulled him to his feet. "This is the most important day of your life."

"It certainly isn't. That day is every day with you."

She grinned and he saw his old Kanza. "Second most important, then. Still pretty important if you ask me. C'mon, Shaheen said he'd send you the job's 'trimmings.'"

He'd always known she was one in a million, that he'd beaten impossible odds finding her. But what she was doing now, the extent to which she loved him, showed him how impossibly blessed he was.

And he was going to be worthy of her miracle.

Aram glanced around the ceremony hall.

It looked sedate and official, totally different than it had during his and Kanza's fairy-tale wedding. The hundreds present today were also dressed according to the gravity of the situation. This was the first time in the past six hundred years that a foreigner had been introduced into the royal house and had taken on one of the kingdom's highest offices.

As Amjad walked into the hall with his four brothers behind him, Aram stole a look back at Kanza. His heart swelled as she met his eyes, expectant, emotional, proud.

What had he done so right he'd deserved to find her? An angel wouldn't deserve her.

But he would. He'd do everything and anything to be worthy of her love.

Amjad now stood before his throne, with his brothers flanking him on both sides. Shaheen was to his right. He met Aram's eyes, his brimming with pride, pleasure, excitement and more than a little relief.

Aram came to stand before the royal brothers, in front

of Amjad, who wasn't making any effort to appear solemn, meeting his eyes with his signature irreverence.

Giving back as good as he got, he repeated the citizenship oath. But as he kneeled to have Amjad touch his head with the king's sword while reciting the subject proclamation, Amjad gave him what appeared to be an accidental whack on the head—intentionally, he was certain.

Aram rose, murmuring to Amjad that it was about time they did something about their long-standing annoyance with each other. Amjad whimsically told him he wished he could oblige him. But he'd promised Kanza he'd share his lunch with him in the playground from now on.

Pondering that Kanza had smoothed his path even with Amjad, he accepted the citizenship breastpin.

Yawning theatrically, Amjad went through the ritual of proclaiming him the minister of economy, pretending to nod off with the boredom of its length. Then it was the minister's breastpin's turn to join the other on Aram's chest. This time, Amjad made sure he pricked him.

Everyone in the hall rose to their feet, letting loose a storm of applause and cheers. He turned to salute them, caught Kanza's smile and tearful eyes across the distance. Then he turned back to the king.

In utmost tranquility, holding Amjad's goading gaze, he unfastened the breastpins one by one, then, holding them out in the two feet between them, he let them drop to the ground.

The applause that had faltered as he'd taken the breastpins off came to an abrupt halt. The moment the pins clanged on the ground, the silence fractured on a storm of collective gasps.

Aram watched as Amjad shrewdly transferred his gaze from Kanza's shocked face back to his.

Then that wolf of a man drawled, "So did my baby brother not explain the ritual to you? Or are you taking off your sharp objects to tackle me to the ground here and now?"

"I'll tackle you in the boardroom, Amjad. And I know exactly what casting the symbols of citizenship and status to the ground means. That I renounce both, irrevocably."

Amjad suddenly slapped him on the shoulder, grinning widely. "What do you know? You're not a stick-in-the-mud like your best friend. If you're as interesting as this act of madness suggests you are, I might swipe you from him."

"Since you did this for me to please Kanza, you're not unsalvageable yourself, after all, Amjad. Maybe I'll squeeze you in, when I'm not busy belonging to Kanza."

"Since I'm also busy belonging to Maram, we'll probably work a reasonable schedule. Say, an hour a year?"

Suddenly liking the guy, he grinned at him. "You're on."

As he turned around, Shaheen was all over him, and Harres, Haidar and Jalal immediately followed suit, scolding, disbelieving, furious.

He just smiled, squeezed Shaheen's shoulder then walked back among the stunned spectators and came to kneel at Kanza's feet. Looking as if she'd turned to stone, she gaped down at him, eyes turbid and uncomprehending.

He took her hands, pulled her to his embrace. "The only privileges I'd ever seek are your love and trust and certainty. Would you bestow them on me again, whole, pure and absolute? I can't and won't live without them, *ya kanzi.*"

And she exploded into action, grabbing him and dragging him behind her among the now-milling crowd.

"Undo this!"

Amjad turned at her imperative order, smiling sardonically. "No can do. Seems this Aram of yours *is* too much like me, poor girl. He's as crazy as I am."

She stamped her foot in frustration. "You *can* undo this. You're the king."

Amjad tsked. "And undo *his* grand gesture? Don't think so."

"So you can undo it!" she exclaimed.

Amjad shook his head. "Sorry, little cousin. Too many pesky witnesses and tribal laws. Your man knew exactly what he was doing and that it cannot be undone. But let me tell you, it makes him worthy of you. That took guts, and also shows he knows exactly what works for him, what's worthy. *You.* So just enjoy your pretty, pretty full-of-himself guy's efforts to worship you."

She looked between him and Amjad in complete and utter shock. "But…what will Shaheen do when Johara gives birth? What about Zohayd…"

"The only world that would collapse without your Aram is yours. And I guess that's why he's doing this. To make it—" Amjad winked at her "—impregnable."

As she continued to argue and plead, Aram swept her up in his arms and strode out of the palace, taking her back home.

Her protests kept coming even after he'd taken her home and made love to her twice.

He rose on his elbow, gathered her to him. "I'll work the job as if I'd taken the position, so I won't leave Shaheen in the lurch. All that'll be missing is the title, which I care nothing about. I want the work itself, the achievement. But contrary to what Shaheen said, I don't need to be always in Zohayd or need to belong here. I already belong. With you, to you."

She wound herself around him, inundating him with her love, which, to his eternal relief, was once again unmarred by uncertainty and fiercer than ever before. "You didn't have to do it. I would have gotten over the last traces of insecurity in a few weeks tops."

"I wouldn't leave you suffering uncertainty for a few minutes. You are more than my home, *ya kanzi.* You're my haven. You contain me whole, you ward off my own demons and anything else the world could throw at me. I haven't lost a thing, and I have gained everything. I *have* everything. Because I have you."

She threw herself at him again before pulling back to look at him with shyness spreading over that face that was his whole world.

"And you're going to have more of me. Literally. And in seven months I'll give you a replica of you."

He keeled over her. As she shrieked in alarm, he laughed, loud and unfettered, then kissed her breathless, mingling their tears.

A baby. There was no end to her blessings.

After yet another storm of rapture passed, he said, "I want a replica of *you*."

"Sorry, buddy, it'll be your replica. In Zohayd they say the baby looks like the parent who is loved more. Uh-uh-uh…" She silenced him as he protested. "I've loved you longer, so you can't do a thing about it. So there."

"I trust this applies only to the first baby. The second one doesn't follow those rules. Second one, your replica."

"But I want them all disgustingly pretty like you!"

He pounced on her, and soon the laughter turned to passion, then to delirium, frenzy and finally pervasive peace.

And through it all, he gave thanks for this unparalleled treasure, this hurricane who'd uprooted him from his seclusion and tossed him into the haven of her unconditional love.

* * * * *